PRAISE FOR *OUT FRONT THE FOLLOWING SEA*

"An absorbing, painstakingly researched read that, like the sea itself, mirrors the beauty, cruelty, enormity, baseness, and wonder of human nature. It is chilling that Angstman's debut novel set in seventeenth-century New England captures the horrors that continue to plague contemporary America, particularly with regard to imperialism and patriarchy. It is heart-swelling that, in these pages and in life, the best of humankind resists and endures. I'll remember this book as a historical tale woven with wry humor, striking detail, lush prose, daring characters, and a belief in glorious possibilities."

—Ethel Rohan, author of *In the Event of Contact* and *The Weight of Him*

"Rich in deeply researched detail, and peopled by complex characters, *Out Front the Following Sea* is a fascinating story that is bound to entrance readers of historical fiction."

—Kathleen Grissom, author of *The Kitchen House* and *Glory Over Everything*

"From the squalor, prejudice, and violence of seventeenth-century America, Leah Angstman has summoned to life the most extraordinary young woman. Ruth Miner insists on surviving, building a life, and being true to her odd independent self, despite the whole world seeing her as worthless filth. Angstman creates a hypnotically real and brutal world and then manages to infuse it with humor and beauty and a moving tale of love. The reader will follow Ruth Miner anywhere, and be the richer for it."

—Heather O'Neill, author of *When We Lost Our Heads*

"Lapidary in its research and lively in its voice, *Out Front the Following Sea* by Leah Angstman is a rollicking story, racing along with wind in its sails. Though her tale unfolds hundreds of years in America's past, Ruth Miner is the kind of high-spirited heroine whose high adventures haul you in and hold you fast."

—Kathleen Rooney, author of *Lillian Boxfish Takes a Walk*

"With *Out Front the Following Sea*, Leah Angstman reveals herself as a brave new voice in historical fiction. With staggering authenticity, Angstman gives us a story of America before it was America—an era rife with witch hunts and colonial intrigue and New World battles all but forgotten in our history books and popular culture. This is historical fiction that speaks to the present, recalling the bold spirits and cultural upheavals of a nation yet to be born."

—Taylor Brown, author of *Pride of Eden* and *Gods of Howl Mountain*

"Steeped in lush prose, authentic period detail, and edge-of-your-seat action, *Out Front the Following Sea* is a rollicking good read. Leah Angstman keeps the story moving at a breathtaking pace, and she knows more 17th-century seafaring language and items of everyday use than you can shake a stick at. The result is a compelling work of romance, adventure, and historical illumination that pulls the reader straight in."

—Rilla Askew, author of *Fire in Beulah* and *The Mercy Seat*

"Leah Angstman has written the historical novel that I didn't know I needed to read. *Out Front the Following Sea* is set in an oft-forgotten time in the brutal wilds of pre-America that is so vividly and authentically drawn, with characters that are so alive and relevant, and a narrative so masterfully paced and plotted, that Angstman has performed the miracle of layering the tumultuous past over our troubled present to gift us a sparkling new reality."

—Kevin Catalano, author of *Where the Sun Shines Out* and *Deleted Scenes and Other Stories*

"*Out Front the Following Sea* is a fascinating book, the kind of historical novel that evokes its time and place so vividly that the effect is just shy of hallucinogenic. I enjoyed it immensely."

—Scott Phillips, author of *The Ice Harvest*, *The Walkaway*, and *Cottonwood*

"*Out Front the Following Sea* is a meticulously researched novel that mixes history, love story, and suspense. Watching Angstman's willful protagonist, Ruth Miner, openly challenge the brutal world of 17th-century New England, with its limiting ideas about gender, race, and science, was a delight."

—Aline Ohanesian, author of *Orhan's Inheritance*

"Leah Angstman is a gifted storyteller with a poet's sense of both beauty and darkness, and her stunning historical novel, *Out Front the Following Sea*, establishes her as one of the most exciting young novelists in the country. Angstman plunges the reader into a brilliantly realized historical milieu peopled by characters real enough to touch. And in Ruth Miner, we are introduced to one of the most compelling protagonists in contemporary literature, a penetratingly intelligent, headstrong woman who is trying to survive on her wits alone in a Colonial America that you won't find in the history books. A compulsive, vivid read that will change the way you look at the origins of our country, Leah Angstman's *Out Front the Following Sea* announces the arrival of a preternatural talent."

—Ashley Shelby, author of *Muri*, *South Pole Station*, and *Red River Rising*

"Rich, lyrical, and atmospheric, with a poet's hand and a historian's attention to detail. In *Out Front the Following Sea*, Leah Angstman creates an immersive world for readers to get lost in and a fascinating story to propel them through it. A thoroughly engaging and compelling tale."

—Steph Post, author of *Holding Smoke*, *Miraculum*, *Walk in the Fire*, *Lightwood*, and *A Tree Born Crooked*

"It's a rare story that makes you thankful for having read and experienced it. It's rarer still for a story to evoke so wholly, so powerfully, another place and time as to make you thankful for the gifts that exist around you, which you take for granted. *Out Front the Following Sea* is a book rich with misery, yet its characters are indefatigable; they yearn, despite their troubles, for victories personal and societal. Leah Angstman's eye is keen, and her ability to transport you into America's beginnings is powerful. With the raw ingredients of history, she creates a story both dashing and pensive, robust yet believable. From an unforgiving time, Angstman draws out a tale of all things inhuman, but one that reminds us of that which is best in all of us."

—Eric Shonkwiler, author of *Above All Men*, *8th Street Power & Light*, and *Moon Up, Past Full*

"A challenging, exquisitely researched, epic, and stunning work of historical fiction that we don't expect but definitely need, *Out Front the Following Sea* magnificently captures the color of its time and settings.

Angstman is an old soul who writes with the same flair that Hawthorne displayed in *The Scarlet Letter* and Jack London in *The Sea-Wolf*. She paints a past America without concealing its flaws, creating a lucid, masterfully crafted narrative and a fascinating fusion of history, intrigue, adventure, action, and romance that will immediately pull you in from the very first page. Angstman is a powerful writer, showing us bold imagery, nail-biting conflicts, and history that comes alive in the paragraphs, including banned languages and interesting dialects. You may forget you're reading a book and feel like you're living with the characters. The pace is perfect, and the action is enough to make you hold your breath."

—Readers' Favorite (five-starred review)

"A sweeping tale of intrigue, romance, and feminist power amidst the tumult of colonial North America. ...Historical fiction, romance, and action-lovers alike will find something to enjoy in *Out Front the Following Sea*. Keeping readers on their toes with ever-changing scenery and vibrant characters, Leah Angstman has recreated British Colonial America with a modern twist... [Her] story will beguile and compel readers, leaving them waiting for Angstman's next book."

—Independent Book Review

"This book moved me in ways that I didn't expect. ...The deeply researched and historically authentic world is vivid and immersive, and it captivated me from the first pages."

—One Book More

"Ruth is an unforgettable strong woman with the independence of Kya Clark from *Where the Crawdads Sing* and the fortitude of Demelza from the Poldark series. I wanted to know whether Ruth survived and, if so, how she conquered the challenges she faced as an orphaned young woman in a harsh, patriarchal environment. ...Angstman uses a broad vocabulary, brutal descriptions, and colloquialisms (i.e. God's teeth!) to immerse you in the time period [and] the characters were phenomenal. ...I recommend this book for anyone who loves historical fiction or stories about strong women."

—Book Picks and Pics

OUT FRONT
THE FOLLOWING SEA

A Novel of King William's War
in Seventeenth-Century New England

Leah Angstman

Regal House Publishing

Published by
Regal House Publishing, LLC
Raleigh, NC 27587
All rights reserved

ISBN -13 (paperback): 9781646031948
ISBN -13 (epub): 9781646031955
Library of Congress Control Number: 2021936003

Interior and cover design by Lafayette & Greene
Cover images © by C. B. Royal

Regal House Publishing, LLC
https://regalhousepublishing.com

Printed in the United States of America

For Mom, my war ship.

If you want to build a ship,
don't drum up people to collect wood
and don't assign them tasks and work,
but rather teach them to long for
the endless immensity of the sea.

—Antoine de Saint Exupéry, translation from *Citadelle*

Every story, new or ancient,
bagatelle or work of art:
All are tales of human failing;
all are tales of love at heart.

—Tim Rice, *Aida*

ACT I

The Winter's Tale

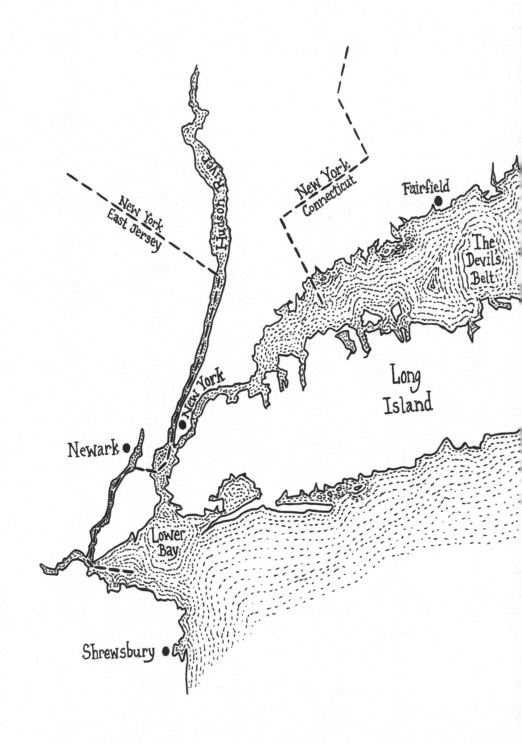

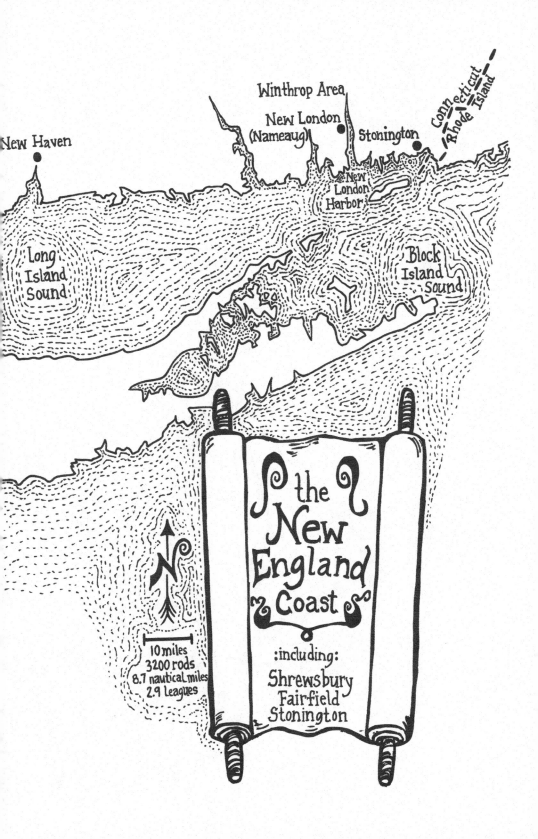

New Haven

Winthrop Area

New London
(Nameaug)

Stonington

Connecticut
Rhode Island

New
London
Harbor

Long
Island
Sound

Block
Island
Sound

N

10 miles
3200 rods
8.7 nautical miles
2.9 leagues

the
New
England
Coast

:including:
Shrewsbury
Fairfield
Stonington

fore
mast

fore
topgallant

fore
top
sail

clew
head

fore
course
sail

bowsprit

bow

forecastle   main   boat de

gun deck

passengers   cargo   galley

ship's
stores   barrel
cargo   supplies

Primrose

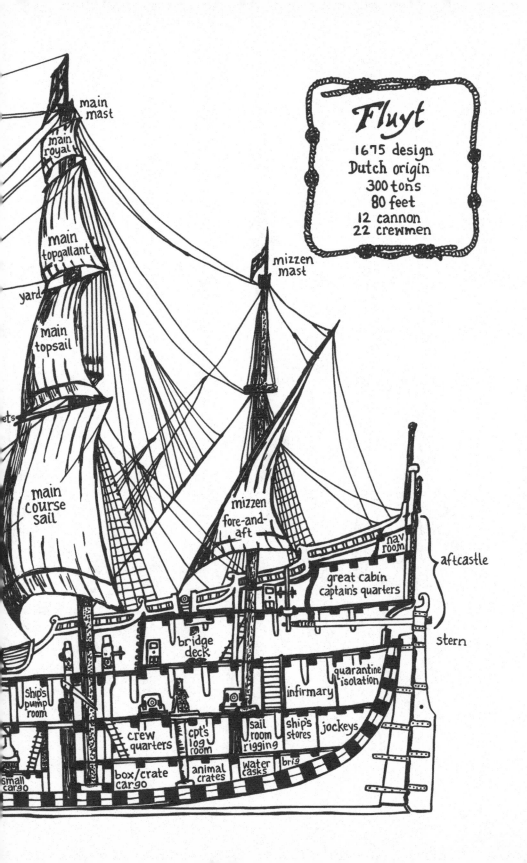

main
mast

main
royal

main
topgallant

yards

main
topsail

main
course
sail

mizzen
mast

mizzen
fore-and-
aft

nav
room

aftcastle

great cabin
captain's quarters

stern

bridge
deck

quarantine
isolation

infirmary

Ship's
pump
room

crew
quarters

cpt's
log
room

sail
room
rigging

ship's
stores

jockeys

small
cargo

box/crate
cargo

animal
crates

water
casks

brig

Fluyt

1675 design
Dutch origin
300 tons
80 feet
12 cannon
22 crewmen

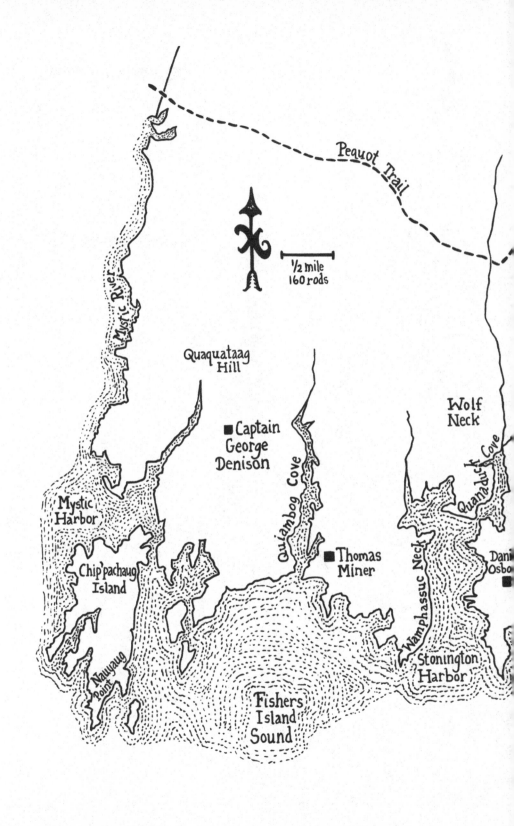

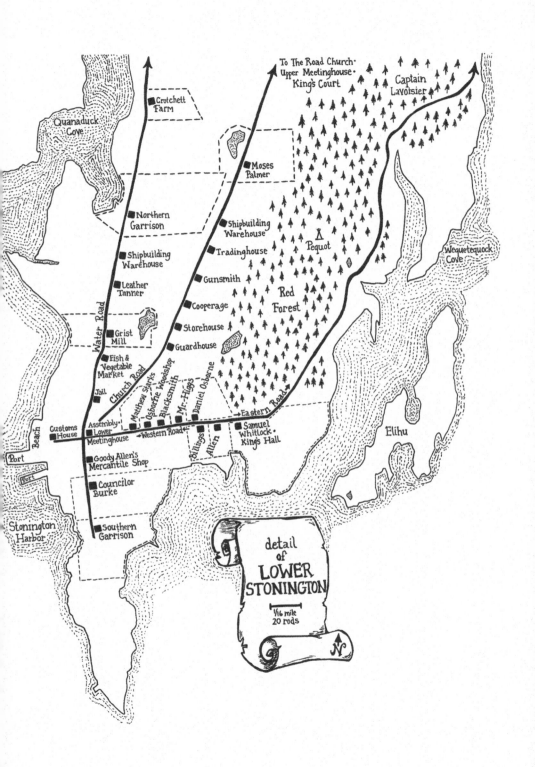

Quanaduck Cove

Crotchett Farm

Captain Lavoisier

To The Road Church·
Upper Meetinghouse·
King's Court

Moses Palmer

Northern Garrison

Shipbuilding Warehouse

Shipbuilding Warehouse

Tradinghouse

Pequot

Wequetequock Cove

Leather Tanner

Gunsmith

Cooperage

Red Forest

Grist Mill

Storehouse

Guardhouse

Fish & Vegetable Market

Jail

Matthew Starks

Osborne Woodshop

Blacksmith

Mr. Higgs

Daniel Osborne

Eastern Road

Customs House

Assembly Lower Meetinghouse

Western Road

Billings

Allen

Samuel Whitlock· Kings Hall

Elihu

Goody Allen's Mercantile Shop

Councilor Burke

Stonington Harbor

Southern Garrison

Water Road

Church Road

Beach

Port

Port

detail
of
LOWER
STONINGTON

1/16 mile
20 rods

N

Chapter First
Autumn goes; or, the exposition

There must be a beginning of any great matter,
but the continuing unto the end until it be
thoroughly finished yields the true glory.

—Sir Francis Drake

November came. Autumn licked flat the fields, blew odors of lye and burning animal fat and manure across East Jersey Province. Ruth tugged at her nose, unable to reach the vinegar of Middle Colonies clinging inside it. Spikenard and staghorn reddened out before her. Sawtoothed panic-grasses crunched beneath hooves along a trail and fanned to the rolling dunes that emerged from the marsh like white chalkstones abrading outward to the Mid-Atlantic seaboard. Blue-winged teal and snowgeese honked overhead, and brant, with their loon throats and beady black eyes, agitated around her with abandon. An early frost that prematurely killed the harvest left only tasteless root vegetables in Shrewsbury's marketplace, where she rode Copernicus from the marsh edge to the mill, alighted, and tied the gelding to the post nearest the few carts of what remained unspoiled. A Dutchman's sneer at the animal—an impressive carting Friesian, blue-black and iridescent as a flea beetle—morphed covetous and violent, hands clenched, balled around a pail. Ruth Miner had ridden a valuable farming horse uncarted through a swamp.

"Mrs. Pieterszoon." Ruth nodded to a frumpy woman sitting behind the first cart. "Parsnips all that survived? What will you trade for them?" Ruth moved her hand toward the cart and got her fingers swatted away.

"Ga weg! Ye'll starve for what I care of it," Mrs. Pieterszoon said. "Ye shrivel them parsnips like ye shriveled the rest of the crop, and ye'll be eating a coring iron."

The woman's chin jutted, a landing rock that ships could spy from sea, and Ruth hastened along to Mrs. Janszoon at the next cart, who wouldn't deign to reply but threw a sheet over the vegetables. Ruth groaned and continued down the line. A father covered his son's eyes; a group of mothers lowered their shawls over their baskets, hurrying their daughters and goats on by. From the upper window of a brick one-and-half story Dutch colonial, a wealthy merchant's daughter laughed at Ruth, then slammed the shutter. Ruth looked up slowly, frowning from the half-door to the double pitches of the gambrel roof to the matching stone chimneys on either end. What she wouldn't give for a house like that. The next and next, their gables rolling into steep pitches, were similar except for the cheaper clapboard, and another building on the end of the row had a wide, wishbone-shaped stone chimney up the front of it, standing in for an entire facing wall. Behind these, a row of tall, slender homes stood gable-out, so close together a body couldn't fit between them, their stonework mounting up the roofs in a series of steps that looked like tiny stairs leading to and from the peak. In front of every fourth house, a post was erected for a lantern that, in accordance with law, had to be hung by the respective resident to light the dirt street at night. Towering behind the row of homes, down near the oceanfront, the clapboard-beam rotatinghouse windmill gazed out at the harbor and revolved without pause. She watched absently, and as her fingers rested on an undersized root, a wooden rod came down across her knuckles. She withdrew her hand, the flesh stinging.

"You fewmet of a boar!" the third cart's proprietor, Kees Karelszoon, shouted. "You stealed one." That embittered widower—undoubtedly, he blamed her for that, too—burst out of his bombast-stuffed doublet while his stockings waged battle with his fleshy legs. He leaned in for another strike with his stick.

Ruth grasped her hand. "Ale-soused applejohn! You could spare a parsnip or three if I had stole one."

The murmurings of the patrons built and shifted her focus, leaving her hand exposed to the stick's unmerciful swing. A second thwack sent pain rippling up her arm. Mr. Karelszoon's eyes narrowed to dangerous slits, and the crowd gathered tight.

"She's a thief and a liar," Mrs. Pieterszoon piped, and echoes of "To hell with lies and liars!" and "Strike down the pettifogger!" followed, chants among pews of circling women. Mrs. Janszoon jeered, wrung her cloth sheet into a whip, and snapped it at Ruth. The sheet spit hard against Ruth's side, then fanned open into her skirt layers, creating a mess of cloth to detangle.

Widower Karelszoon snarled. The man was a hound of teeth and mange. Before Ruth thought through her action, she picked up a parsnip and lobbed it at his face. He bounded toward her with his walking stick thrust high—Moses parting naught but air. The hissing sounds that slithered through his lips would have rattlesnaked a horse, and Ruth's eyes widened. She swiveled, narrowly avoiding his grasp. Her feet led her behind another cart, dodging, then back toward the marsh dropoff at the edge of town. The townspeople at her back rallied in support of Mr. Karelszoon's pursuit, and he gained on her in the marsh, swinging his stick wildly at every turn, ensnaring the seams of her dress and tendrils of her hair in the bellicose motion. Her dress snagged and tore at the hem.

"I stole nothing, you, you mule-brained pumpion. Were your parsnips as plump as you, they still wouldn't be worth stealing." Her words fueled him. The marsh slowed her down, and she sank to her ankles as Mr. Karelszoon descended upon her.

"You've stealed enough—God's mercy from us. His good grace. Replaced it with dried-up parsnip rubbage! You've brought the Wrath down upon us."

He lunged at her, knocking her off balance. Her boot stuck in the suctioning mud. She lifted her stocking-clad foot out of the boot and stepped down into swampwater. The unexpected coldness of it surprised her, and she wobbled, fell into muck, then sloshed to find something to wield in defense. She anticipated the stick cracking down upon her back, and then her fingers struck a rock and worked it forth from the mud, prying, her knees sinking into the wet marsh grasses. The rock loosened from soil, and she clenched it. At the edge of her vision, the stick sliced through the air. She spun out of its path, hurling the rock at the widower. It smacked against his knuckles, and the stick flew from his grasp like a marsh sparrow. Both the snarling man and Ruth dashed for it, but she reached it first, swung it, clipped him at his knees. His footing slipped from under him, and he landed gracefully as an ox in the mud. When he wiped the splashed swampwater from his eyes, he opened them to find his walking stick level with his nose, the traced length of it leading to Ruth's grasp.

"God's teeth." She punctuated her words with the point of the rod. "Get up."

Widower Karelszoon swallowed audibly and shook. Seizing the reprieve, he lumbered to his feet, then inched backward toward the town. He took off at an approximation of a run when out of striking range but fell in the mud once, twice, before clearing the marsh at the end of the town street.

The sound of sardonic, slow applause came from behind her, and Ruth turned, cupping her palm over her eyes, to confront her taunting audience. She blinked, then blinked again. The windmill chopped the salty air and made a repeated click-creak where it hooked on a catch with each rotation. Silhouetted against it, the buildings rose like a line of jagged mountain peaks, their matching A-slant roofs like fangs against the sky. And there, a sailor, clad in a cap-sleeved, bluish-russet jacket with brass buttons in a line down the front; thigh-high, beaten-leather boots pulled taut over hose up to cottonade breeches; baggy ivory sleeves rolled into cuffs across worked upper arms; and a billed woolen cap stretched over black hair that hung shaggily around his ears and neck. He was still clapping. Ruth blinked again, then threw her eyes toward the harbor, beyond the windmill. There she saw the freight fluyt *Primrose* anchored outside the eastern dock. The great square-rig was never docked at Shrewsbury so late in the season. *So, he wasn't an apparition.* The sailor's attention flickered between her kneeling in the mud and his ship's shallow bateau unloading at the dock, and Ruth's eyes collapsed to quick, thin lines.

"Thank you for the help," she said.

"Didn't appear you needed any. You scrap like a sailor." His smile was brash, genuine. "I had this niggling suspicion you'd light to that stick before the fat man could." He hooked his thumbs into the waistband of his breeches. "Right, per usual."

She grunted and tossed aside the stick.

"A grunt is all you got for me? Hello to you, too. What are you doing out of your cage?"

"Scavenging." The cold dampness clung to her stockinged foot, and she rutted around in the mud like a farm animal, hoping to find her sunken shoe. She shook the remaining tremble out of her fingers as she laced them through the muck.

He watched her steel herself. The corner of his lip twitched. "You're unscathed, though, aye? Say you're not, and I'll stock-iron the brigand to Antigua on the next breeze."

She gave up on the boot and stood, flipping mud from her dress. "Unscathed." The throbbing of her knuckles reminded her she was a terrible liar.

"A jaunt, then?" He removed his cap and took an unnecessarily long bow, lifting her muddy boot from the marsh on his way back up. "To the dock. I've items."

Scowling, she took the boot. A glance inside didn't promise comfort, and she shook the miserable thing upside down. Mud oozed out onto her dress. She frowned toward the harbor's small incoming boats only a short distance away, dwarfed by the mighty *Primrose*, then back to town equidistant behind her, then down at the mud caked on her arms and along her hemline. "Like this?"

"Like what? Something different about you, mon petite amour?" he said with charm only a licentious Frenchman could exude. "I'll feign for modesty that all the mud covers what you think you're hiding. Consider this: Widower Karelszoon might have been chasing you for another reason entirely."

"God's teeth."

"I swear you was a scrawny mutt last I saw you."

"God's teeth," she muttered again.

They reached the harbor, and he guided her toward the flatboat, where he withdrew a bundle, looked both ways, and slung it over his back. He tried not to think of it as reparations, but he knew they'd get to that later. The pilings stretched out into the Atlantic at the end of a long dock that flooded over with each wave. Fog moved in and gradually turned the land into fuzzy, gray felt. Grazing among offloaded firkins and kilderkins, he kicked the staves and pretended preoccupation, but his attention rested on the young woman, dressed in shades of murrey and lace and mud, shoulders curved away from the mirth of the sun, too old for her time. Her hair draped in auburn rivulets, not pretty, not unpretty, about her angled features. *Wild*. She looked feral and unbound. Her slender sixteen-year-old frame was adorned in colors too dark to be worn so soon before winter, as if in mourning or expecting to usher in the cold with her very presence. No other townswoman would have been caught entering the busy marketplace or harbor without her hair drawn beneath a coif, but convention escaped Ruth, and she, it. From the corner of his eye, he saw a deserter running inland, to the south, dodging behind the windmill, but he thought: *Let him go*, and couldn't break his gaze from Ruth. He watched her, just standing, stark and cold and breathing, shivering somewhat. Hair down, dress muddy. What a creature to reckon with. He would, someday. Not today.

"It's been a turn since I rescued a demoiselle en détresse."

"Was that rescuing?"

He smirked. "I oversaw. Overseeing is crucial to the rescuing."

"Perhaps you'd like, then, to oversee," she counted off on her fingers, "stuffing rags in the wall cracks between planks, binding shutters in place, making vats of candles, scraping ash from the fireplace to reap enough soap for winter, bringing maize garlands from the shed into the pantry, soaking the salted pork butts overnight—"

"Removing caked mud from your dress didn't fit that list, eh?"

"I'll not ask you to oversee anything that involves 'removing' and 'dresses.'"

He laughed, but his eyes darted to her hands as she wrung them. "That crawthumper did hurt you!"

She shook her head, sliding her hands behind her back. "Just mud. Mud washes." She bit her lip and stood straighter. "Tell me what I owe your unseasonal company to, First Mate Townsend. I assumed your slippery mouth would be on its way to Antigua by now."

"Are we to titles? You only get particular when you're sore at me."

She *was* sore at him, the scoundrel, the rat, the knave. Owen Townsend, the captain's son. He'd been her neighbor in another life; she'd known him as long as she'd known anything, and he'd been a scoundrel for all that time. She couldn't remember a time she wasn't sore at him, the scoundrel.

Owen grinned. He glanced about the docks and stepped closer to her, turning her toward the budding port settlement and away from the freightmen who watched her alarmingly. "Surely you know no painted Indian lady could keep me away while witch hunters are after my charming First Mistress Miner with sticks, aye? What theater I'd be missing." He winked.

She hrmphed. "Sakes! Out with it. I hadn't set to hear your squalid profanity again this season. I'd planned on having until spring to purify my ears. There's enough wind blowing in your sails to send you back out to sea without a boat—"

"Ship."

"—ship, if I'm unfortunate enough to hear you warble on about it—"

"Her."

"—her. This is not your choice port for evading alcohol duties."

He put a finger to his lips, and his brows V'ed. "A sailor can't pass a chance to muss a skirt."

"Achh. You're impossible." She threw her hands up and walked faster ahead of him, then stopped abruptly and looked back. "Then you came for me."

His smile dropped. "No. Emphatical no. Hors de question." He made an effort to look disinterested as they waded back through the marshy meadow, but her mouth snapped shut, and he winced. "Not yet. Not for some time. Don't be in haste to spend a lousy turn at sea with a sailor. You're not exactly a pick, all smelly of marshwater and salted fish."

"And you don't smell like fish?"

He wiped a wet glob of mud from her shoulder, held it toward her face as if in evidence, and shook it to the ground before drying his palm across his breeches. "You'll be a spinster before a man took a witch like you for exchange."

She missed a step. "I'd rather be a spinster than a—"

"Aht. Don't say coward. I won't be punished for it today. You got the rest of the town to chase you through the mud. Today, I'm just a missioner who heard Grand-maman wasn't faring good."

Ruth froze.

"She's not, is she," he said, not asking. "She's…"

Ruth at once appeared faint. She wrung her hands again and concentrated through an unwelcome daze. His face. That face she knew too well. It turned so quickly sullen. His mother's French cheekbones, angled jawline, dark features. Rosalie's same pointed nose. *What words did he say?* Ruth stared voidedly into his hooded gaze, masked with thick, black lashes and dark brows of his mother, making him appear ever quizzical. Had he spoken? His mother's replicated robin-egg eyes intensely flashed like Banded King Shoemakers he'd once brought to shore from the Indies. He'd been his mother's son for all of his twenty-one years. Images of Rosalie flitted through Ruth's mind, to distract. What words had he said? She sputtered to find her own. They weren't found.

"This coming cold will be hard for her," he said. "What if…"

"Aye," she finally managed.

Grandmother Helen was her last tie to this town, this land. The woman had been a founding member of the colony, and her husband its first selectman. Their lastborn son, Ruth's father. Out of the town's residual respect for Helen Miner, Ruth was only relegated to the mere trifling of wooden rods and marketplace snubbing, but the elder suffered from a crippling dementia brought on by contaminated water and too much mercury in her bloodstream, and if. If she died. *When* she died. Ruth shook her head of the thought. The people would not be so compelled to trifles.

Owen said, "Have you still got that barrel of aqua vitae I gave you month-last? Enough wood? Haven't much time, but I could hew more on the heel. Food?"

She snapped-to. "Yes, yes. I manage. If you could by grace make a goat appear, I might believe in miracles."

"You'd durst not believe such frivolities." He poked her shoulder.

She'd had to slaughter the goats right after he'd come, month-last. She couldn't milk them both morn and night, so they stopped producing. Mutton became all they were good for, and she had been without milk since. The weakness from it replaced her bones.

"Gran's got this stubborn fever, and she's talking in circles, sometimes thinks Fa—hpmm—Father is still alive." She looked again to the marshy ground, but no answers came from her soaked feet. Her eyelids fluttered closed. "I'm laboring on the Sabbath, heaven forgive."

He took her hand, and she startled at the feel of human skin that wasn't her own. His hands were callused, his grip as if yanking a halyard. "Just don't eat blackberries after Michaelmas, Ruthie, even if you're starved. That'll land you in the devil's briar for good." His fingers played over the swollen knuckles of her hand, and he scowled. "Why don't you get the reverend?"

"He won't come."

A growl thrummed long through Owen's throat. "I'll be back for Gran in the spring. I'll take her to Fairfield. To my mother."

"Take her now." She squeezed his hand and ignored the throb. "Spring is too late."

"I can't. Please don't ask it of me now. We won't be back to Fairfield before the cold is out. She'd be a winter at sea before I got her back to the colonies."

Ruth stared off, over her shoulder, through the low incoming fog clinging to the edge of the dock, at the gray turreted altocumulus forming over the ocean, virga shafts threading below it. Winter skies. They'd sweep over the land, blot out the blue, wrack what remained of the glasswort and narrow-leaved cattails of the saltmarsh, and freeze the mud solid with all its lumps and bumps until the uneven paths broke a horse's pastern. Saltmarsh sharptails that hadn't yet flown south probed through the mud for insects and seeds. Their raspy trills blended with Owen clearing his throat. He slung the bundle from his shoulder, eager to divert further talk of winter travel. The winter ocean would be the death of him someday; they both knew it, but only one of them accepted it.

"I took some of the downs bound for Boston, this heavy cloak—"

"Of course you did, you thief." She jolted out of her mope. "You're the one who should've been on the receiving end of Widower Karelszoon's stick." Her face lit as she perused the goods. A copper kettle, a thin cast-iron flatpan. A blanket of feather down. "What if they find out you took this?" She rubbed the soft material against her cheek, and it caught on rough skin. "It doesn't feel English-made."

"French. Only the finest for my doxy. À ton service." His pride shone like a banner on a new ketch. "Leave a man to his trade without question, my blush. I dare just one of them to accuse the," he emulated the captain's gruff voice, "honorable Captain Jacob Townsend of shorting the order, when it could just as right have been one of their own deck hands."

"I should think your father was not so pleased to come back here."

"Nay the slightest. It was my mother guilted him by reminding him Grand-maman was midwife to all his sons. In fact, Captain's glassing me." He looked back at the ship. "I can't afford to dally on these grounds, or the English loyalists, thumb to 'em all, might keep me docked a bit more," he made a guttural sound, "permanent."

Her brow arched. So dramatic he was.

"You haven't heard? King Louis besieged a Philippsburg fortress and took Mannheim. Him and Louvois have set out to destroy the Palatinate, Baden, Württemberg. Land expansion."

"You can't know what any of that means any more than I do. I'm inclined to say bless you."

"It means the English and the French are at war. It means the Treaty of Whitehall is dead. New France will surely war with New England, right here, beneath our feet, despite the treaty's promise of keeping Old World conflicts off these shores. William of Orange took Torbay, but if Louis attacks Dutch lands, then even Shrewsbury will join the fray."

"Bless you."

"I plan on keeping my French feet far from here."

"Not too far, I hope." She grinned. "You're only half French, so you have only one foot to worry about." Then she looked as if struck by lightning. "That means Governor Andros' Dominion of New England can no longer enforce the quit-rent for Gran, nor the Navigation Acts for you, aye?"

"Snuff that thought." He glanced around himself quickly. "Nicholson won't allow dissent on these grounds, and his fellow Andros is all too happy to extinguish anyone, dissenter or no. And half French, well…that depends who you ask." He tapped the tip of his pointed nose, looked toward the woods to her grandmother's halfhouse tucked out of sight, and felt Ruth's eyes follow his lead. "I must be off to the marketplace to pick up a barrel of oats from Willemszoon's. Then, quick to the dock to rally deserters."

"I have to go back to the carts, too, much as I dread it. Copernicus is hobbled there."

"You rode him into town? Sakes, you really don't want friends, do you. Walk with me, then."

He splayed his hand in the direction of the marketplace as they left the marshy meadow that connected the harbor dock to the edge of town. The row of Dutch houses loomed, and the slow churning of the mill wheel made a grinding whine, followed by a clunk at the end of each rotation. He felt his breaths synchronize with it. A young woman, too close to the harbor for modesty's sake, stared hard at him beneath her starched, triangle-flapped bonnet, until an elder scolded her loudly and dragged her back to the row of houses. The mill wheel continued its whine-clunk, whine-clunk.

"Have you thought on what you'll do if I can't come back?" he said quietly.

"How have I had time to think on it? This is the first I've heard of it."

"Well, then, have you thought of what you'll do if this winter is too hard? How much longer can we keep meeting like this before your reputation is questioned and we're not just a couple kids getting reacquainted anymore?"

"My reputation? Questioned?" She rubbed her swollen knuckles and gasped deeply. "Heavens, no. What will they think of me? Do you think there will be rumors? Perhaps wooden rods? My, what if they prejudge my character?"

He smirked. "You should go get married, Ruth."

She stopped.

"Find a warm house to move Grand-maman into, get some of the burden of providing off my shoulders." He didn't notice that she'd stopped.

"Who else would marry me?" she retorted too loudly behind him, not caring that the Dutch women of the vegetable carts could hear every word. She marched up to him. "Don't tell me to go get married as if it's that easy." Her arms flailed like an injured bird. "Look at me!"

He did look at her, always did. Mud didn't hide her.

"I can't trade a parsnip! Or shall I remind you of that day when you—"

"Cease." His eyes flashed, then darkened. He didn't need to remember what never left his mind. "I didn't come here for that. Let the past have the past." He had the good grace to look away. "You're a stubborn one, Ruthie. It's no wonder no man'll have you. I'd be like to find his body floating facedown at sea, closer to me than he ever got to you."

"Hmph, go get married. No one in this town would have me."

"Then get out of this town." He ignored the hollowness of his advice as he entered Mr. Willemszoon's shop. He focused instead on oats. A load much easier to lift.

Ruth paced. *How dare he?* She had no means to leave the town without him. She'd die from the elements before she reached the closest settlement, wherever that was. She waited while Owen was inside, treading dirt, tapping her foot, switching the gift bundle from shoulder to shoulder. She thought about taking out the flatpan and cracking it across his nose, the blackguard. When the door opened, she spun to fire another salvo across Owen's bow, but was met instead with Kees Karelszoon walking out of the shop, his puckered, red knuckles holding a cheesecloth over a freshly bloodied nose. She took a step back to bolt for Copernicus, but Mr. Karelszoon nodded his wide-brimmed hat and stepped past her, averting his eyes, mindful to avoid brushing shoulders. She exhaled the breath she'd been holding and eased.

When Owen exited the shop with the barrel of oats thrown over one shoulder, he pulled something from his breast pocket and dusted it on his breeches, feigning ignorance to Ruth's chagrined new expression. He placed a fabric-encased book into her hands. "I near forgot this."

"Oh! A new one." She read the inscription: *The Injur'd Lovers, or The Ambitious Father*, William Mountfort, London, The Year of Our Lord Sixteen Eighty and Eight. "A drama—dreadful! How did you ever afford—"

"Avec plaisir. I didn't afford it."

"Of course you didn't. You can't just—"

He rested a finger over her mouth. "It'll be our secret. Like everything between us."

The touch didn't go unnoticed by the town's Dutch women. One of them pipped like a surprised mouse. Another tapped the tip of a butter churner onto the side of her cart like a schoolmarm getting the attention of unruly pupils. The Dutch-Reformed, with their identical broad-brimmed, low-crowned hats, stood in a line outside the meeting-house and shook their heads in unison. Ruth collected herself under their judgment, but the onlookers didn't faze Owen.

"Why, hello, ladies." He removed his hat and set the barrel of oats on the ground next to their carts. "Looks like you got some fine parsnips here and, I must say, a deft green thumb to keep them alive during the frost. Almighty impressive."

The women blushed.

"How much for a parsnip today?" he asked.

"For ye," Mrs. Pieterszoon fair hummed, "there be no cost." She cast a superior smirk at Ruth, who scowled in return. To Owen, she added, "Do tell your father good day for me, will ye?"

"I will, indeed." He lifted the fattest parsnip he could find in the cart and nodded. "He will be most delighted to hear it."

Mrs. Janszoon said hastily, "Ye can have two parsnips from me, dear boy, and do tell your father that I gived you twice the bounty as Betje." The woman piled two plump roots into Owen's hand.

"Oh come, Saskia!" Betje Pieterszoon retorted. "Don't listen to her. Take another parsnip from me, too, Mr. Townsend."

"Thank you ever so kindly, ladies. Shall we make it three apiece?" He took two more roots without waiting for a reply, pressing the six dirty parsnips against his chest in one arm and squatting to lift the oats in the other. "The captain will be delighted. Have your lovely selves a lovely day." As he stepped away from the carts, he dropped the six parsnips into Ruth's apron, avoiding her disgusted glare. "There. I got you six parsnips and had not a time of it. Heaven knows what you thought was so hard about that."

He walked her to Copernicus, then helped Ruth strap the stolen material bundles, copper kettle, and down blankets across the horse's back. His eyes settled on a branded W that marked the animal's hindquarters. A breath left him sharply. He knew the derogatory brand wasn't a chosen monogram and was the reason Ruth still owned the valuable horse that could otherwise have purchased her years' worth of comfort, could she only find a buyer of little enough superstition not to consider the beast cursed.

"I still can't believe you rode him to town."

"I can't spend all day getting here just to return home empty-handed. There is naught faster than a good horse."

"My ship is faster than a horse."

"Impracticalities excluded," she laughed, unroping Copernicus, then walking, the three of them, back toward the marsh. "I can't very well boat across these saltmarshes, now can I?"

"I spoke nothing of a boat. Your horse is faster than a boat."

"Ah, boat, ship: when will you ever get over that nuance?"

"When you've finally corrected it." He turned, and his second mate's voice called out across the marsh. "Ah." Owen's crest slumped. "Looks like *Primrose* will be first mateless if I don't go…although you'll be mateless if I do go. Quite the predicament for a man with any conscience. Lucky for me, I haven't got one of those useless things." He grinned, but not quite. "Adieu, Ruth Miner, you muddy creature. Until spring, doxy. You fare well, you hear me?"

She watched him walk the short distance across the marsh, silhouetted by the harbor, creating a bustling halo around his figure. The birds stopped chirping, and he kicked up flocks of sparrows from the tall spike grasses and bulrushes. They swarmed like dark winter clouds around him, until they separated and darted after waterbugs and dragonflies that hadn't yet migrated. She was still watching when he shouted across the meadow.

"Go get married, Ruthie! You'll never last the winter!"

Abashed, she turned her focus to the few harbor patrons and marketplace women who had heard his shout. When she looked back to where he had been, he was a speck of movement and reflected light on the dock, some glinting buttons, a wash of russet, climbing into the last loaded tender headed toward *Primrose* with the surefootedness of a cat on a ledge. Ruth made herself turn away.

She mounted her gelding, cast Copernicus' muzzle toward home, and came back into herself when she neared the entrance of the marshy woods that led to Grandmother's halfhouse. As the horse hit the first soggy steps of the woods, Ruth looked back toward the harbor. *Primrose's* sails were much smaller now, dollhouse-sized and floating with a ghostly ease. The fluyt would not return until winter's icy waters gave way to spring.

At the sobering thought of winter, she shivered and released a desperate sound, the chip-note of a caged swallow. Her horse continued on, unguided, toward the wooden halfhouse nestled in the clearing, its faded clay-red paint coming into view, dulled on the southern boards that received the sun's waning rays. The sun, though, was of little matter: the house would be unbearably cold in a week's time, and that dear fireplace had to be filled faster than the heat could surface from it. But the smoke rising from the chimney and the floating scent of soaking salted alewife and clippers mixed with her spicy gingerbread, sugary olykoeks, and barleyloaf gave Ruth the bones she needed to stable Copernicus and leave the harbor behind for the season.

CHAPTER SECOND
In the bleak midwinter

And, thou away, the very birds are mute;
Or, if they sing, 'tis with so dull a cheer
That leaves look pale, dreading the winter's near.

—William Shakespeare

Ruth started awake. Grandmother's cough proved the walls useless, and she called out for her son—Ruth's father—in breaths that caught nothing. Early yellows sliced through the slats. First morning in a month that the clouds had lifted. Ruth dragged herself from the bed, and the twisted roots of her body burrowed, planted into place, unable to lift, upward, outward, until Gran coughed again, and Ruth jerked upright as if chained to Gran's breath while it left her.

The rags from Ruth's mattress padding had been removed and wrapped around the reeds in Gran's bedding, cushioning the sickly woman above the oil pan that sat beneath her bed, needing new flame. Ruth's mattress now comprised nothing but raw banded sticks, one top layer of cloth, a few wraps of failing twine. She was sore and had slept little, the last two weeks having a cold to them too stinging for sleep, even by February's standards.

The dirt floor didn't welcome her stockinged feet. Her cloak draped ineffectual. She shuffled to the hearth, prodded the remains of the fire with an iron, and watched sparks shoot in bursts, landing without promise. The cold felt solid inside her, firm, immovable, and it met a winter ague that she dismissed out of necessity to move forward. Every joint pleaded against it. She posited a crucible of water to boil, then set to dressing for winter—layers of skirts, aprons, several shifts beneath her low-waisted bodice, a hooded woolen cloak, bundles of stockings. More grunts and writhings than a barnyard beast. When finished, she couldn't bend to lace the calf-high boots that she wished she'd put on first.

She removed the draft cloths wedged under the front door and lifted its wood bar. Wind keened through the trees, and when it changed at once to a low howl, it stung her cheeks like a snapping gutwhip, and she low-howled back, hurled away from the door. Her ribs seemed to freeze to her lungs before she got to the closest cedar with her wedge. With one hand she pulled her apron into a net, and with the other, she shaved the wet bark into the net with the wedge until she had enough for kindling. So cold she couldn't feel her toes in her worn boots, she slogged to the woodpile and reached to brush ice from the wood. Nettles tore through her arm. Her ignored sickness racked her with lightheadedness; she finally knew its identity and felt the choler coat the roof of her mouth. She let out a loud "Ahhyh!" to get her adrenaline pumping, then swooped and cupped a log to her chest one-handed.

Back within the house, she removed her wet layers, her stiffened fingers uncooperative. Inside was no warmer than outside. Everything was damp. Puddles came in under the doors and onto the window ledges. The hot water scarce hissed. She dropped down in front of the hearth and cradled the log, laid it so carefully against the weak flame to dry one side of the wood slowly. But the dampness was too much; the log quelled the infant flame like a wet blanket before she could even retrieve the kindling. She lowered her head onto her forearms and stared. Her sickness flared in her, and she thought about how easy it would be to stop moving and freeze to the ground.

From the borning room, Gran's wheeze filled the house, then collapsed, again, collapsed, rose, collapsed—an eerie rhythm of death's footsteps. Ruth pulled herself to her knees, grabbed hold of the fireplace grate, and reached for the iron to poke for any lingering hot coals. A quarter of an hour later, despite the new log's wetness, a budding flame was nursed to health. Eventually, the crucible boiled with melted snow.

Ruth sat at Gran's bedside and soaked hot calico into a wooden bowl for the woman's clammy head, then readied a droplet of mercury to dot the woman's tongue.

"I remember at your age. In Woodbridge—" Gran grasped her granddaughter by the wrist. The woman's eyes were sunken like dark cherry pits, strikingly contrasted against saggy eyelids of old linen. Jowls, rich of age, laid against her neck in one continuum.

"You've never been to Woodbridge. You're thinking of my mother."

Gran shook her head. "I do not know your mother, child."

Ruth sighed and forced a patient smile. "She married your last son."

"Why has he nay come?"

Ruth studied the flower print on the ewer. The blue porcelain came from the Old Country, the flowers not native here, their blossoming colors an insult to the season's starkness. The spot of life deadened Gran by comparison. Nothing but death flourished in a New English winter.

"Who'll take care of you?" Gran said.

"I will," Ruth replied flatly.

The old woman winced at the application of a new hot cloth to her forehead. Her mind trailed beyond the shutter cracks, and Ruth knew where it went. That path that led to the false hope of the harbor— Gran's mind walked it, too.

"Pray, then," the elder whispered.

"Praying makes no more of an end to this than discussing it. Owen will be back in spring to see you. You'd like that, wouldn't you? He will take you to his mother in Fairfield. In Connecticut Colony. You do remember Rosalie?"

"Your mother."

"No, she's not my mother. Rosalie Townsend, Captain Townsend's wife."

"You're Captain Townsend's wife?"

"Oh, heavens. How dreadful a prospect that would be." Ruth snorted. "Rose is Owen's mother. He'll take you to stay with her until you get better. Along the Long Island Sound, on a bowery near the water. It will be good for you."

"Oooh, that's too hot."

Ruth pushed the woman's hand from the cloth. "It's not that hot, so stop. You're freezing. You look—"

"You should see how you look." The woman chuckled, then coughed. Her chest heaved beneath the weight of it. "Where is my son? He hasn't come for me."

"He's not here now." Ruth felt the fever swell inside her. Her father hadn't been there for a decade. "You won't see him. He won't be coming."

"Who'll take care of you?"

"I will."

"But who'll chop the wood?"

"I'll chop wood. Gran, please." She faced away and whispered to herself, "I always chop the wood, always."

The elder closed her eyes and nodded reluctantly and fell into sleep. Ruth retreated into herself, maddened. Color drained from her eyes and cheeks and hands, from the wallpaper on the one wall that had it, from her fingers, clutching cloth that felt neither warm nor cool. The candle's flame like a tarantella and her dancing inside it and around it and in it and around. The bubbling of a boiling crucible, the howling wind. Stoke the fire, stir the pot, mash the peas, heat the kettle, wet the cloth, chop, slice, wrap, heat, cook, sweep. Dizziness overcame her, and her forehead burned, throbbed. She stood to her feet, but her balance gave way; the sudden motion swept blood from her spinning head. Her body crumpled against the wall, where she slid down to the cold floor into dark.

❧

Ruth awoke in a fever spell with metal in her throat, her body itchy hot and chilled. A crawling like sumac spread beneath her skin. She peeled her face from an icy pile of vomit that had frozen to the floor, to her hair and clothes. The fire was out and appeared to have been dead for at least a day. Ice crystals formed around the front door, and a cold vapor rose from the iron gate around the fireplace—winter's breath.

The room stood so frigid she could hardly breathe in it. She heaved herself up along the frame of the doorway and moved toward the hearth, bracing herself on chairs, the blood flow returning in tingles. Water dripped down the chimney and dampened the logs and kindling beneath it. The pieces of char linen from a wooden box were wet, too, a layer of water sitting in the bottom of it. She blew against the kindling and char and strips of flax tow nesting until her head floated languidly back from the effort, spent, but the nest still wasn't dry enough. She smashed her knuckle-branched steel striker at a sharp angle against jagged flint until her knuckles went red with rogue strikes, and she watched the sparks evanesce into nothing. It took twenty minutes before the char cloth caught a spark. Ruth gasped in disbelief and almost put the little flame out with her burst of breath. She sucked in, then blew against it steadily, lowly, for ten more minutes before the flax tow was dry enough to take the flame. Another ten minutes of steady blowing and the cedar shavings finally caught, then Ruth could fan the flame carefully with a bellows until the logs were dry enough to catch. She felt her fever at full pitch. It afflicted, but at least she could feel it.

The water eventually boiled, then Ruth carried the bowl to the borning room and stared at the ice crystals that had formed around Gran's nose. Her body, now a jaundiced yellow that had been a pale pink, lay still. Ruth leaned closer to Gran's face and could see the tiniest breath rising from the sick woman's mouth.

"Gran, we need help. We need someone to help us."

Gran's fragile voice returned, "Where is your father?"

Ruth let out an unexpected, violent dry heave—her stomach empty, vision blurred, hands sweaty from sickness, body recoiling from the throat burn. "He's dead. He's been dead for near ten years."

"My son?" hoarsely.

"Dead." The word sounded like someone else saying it. Her eyes scanned for something to throw, to break. She clutched the bedpost and thought she'd rip it loose from its moorings. "He is dead. They're all dead!" She got up from the bedside, ambled down the hall, and bundled. Her head spun, but standing in the doorframe, she could no longer hear Gran's faint breathing, and this galvanized her. "Do you remember Reverend Morgan? I'm going to get help from Reverend if he will help me. Please. Please, hold on. Just a pitter longer. It will be spring soon."

She stared at her unresponsive grandmother, then forced herself to move toward the door. If she approached the reverend, he'd have her head on a pike. If the townfolk learned about Gran—*but it had to be done.* She swallowed and grabbed the wooden maul from the hearthhook. Heavy winds ripped the door from her, and she labored to close it behind. The cold numbed her fingers and toes within minutes. She made her way to town, through drifts near to her knees, and each step slowed her down so that it took her an hour to get there. She eventually found Shrewsbury deserted, its families tucked inside their daubed homes. The tips of the Dutch colonials no longer looked like mountain peaks, but knives thrust into the gray carcass of the sky. Carts and wagons and mobile sheds were winterized in heavy burlap and pressed against the homes like scared children to mother's thigh, so coated in snow they were nearly invisible in the white.

Ruth knocked at the back of the meetinghouse until Reverend Morgan's new apprentice, John Crawford, pulled open the door and stared at the unkempt figure before him.

"Good day, Apprentice Crawford." Ruth curtsied clumsily, her body bending poorly in the cold. "I am in need of Reverend Morgan, please."

"You appear ill. Are you sick, miss?" His voice was without urgency while he eyed her maul.

Miss? Could he really not yet know who she was? "It will pass." His calmness irked her. She thought of her appearance, how much better her prospects could be with the young man if she looked presentable, pleasant. *Go get married.* There were far worse things than being the wife of a future reverend, but she rid herself of the notion. One word, and Crawford would learn of her, and that would put an end to that. "I'm Ruth," she hesitated, "Miner." *There was the word.* Just mention of the name sounded like a curse to her. As soon as that name got back to the reverend, help would no longer be offered by his naïve apprentice. Her only hope then would be to speak to the reverend face to face, to plead for his mercy for her grandmother, a woman who'd once been a cornerstone of the town. "Please, my grandmother is dying. Might you come yourself?"

"Mistress Miner, I shall inform Reverend Morgan, and we'll set out for your home immediately."

Her face drooped. "Please. Hurry. I beg you."

He shut the door, leaving her to stand in the snowbank as a precaution. She didn't blanch. The snow fell in fat, quick flakes and piled around her. The white blinded. With each breath she was reminded of the sickness that squeezed her lungs but didn't reach her outer limbs. She tried to flex her toes but couldn't. The bootnails in her worn soles poked through to her heels, and her feet squished in numbing water. The minutes passed, and she thought the ground had swallowed her up to her shins, where feeling began again. She gripped the maul and glanced over her shoulder. When Crawford reappeared, he opened the door only enough to press his mouth against the crack.

"Reverend Morgan is not in," he said.

"But you just went for him."

"He does not wish to speak with you."

"Is he not in, or does he not wish to speak with me?"

"Yes."

"Yes?"

"Please, go," he whispered.

"You're turning me away? What wrong have I done?" She lodged her foot between the door and the frame and didn't feel the slam.

"Please, go," he repeated, and nudged her foot loose of the frame and closed the door between them.

"Apprentice Crawford, I beg you." She pressed a hand to the door as if she could reach through the barrier. "It is not for me that I ask; it is for my grandmother, Helen Miner. She's a humble, God-fearing servant of the Lord, sir. She was a founder of this colony, was a midwife to half the folk in this town and their children after that and after that."

"Please, go." Crawford's voice was muffled through the door now.

"Helen Miner has always attended this church. She is ill. She helped your needy when she had nothing herself, made food and clothing for your poor. You ought repay her!"

At this, Ruth heard the door of the meetinghouse barred from inside. The clicking sound of hypocrisy's hasp echoed loudly in the dusk. Looking up, she saw the foreboding figure of Reverend Morgan through the oiled-linen windows, backlit by candle glow, and her indignation overcame her. She shook her maul at him.

"Reverend Morgan, I willn't go. I know you hear me. God will damn you for this! Come down from your cowardly tower!"

But the reverend's figure moved away from the window, and Ruth stood alone. She waited, but the door didn't open. Her ears tuned to the whirring wind, one lone horse's whinny, the latch clicking over and over in her mind. Her lips quaked with shivers.

"Is that it, then? You will not come? You will not aid one of your flock with your blessed healing hand of God?"

She turned toward the street; the center of town stretched before her, empty and quiet. Poles struck the sky, naked of lanterns. The windmill that loomed in the distance was bogged in snow and couldn't rotate, rocking in place too shallowly to dislodge drifts from its propellers.

"Then damn your god!" she screamed in a cry that bounced against shop windows and candlelit homes. "Damn your false god!"

Only quiet returned.

"Who will help her? She is dying. She has clothed you, fed you, dripped for you those candles you're burning, made bedclothes which bundle you! Who will come?" She heard shutters snapping, furniture sliding behind doors, wood bars dropping into hooks, hasps bolting home throughout the streets, from one side to the other, reverberating off the dampened homes. "Then damn you all!" Her fingers curled into a fist at her side, breaking open the damaged skin. "You fear me? You condemn me from your pedestal? It's you that hath sentenced the innocent to death this night! Sinners, all of you!" Her voice grew hoarser with each breath. "You think I am a witch? This you call me? Then witch I am! I'll be that devil conjuror you must blame for your deaths and poor crops and sick children. You want to burn me? Come and get me! I'll curse you as the witch you've made me. All of you! In your tight houses, curse you. Curse your children and their children. Curse your Bibles and your cattle and your goats and your fields!"

Silhouettes filled the windows of homes. The ticking of the windmill as it stuck in place beat its rhythm into her head, her heart.

"Might your candles go out and your flint disintegrate to flakes! Might your yeast not rise and your beds be infested with lice and your roofs all leak and your mules run off to Woodbridge! Might savages and Quakers plague this town and burn your church to ashes! Curse you. Curse you all!" Gasping for breath, she fell to her knees in the snow, diaphragm pulsing.

※

Ruth hauled herself through the door of the still house two hours later, exhaustion coroneting her head. All lay quiet, save for the dwarfed fire toward which she moved, then buckled, resting her head against the hearth wall. She squeezed the bellows to bring up the flame. As she thawed, sharp sensations shot through her hands and feet, and she found herself whimpering like an injured puppy. When she removed her boots, her stockings stuck to her feet like a second skin. Beneath the bondage of the wet socks, her toes were spavined with red, dull yellow-gray, and white spots surrounding swollen tissue and blisters. Piece by piece, she took off her soggied articles, her hands not recognizing the feel of buttons or laces. She was thawing out, a misery unlike anything she'd ever known.

She crawled to the pantry for mustard seed and ground wheat and mixed it on a cloth with water from the floor puddles. She laid the poultice over her red feet, and when dark fell, she slumped with it until the mustard plaster burned her, then she pulled it off to find more blisters. Through the dark, she felt her way along the walls, hobbling on her freshly bandaged heels to the ledge containing the candlesticks. Feeling around for what was left of her supply, she found a taper and carried it to the fire. Each step took minutes. It had never taken her so long to light a candle, and she cursed the damn thing's necessity with every movement.

She hadn't durst enter the too-quiet borning room since her return. The stillness there bathed her in unease. But with her lighted candle, she drew up the courage to make her way to Gran's bedside and held the light to the cold, white face. No tiny breaths stirred in the candle's glow. The air was heavy with a lulling static, and Gran's body lay still in it: her hands folded across her chest, her wrinkled lips turned up at the corners, her heart and suffering having stopped. Ruth's lip quivered, and she took the candlestick and the heavy comforter from the bed and walked back to the fire, staring into its flame. She extinguished the candle with thumb and forefinger, not noticing her burned fingers left pinched too long over the smoking wick.

᷇

The next morning, beads of sweat gathered around her hairline and had soaked through the cloth at her armpits. For the first time in days, her hunger returned. There were canned jams, prunes, peas, dried figs, and mashed cornmeal, but little of each and little else. The pantry boasted boiled cookies and fruit-and-nut jumbles left from autumn, neither of which would be sustaining, but seafood could not be acquired until the waters broke for fishing. Breakfast would have to settle for jam, boiled dried cedar leaves, black coffee. Supper would be tasteless pea mash. She was out of fresh salt. Ruth set the kettle to boil and a pot to soak the salt-cured, dried peas until supper, then bundled again. She would harvest the pea salt from the water after it boiled dry, but she craved something heartier; her feet throbbed, and exhaustion had weakened her. She ate in silence, prolonging the inevitable, taking ample care to finish the last drop of her coffee, to cherish its company like a visitor.

Stiffly laced and buttoned, she could scarce bend down to where Gran lay in the borning-room bed. Ruth took a comforter from the top of a trunk and worked the blanket beneath the feet and backside of the body, the deadweight difficult to lift. When she had the flock under the body, she pulled it closed and grabbed hold of the bottom ends with Gran's feet. She rolled the body, inch by inch by inch, until it dropped from the bed. The dead woman's head cracked against the floor, the sound skeletal, primal. Ruth cringed and dragged the covered body through the house, stopping every few steps, her sickness still weakening her. At the mudway, she took two iron-jaw leghold gin traps from their wall mounts and dropped them down on the bundle. She managed to heave it through the door and to the field past the woodpile, where she dropped the body into a large drift. She stood for a moment, cold but sweating, eyes to the woods that were brighter than usual, cast against the gleaming snow, then faced back.

"You ate all those sweetbreads, Gran," she said aloud. Her own voice shocked her in the silence.

It was then that she saw in Gran's sunken, gaunt face, for the first time, her father. She'd always held them so separate, so different they were. But now how they likened one to the other, how she saw in this face what her father would have looked like old, had grace granted him time. She thought of being as close to his death age as to the years she'd known him alive. Eight on both counts. She thought of outliving him, what a scar that would leave on the soul of a being. Two years junior to that, she would have already outlived her mother. Ruth's nose burned from cold snot, and she sucked it in and spat like she always chastised Owen for doing, then she kicked piles of snow up over Gran's covered body, packed it all down. The snowy burial mound would have to suffice in advance of spring's thawed ground.

The burred gin traps felt like anvils in her cold hands, but she carried them a distance away, hooked the chains around the horse pulls, and buried the stock bars in the snow up to the spring rivets. She stepped the steel jaws open with her feet, set the spring neck, then snapped the jaws back to the tongue and clamped the till. The iron stuck to her fingers when she touched it. A dab of jam and dried figs wouldn't attract much, but it was all she had to set on the iron plate. She kept her back to the crude stable all the while, knowing that Copernicus could not have withstood the snowdrifts up over his knees that blew in through the hayledge, nor could she yet bear to face that awful truth: that she'd been unable to care for him, too—trapped, alone, and for all his tremendous strength, helpless.

Once back inside the house, the silence draped like a noose around her neck. There was no one now, human nor creature. And Gran, Ruth's last asylum from the town she'd cursed, was gone. All that was left was to wait for them to arrive. And it wouldn't be Kees Karelszoon with his walking stick and Betje Pieterszoon with her hands full of rotted parsnips. They'd come with torches and muskets and stones and appled faces. Would they hang her? Drown her? Tie her to a chair and lower her into the ocean? Lock her in the stocks or force her into the pillory? She feared her fate would likely be worse: they'd burn her alive in her own cabin.

She looked about the house, pocked with dried vomit and discarded cloths. The room was in disarray, and she had few weapons with which to defend herself. Wincing, she stepped gingerly on her frail feet, holding herself upright on the bedstand as she worked her way back to the mudway. She took the last two iron-jaw gin traps from the wall mounts and headed outside to the path leading in from town. When they came, she'd be ready.

⦈

But no one came. They couldn't get through the snow. For weeks, Ruth awaited the warmth of spring with the terror that the townspeople were waiting for warmer weather, too. The sound of the hammer was violent in the stillness when she pounded nails into new strips of wood on the bottoms of her boots, then chiseled down the edges with a whalebone file. She spread heated birch-pitch into the seams and left the boots upside down to dry while she examined her foot. A wound along the big toe still blistered and refused to heal. She rinsed it and applied another mustard poultice. Her stomach growled, but all she had was a prune-and-fig pottage that she kept stretching with snow water. While she waited for her boots to dry, she packed her belongings into a trunk, taking stock of each item, selecting what she'd leave behind. What she couldn't carry, she would forsake to be burned. There wasn't much of value, but she only needed enough to purchase her safe passage to any-where. *Anywhere else.*

Like a banshee wail, a shriek came from outside that sent Ruth staggering a few steps. It was followed by a monosyllabic bark and then another, and she righted her boots, shoved her bare feet inside, poultice and all, and grabbed her cloak and her maul and a flencher. She bounded out the door and toward the woodpile. At the stock head of one of the traps, a red fox gnawed his foreleg and gekkered at Ruth with ratcheting throat sounds. His hazel eyes caught her movement, and he stilled and laid back his ears and went quiet. She came closer, and he didn't move. Blood stained the white underbelly of his neck. She moaned sadly. Her heart lurched, and she looked away and brought the maul down on the bright red head. It was as merciful as she could make it. Snow seeped into her boots when she knelt. The poultice burned on her toes. She stabbed the flencher into his belly, slit up the gut, and reset the trap with the discarded organs. She lifted the fox and turned toward the house, then stopped. Somewhere near her was another set trap that she couldn't see beneath the snow. The ground was liquidy around her, and she felt the thaw coming. Carefully retracing her same steps, more difficult this time without her bounding stride, she made it back to the halfhouse with her kill.

The mock meat tasted gamey and rough, but it gave her nourishment. She felt her strength return as she finished the canidison fig pottage, licking the wooden bowl. With food in her stomach and the thaw upon her, she went back to the stable for a shovel, shuddering at the sight and smell of the dead, disintegrating horse, then turned to face what re-mained of the mound where she'd left Gran a month before. There was not much left of the high snow, and the blanket was lifted open in its half-frozen corners, peeled back to reveal chunks of skin torn loose and hanging from the body. Ruth could see fleshy bits of limbs, toes, and strung-out organs where animals had eaten what they could uncover in the unproviding winter. She quickly looked away, choked down the bile that stung her mouth, and jammed the shovel into the barely softened ground, striking a piece of decamped bone.

Hours passed. She'd scraped a foot and a half of hardened soil and could dig no further. Her arms drummed with taxation. She covered her mouth, chipped the body away from what remained of the snow, and unceremoniously dragged Gran into the shallow grave. She kicked the soil back over the top of the body until she realized there wasn't enough dirt. When Ruth gained nerve enough to look, Gran's body still peeked from under the soil. Ruth dropped the shovel and cursed it, then glanced toward the harbor. Mares' tails dappled the seascape in an otherwise vibrant cerulean sky. A solitary blue-morphed snow goose dived for something and came up with a moving throat. The ships would be in soon. On the path that led to town, patches of brown poked through the snow, and her neck tightened. The snow couldn't protect her now.

⚮

Before dusk fell, she saw the torches. The town was restless, awakening with the thaw and the coming new year, and with the planting of the next crops, they were anxious to be rid of Ruth's curses over them. She figured word had spread about Gran, the land, the forfeited quit-rent. Two silver serving dishes, a set of four pewter spoons, some imported beads, and six full bolts of cloth. This would have to do. She slammed the lid of her trunk, but it wouldn't click. Inside, her Bible protruded in the way of the clasp, and she sighed. She pulled out the tome, tossed it onto the bed, and the latch clicked as if the smith had newly fashioned it. Her blood raced when she heard the villagers' voices shouting, closer.

After finding a wedge to budge the trunk, she towed it, partially bolstered by a piece of wood, out the back door. It was a slow limp to the stable, but when she got there, she flung the door wide and battled with a hanging wooden sled to shake it loose from the pile of stacked metal prods, ropes, and tools that had once belonged to her father. She untangled the sled from the stable wall, then paused in the doorway to look toward the grave mound.

"Adieu. You fare well, Gran," she said, "Copernicus," nodding. The animal's shape was hardly recognizable as a horse, the remains not much more than fragmentary. She squatted to lever the trunk onto the sled. She could make it the long way to the harbor, in and out of the woods at the foot of the marsh; they'd never see her, she reasoned. Then, on the path in from town came the sudden snap of iron and a crack, a human howl akin to a wolf's, and she knew exactly where they were. The lights of torches came around the far side of the house, and she hunkered down and jerked the sled forward into the trees behind the stable. The rolling marshlands were frozen solid in some places and thawed soft in others, rendering smooth maneuvering of the sled impossible. She stopped frequently to push one side or the other out of a defrosted marshy rut. Emptied and fatigued, she looked toward the harbor to see that she'd only made it a quarter of the way across the meadow, sheltered by trees. She could still go back; the house was closer. But as she watched it, she saw the figures, the black smoke that rose from somewhere near them, shadows attached to angered voices. Animals rustled in the woods at the scent of fire, acrid, overmolded loaf mixed with that blackchar when it burned to the bottom of the flatpan, sour at the back of the nose. She pressed on toward the shore. Tying the sled's rope around her waist and hunching into a workhorse position, she sloughed across the uneven field, stopping periodically to wipe her drenched forehead, to flex out the pinch in her pained toe, then finally arriving in a blur of paradoxical fury and weakness at the far corner of the harbor.

She panted and stepped to the counter of a makeshift, crude customs house built on four oak stanchions with uninsulated wood slats nailed from post to post. The room was no bigger than a backhouse, and behind the counter, one immobile man leaned over a ledger, and Ruth approached him. "I need to pay my passage."

"To where?" he replied. He couldn't take his eyes from his ledgers, where he had scrawled customs records in accordance with the Navigation Acts, ensuring that merchants carried only goods that benefitted English tradelines, and were therein properly taxed for them. He shivered in the winter air that seeped through the undaubed wall cracks.

"To anywhere."

He looked up. "Alone?"

"Aye." She stared at him, and he stared back. "Is that the wrong answer? No, then. I won't be traveling alone."

"Who'll be traveling with you?"

"My trunk."

The teller did not relax his face. "There's no passenger ships until the waters break."

"How long?" The waters had broken; she knew it. Small rowboats were already starting adrift.

"Maybe two, three weeks. Hard winter, maybe a month."

"No, that won't do. I can't wait that long."

"Got nothing for you." The teller stopped looking at her.

"What's that list on your ledger?"

"A list of ships due for arrival."

"Put me on one. I got payment. Two silver dishes—"

"There's no ships."

"God's teeth, I see them!" Ruth shouted. "On your list!"

He glared at her and would have walked away if such movement had been physically possible. "Only freight can guarantee to break through them waters in the coming week."

"Freight, then."

"Can't go on a cargo ketch without the captain's permission. That must all be cleared months in advance in writing, no vagrants. Must meet an assurance of weight distribution after making certain that all passengers have a clean bill of health."

"What if we don't tell the captain?"

"Why would I not tell him?"

"Because you're a keen fellow taking pity on a lone-traveling female."

"No one takes pity on you, Mistress Miner."

She paused. Her reputation had preceded her. "Bribery, then?"

"Certainly not."

"Well, then, how about simply to get rid of me?" She hated to admit that having any exchange with another human being, even this one, was stimulating. She'd scarce heard herself speak for months. "I'm not leaving until I have a ship."

"No ships."

Ruth looked at his scribbled upside-down ledger. "*Sparrow*."

"Her passenger slot is filled. She's only freight now."

"I will take freight." She glanced again at his list, straining to see the next ship name. Her pulse quickened. "*Primrose!*"

"Filled. Them passengers have had their places for months now, waiting for spring. Freight ships have little room for the wretched of the earth."

"But there's room for freight?"

He conceded with satisfaction, "Plenty of room for freight, yes."

"God's teeth!" Ruth slammed a fist down on the counter and grabbed the teller by the collar, pulling him against the desktop. "I'll curse you to contract a deadly plague from hidden fleas in a cargo of fabrics that will wipe out your entire household and half this town and cause your children to die such horrible deaths, they'll be—"

"Stop!" He wrenched free and pulled back.

"Don't you want me to leave this town?"

"By all the might of God, yes!"

She smacked her pointer finger down on his ledger. "Freight."

"Freight," he repeated and penciled her in.

She slid the payment bundle of fabric-rolled goods and one fox fur toward him. "Fret not. There's no fleas." Then she limped from the stall to sit with her trunk at the far end of the beach—chilled, tired, and hungry—to wait.

CHAPTER THIRD

Primrose sets sail

> *I must have the gentleman*
> *to haul and draw with the mariner,*
> *and the mariner with the gentleman.*
> *I would know him that would refuse*
> *to set his hand to a rope,*
> *but I know there is not any such here.*

—Sir Francis Drake

March stung Ruth's face as she took in seaspray from the side of *Primrose*. The merchant vessel weighed just over three hundred tons, fitted with enormous cargo holds and four full decks. She was a newer, experimental model of the Dutch fluyts, distinguished by her extra sails on the foremast and mainmast more typical of barques. *Primrose*'s wide, boxlike hull allowed her a narrow weatherdeck, which proved convenient for avoiding higher deck-surface-area taxes, yet her full-sized holds could still be packed with hundreds of tons of goods. Her high, proud bow was matched by an elegant aftcastle at the stern. The ship lacked only in firepower, although Captain Jacob Townsend had several false gunports painted on the sides to look foreboding from a distance. With a mere twelve cannon on the gundeck, she was not well suited to fend off privateers. That is, if they could catch her. The nimble vessel could cut through the water like a shark fin.

They were into the two hundred miles to Ruth's destination of Stonington, Connecticut, which was as far as her pewter and fabrics could take her along the banks of Long Island, a stretch the sailors called the Devil's Belt. Idle winds meant the journey could take upward of a week, skirting through the Devil's Stepping Stones, a shallow reef of boulders edging the Sound that Siwanoy legend claimed were thrown there by the devil when he made an escape from the island. Make no mention of the Siwanoy, themselves. They'd come for Anne Hutchinson at Split Rock; they could come for *Primrose*, too.

"Ah, so it's true; the ledgers don't lie. How are you, my lovely piece of freight?" The voice of First Mate Owen Townsend pealed across the weatherdeck. Ruth didn't turn to acknowledge him as he toked on a carved soapstone pipe. "Is that it? Not even a little happy to see me?"

"I would have been happy to see you month-last."

"Aye. I'm sorry to hear about her." He fiddled uncomfortably with his soapstone.

"You could have taken her with you."

"Aht-aht, Ruthie, now, no grudges here. You're not near so powerful on this deck as you imagine you are." Owen glanced over it, then back to the woman who graced the bow. His sweeping gesture was half-hearted. "You like arithmetic, so configure this: The bow you stand on has the volume to carry the foremast sails. If there's too much bow, then the girl won't get enough speed. If there's too little bow, then there's not enough support for the ship. If the bow is too slender, then the hull won't keep her shape against the constant pressure, and the keel will warp out of alignment. But if the bow is too thick, she will drag through the water and be more like to upend in inclement weather. So, you see, it's the balance what makes it work." He turned to look at her. "You are causing unbalance, Ruth Miner."

The sails creaked and clanked above them, and the windlass turned with a clicking rhythm like Shrewsbury's old windmill. He peered again out over the blue-green ocean water. She was too pretty for this ship, despite how the winter had tolled her. And women traveling alone seldom ended up where they set out to go.

"You told me to get out of Shrewsbury," she said. "I got out of Shrewsbury."

"I told you to go get married, too. All the hundreds of brilliant ideas I've had, and you have to listen to the one terrible one." He indicated her hands on the rail. "Rough winter."

"You should have taken her."

"Aye, I should have," he conceded. "Should have taken you both. History says there be a lot of things I shoulda did different." He paused and reluctantly admitted to himself that there was something exciting about seeing her decorating the bow of his ship like some carved figurehead. And something equally frightening about it. It wasn't *his* ship, and he wasn't captain; he had little say in what happened to Ruth here. "It does me good to see you, even knowing the trouble you'll cause. An unmarried woman sans escort. Between the hungry men on this ship, the Metoac on that island," he pointed across the Devil's Belt, "and the pirates off this bay, a pretty lady be in trouble." He cleared his throat and muttered, "I need a stiffener."

"A mite early, no?"

"A stiff never hurt anyone. It's either flip or saltwater out here, so make your pick and make it wise. Keeps you from the scurvy." The pipe turned to lead in his mouth when her lip twitched into the tease of a smile. He took a long drag and leaned into the rail. "I ran to your cabin when we docked at Shrewsbury." They were both quiet, and the block and tackle wheezed with crates behind them, straining like an old man bending over. "Were you in it when it caught?"

She pictured that black smoke that billowed behind her as she crossed the saltmarsh. "No."

"Thank Christ. They only got half of it. Too damp. You could still rebuild—"

"I'm not going back." She squeezed the rail.

"Aye, all right. But you shoulda packed two trunks. Some of them items could have been handy to trade until you were established in Stonington as a woman to marry."

"I've no desire to be a woman to marry, and I couldn't carry two trunks."

"You carried that trunk yourself?" he said, his voice high in disbelief. "Even I strained at that damn heavy thing."

She scowled. She hadn't wanted him to see her board. She didn't want his objections and lectures about how his ship was no place for a woman traveling alone, or how she should've gone and married a stranger, or how she upset the balance of his apparently precarious ship.

"This is no place for a woman traveling alone. You should have married."

She rolled her eyes. "I've family in Stonington."

"Your family could have used—"

"I couldn't carry two trunks."

"What family do you have in Stonington?"

She clenched her jaw. A makeshift box-lighthouse hung with lanterns disappeared into fog, and she watched it until it looked like tiny fireflies. She could feel the sandy shoals scraping against the hull of the ship, and Owen muttered something about being too close, and then brown pelicans dived at open waves in the water, one coming up with a crab flailing from the hooked bill and throat sac that jiggled from thin bones in the pelican's lower jaw. A male clapped his bill together repeatedly, rippling his pouch like a gonfalon as its color turned to a blue-pink to impress the female, but she was preoccupied with her crab.

"Ruth," Owen said flatly. "Who's in Stonington?"

"My aunt…Anne."

"Why have I never heard mention of her?"

"It's a dull name. You probably forgot her mentioned."

"I don't forget anything, and you know it. Your father had no sisters, outlived his brothers, no other wives, no other children. I know your family as I know my own. You are the last grape on the vine."

"My mother's side."

"Your mother's sister Constance has been estranged for as long as I remember," he pressed. "And wouldn't she still be in Woodbridge? What would have brought her to Stonington?"

"Why so many questions?" Ruth fired back, throwing her elbow into him and knocking some of the leaves from his pipe; he absently swiped at the wind to catch one. "Do you think I'd make this journey if I had no destination?"

She absolutely would, he knew. She'd make any journey without a destination. He thought of her in Stonington, how the men, ignorant of her past, would line up for her hand. He thought of standing at the back, the wave of them, and disappearing against the sea, forgotten by all but her pain. When she hurt, she'd remember him; that he knew. That's the legacy he'd leave hanging on her when he set her free. The English settlement of Stonington had invoked laws against the French, and *Primrose* hardly paused there but half an hour on its route through the Sound. He wasn't ready to think about that yet. How little time they had, and would have. He'd explain that to her another day. He wanted to see how long she'd hold out on this family-in-Stonington tale first. It would give him a game to play.

"See to it that you take care of yourself here," he said. "*Primrose* is not Shrewsbury. This ship, beautiful woman she is, has her ugly side."

"Oh, I assure you, so does Shrewsbury."

"Not anymore. Its ugly side just left." He laughed alone until he caught Ruth's glare. "Don't wander."

"You're leaving?"

"I work here. This—" he flicked a finger back and forth between them, "—is not work."

"You're headed toward cargo boxes of things I'm not allowed to see?"

He crossed his arms. "Ruuuth. Don't you undermine me here. Those are my crates." He put the back of his hand to his mouth and whispered, "You're not to know that I got a ledger in my pocket with inventory items, and the control of its numbers go through me. That would be a very dangerous thing for you to know." He paused, chewed at his lip, then smiled broadly. "Don't make a habit of it."

She pressed in conspiratorially. "Have you parchment?"

He'd goddamn well make some if he couldn't find it, the way her mouth creased upward. "Shoulda packed two trunks." He pulled his pipe from his mouth, dumped the crusted tobacco remains over the bowsprit, and replaced the soapstone in his breast pocket. "Aye, I can provide that."

"With no consequence?"

He leaned to her ear: "No more consequence than leaving your Bible behind, Miss Miner," then passed her and headed below deck.

❧

Returning with a roll of paper tucked in his armpit and his hands busied with a carving knife at the end of a quill, Owen stepped on deck to find Ruth surrounded. "Pour l'amour du ciel!" He slid the paper and quill into the pocket of his jacket and advanced around the heady foremast. Rounding it, he saw what he'd feared. It hadn't taken but minutes for Ruth to be cornered by two of Owen's crewmates.

"Where ya headed, purdy thing?" the taller of the two crewmen asked.

"I'm strolling your dirty little boat." She thrust her chin in the air. The smell of stale fish and rancid body odor and halitosis filtered over her.

The second crewman came up against her, brushing his groin on her skirt. "Now, I doesn't think it'd be none too gentleman of us'n to leave you strolling alone. What do ya think, Kingsley?"

"I do quite fine on my own," Ruth said. "I've practiced for years."

"My, no, no, no, she can't be left alone." Kingsley put one finger in the air in a motion that would scold a child and put his other hand upon her dress.

Ruth sunk her fingernails into his arm. "I haven't had a clean dress all winter, so you'll not be soiling this one."

He opened his mouth, but the shorter sailor tapped him at Owen's approach. Kingsley tipped his hat to Ruth, and the two sailors scattered like crabs on a seashore.

"Did they hurt you?" Owen said too harshly.

"Grease on my dress! If you *knew* how hard it was to clean."

He narrowed his eyes. "This is not a 'little boat.' I heard that." He loomed over her. "Don't wander alone."

"Who might I wander with instead?" She waved her arms at her sides. "Oh, wait. The imaginary friends in my trunk. I always bring them along for these occasions."

"Then there's your answer. You can join them in there." He'd lock her in it. "Look, just stay put. The bow or the passenger hold. Those are your choices."

"I was at the bow."

"Then the passenger hold."

"That narrows my choices considerably."

"Ruth—"

"I like to have choices."

"Ruuuth."

"I'm going. I won't be causing any mutiny."

"Splendid. That's my job." He doubted she'd understand the nuances of it. Back in the Old World, the Count of Tessé had torched Heidelberg, and Montclair had leveled Mannheim. Here in the New World, word was the Iroquois were joining with some northern New English garrisons against French settlers. It was not a popular time for a Frenchman on an English ship. Off to the right of them, he espied an East Indiaman, a slaver, probably bound for Boston, all her flags down save one: the yellow flag of a quarantined fever. He skylarked, guessing the time by the sun, and made note to mark it in the log. "Best go below with the other living cargo."

"Living cargo?" Ruth snatched the quill and paper from his outstretched hand, blunting the point he'd so carefully sharpened. "That's a fine thing to call me."

"You prefer freight? I believe that's how I've got you marked." He stepped around her, pointed off starboard, and yelled loudly, "Hoay, the ship ahoay! Yellow jack!"

When he turned back, relief washed over him to see she'd headed to the lower-deck companionway, and again when she turned toward the stairs to join the other passengers. Why was everything so suddenly changed? He was defensive, so tight-chested. She was on his ship, devil take it. Part of that was what he'd always wanted, but not quite like this. Not this ship. This was dangerous. Women disappeared on ships. He let out his breath slowly. Her footing was steady aboard the moving vessel, but he could see a new limp as she walked along. A winter injury, he imagined. Three sailors passed her, led by Second Mate Thomas Hewitt, a sandy-haired, squinty-eyed ruffian, built no larger than most, but hardened, spraddle-legged, and weathered from years of salty air corroding his sorrel skin. The crewmen walked toward Owen making overt gestures in Ruth's direction.

Owen scowled. "Eyes in the ship! Don't you have work to do?"

"I could ask same to you, mate," Thomas replied. "You found plenty'a time to pluck pearls from the wench's oyster yourself."

Owen's hand opened toward the dagger he carried in his boot.

"Relax, mate," Thomas said. "She's doxy 'nough to go 'round. I seen no dowry on her. She's fair game, and you know it."

Owen stepped to Thomas. "She's in my care." He said it loud, and the men perked, then backed away, until it was only Thomas and Owen, boot to boot. "You are a good mate, but you'll make an enemy of me."

Thomas sneered, "Better see that you get her first, mate," then took a step back and slinked away.

Owen relaxed his fists, but fear gripped his chest. His eyes sought the area where Ruth had been, but she was no longer in sight. He quick-stepped to the bow, searching, too afraid to call out for her, in case he should draw further attention to a young woman traveling alone. Damn her for this. Any other ship, any other ship but his. The stairs to the passenger hold were no match for the hurry that overcame him. He took them three at a time and pushed open every door. Heaven help him if Thomas found her first.

Thin shafts of sunlight highlighted rows of tea boxes, gallons of cooking oil and vinegar, piles of doeskins, mace and pepper jars, and handcrafted tools. Ruth couldn't resist a step inside the enormous cargo hold before joining the other passengers. She'd never seen anything like it. It creaked like a dozen unoiled doors, and the boxes made a *tchhr-tchhr* sliding noise as the ship rocked. She pried up a nail in the corner of a slatted crate and pulled out a handmade violin crafted from lightweight tin. The horsehair bow made a hissing screech when she trailed it across the strings, and she laughed, plucking at them again and again.

Replacing the violin, she was struck by a sparkle of light inside the box. She gasped and picked up a tiny mirror set in a heavy metal frame. Her reflection was ghastly! The winter had left its mark, she imagined, although she had little in way of comparison. Tugging at strands of untamed hair, she puckered her mouth and pinched some color into her cheeks, until the mirror caught the reflection of someone over her shoulder. She spun and drew in a sharp breath. An unfamiliar, half-shadowed sailor stared at her.

"Well, well. Looky what we got here. A she-pirate in our midst, huh?" His voice snaked through the room on the belly of a serpent, and his blackened fingernails curled into claws.

"Oh, no, I was just—"

"It's all right. I wunnot peep a word'f it. But silence will cost you." He proceeded toward her with his fingers protracted like a tentacled sea monster.

"You stay away from me!" Ruth reached down to the crate of tools and grabbed a claw hammer, extending the cumbersome thing out in front of her. She wished she'd grabbed the iron wedge, but she'd too hastily committed. "I'm warning you."

"You doesn't scare me, cunnywench," he lisped through a crooked grin missing more teeth than not. Pockmarks mottled his sneering lips and cheeks like burning welts.

"I mean it. Stay back. I…I'm a witch! I've cursed a town to unsavory ends, and I'll do the same to you and your ship."

"John!" Owen's voice cut through the main cargo hold as his crewmate lunged for Ruth's arm. "Belay!"

The sailor turned to Owen, and Ruth flung the hammer into John's gut. John fell back against a crate, winded. Ruth plucked the quill from her apron and drove the tip into his neck at the seam of his ear and jaw. John howled, and Owen grabbed for the downed sailor's jacket.

"Go, Ruth! Get the hell out of here!"

She picked up the hammer and was breathing heavily with it poised in one hand, the quill in the other. More men entered the hold to investigate what commotion they were missing. Owen lifted John to his feet by the collar and pushed the knave back away from Ruth and toward the incoming men. Ruth searched the dim room for other exits, dropped the hammer, and fled.

Owen faced his men. John stared him down, listing, blood seeping through his fingers held to his neck. Kingsley spat tobacco juice onto a crate, the spittle landing on the sign-of-four on the box's East India Company brand, dripping down the staff of Mercury, and stopping on *Primrose*'s initial P in the heart engraved with EIC. Owen couldn't fight

them all, but his fists were clenched, his body crouched. From the back
of the group of sailors, Thomas came forward, his expression one of
cynical platitude.

"We got no battle with you, mate. We's just taking the girl."

"She's not for takes," Owen said quietly.

"All women is for takes. Play the game."

"Not with her."

"Then step aside! Her meat's tender. We's lookin' for a scopperloit,
then you can have what's left of her. We'll wide her out for you." This
was punctuated with a chortle that showcased a row of broken, rotted
teeth. "The code goes for you, too, ya frogleg. Gotta peg her first."
Thomas locked eyes with him. "Or I will."

"And if I do take her first," he swallowed dryly, "you'll honor the
code?"

"If she means that much to ya, we'll give you a running start." He
swept his hand to the side.

The crew laughed uneasily. It wasn't like Owen to interfere with their
code. They parted for him as he walked through. He felt his balance
shifting with the ship.

∽

Owen studied his living cargo from the door of the passenger hold.
There were two other women aboard *Primrose*, each accompanied by
men and neither worth fighting over. Even this was atypical of the usual
roll call of male passengers. He searched their heads for Ruth, until he
found her sitting apart from the crowd, clutching the mirror in front of
her face, but staring right through it. He locked his jaw, caught her eye,
and motioned for her to follow him.

"What is it?" she asked.

"Just come with me." Clutching her by the arm, he led her away from
the passenger cabin and closer to the shipmates' hold, stopping in the
darkness near several doors marked Crew on signs gone over with ink
in etched grooves. He pivoted to look at her closely, his eyes no longer
butterfly blue in the darkness, but a solemn shadow, heavily dilated and
panicked. "I've got to make you understand me. Something. Hard to
explain. I told you that you got to be mindful. These men." He paused.
"I'm devising a plan you won't like."

"I usually like plans. Why won't I like—"

"Merde!"

Owen saw three crewmen moving toward him, recognized one as Thomas, and words escaped him. He cursed Thomas for putting him to this, the blackguard. Before Ruth could refuse, Owen held tight to her arms and pressed his mouth down over hers. Passing one arm around her back, he dragged her through a crew door into natural darkness. She struggled against him, but he didn't remove his mouth from hers, pressing thoroughly into her. Inside the room, he snapped her loose and slammed the door shut behind him. She spun around and slapped him across his face.

"What on earth ever made you think I wouldn't like that plan?" she hissed. Another wild palm flew toward him.

He grabbed her wrist midair and came in close to her. The slap stung more than he wanted to let on. She had a hand on her, this one. "You've got to scream like I'm hurting you."

"Not on your life."

He grunted and poked her hard in the ribs. "C'mon, scream a little."

"Tell me why I should."

"Because, contrary to everyone's expectations, I don't actually want to force myself on you."

"Oh." She stilled. *So that's what this was.* Some kind of initiation of manhood. A woman as possession. Had he done this before?

He poked her again in the ribs, and she let out a pathetic shrill no louder than the yelping mew of a wounded kitten. "Scream, and get this over with."

She said plainly, "Owen. Stop. You're hurting me."

He smirked. "Louder."

"Owen! Stop!"

His hand flew to his ringing ear. "Not in my ear, you caitiff."

"Stop! You're hurting me!" She added some panting and whimpering, then thrashed about the room: tearing into crates, knocking over objects from an accounting desk, winging a ledger at a lamp that teetered and fell and shattered. She feigned sexual grunts and thrusts. *How dare he?* "Owen! God damn you!" Her hand covered her mouth in alarm at how easily the curse spilled forth. "God's teeth!" This time, she stifled a laugh. "Stop! Don't touch me!" Awful gagging sounds left her throat, somewhere between choking and giggling, and then she ran back to him and kicked him in the shin. He yelped and glared at her. Her eyes chided as she reached toward his frame-and-prong belt buckle and began to unfasten it.

Owen froze, then gripped her wrists when her suggestive motion registered. "What're you doing?"

She loosened her hands from his grasp and brought one of her fingers to his lips. Taking his buckle again, she rattled it loudly, the metal pieces clanking into each other, and Owen stood stock-still, his eyes fixed on her, his body tense. Each brush of her fingertips tickled him. As she pulled her hands away, he shook his pantleg to adjust his discomfort, but when he glanced back up at her, she was unthreading the laces of her dress, lowering her lace collar so the rounded tops of her breasts budded forth.

"Ruth!"

She pointed to the soft flesh at the curve of her breast. "Bite me here."

"Absolutely not."

She drew his head forcefully to her chest. "Bite!"

He set his mouth at the crown of her breast, but he couldn't go further. He caught the scent of the dried flowers crushed on her neck and was in a daze, until she slid her cupped hand between his thighs and clenched her fingers around his plums. He clamped his teeth together. On her breast shown two reddening crescents, and she squealed.

"I'm very uncomfortable with this," he whispered.

"Good. You should be. Did you spare a mind for my discomfort when you dragged me in here?" She looked toward the door and back to him. "You'd never last this long. Better bring this to a head, or they'll be on to you."

"Are you challenging my pulsion sexuelle?"

"Not challenging, just pointing out its shortcomings."

Before he could respond, she stuck another forefinger to his lips. He turned to the door, hesitant and confused, fumbling with his belt.

"Leave it unfastened," she said. "They'll be impressed."

꿍

Owen entered the hallway to his proud crewmates standing semicircle around the door. He squeezed his hands into fists and fastened his belt buckle in front of them. To his dismay, they looked impressed. "C'est fini. Honor the code."

Thomas affirmed, "All right, you earned her, mate." He slapped Owen on the back with a wicked smile.

Owen tried for a smirk, but he was crestfallen. "Disperse." His stomach clenched, and he pushed past them and headed down the hall.

When he neared the hallway corner, he stopped and leaned his back against the wall, trembling while he readjusted the constricting carriage of his breeches.

The men still circled the door when Ruth pushed it open. At the sight of them, she cried out and slammed it shut, pressing her weight against the inside. Owen's guts twisted at the sound. Whatever was going to happen would have to happen, he knew, and he rocked restlessly on his heels, praying his crew would walk away from it. Going back was out of the question. Her presence created a thin line between the honor of a man and the honor of a woman, and Owen feared he couldn't have both.

The crewmen crowed exaggerated, mocking laughs, and Ruth could hear their chortles getting fainter as they finally exited the hallway. She peeked through a crack in the door. The men walked toward the passenger cabin, away from her door and away from where Owen stood near the other end of the hall. The ship rocked, and Ruth held to the doorframe for balance.

Owen breathed out, steadying himself, until he heard footsteps coming down the connecting hall toward him. He jolted erect.

"What is the bother here, son?" the captain's voice sliced the darkness. "I heard screaming."

"It's nothing, Captain."

"Our master pilot is stabbed in the neck with an inconsequential spike. You wouldn't know about that, would you?"

Owen chewed the inside of his lower lip.

"You knaves are worthless. Insolents run my ship." The captain peered around the dark hall and made out the figure of Ruth slumped against the door. "Goddamn. Did someone lay a hand on her?"

"She's good, Captain."

"She doesn't look good to me. Who lain a hand on her?"

"She's shaken. She'll be all right, Captain." Owen studied the planks. *Coccifera*. Kermes oak from the south of France. Long, beautiful planks. He thought of the kermes scale insects that ate the tree on land and created the red cochineal dye the crew used in their uniform wool, back when they had uniforms, when the ship was new. On land, *coccifera* dropped acorns, and he thought of the acorns, thought of dropping them in the sea like they'd grant wishes. He'd wish to go back eleven years. To change it. To change her. And then he lit on a tiny bored hole from a *Teredo* shipworm, a softshell mollusk that could eat the entire ship inside of ten years. He'd have to coat against them now, the boring devils.

"Answer me, son. Who touched her? I want a name."

He met the captain's eyes. "It was me, sir."

"You? I didn't raise you better than that? Nay to partake in these brute obtainments, even with someone as lowborn as her?" He gestured down the hall as if she disgusted him.

"She's already ruined, Captain." He quailed. What awful words. "It was my doing."

The captain backhanded Owen across the face, splitting his lip. "Get out of my sight, son. And right smart." He about-faced, hovered a moment, contemplatively, then left.

Owen lowered his head and tongued the speck of blood coming from his mouth before making his way toward the upper deck.

Ruth wasn't situated in the passenger hold but ten minutes before he came around the corner of the doorway again and stood before her. A scowl burned across his face—his lip puckered, his hands resting on his hips. He moved forward and grabbed her about the waist, then threw her over his shoulder. Her petticoats rustled in his face, and she scrambled to hold on to the pilfered mirror she still clasped. Despite how she pounded on his back and demanded to be put down, he weaved through the maze of cargo holds, past the galley, sail room, and ship's stores, and dumped her into a cramped space.

"Oh, daisies!" She clamped her nose. "It smells awful in here. What is it?"

"Your new bedchamber."

She pulled herself to her feet. The ceiling planks met the walls in a slope at a space just above her head. The floor, covered in damp, mildewed straw, was still wet underneath from flooding and horse piss. It reeked of lathered sweat and excrement and a powder used in killing lice. A calico cat pawed through a pile of straw before scratching vigorously at fleas, then leaping from the trough up to the rafter, balancing his way across, and jumping over the far wall at the height of the slope where a thin crack showed.

"That's Mäuschen," Owen said. "He comes and goes."

"Where am I?"

He glanced from the place the cat disappeared, the wooden trough bed that lined one side, then to her. "It's a jockey. A horse stable suits you right."

"A mule couldn't even fit in here!"

"You're fitting in here now, yeah?" He shrugged. "This'll do."

"This will do?"

"Aye. It's nice to have the upper hand again. I'll find you a book." He slid the wooden gate closed, and the heavy bolt clanked behind his exit.

When he unbolted the door minutes later and pushed back the gate to hand a book through the door's crack, her flailing palm snaked through and smacked him over the ear.

"You want the upper hand?" she said. "There it is."

"All right, I deserved that," he conceded, and Ruth went in for another smack to his face. He dodged. "Tu êtes impossible!" He pushed open the door to the stable and drew it closed behind his entrance. "Now, you listen to me: You don't know what your run-in with John cost me, but bastard he is, he's still one of our master pilots, and you stuck a quill in his goddamn neck. No one is familiar with sand banks or hidden shoals like him, so I can't afford to lose him to a rift." He threw his hands in the air. "Make no mention of Tom."

"But this is enslavement. This is a cage too small for...for a mongoose!"

"You should be used to cages." He stepped toward her, then back. "Pretty, unmarried women are rare. Pretty, unmarried, virgin women aboard *Primrose* are even rarer." He heard how whiny he sounded, but he couldn't help himself. "Why did you get on my ship? There is a half dozen other ships leaving your harbor; why would you take *Primrose*?"

"I had to. I figured you'd be kindest to me."

"Kind? I'm not kind. I've never been kind to you. I robbed you of everything. I murdered your parents; how could you think I got kindness in me?" He watched her expression change, and oh, how that drove iron into him. He felt the heat of it as it cored through his insides and spread numbness as if troweled. "I owe you being your guardian, but it's not out of kindness. You never spoke against me, never told a soul you didn't start that fire—do you think I live with that well, that it doesn't haunt me? That you don't haunt me, witch that you are?"

"Stop!" She reached a hand toward the wall to steady herself.

"You being here is a constant reminder—"

"I beg you, stop!"

"—of all I tried to outrun. I took everything from you, and now I got to feign take more." He pulled down on the cloth around her collar to reveal the bite marks at her breast, lightly purpling, then turned abruptly for the door. "Brush them marks with lye. My bite is poison."

Her vulnerability gave way to righteous ire, and she kicked the trough, kicked the straw into the air, and kicked it again, the odor disseminating anew. "I won't stay in this box that smells of horse piss because you can't handle pressure from your men. Oh, poor, pitiful you in your sorry little lot, sitting like a magistrate on a boat you'll inherit, boohooing that your crew mightn't listen to your orders, and you can't run to Father to tattle. Well, I'm not listening to your rules, either!" But Owen shut the door and latched the bolt, while Ruth threw her weight against it.

"She's a *ship*, bloody curse you," he retorted through the closed door. "And the next rule I'll give you is that the grate on the floor at the back empties into the sea. You'll find that very relieving in a few hours."

"I don't see how that's a rule." She lowered her tone. It dawned on her then that he really wasn't going to let her out.

"Friendly advice, then."

"It wasn't particularly friendly."

"Ça suffit! Merde! Comme tu veux. J'en ai marre," he cursed to himself, then stalked off in a huff.

"I don't know what you're saying, but don't take it out on me because I pointed out that you're not friendly."

But there was no answer. He wasn't bantering today. There was no humor in it. In any of it, now. She heard his footsteps wind back through the maze until she stood alone, the grinding of the boards where their warped edges rubbed, the only sound. The occasional scraping of a softbank like a gray whale's low moan. The stench of stale urine overwhelming.

CHAPTER FOURTH
Un marin français et sa sorcière

A man may imagine things that are false,
but he can only understand things that are true.

—Sir Isaac Newton

The rafter almost slipped from her grasp for the third time, but she managed to hold on and to walk her hands the rest of the way across the beam, then to swing one tiptoe up over the edge, into the crack Mäuschen had disappeared into. A little farther, and her kneecaps were over; she inched in, ignoring the throb in her foot. The slender open-air ventilation crease parted the stable from the ceiling slope, and she slid down it and rolled, dropped onto a new pile of straw on the other side of the wall. Another stable. So much for keeping her only tidy dress clean. Her initial luck held for a moment, however; this jockey wasn't locked.

In the hall, she peered through the doorways, the peepholes at the green ocean. Crates spilled into the hall from the overstuffed holds, strapped to handrailings to keep from sliding, their sides branded with respective destinations. She pressed open a door to a crew hold. A few men were cast upon their bunks like lumps of sod, in deep sleep. No one else stirred. She squeezed her body through the opening, her curiosity getting the better of her. Sneaking past the sleeping men, she hunted for any sign of personal belongings. The partitioned quarter near the back of the crew hold looked to accommodate the senior-ranked sailors, and she ducked through the cavelike corridor.

The room was empty, save for nine bunks and one meager round table, shoved against the wall as if only temporary until it could find a better home. The table's reddish wood lay unfinished, covered in knife gouges, drink stains, and burns. Upon it sat three candles, a box of cards, some rolled and half-smoked tobacco leaves, and a wooden cup. Few possessions lined the runners of the dark room. No pillows on the bunks. No closets, windows, shelves, chairs. In the corner stood a keg of what smelled like rum, but the thick puddle that collected under the barrel's spout looked much darker than ordinary grog.

Ruth stared from one bunk to the next, each in replication and none having any indication of personal identity. At the head of each bed was a wooden chest, attached with slats to the wood of the bunks, for the sailors to store all they owned. She wasted no time in walking to the first bunk. Then, something caught her eye. There was a difference in the lower bunk straight ahead of the corridor. It was the only bed that was made. She was struck by the wool blanket hugging the thin flock mattress without a wrinkle, its flawlessness compared with the others. Only one sailor here could respect a meager, dilapidated bunk enough to smooth out every wrinkle with such care.

Ruth walked to the bed, crouched her head beneath the low-hanging bunk ceiling, and scooted her butt onto the mattress. It was horribly uncomfortable, lumpy and thin and cold, but it beat the straw pile of the stable. She kicked up her feet and laid her head back on the flat bunk without a pillow, breathing in the familiar smell: his greasy hair, his sweat. She shuffled to wrinkle his blanket. A warmth stole through her, and she thought of home. What that meant—what it meant now. His scent was home, and there was now no other.

Her eyes lit on the wooden chest pressing against the top of her head. She touched the rough, unfiled teak. Tracing along the edge of the lid, she gave it a push and was surprised to find it opened easily. She flipped onto her elbows and pried up the cover of Owen's box. To her dismay, it was sparse of anything intriguing and smelled of musty mold and stale fish and animal-fat wax. A spare change of clothes, including an unworn pair of fallfront galligaskins; two bars of glycerin soap; a few fat and spermaceti-oil tapers joined at the wicks; some flint stones and chunks of steel; a blade-sharpening bar; rolled tobacco leaves; a few dice; Fuller's Earth hair clay—the fancy kind from Vale of White Horse in Oxfordshire; a few bottles of panchymagogue and medicine oil; a soapstone pipe; a foul-smelling pig's bladder stuffed with vanilla pods and cheroots from the Southern Devil Coast; two bundles of hardtack reserves wrapped in discolored linen; a straight shaving blade sheathed in a plain-leather scabbard; a fractured piece of mirror glass.

For a man who showered her with lavish thieveries, he didn't take much for himself. She rummaged down beneath the functional items, and her fingers struck a wooden box in the back corner, no larger than a man's fist, bound with a leather cord. She pulled the box out of the chest, unraveled the cord, and opened it. Her breath tripped. The box was filled with pieces of her. Her childhood. Things she'd forgotten. A swatch of lace from the collar of a dress; a carved arrowhead that she'd found along the forest path of Shrewsbury, still attached to the rotted leather cord that Owen had used to wear it; a dried wildflower, now almost completely turned to dust, that she had slid into the button hole of his jacket before he returned to his ship; the wish-half of a wish-bone, heaven knows with what merrythought imparted on its furcula; notes in Ruth's hand scrawled on thin strips of birch.

She turned again onto her back, clutching the box and examining each item, then she slid her body down into the dented form his back had canyoned in the mattress, and melted into it, into him. Just when she was getting comfortable, a disagreeable lump shifted beneath her. She rolled back the edge of the mattress to reveal Owen's dearest possession that he would never house in any unlocked chest, even if it could fit.

With two eager hands, she drew forth the scabbard from beneath the mattress and unsheathed the beautiful sword. Its blade slid out of the oiled, fur-lined throat with little effort, and it was lightweight. She set the metal-tipped leather shell across the bed and clasped the haft, swinging it around the cramped room, pretending to be an actor in a Shakespearean play, reciting what lines she could remember from her personal collection of literary contraband, until the sounds of men's untimely voices filled the main crew hold.

Ruth froze with her hands still gripped around the sword. *Between deck.* The sleeping men were relieving the incoming men, and they were blocking her exit. Time had slipped away from her. Clutching the sword to her chest, she tucked herself behind the corridor frame and prayed the voices would disappear. But they didn't. Footsteps headed toward the private quarters, and Ruth had no choice but to keep still.

Her eyes darted to the bunk where she'd left the wooden box and scabbard haphazardly strewn on the wrinkled blanket, but it was too late. Owen fixated on them when he walked into the quarters. Instantly, he flung himself around, and there was Ruth, huddled against the wall, grasping his saber. His nostrils flared as puffed by bellows.

"What do you think you're doing?" he hissed. "She is not a toy."

He wrapped one hand around the ricasso and tore the blade from her as if it were no heavier than a twig. Her hand smashed against the knucklebar.

"Why are you rummaging through my things?"

"It's just a sword."

Just a sword. He curled his lip. She was a single-edged, single-fuller, custom-forged steel saber, with a rapier-hybrid swept hilt, curved guard, knuckle branches, and thumb annellet, a hand-and-a-half ricasso with full tang running through a soft-curved flatback and custom-fitted waisted grip covered in helix-wire-wrapped shark skin, held together by a rounded thrust pommel and a metallic-gold-and-red passemen-terie sword knot for distraction and recall. She was not *just* a sword. Foolish girl. "Her name is Égard. It means *respect*, if you still know what that is."

"I heard of your saber back in Shrewsbury, but I've never seen it—"

"Her. Good. That means I've never had to kill you."

"She's killed men?"

"She's killed pirates and Indians, raiders, crusaders, privateers. But no, never men." The box on the bed lay open, and he looked at it now. He hadn't seen that lace in years. He thought of running his fingers down her lace collar, how soft it would be, whether he would even feel it against his calluses. He glanced swiftly away. "A gift from Uncle Étienne if you remember him. He tutored me."

Ruth pondered, sliding her hand along the fuller. "Expensive gift."

"Where gifts are concerned, I don't inquire about attainment. In Fairfield, I've got a cutlass, a Claymore, a court sword, two rapiers, and another saber, attained from fallen men. Someday, they will go to my sons, and my boys won't ask where they came from."

"And if you only get daughters?"

"Hmph. You would use your witchcraft to curse a man thus, wouldn't you."

She smirked and eyed the blade. "Will you teach me?"

He shook his head. "Putting a sword in your hand would cost a man his life."

Ruth touched the hilt and traced the curve along the knuckle branch-es, grazing his fingers as he extended the saber. Her hands tripped lazily along the blunt ricasso, then onto the edge, tempting fate's sharp tongue. His gaze fell to the bite marks at her breast, and his judgment crumpled like an enemy at the tip of his blade. He inched his face closer to hers, his eyes answering her invitation, shifting back and forth between her gaze and her lips, full of uncertainty.

"What are we doing?" he whispered. "I'm one of these blackguards, y'know." He thumbed over his shoulder. "No one in Stonington will know your past, and you can start over without me, without all I mussed for you. We aren't shackled now to one day in history. You don't have to curse me with no sons. You can curse some other man."

"You'd run him through with your sword."

"Aye, I would."

She did not increase her distance from him. He felt himself grow tense, then a little faint, then tense again, and she the same, and his hand was on her waist, then how it got to the small of her back he didn't know, but their bodies pressed in. The instability was alarming, and with the feel of her breath at his neck, he lost his grip on the saber's guard, then recaught and stepped back.

"You can't be in here," he breathed out quietly and faced Ruth's softening gaze. He pointed to the door. "Get out, and grant me sleep."

She lifted her chin, but he shook his head, and she walked past the men with her eyes lowered to the floor, then out. Disappointment gnawed at her, and she couldn't tamp down the warming sensation that rushed through the V of her neck. Was it supposed to be like that, like this? She hadn't made it far outside the door when she heard an incoming sailor's voice ring out, and she jumped.

"Townsend! Captain requests ye in the log room."

The door swung open and closed and open and closed. Ruth hunkered into a shadowy spot in the hallway. Within seconds of the command, the door swung open again, and Owen walked through it. Ruth crept out from around the corner after him as he hoofed it to the captain's log room. Once he was out of sight inside the door, she listened in the hallway as the two voices spoke, formally at first.

"Reporting, Captain Townsend."

"Do you know why I called you in?" Jacob Townsend asked coldly.

Outside the door, Ruth held her breath for the answer.

"You're either mad I fucked Ruth, or you think me a traitor," Owen replied.

Ruth exhaled hard. Through a crack, she peered into the room.

"Son, I have nay said such a harsh word—"

"Well, go on, say it then, and get it off your chest, so I can finish self-polluting. You can berate me and split my lip when I'm on your hourglass, but not when I'm between deck, with all due respect, sir."

Jacob's voice was leached of warmth. "I didn't raise you to have such a vulgar mouth."

"No, sir, you didn't raise me at all." He shrugged and sighed. "I acquired the sea letters of neutrality and safe conducts issued from

Fairfield to permit our safety without the bother of this war, sir. I acquired them in lawful manner."

"The men speak of alliances. There is visible undercurrents and could be uprising."

"Aye, there could be a tidal wave what kills us all, too. We could get tipped by a whale. I can't go around fearing what could be." Owen pulled his pipe from his breast pocket and packed the tobacco down into the bowl, holding the soapstone over the candle on Jacob's desk. "They know your stance. It can't get as far up the line as you."

"You are my son. There can be no difference in our view on the same ship."

"I am my mother's son, sir. I cannot brush her aside so easy as you." Owen thumped his pipe against the desk, then held it again to the flame.

"Don't make this a personal matter."

"How is it not? She is your wife. Have you no loyalty to your wife? I know how little I mean to you, Captain. But what of her? She birthed your boys. What of the rest of your family? Your brothers by marriage. This is, too, your family."

"And what about your own brothers? You are oldest, their model of a man. This is what you let them see?"

"They see the man who raised them in your absence, sir."

Jacob finally balled his fists and threw one against the logbook, tearing a corner. "Insolent boy! I shoulda let them hang you back in Shrewsbury!"

Owen fell quiet beneath the weight of the captain's words, and outside the door, Ruth drew in a sharp breath.

"Your mother can't help it. It's her blood; she's all French. But you! You were born in these English colonies. Rule is shifting, son, and you must shift with it."

"J'ai honte d'être ton fils," Owen muttered to himself.

Jacob raised his hand, threatening to strike Owen again. "Nay spake that language here. It's filth she taught it to you."

"Je ne me considère pas comme ton fils," Owen said louder and blew a puff of smoke into the agitated captain's face. "You will not lay a hand on me on my own time."

"General Whitlock is commanding militia brigades in Connecticut Colony to aid the English, and he demands us for a gun ship. Do you know this? Do you know how dangerous that could be, how powerful a man Whitlock is?"

"Tell him no. We have safe conducts."

"How could I tell him no if my own son is his enemy? We'll be a mark for every buccaneer in the bay if we carry munitions, and I'll nay have foreign ports think we chose a side."

"How noble." Owen shrugged. "She's your ship, Captain. He cannot own you if you do not let him."

"Unless he blackmails us." Jacob slammed his open palms onto the table. "Every English port could turn us away."

"Poppycock. As long as they're getting their goods, they'll not care about one merchant Frenchman."

"We could be ruined. And my own son will be…"

Owen grinned. "Say it. *A traitor.* Say what you mean."

"You *are* a traitor. To me, to this ship, to this land, to your king, to these waters, to England! A traitor. A bloody traitor to the Crown with no cause. No cause."

Owen stood as still as the dead wind that left the ship idling along the Sound, then dumped the tobacco from his pipe onto the captain's desk and pocketed the soapstone. He leaned in, a smirk tugging one side of his mouth. "Then if there is to be mutiny on this ship, sir, it will come from me. Cette conversation est terminée."

Owen pushed open the door so quickly that Ruth didn't have time to move from her place. Surprised by her sudden appearance, Owen grabbed hold of her arm and yanked her to her feet, dragging her with him through the hall. When they rounded the corner, he pushed her against the wall, and it knocked some of the wind out of her.

"What are you doing here now? Spying?" He took hold of her as if handling a brawling man. "What did you hear in there?"

"Nothing."

"Menteuse!" He gritted his teeth, and his jaw locked with such tension that Ruth could see the blood rushing to his face through leaping veins. "Don't get involved with what you don't understand." His hands flexed into fists at her arms, and Ruth turned her face to the side and closed her eyes. "Don't let what he spoke in there scare you. I'm no one's enemy." He pulled her hard into his chest as he backed against the wall. "Just breathe. I'd never strike you, ya fool. Breathe. I'm angry at him, not you." He gripped her, enraptured by her soft, pale skin on his browned arms, fingers trembling. Her tense body relaxed and eased into his, her head in the cove of his neck. "Do you trust me?"

She nodded into his chest. Her feminine floral scent played against his nose, and he lowered his lips to her shoulder where he could feel her heart pounding against his mouth.

"Suppose I hadn't set fire to your barn, Ruth."

"Don't." She tensed again, but he held her tighter.

"Shhh, hear me. I need to say this. I relive things." He realized his knuckles were white around her arms, and he let up slightly, only slightly. "Suppose your mother hadn't been inside it. Suppose all this… Suppose she'd been inside the house. Suppose your father hadn't come out after her…" *As the barn collapsed*, he almost said, but he couldn't finish it.

She waited a long time before she responded. His regret had physical weight that pulled the air down around them, but she wasn't sure if she was expected to answer, wasn't sure if the weight was hers. "I suppose this all the time."

"Suppose I come forward that day you were accused of my crime, had spoke the truth. Suppose you had let me." He ran his cheek and nose through her hair, his grip around her loosening further. She could pull away; he'd let her pull away. She could run down the hall; he wouldn't chase her. He'd let her run from him; she should run from him. His voice shook. "I never meant to hurt anyone."

"Shrewsbury is not so forgiving as that. You were a breeched boy, and you would have hung. It was easier to take pity on an orphaned girl."

"There was no pity for you, neither."

She blew air out her nose. "Wasn't your doing—that. It was Dan Miller's sheep what did me in, you know. You were gone by the time this came down, but his flock took sick and died same day. Bad timing requires blame. I had taken the blame for the barn. So then I was blamed for them all, every last dead sheep and soul. Fear will do that to men."

"If I'd not started that fire, my home port would still be Shrewsbury. Captain wouldn't have lighted out so fast with us." His palm found the back of her head, and he couldn't cradle her to him close enough. "I would deserve you. You'd have been my wife by now."

"Boiling cookies for French soldiers and a treasonous prattlebum." She felt his smile against her head, and she pulled back to face him. "If I didn't know any better, Owen Ward Townsend, I'd think you were about to turn romantic on me."

"All sailors are romantic, Ruthie." He beamed. "Just not with one woman."

His inviting eyes, his mouth so near, betrayed him. He found her lips brushing lightly against his own. She covered his mouth with hers, chapped and windburned, callused yet soft, and she drifted into his scent, *home*. Owen felt lighter, his insides floating outward, unraveling. When he realized it wasn't just his own chest pounding, he pushed her away at the sound of the captain's boot heels clicking down the hall.

"Go." He turned, ready for another fight, a bigger one. The big one.

She tugged on his shoulder. "Come with me. You don't need to prove a thing to him."

He shook his head. "Leave me. This has always been my fight."

"It doesn't have to be right now. Come."

Hesitant to drag her into it, he turned and ran down the hall with her, unsure where they were headed. But Ruth knew only one place that was safe.

◈

She broke through the door of the tiny stable and spun around to face him as they succumbed to adrenaline-tinged laughter at the spontaneous flight.

"Of all the places to pick, you choose here," he said, waving around the cramped stable.

She pulled his waist toward her. "I thought you'd feel more at home in a dirty jockey, you stubborn mule. I intend to invoke the shipmates' code and claim you, so other ladies cannot have you."

He groaned and glanced around the stable and tensed. The smell of urine and lice powder was potent. "In here?"

"Where else would you suggest? I know we're safe, or you wouldn't have me caged here."

"I don't have you caged now."

She took both of his arms around her, placed his palms flat against the planks on either side of her body, boxing herself between his chest and the wall. "It looks to me like you do."

"Not like this. Not in here. I—"

"I've got no desire to hear your whinnying." She lifted herself to his eye level on the trough. "There is no bed of roses on this ship. I saw your lumpy bunk, and I slept in piss-covered straw." She grabbed hold of his collar and pulled him into her, and he involuntarily moved one hand to her leg as his passion urged him.

"Ruth, I can't—"

"Perform?"

"What? No, yes—"

"Is it no or yes?"

"Yes! Yes, I can perform. Everything works good. It's just that—"

"It's your first time?"

"No, of course not," he dismissed quickly, but then grasped for some sensitivity. "But it's yours, isn't it?"

"Standing upright in a stable? Heavens, no! I do it all the time. You mean you can't handle a chaste woman in a horse trough?"

"Aye, I can handle you—and the trough—plenty fine. But I—"

"Am afraid you'll hurt me both emotionally and physically, yes, yes, I know."

"Yes." He grinned. "Finally you finished a sentence correct."

"By God's teeth, I'm standing in a trough with your hand under my petticoat. Stop worrying if I'm hurt or not, and kiss me."

He raised a brow, and her mouth met his, and all hesitation left him. He lifted her thigh up over his and ran his hand along her leg. She braced herself against the wall, and he pressed his mouth over hers and traced his fingers down the inside of her thigh, until he stopped with a start when he felt a deeply engraved wound. He brushed away the layers of her petticoat to reveal the same large branded W burned deep into her inner thigh that he'd seen upon the hindquarters of her horse. She watched his face as his curious fingers curved around the W, and all other motion stopped.

"I've got a matching pair," she declared when he could say nothing. She moved aside the petticoat to reveal the same brand on the inside of the other leg. "They're really quite fashionable."

He stood in shock. "How do I perform after seeing that?"

"I suppose that's the idea. In case any unsuspecting man might not know, the townfolk thought it best he be warned."

He held her leg firmly and moved to pull himself from her, but she kept him in place. "Why did you never tell me?"

"I wear these marks because of you, so you better not let them stop you."

He looked hard into her impassioned eyes and pushed himself back against her, gripping a beam overhead and bracing his balance on the trough and the wall. "I won't let your witchery stop me, if you won't let my French stop you."

"I would think the fact we're standing in a horse trough would stop us both first." She laughed and pulled him closer.

CHAPTER FIFTH
Yo-ho and a bottle of rum

I would rather have
a plain russet-coated captain
that knows what he fights for,
and loves what he knows,
than that which you call "a gentleman"
and is nothing else.

—Sir Oliver Cromwell

Ruth awoke abruptly to the sounds of her jockey door unlatching. It was too early for Owen's arrival, and there were no salutations from his familiar voice. She hopped to her feet, thoughts of her run-in with John flashing through her mind. Those teeth and dirty fingernails. This time, however, she had no claw hammer. Only a book, a small stick, a mirror. None of those was likely to provide much defense. As the corral door heaved open, Ruth crouched behind the frame. In walked a smallish, wiry man dressed in rags with a wool cap pulled snug over his ears and eyes, near to his cheekbones. On impulse, Ruth threw her book at the man, striking him between the shoulderblades. He squealed and faced her, just as she flung the mirror at his face like a discus. It hit him across the bridge of the nose, knocking his hat from his head.

"What th' blast'd devil?" he said, raising one fist for a brawl and catching his falling hat in the other.

Ruth drew herself upright and stared. "You're a girl."

"Am not."

"As one to another, I know a girl when I see one."

"Ye'h, so what'uv it?" The girl had beady eyes and was covered in dirt from cheek to shoe. The jagged ends of her short hair had been crudely chopped with a knife in a futile exercise not to give her away. A series of patches cobbled together with mismatched thread stood in for clothes, and her shoes were little more than soleless slippers. Layers of stuffed shirts swathed her beneath two threadbare jackets.

Ruth laughed. "How'd you get here?"

"I d'nno." The girl shrugged and picked at a scab on her wrist.

"What's your name? How old are you? Why are you in my stable?"

"Y'r stable?" the girl grunted. "I's in charge'a jockey." She thumbed her chest and puffed it up, kicked her foot against the trough. "Name's Frankie. I gett'd no ovver name. No day'a birf, so I d'nno, maybe thirt'en. I's put on a ship t'be some rich man's serv'nt some'eres, but I ne'er gett'd off, just stowed in some crates 'til I end'd up 'ere." Frankie rubbed her face where the mirror had hit her.

"Sorry about that."

Frankie shrugged again. "I's stuck 'ere. If I step off'a this ship, I be a slave 'cause I gett'd nut'in'. N'fanks. 'D'ruther drown or get beated by th' cap'n than be a slave." Frankie turned to go, setting a hand on the corral door. "Leave 'is jockey 'ow y'finded it. We pickin' up 'orses next port."

"Wait," Ruth said to Frankie's backside. "Will we be friends?" But the girl walked off, and Ruth stood in the center of the stable and watched her go, felt the vibration of the sliding door through her shoes, and heard the footsteps walk away.

She was still thinking about the sailor girl when the filtered light of afternoon streaked through the deck cracks, and Owen appeared on cat paws at the corral door, leaning against the framepost, puffing on his soapstone and setting down a bundle of hardtack from the galley.

He took a long drag of tobacco, then another. "Come with me."

He held her hand and led her past the ship's stores, the sail room, the crew's quarters, down a flimsy ladder to the lowest cargo deck. It was dark and quiet, deserted. He took her in his arms and kissed her deeply, and Ruth felt his heart thudding through his mouth. The sound of waves slapping against the larboard planks was amplified in the lower levels. The rocking tested her limp, and she stepped gingerly from him. At the base of the stairs and further spread out before her, lay multiple partitioned rooms of cargo, both small and large.

"Help yourself to a thing or two," Owen whispered and grinned.

Her eyes lit up. Each compartment wove around in an intricate systematic maze. She lifted the dusty blankets from atop the boxes and peered at each in turn, all labeled for different ports, smelling of spices and straw. One side of the ship held rations: crates of meal, preserved pork, beef tongue, salted codfish, flour, oatmeal, peas, rennet. The other side held materials and goods: nickel horse bits, sewing needles, tobacco, and vibrant West Indian fabrics. Mäuschen leaped between the boxes and scurried off.

"There's over 20,000 biscuits and 60,000 gallons of beer on this deck, alone," Owen gloated.

But Ruth was not interested in biscuits or beer. Her eyes fell on the words Sun Hats painted on the side of a crate. She pried it open, reaching for a wide-brimmed hat reinforced with split-cane ribs and a blue ribbon that complemented her dress. "Boston gets the best things," she said.

"They do."

"Why did you never tell me there's a girl in your crew?" She picked at the ribbon that had been crushed by the lid of the overstuffed crate.

"There's no girls in my crew."

"I met her. Frankie. She was inspecting the jockeys."

"Like I said, there's no girls in my crew." He smiled. "Frankie's not on my payscroll. But she's good luck when it comes to bad luck. Pirates won't jump a ship what has female sailors. They deem it cursed. They think she's a Jonah what'll sink 'em. We know her to be better luck around here."

Ruth smiled at that. She liked Frankie already. Then she motioned for him to come to her. He seemed so disheveled, flustered in her presence. "Why stand so far? It isn't like we're strangers." She blushed.

He grunted and took a deliberately long puff of his pipe. "That hat suits you."

She put her hands on her hips.

"Look, I spent the last decade contemplating the way we'd…" It was his turn to blush. "I didn't exactly foresee us in a trough."

Ruth went back to the hats. "How's this one?"

"Same as the last or the next. Just pick one. And here." He pried open a tightly nailed box with his bare hands, rifled through, and handed her a pair of soft-knitted stockings. "Take them, too. Yours are starting to look like Frankie's."

She put the stockings in her dress pocket, and he ushered her back up the ladder before him, stealing a glance up her petties, thinking how the chivalrous *ladies first* was invented for just such scenarios as this. He escorted her back to the jockey and left quietly, while she studied her new wares. By the time she turned her attention to the door, he was gone, and she was alone in the stable. His scent lingered, and she felt a hint of sorrow for this; he was waiting for dry land. She might have to wait forever.

Moments later, she heard voices whispering in the hallway between the ship's stores and the jockeys. At first, she thought Owen had returned, but the sound didn't come closer. She put her ear to the door of the stable and tried to discern the voices, but they were drifting farther off.

"I got no wish to go agin him, sir. He be a good mate, loyal to this ship."

"I'm not asking you to go against him, Thomas. Just pay attention to his alliances."

Thomas! Ruth took in a sharp breath. Who was he talking to? She listened closer, willing her ear to leap from her head, through the wooden door, and return with the answers.

"You's nay asking me to go agin him…yet. But we both know you will. A scrap is one peg, but what you spake is nay honorable, sir, and I can't partake in it."

"Then I'll find someone who will," the voice rose loudly over the quiet air, and Ruth's chest tightened. The captain.

Her heart pounded as the words dimmed. She paced the floor of the stable, counting the men's footsteps until they disappeared down the hallway toward the crew quarters. She paced that way for hours, unable to sit still. Where was Owen? With each passing hour, her nervousness grew. Was he in danger? She watched the filtered rays of sun pass slowly across the stable dirt, then evaporate into night, yet without sight of him.

It was too late at night to be stirring on the ship when she set out. She made her way down the hall and knocked sheepishly at the crew hold, a knock so faint, only someone close could hear it. Thomas opened the door from inside, standing indecently before her in his undershirt and hose. Ruth stared at him, untrusting.

"Owen here?" she asked timidly, her eyes shifting to his undershirt, then down, immediately back up.

"I's sure he'll have no objections to you entering the men's berth and interrupting his drinkin' and gamblin'. We's having a fine conversation about whoring at the brothel rooms of Bendell's Cove, whether there be more knocking shops on Court Street or Fish Street, and how much the new dark-haired harridans costed in the hush houses 'bove Ship Tavern. You'll add to it nice, I's sure."

"I just need to—"

"At the back. Gamblin' for knocking money."

"Can you retrieve him?"

"Retrieve him yourself. Them men would trade in some of their earnings set for Old Amsterdam's jilt shoppies and Town Dock's sailors-welcome to drop their galies on a look at you instead."

Her eyes widened. "Please. I don't want to—"

Thomas yanked her by the arm into the hold. "Sure the sight and smell of men don't bother you none." He patted her on the butt as she inched past.

He led her back to the quarters where the men were smoking West Indian cigars and pipes, drinking stolen rum from the cargo hold, and gambling with dice, cards, and meager possessions around a makeshift table. She wondered if perhaps this was where Owen acquired half the items he bestowed upon her. She was relieved and contented to see him alive and turned to leave before he noticed, but Thomas grabbed her again by the arm.

"Look what little nosy mouse I finded creepin' 'round," he said, "twitchin' her whiskers and skirts, scurryin' 'bouts, searching for Owen at this late glass. How dear."

Owen shot her a glare and went back to making his bet.

A voice rose: "No dames, 'less there be 'nough to go 'round," and it seemed Ruth wouldn't be the only recipient of Owen's glare.

"This is no place for you." He didn't look up from his cards. "Can't stay here."

"But it looks fun," she responded, surprised at her own words.

Another voice bit through the air, "Awww, let the girl stay! 'T'will be something novel in this cabin." Bawdy laughter followed.

Owen threw his cards to the bed and stood. "You won't speak that way, Lordfellow. Follow the code. Ruth, go on, get out of here."

She didn't move. Her mouth curled into a tight grin. Owen grunted and shoved a sailor out of the closest seat, then patted the corner of the bed. This time, Ruth went where he instructed, relieved to find the familiar, unintimidating Frankie next to her, jug of flip and a bet in hand. Frankie scowled when their eyes met, but Ruth smiled.

"Takes a stable lockdown, and you get yourself a broke mare," Thomas sneered.

"She spraddlin' like she been rode good," another laughed.

Owen watched as she settled into the seat next to him. "Are you still limping bad as all that?"

She didn't say anything. The winter was long behind her. But in her mind, she felt that cold again, the ice at her toes like she'd stepped into a brick of it that had congealed around her. Gran's yellowed face, sunken in. The snow piled around Copernicus in a wintry grave. She forced a pleasant face.

Frankie said, "Mayb' she'll bring yeh some bett'a luck."

"She better. Why else does a man keep a doxy around?" Owen held out some dice in his fingers to Ruth's mouth. "Give that a little blow." Ruth complied as the rum jugs came around, the room awaiting Owen's toss. "Hell, whuddyaknow?" The first sign of delight in his voice since Ruth's intrusion, was met with his shipmates' boos. "You are good luck, doxy. You just winned me back everything I lost."

"Surely it wasn't yours to begin with, you swindler." Ruth felt the tension in the air easing as Owen visibly relaxed. Somewhat. She watched him closely now. He never really relaxed, she thought, not really. She pictured him sitting by a hearth, pipe in clenched lips, a beard long and gray, but even in her mind and old of age, he was a restless spirit. She imagined that was what she'd always admired in him. And how she wanted that wanderlust for herself, so captive to all that had tied her in place.

Frankie tapped her on the shoulder as the jug came around. Ruth hesitated, then took the jug when she noticed Owen's look of disapproval. She tilted her head back and took several chugs, guzzling as much as she could before he snatched the jug from her eager hands. The thick rum contrivance went to her head and warmed her body all the way to her toes.

"You're not used to this heavy stuff. Keep it to two gills. If you go soft on me, I'm swindling you while you're knocked out."

The men cheered, and Ruth hid her fuzziness as she focused on the game, first looking over Owen's shoulder at his cards, then slipping her hand into her dress pocket to find the pair of knitted stockings from the cargo hold. As the jug made its rounds again, she stole the opportunity to place the stockings into Frankie's hand in exchange for the liquor. Frankie unfurled her fingers and smiled bashfully, pocketing the gift, a fresh glint lighting her eyes. Her face rosied, but her smile remained. Ruth returned her muddled mind to Owen's cards. The jug kept passing from one hand to the next, around and around again, until she felt sick, looking at the game and the men and the game and the men and the jug and the game and the men, then the floor.

As the cards flew on the table and the jug came back around, Ruth barely passed it to Owen before landing with a thud on the planks, nearly knocking Frankie over in the process.

"Deal me out this round," Owen laughed. "There's swindling to do." He put her arms around his neck and hoisted her up onto his bunk, laying her head back, pulling her feet up, and unlacing her boots.

She snapped-to and stopped him with a thrashing arm. "No! Leave the boots."

"Boots off in bed. This might be a ship, but for heaven's sake, we aren't heathens."

"I don't want to be a bother." She tried to get to her feet. "I'll go."

"You're slewed as a sailor. You'll stay right here until you don't talk fuzzy." He began to unlace her boots again.

"Please, don't take the boots—"

"Why not? You don't want to show off your new stockings?"

The men chuckled, but Ruth drunkenly pulled the laces from Owen's hands. "At least leave my stockings, please. I beg you."

"You beg me? What's under your boots to warrant begging?" He remembered the limp she'd displayed since the beginning of the journey. It had seemed insignificant, but it hadn't improved over the passing days. A concerned look paled his good humor. "Are you hurt under there?"

He pulled off her boot and stocking together in one tug, and the odor shot down to his gut, so potent he could taste it. Her toes were red and gray, one blackened. The wound that had refused to heal had reopened and become infected. The stench of rotting flesh filled the berth, and the men drew closer to see.

"Merde! Good God in heaven. You got frostbite dreadful."

"It's embarrassing," Ruth said. "Give me back my stocking." She lunged for it, failing. Her hand landed against the wood of the bunk, and she felt the sting in her fingers.

"Embarrassing? Do you not know the rot is deadly, you mulebrain? Sakes, Ruthie, that doesn't look good." The men gathered, and Owen called out, "Edmund! Medical assessment!"

"Edmund?" Ruth said, somewhat relieved, somewhat terrified. "Is he a doctor?"

"A barber. But close enough."

The men rallied as the barber inspected her foot. He pushed on her big toe. A squirt of foul-smelling discharge left the dark ulcer on the tip of it, surrounded by bluish skin. A crepitus crackled from air in the tissue, and she drew in a sharp breath. He put his hand to her forehead, and his face scrunched with disapproval.

To Owen, Edmund whispered, "She's warm." To her, he said, "You inn't feels lighthead or tired or sick or nothin'?"

"Not too much," she said.

"God bless the kitten. She inn't get the septicks yet," he said to Owen and declared after examination, "but she's gonna have to lose it."

"The whole thing?" A horrified Ruth retracted her foot from the barber's grasp.

"Nope, jes the big dead'n on the end, there. He's spreadin' his rot. Better to take'm now than getted the whole foot tooked later. Nay, the whole leg."

Ruth searched Owen's eyes for sign of a joke, but his face bore no humor as he eyed the barber intently. "You sure?" Owen said. "She's been through a lot. I'd hate to—"

"I's sure. Seed enough to know. Nature be cruel, but that's the nature of it. I'll get my tools; you get her bricked."

"More rum!" Owen yelled to the men. "Oldest barrel you can find, and mix it with the heavy brandy."

"Right now? Right here?" she squeaked, but Owen was instructing the men in the operation briefing, sending someone for rags and someone for water and someone for needle and thread. "Please. I don't want to lose my—"

"Rest your head back." He took the newly opened jugs of rum and brandy and mixed the concoction into a handled tin cup. "Tilt."

But she wouldn't budge. Her head already swam with it, and the scent alone made her queasy. She felt the sea roil beneath her, and the cabin seemed to shrink and swell like it was breathing around her, and she, a feather lodged in its throat.

"Listen, you're going to lose it, and that's done with it. Drink." He lifted her head and forced her mouth open until she was drinking.

"I can't." Half the rum dribbled down her chin. "You're asking me to lose a big toe."

"Not asking you nothing. You're losing the toe."

"I'm going to be sick."

"That's all right. Go ahead. Bucket!"

With his instruction, a crewman ran for a bucket, and Ruth marveled hazily at the way Owen directed his crew, how limpid his eyes could be after drinking the same heavy stuff that had wrought her dizzy. Within moments, a pail sat by her head, cloth rags spread beneath her foot, and a fresh bowl of seawater rested on the makeshift table where only minutes before cards had been merrily strewn.

Edmund hurried back with a wooden box of picks, scalpels, and miniature handsaws. He placed a thick wedge of wood beneath her big toe and another wedge separating it from the other toes. The men fell into place dutifully, holding down her legs and body, while Ruth dug her fingernails into Owen's arm.

"Please, don't do this."

"You'll be all right. Je te promets. Tu avez ma parole. But it's going to hurt dearly. Let it knock you flat; don't try to fight it." He shifted his legs to stand and assist Edmund with the debridement.

"Don't leave me." She clutched at his sleeve, until he knelt back down beside her.

"I'm here. Shut your eyes and breathe. Be calm now. Shhhh." He put his hand over her closed eyes, held her fingers tight with his other hand, and leaned in close to her ear. "Think of someplace beautiful, and tell me what you see." He gave a nod to Edmund, who waited with hands on her toes and a sharp handsaw in grasp, for the cue.

"The meadow in Shrewsbury in spring, right when the ships finally come in."

"All right, the meadow. Riding on horseback as the marshlands are turning green and watching the sails over the harbor that—"

Ruth let out a cry that caused the crewmen to wince. She convulsed, and her lament pealed through the tiny room. Owen covered her mouth, but she bit down into his flesh. He bit into his lower lip in turn and bore it. For too long she remained lucid, and Owen grew squeamish waiting for her tolerance to yield, while blood spurted from her toe, and the men talked reassurances to her in low, indistinguishable voices, some of the crew exiting to give space when they were no longer needed.

"I said don't fight it!"

Her hand squeezed tighter, and her wails grew louder as the handsaw made its tiny slices back and forth across her toe—popping sounds she could hear, metal backed up into her throat—until finally, she passed out. Owen stood from his place and hastened out of the room. Outside, he leaned against the open partition to the next room and breathed deeply to calm his pounding chest.

"It's did now, mate. Ed's stitching her up. She's still flat." Thomas slapped Owen on the shoulder as he stepped out after him, then studied his first mate closely, nodded, and turned away to give them privacy.

Owen stood there too long, then collected himself and reentered the room. Edmund was applying heavy bandages to the stitches and wrapping her freshly salved foot in cloths. The barber folded the hacked, frostbitten toe in one of the bandages and handed it to Owen.

"I knows 'bout you twisted Frenchmen and your frogleg fetishes. Figure one foot's tasty as another." Edmund laughed at Owen's bunched face, cleaned up the bloody cloths, and put the used tools in the water dish. "She'll get them night sweats in a split. Break through clear by morn, but she'll be in considerable pain, poor kitten. Bum feet hurt to almighty hell, so see them bandages stay dry. She's in your care now, less'n you need holler for emergency, 'course."

Owen nodded, took a seat on the edge of his bunk, removed his boots, and kicked up his feet next to Ruth's body, laid his head back onto the flock mattress beside her. The barber packed and left. The other men in the partitioned crew quarters had gone to unclaimed bunks and hammocks behind the adjacent partition for the night, giving Ruth the comfort of a private recovery under Owen's watchful eye. He scanned the room. The table was overturned. Black blood spotted the floor at the foot of his bed, and more soaked deep into the flock at his feet. An upturned card sat in the blood spot, and though he couldn't see it, he imagined it was the queen of something. She stirred, and he nestled her into him and whispered things she wouldn't hear and longed for a pull of the grog in the corner keg.

❧

He lay on his back, staring up at the bunk ceiling. The night lifted its veil to reveal orange-hued shafts entering through the deck cracks. Ruth slept peacefully now. Her head was tucked in his armpit, foot elevated, face burrowed against his breast pocket, damp with her sweat. As he shifted, she opened her eyes and rubbed her face into him.

"It's dawn," he whispered. "I must go."

"Am I dead?"

"Of course. Don't you feel like it?"

"I feel the dregs and dross of my divine punishment with a busted brainbucket."

He chuckled. "We call it brown-bottle flu. You'll be fur-tongued and throbbing for a spell, but it'll wear."

"I...I came here last night to warn you. There was voices—your father, I think. You might be in danger."

"I don't want to know."

"But—"

Owen put his hand over her mouth. "I really don't want to know." He knew the man she warned him of. He pictured so plainly the captain who charged a cabin of passengers stricken with calenture or phthisick to be locked in the hold with no intention of their release until every last one of them had died. Owen could still hear their cries, remember their hunger, how the captain let them starve and scream and murder one another, hung a yellow flag at the mast, and never unbarred the door once in the nine-week passage to keep his own working crew from contracting the fever. Owen knew the man who'd never been a father to him. The captain would do what he had to do. On different occasion, that might have been Ruth in that passenger hold, stricken, and Owen would have been instructed to do nothing to save her. He'd have been locked in the brig for good measure. A shiver ran through him. Her cries would have haunted him for all of his life, more so than they already did.

She sighed and shrugged. "You'll need teach me French."

"Hors de question." He shook his head.

"I won't be a mourning widow."

"Oh, come, you've perfected that look for years." He sat up. "If the captain finds out I'm not on deck, he'll make fast widow's work of you. And we aren't even married."

"Yet." She touched his hip. "But you will, won't you."

"I have to," he said with a grin. "I'd hardly be honorable not to, what all I know of you now." He scooted to the edge of the bunk and tugged on his boots. "But you'll have to wait until the house is built, and until—"

She caught his hand in hers. "Teach me some words. I'm not asking for everything you know. A few phrases to begin, and I'll study the rest."

He paused, considered. "One condition." He waited until she looked him in the eye. "You got to promise me that you wouldn't use the language with anyone else."

"I can do only my level best."

"Alors, pas de français." He shrugged and turned.

"All right! I promise. I'll do whatever you say."

Owen melted into an easier grin. "Now that's my language." He pulled his cap down over his head and left for the deck.

❦

The days passed quietly as *Primrose* approached Stonington. Ruth's foot healed day by day, and she kept it bandaged beneath her boots, her limp getting worse before it got better. She met with Owen for hours each morning and night to learn his forbidden language, reading from French poetry books he gave her for practice, and stealing his precious waking hours and often his bunk space. He would correct her when she stumbled over unknown words, and he'd translate each line as she read until she picked out repeated patterns. Above deck, he kept a watchful eye on her, a task eased by virtue of the fact that the sailors had come to accept her as his charge. Each small port and settlement they passed looked bleaker than the last, and she prayed each one wouldn't be Stonington.

At long last, the crew bustled in preparation for arrival. Ruth grew impatient to touch land, having little expectation of this new, sterile place, except that she'd find freedom there. She'd pictured for years the lush greeneries of *anyplace else*. Any expectations that might have surfaced, however, were quelled by the fog that draped the port in mourning and the wealth of biting gnats that expertly found each sliver of bare flesh. Dampness clung to whatever clammy skin the gnats couldn't reach, and she longed uselessly for the warmer, drier, sunnier spring of the Middle Colonies. Her swift impression of New England was that of a breeding ground of misery and insect infestation, sandwiched between slabs of wattled gray water and sky, an endless lamentation cloak of sables and widow's weeds, where neither sun nor moon rose. Depressing, to be sure. She could think no other word for it.

Owen hurried around with arms full of crates and barrels, rolling and handing them off to each man with the wiry movements of a muscled hound. When the men went below for the next load to heft up on the block and tackle, he counted each item and marked it on his ledger, fluidly grouping materials together along the deck. Ruth observed him picking up a few small items and putting them in his pocket when he thought no one else was looking.

He cut toward her with his ledger in hand. "It's probably time you put a bonnet on this wild head and looked a respectable girl for your aunt—what was it?"

Ruth searched her mind for the name she had given before.

"Anne," he supplied. "So dull I'd forget it?"

"Yes, Aunt Anne."

He raised an eyebrow. "We'll be docking sooner than we figured. The winds gave us a dead run. Just enough to get us here."

"Where is it?"

"That tiny set of white specks up ahead." He pointed his finger in the direction she'd feared.

"Oh, how miserable."

"Eh, it's Connecticut. They're all miserable here. Will your uncle be there to take your trunk?"

"No."

"No?"

"I mean, yes—I don't know."

"You don't know?" Owen pierced her with a glance and fingered the pipe in his pocket. This woman. "Do you have an uncle?"

"I don't know. I mean—I don't know...him."

"Comme tu veux." He smirked. "You're swimming upstream."

"Oh, there's my trunk now!" Her eyes skipped past him.

"Ah, so it is. That marks the end, then." He tipped his hat toward her.

She tucked her disappointment away to part with grace and curtsied clumsily. "À bientôt." But she didn't feel it. This dismal place? He'd never return for her here. Her dull pallor would blend in with the gray sky and the gray beach until she disappeared. She huffed. *So be it.* She'd focus on her liberty. She'd make new friends. She'd build her own home.

He walked with his ledger over to her trunk, looked around, reached down to unlatch the lid, and placed inside the trunk whatever small contents he'd collected in his pockets. Ruth smiled, then felt the ship's hefty anchors drop like a sea kraken had kicked its underbelly.

Cargo and people went over the larboard side of the ship and headed for shore in small tenders and flat-bottomed dinghies, arriving at the two solitary docking points and offloading to an excitable crowd of a dozen or fewer people, over half of whom were getting back into the emptied boats to come aboard *Primrose* bound for Boston. If only she could have afforded Boston! But it was too late to regret her haste. She leaned against the rail and searched for any signs of color on the milky horizon. A horse hoist lifted a stallion by its undercarriage from a flatboat into the air and over the side of *Primrose*. She peered back at Owen, but he was preoccupied with hauling a full boat of new freight and passengers up the side of the ship. As the boat lifted, she saw him clutching the arm of a beautiful, young, upper-class woman and helping her over the side, removing his hat as he instructed her across the edge. Ruth looked away, scoffed, disengaged from her current line of thought just in time by the sound of Thomas calling out her name. Her own boat was being lowered, and there would be no goodbyes. Owen didn't glance in her direction. She frowned but endured the dinghy quietly.

Thomas extended a surprisingly gentlemanlike hand across the gap created by the landing piles when Ruth stepped from the small boat to the dock. "Pleasure having you on board, Mistress Miner," he said, roguishly kissing her hand. "Your trunk be on shore. Best take out the dead bodies before they stink."

She smiled and stepped. The land underfoot shifted as if water currents coursed beneath the sand's surface. She thought she saw ripples. Her first step jellied, and her legs disappeared, and Thomas caught her without a word. The ocean now seemed perfectly still, and the dry earth rolled in waves. She took another step.

"You'll get it," he said, and turned back to the boat.

She wobbled down the dock to sit with her trunk, her legs slowly floating back under her. She expected *Primrose* would be gone soon and hadn't thought about her next action. One wobbly step at a time.

⤦

The last bundles of trade passed hands. Passengers with families to greet them left reunited, and the final boat crew rowed back out to the ship. Ruth sat in silence against her trunk, waiting to be completely alone, to see *Primrose* again set sail, catching a dead run north. But the ship didn't move. After almost half an hour of no activity in perfect tide, *Primrose* was still there.

Then Ruth saw the shallow coming back toward land. *Must have forgotten someone*, she thought. But she made out the familiar figures of Thomas, Owen, and the captain in the boat, the latter with a glass up to his eye. A lump formed in her throat. She waited, swallowing hard.

"No one here to greet you, then?" Owen called, securing the hawser to the dock. The men jumped out of the boat with no help from one another. Their legs seemed fine.

"They'll be here soon. I'm only resting until I get my land legs." She peered down the road as if expecting someone.

"I'm not taking the chance you'll have to lug this trunk again all by yourself. You'll lay your back flat out."

The captain said, "Where's your family, Mistress Miner? You been sitting here for half of one hour. Isn't someone coming for you?"

"Yes. They're coming. They'll get my trunk."

"What is the name? We'll find the house—"

"No! No need for that." Ruth tugged at her sleeves. The damn biting gnats were worse on land, and she'd forgotten how imposing Owen's father could be. He'd never agree to—

"The name!"

"Don't raise your voice to her, Captain," Owen said. "Can't you see there isn't a name? She has no family left." Owen cocked his attention toward Ruth. "What were you planning to do now? Just going to sit here until someone took pity on you?"

She stayed silent.

"Didn't think that far ahead? Thought I'd leave you here?"

She looked defiantly at him, yet tears threatened to betray her. Of course she thought he'd leave her. He always left when the ship left. And when he came back, she would have had something figured out by then. She needed time.

"Get her trunk," the captain said. "Haul it aboard. We'll deliver her back to Shrewsbury in weeks-next."

"No!" she cried. "I can't go back there. They'll kill me! Owen, please. You saw what they did to the place. Tell him I can't go back."

"I've thought of taking her to Fairfield," Owen said. "Mother could look out for her until I could return—"

"Return?" Jacob interrupted. "Return and do what? Have a garden in the spring? Grow some vegetables, raise some cattle? Make merry babies and work the docks, while supping ale in the hot August sun of halcyon days?" He threw his hands up. "Do you intend to marry her, then? This…thing?" He gesticulated rudely. "This meager, unkempt, undomesticated girl of no kinship or class, no education?"

"It's a thought, Captain."

"It's nay for you to provide for her. Don't make the mistake I made."

"You'll not say my mother's a mistake any more than you'll say Ruth is."

"Stop!" she shouted. "I'm nobody's mistake! I'm not a piece of cargo waiting for a customs tax. You don't get to make my choice or shove me around from shipload to shipload like a crate of cornmeal. I paid my way from Shrewsbury to Stonington. I'm staying here, and it is of no concern to anyone." She pointed both forefingers to the ground and realized her shoes were sinking into the muddy shoreline. So much for something different from Shrewsbury. What a sorry marsh she'd chosen.

"You heard her," Owen said. "She's not budging."

Thomas asked, "What now? Does we just leave her alone on this beach?"

Ruth sat back down on her trunk and nodded.

"No." Owen's gaze softened upon her. What a sight she was, so defiant. "We help her."

Thomas chipped at rough soil with the toe of his boot. "What be your suggestion?"

"Why don't you ask me what my suggestion is?" Ruth said. "Why is it up to him?"

"Women doesn't get suggestions."

Owen cleared his throat.

"Very well, Mistress Miner," Thomas said, "what be your suggestion?"

"Knock on every door until someone takes me. I can cook, clean, read to children."

"And your trunk?" asked Thomas.

"It isn't so hard to lift for two big, strong men," she hinted.

"Now, wait a minute! That trunk be heavier than sin. You might be able to talk softheart, here, into doing what you like, but I willn't—"

"Tom," Owen said, "get the trunk."

Thomas gaped. "You's a real bit of work, mate, you know that," he muttered under his breath, then caved, and the two men took opposite ends of Ruth's trunk and moved toward the road.

"No one will take her, low-class nuisance she is," Jacob called across the beach.

Owen bristled but turned his focus to the road and the trunk.

⌀

They knocked on several doors to no avail. Many had no answer, as their inhabitants were out in fields or working the dockyards. They traveled as far as they could down the road, then doubled back, this time coming upon rows of tiny coffins lined at the outskirts of town. Owen glanced worriedly at Ruth, but she looked away like she hadn't seen them. No one spoke about it, but the boxes felt heavy as a harbinger looming behind them. Ruth peeked over her shoulder. *They were nailed shut.* She whipped her face forward, eyes wide, and the three of them finally came to a cottagelike, small-frame home backed against a modest field and a great forest. The home was built of heavy oak timbers, each half a yard wide and upholding a wealthy loft and side walls covered with irregular oak clapboards. The boards had been smoothed over with a shaving knife around sassafras window frames that held windows of thin linen soaked to transparency in linseed oil. An elderly woman opened the door, and Owen removed his hat.

"Hello, miss. I'm First Mate Owen Townsend, and this is Second Mate Thomas Hewitt, of the freight fluyt *Primrose*. This young woman is orphaned with no other family and needs a place to stay, for as long as she is allowed." He pointed to Ruth, who tried her best to appear pleasant. "She has nothing but this trunk. She takes up very little space and will work hard doing whatever is needed. I know this is a burden, but please, if you can spare it or know anyone else who—"

"We can spare it," the elderly woman said without hesitation.

Owen stopped short, surprised to hear the words.

The woman continued, "We've been blessed with more than we need for the two of us, save that we buried all our babes many a year ago."

"She'll be no trouble. You have my word."

"Is the word of a sailor any good these days?" She exchanged a smile with Ruth. "Heaven knows we could use the help at our age. Would have been nice if you'd brought us a hale boy, but alas. Come here, child. I'm Isabel, and this is the Osborne home. What is your name?"

"Ruth." She stepped forward and without her usual shame, added, "Miner."

"Miner? Of Lieutenant Thomas Miner, selectman and brander of horses, who founded Stonington and The Road Church with his son Ephraim and now lives across the Quiambog, Miner?"

"No, Mistress Osborne," Owen answered. "Might be coincidental. She has no known family left to claim her."

"I suppose we'll claim you, then, Ruth of the coincidental Miners. Do come in. I don't believe for a second you'll not be trouble, but do warm yourself by the fire and have some bread. You must be a tired thing." The woman eyed the trunk and held open the door as wide as it would go. Her gaze traveled down to the coffins, and she murmured something silently, then said louder, "Well, come on. Inside with you all. You'll have the whole town humming and Goodwife Crotchett's sinful tongue wagging before the sun gets setting."

The sailors heaved the trunk through the door with difficulty and pinched fingers. Thomas cursed repeatedly, checked himself, and each time, Isabel laughed. When the old woman laughed, Ruth saw her grandmother, in the days of merriment, when Father was alive, when she'd laugh like that, and her sagging cheeks would pull back the same, her neck wiggle alike. Isabel was slighter than Gran, looked healthier and hardier, but there was a warmth to her that radiated equally. Ruth prayed it was real, that it would stay, that it would wrap around her like a cloak. The sailors set the trunk back in a far corner where Isabel was laying out some quilts for Ruth.

"I'll see what Daniel has in his shop for a proper bed for you, but this should be fine for tonight."

"I reckon I could sleep on the hard ground I'm so spent."

Ruth looked to the quilts and around the house. Tidy and small, not much to misplace, less cluttered than Gran's. Walls bare and the linens plain. The only thing ornate was the woodworking—large European handles on cupboards and extravagant finials at the apex of every post and wooden base.

"A quick goodbye," Owen said sadly and came toward Ruth, shaking her from her reverie.

"Did you mean what you said to your father?" she whispered.

"Not a chance," Owen chided loudly, then hushed as he closed in to kiss her forehead. "Wait for me."

"Not a chance." She felt the heat of his breath creep in, pull away.

Too soon, he directed his boots toward the door, passing the disapproving gaze of Thomas.

"I'll watch out for her well, boys. Fear not. You come check on her now and again," Isabel said, and she closed the door behind them.

Ruth shut her eyes, squeezed them tight, and tucked it all away to sit down with Isabel and start over. All life began anew in spring.

ACT II

The Tempest

CHAPTER SIXTH

A spirit in the woods

Learn how to see. Realize that everything connects to everything else.

—Leonardo da Vinci

Ruth stirred under her pile of quilts. She was nestled in the corner of a small room long ago converted into a handiroom. The crisp near-spring air hummed with chirping birds and cool, windy gusts that streamed over her cheek, mashed into the cattail-stuffed pillowbere. Reluctant to leave the warmth, she forced herself to rise. This was a new start; she would mind her tongue and make new friends and be respectable. For the first time in too long, she would fit in somewhere. Her wool stockings took some effort to secure at the knees with bits of fabric that served as garters, and her coif had shrunk in the sea air and fit too snugly about her head. She rolled her bedding from the floor, slung it over her shoulder, and dragged it up the ladder to the loft where she would store it near the dry goods until needed again.

"Ah, there be the girl. Thought you'd never join me," Isabel chuckled from the kitchen table where she was thickening liquefied cornmeal into dough with one hand and mashing lima beans, corn, and tomatoes into succotash with the other. "I durst wake you, after the journey you'd had."

"Bless you, Mistress Osborne." Ruth rubbed her sore back and limped into the kitchen on a still-tender foot.

"Just Isabel. Sit. Have your morning meal." The elderly woman pulled a chair out for Ruth, seating her beside the cornmeal mash. "Tell me about the sailor boy what dotes on you."

Ruth demurred. "Why, that's awful forthright."

"Is it? Women talk on these things here. Pin him down and marry the lad and be done with it, I say." Isabel placed a plate of warm biscuits and salty cured bacon before Ruth and watched the girl's eyes light. The woman wiped her hands on her apron and made a round through the kitchen, stirring one pot of broth, poking the fire, two strokes on the churn, a couple clumps of lye broken up and sprinkled into the vat.

That's what the chemical smell was in the room. Gran would never allow a lye vat inside the house, Ruth thought, before diving into the meat like a malnourished animal.

"A passion for the sea takes an enduring heart." Isabel went back to kneading the doughs. "'Tis a noble trade, that."

"You'd never agree to him if you knew him," Ruth replied, then bit her tongue. She ate and didn't look up until she had finished. Gran had adored Owen. But then, there was history there. There was no history here. And Gran didn't even know who he was at the end.

Isabel murmured and stood. "You'll be in the field today." She led Ruth to the window facing behind the house and lifted out the removable shutter to reveal an unkempt, underworked field. "Building the stone fence."

"You mean lifting those massive stones piled out there?"

"Yes. Hard labor maketh the Lord proud. We need a fence to delineate our property before Mr. Higgs tries to say it's unclaimed, the knave. The…dullycock." She bit down on her knuckle and made her rounds again.

Ruth heard the swishing of the stewpot and the sprinkling of the ashes, and she kept seeing her father's cabin, how she'd maddened on singly running the household. She stared at the pile of stones and the ugly field. It was half-tilled, sloppily as if by old hands and a crude sodplow, half-muddy with tufts of crabgrass and weedtails cropping up in patches all over the untilled side.

"Take heed to stay within our property," Isabel said, rounding back. "Do you see the line where the soil be shoveled hence?"

Ruth nodded to Isabel's pointing. A shallow trench separated the ugly field from beautifully tilled rows on the other side that must have been that accused dullycock Mr. Higgs'.

"Do not venture further into Mr. Higgs' land."

"Whose land is that?" Ruth asked, pointing to a spot directly behind the Osbornes' lot, butted up against the woods. It was a small plot, undeveloped, wedged between the back of the guardhouse and a wee pond at the edge of the woods, some twenty rods past the end of the Osborne property.

"The Company of Merchants owns that. We lain money aside for it for a while, but once our last boy died, we gave up on it. It's held at the tradinghouse. It's mostly marsh. No good for most planting."

Ruth smiled. She knew about marsh planting. "How much is it, if I wanted to purchase?"

Isabel's brows bridged. "Women don't purchase property. You mean to say on your own?"

Ruth nodded. "But say I did?"

"Well." Isabel shook her head. "The Company of Merchants will trade with you. They'll take some of your crops for a dozen years, or let you sew uniforms in exchange, or that like. You'll have to ask."

Ruth beamed. She'd get the land. She'd build her own house. She'd work odd jobs and learn a trade or have a shop. She'd buy a horse and chickens.

"But you must take care. It's close to the trees. Absolutely do not go into the woods. My, the woods." She bit her knuckle again and muttered low. "The devil be in that forest."

"The devil! What kind of dark wood is it?" Ruth peered curiously toward the burgeoning woods filling with greens and buds. The forest had a red glow from the maples that looked like a dulled wildfire under a haze of fog. The dreary place at once came alive.

"Savages, dear. Among wolves that steal our livestock, bears, and black witchcraft what lurks in wait for the unknown." Isabel wiggled her fingers before Ruth's eyes as if conjuring something. "You watch yourself now. Redmen won't tell you twice. They don't fear Our God's wrath."

Black witchcraft, indeed. Ruth stifled a giggle, but there was sadness in it, too. She knew too well the kind of folk who believed in witchcraft and what they would do to stamp it out. Indians, though, had never fallen upon her port in Shrewsbury. Some of the Dutch had even traded with them. They were a curiosity not to be feared. "Savages so close? And you're afraid of them?"

"Not if we stay on our side of the line." Isabel looked at her peculiar new ward, pondering the recondite mask that played across the young woman's face.

◆

The tradinghouse was a dilapidated shack, one of the first buildings in town and not a fixed plank since. The damp, salty air had rotted most of the boards through. Ruth stepped inside to see rows of dried herbs, labeled foods in crock jars, and a table piled with slabs of dry meat. Char linen sat in a neat stack by the door, next to two leather-bound Bibles, next to woven weed baskets, next to strips of homespun wool.

She lifted the set of heavy nickel-plated knitting needles, and a man appeared beside her with startling efficiency.

"They will not rust," he said with a smile. "I am out of sheaths, but we'll have more in a month or two."

"I could sew myself a sheath," Ruth replied sharply, then reddened at her haste. She set the needles down. "I'm inquiring after the empty land between the guardhouse and the pond." Her finger pointed through the wall thereabouts.

"The marsh?" The man made a face, then quickly erased it. He arranged the knitting needles back to straight lines. "Who is your husband?"

"I don't have one."

"Then, who is your father?"

She looked down, stroked her fingers across a tube of beaverskin. "The land is only for me."

"It requires a male purchaser."

"I don't see why. Just bid me a price." She didn't take her eyes from the beaverskin. She feared what the price might be after her admission.

The man sighed. "All right. Have you money?"

She shook her head.

He sighed again. "We'll take twenty percent of your yield, including livestock and eggs, and you'll sell us six sterling per month of whatever goods you can produce that we can put on our counter. Wool, furs, bread. We set the price."

Ruth narrowed her eyes. "For how long?"

He grinned slyly. "Until we're satisfied."

"Five years."

"Ten."

"Seven. It's a marsh."

He put his hand out, and she took it. He held it too long.

"And I can start right away?"

He smiled again. "Sure. I'll have Stanton blot papers. But you'll have to convince the magistrate the papers are real if a man of the house don't sign them. If a magistrate agrees a woman can't have land, then it comes back to me, no matter what's been did to it."

⁓

Ruth lifted the cumbersome stones into place one by one, finding the perfect resting spot for each shape against another, lining them along the property's edge nearest the house. Her foot throbbed. She thought it might be swelling again, pressing inside her boot. It had taken her most of the morning to sort only a fraction of the stones into like shapes and sizes, setting flatter ones aside for tie stones and rounder ones for risers and capstones. She dug away the topsoil into the first of many rectangular fence beds, ten foot by three foot, and filled a fifth of it with a layer of larger flat stones. She couldn't decide which hurt worse: her foot, or her shoulders from pounding each stone into the soil with an unwieldy mallet.

"God's teeth, this will take me a year to go one length of this field," Ruth cursed aloud after hours of work, looking over her pathetic beginnings. "God grant me patience, just this once." She nudged a stone with her foot. "What a miserable virtue."

A motion caught her eye near the forest's edge. She looked over the piles of stones to see a man standing before her, backed against the bursting red of the forest, dressed in a colonial tied-linen shirt and crude, worn breeches tucked beneath knee-high English-leather boots. A necklace of carved wood and beads dangled down his chest, and his long, black hair was pulled back at the top of his head, falling most of the length of his back. His titian skin made his dark eyes appear wild, the white of them snowlike with brightness. Ruth gasped and stepped back, stumbling over her mallet on the ground. But the man didn't move or speak as Ruth locked eyes with him and gazed silently. It appeared he didn't mean her harm. *Did he?* No. Surely he would have struck out. She smiled, timidly at first, but she so desperately wanted a friend. He tightened his eyes and stepped away when she neared her side of the stone fence.

"Hello." She curtsied, then extended her hand. "You must be an Indian, no? Although, with that shirt and those boots, you look confused."

The Native remained still and didn't take her offered hand.

"Well, come on then, are you a statue? Are you a Delaware? Do you speak English?"

He seemed to be memorizing her, his face continually scrunching.

"No English? Ennnnglish?" Ruth said slower and lamprophonicly with hand motions. "Parlez-vous français?" Not that she could hold that conversation well, either, but she knew enough phrases to get by and was learning. If he spoke French, she swore she'd learn even faster.

The Indian stayed quiet, fixated on her.

"I'm sorry. That's all I know. Whatever language you hold, I don't know it." More sweeping hand gestures. "You don't look very scary to me. Isabel bade you a devil in the forest, but you don't look a devil." She laughed uncomfortably. "Are you hungry? Can I fetch you something? Would you like to come in and sit? I'm sure Isabel wouldn't mind, despite her talk. After all, she took me in. Once she sees you're not a devil, she'd be delighted to know you, certain." At least, Gran would have been delighted. "Are we neighbors? What is your name? Do you have a name? Oh bother, I shall name you, then. Let's see, something easy. I shall name you James. I hope you've no objections to my calling you James. I'm Ruth. My name is Ruth," she accentuated, pointing at herself. "Ruuuuuuth. I hope we'll be friends. Are you going to say anything?"

The leaves rustled like unsettling whispers. Flits of orange darted through the red, and the cheerful chirping song of a robin wove intermittent around them, excited units repeated and broken by pauses as if listening for a returned song. A male skunk-duck coasted by, his orange and black beak working open the shell of a mussel in midflight, dropping the casings into the forest below. Without a word, the Indian looped back into the woods.

"Wait!" Ruth hailed after him, but he sank deeper among the trees. She watched where he'd gone, then examined her fence and stared off to the plot of land that would be hers, and hunger overcame her. The hanging sun said it was well past midday, and she headed for the house. One final searching glance over her shoulder. The stranger was gone.

Back in the house, Isabel stood over a cast-iron pot of boiled-grain pottage, mashed vegetables, and chunks of heath hen and cod. Ruth could smell the hearty meal from the door. Saliva flooded her mouth in anticipation, and it stung and tightened her jaw. Her arms were so leaden she thought she couldn't lift a bowl, and her thighs, abdomen, and foot quopped with ache.

"Oh, thank goodness. I'm so famished I could eat the whole pot."

"You got quite a appetite, young lady." Isabel arched a brow.

Ruth approached the steaming pot and reached for an apron draped beside the hearth. She smelled her own sweat and wiped damp ringlets back from her hairline. "How might I help you?"

"You can place the table, and then stir this. It will be the two of us until Daniel returns from the woodshop late tonight. He's had his hands filled there of late. Coffins, mostly, poor man."

Ruth counted herself blessed that she'd missed the fever that blistered the skin, pocked the face with red rashes. She thought of the rows of coffins she'd seen lined along The Road. Small coffins. Children. When it finally ran its course, half the town had been lost, and nearly every home had buried a child or two. Many still draped themselves in the black dresses of mourning. The men wore arm ribbons. Dark curtains shrouded their doors. Ruth shuddered and thought of the nails she'd seen in the coffins, that moment when she truly realized they weren't empty. Such preparation for the dead.

She laid two large wooden spoons at each setting, then filled the holes in the top corners of the treen trenchers with four crumbs of salt from the block. The handmade trenchers were carved of sycamore, giving them no smell or taste to spoil the food. The centers were curved into circles for holding full meals, and a small, formed handle protruded from each dish's side. She wondered if the craftsmanship was Daniel's. She'd heard him wake in the dawn, but he'd been out the door before she roused.

"Will I get to greet him when he returns?" She met Isabel at the pot to take over the stirring, and Isabel made her usual round, to the fire, the bread loaf, and back.

"He'll keep hisself to hisself. He's one of God's quiet men. Makes all the woodwork for the town and nay a fuss more." As she said this, she put her hand on the butter churn for her two strokes, and Ruth saw for the first time that its tall churn had a regal wire-filigreed lion's head filial that looked like it would be at home in the Orient.

A knock arose, startling Ruth so that she almost dropped the wooden ladle into the pot of mash. Isabel opened the door to a tall, sovereign man with a thick chest, middle-aged but handsome and distinguished, fitted in a pressed leather military jerkin with gold-buttoned epaulets at the shoulders. Crow's feet marked the speckled-hazel eyes that reminded Ruth of the trapped fox, and salt streaks peeked through the sandy-brown hair around his slicked temples. He stood straight as a bitternut hickory, as if a soldier at attention, and made a polite formal bow to Isabel when she opened the door.

"Lieutenant General Whitlock." Isabel pressed her hand to her bosom. "What can I do for you this day?"

"Mistress Osborne, good day to you. I hear told you have an unmarried woman in your household."

"Why, yes, I do." She reddened. "You certainly didn't waste any time, Samuel."

"Is she of child-bearing age?"

"Mind your tongue. She can hear you," Isabel said. "Yea, she is young."

Through the crack in the door, Samuel peered around Isabel and saw Ruth, squinting back at him with curious eyes. "She is a small, pretty thing. She'll do."

Isabel protested, "Certainly you don't intend to—"

"Why not?" Samuel held up his arms stiffly. "I need a wife, and she is young and unwed." He looked around the door again, but Isabel narrowed the gap.

"Because your last wife's not a week in the ground, and this girl is half your age."

A bolt of sorrow shot through Ruth. The coffins. He must have lost his wife to the fever.

"I'll call on her tomorrow," he said, "and I'll go now to visit with Daniel regarding arrangements."

"Samuel, you didn't even ask her name."

He looked at her blankly and gave a small shrug. "Soon enough it will be Whitlock. Surely I've enough to offer her, and you'll be pleased to have her out from under your roof." The lieutenant general nodded toward Isabel. "Good day, Mistress Osborne."

Isabel stayed at the door, watching as Samuel headed down the road toward Daniel's shop. She turned to Ruth, who stood quietly with two bowls of steaming soup in hand, staring back at Isabel, a pall marking her face.

"Must I marry him?" Ruth anxiously whispered.

"Not if you don't want to, child. Hath no man called on you before?" Isabel seated herself at the table and patted the place next to her. "Did you live in a town of blind men?"

Ruth offered up a tight laugh. "Most certainly." She set the bowls on the table and drew a chair next to Isabel.

"That's Lieutenant General Samuel Whitlock, the commander of the garrisons. You ought to know him in this town. He'll have to make you an offer, same as any man. Still." She tapped her fingers on the table. "He hath gone about it the proper way. If Daniel gives him permission, then Samuel calls on you tomorrow."

Ruth's stew stopped halfway to her mouth. Hungry as she was, she couldn't force it further. "Would Daniel give him permission?"

"Of course. A man of Samuel's stature doesn't really need permission. He's just being formally polite."

"But he's so…old."

"Nearing forty, I'd wager. Owns King's Hall and the land surrounding it down the way, there." She waved her spoon in the direction of the coffins, and Ruth pictured them buried beneath his mansion. "You wouldn't have refused him when he was younger, I tell you. He led the colonial militia attack on the Narragansett fort during the Great Swamp Fight on a bitter cold day. Hath much lauding for it ever since. The man's got tough bones. Tough bones and iron nerves. It's a miracle he had the strength to get us through it."

"It's not a miracle." Ruth disliked how people used that word so loosely. "It's human nature. I believe it might be worked out logic-like, something philosophical if one only thought about it, like a natural physical process."

"Nay speak of sciences here. I'll have no such blasphemy in this house."

Ruth snapped her mouth shut and stared. Gran had talked of sciences. Her father had always been the curious sort, and it had once been encouraged. She lowered her face toward her bowl. Isabel wasn't Gran. The warmth she'd felt would not stay. "My father told me Narragansett never fought on the settlers first. We didn't fight savages in my town. We traded openly with many of them."

Isabel thumped her spoon on the table then rattled it around trying to take hold of it again like it had become a hot coal. "This be men's talk. We don't tolerate those what take the side of savages against fellow Englishmen. If this town had been unable to defend itself against savages, the appointed cape merchants would have long ago took over our settlement and demolished it as substandard."

Ruth whispered, "But it is only defending if you are under attack. It's well known outside of here that there was no attack."

"Hush that mouth! What you speak is a capital offense, so nay forget it. Seems you like to fill your head with stories. Samuel will tell it to you right. It would be good for you to learn your place."

Ruth stood and went back to the pot for a second bowl of mash and turned her back to Isabel. The nerve. And why couldn't she mind her tongue in a stranger's house? What stake did she have in the Indians of the Swamp Fight? She thought of the stranger she'd seen—maybe he was black magic after all. Or maybe he needed someone to plead his side. Or a friend, like Ruth needed. Moments passed between the two women before Isabel came to rights, quieter this time.

"Give Samuel the chance. If he doesn't win you, at least he will feel he had a fair shake, and you will have had a stimulating conversation."

"I'm sure," Ruth said beneath her breath. "As stimulating as stone fences."

❦

By the light of the evening fire, Ruth prepared yeast, flour, salt, and water in an oblong pan, then kneaded the dough together with her sore fingers, straining against the weight of her eyelids. She made twice as much bread as necessary, to take a loaf to the tradinghouse for her land. Her arms ached from hefting stones, and her back had a sharp pain that pinched whenever she leaned across the bread pan. Isabel noticed Ruth's wince as the tired girl labored over the yeast without complaint.

"Child, surely you made enough bread for a week. Come, sit by the fire for a spell."

"Someone wise once told me that hard labor maketh the Lord proud. This dough won't rise itself."

Ruth set the pan on the top of the hot wrought-iron flat grate propped on feet over the fire and took a metal spike and hammer off the hearth wall. The night was already black when she set out to fetch the next morning's cod from the outback barrel. Placing the metal spike at the base of the iron band circling the width of the barrel, she walloped the spike with the hammer until the band loosened enough to be pried off with gentler effort. When she'd wiggled the band free of the barrel, she lifted the top. The overpowering smell of rancid cod rushed out of the barrel like a mighty gale. Its potency made her instantly nauseous. She focused on the end result and reached into the barrel in the dark and groped a chunk of slimy, moldy fish until she recognized the feel of a single tail and lifted it up. With it came a burst of putrid odor. She slammed the lid over the rest of the fish to keep from vomiting into the barrel. The cod slipped onto the ground, but she could still feel its carious slime coating her fingers while she fumbled with the iron band and the hammer. She felt around for the fish on the ground, carried it back into the house, and slapped it on the kitchen table. There was no need to wrap it to keep it from spoiling. It was already spoiled. She imagined the morning when they would gather and eat it anyway. Her mouth soured.

She wiped her hands on her apron and returned to the hearth with a pot of salted water to soak the fish overnight, hooking the pot onto the hinged arm over the fire, and kneeling next to the blaze to prod her rising dough with a thin testing stick. She pulled her arm away sharply as a spark caught her hand.

"Child, you are tired," Isabel said. "You're getting careless. Come, rest now. Read to me from your Bible before you set the house afire."

"I...I don't have a Bible." Isabel's forehead rose, but her hands didn't miss a beat on the wool she spun. "I couldn't bring it. There wasn't room."

"But there was room for those other books I saw you rummaging through by candlelight eve-last?"

Ruth wrung her hands. How could she make Isabel understand the importance of the books? Gifts. From someone who never told her that Indians and politics were men's talk, that science was blasphemy.

"Read to me from one of those other books, then," Isabel said. "I don't see the words so good anymore."

Ruth's gaze drew upward. "But they are—"

"—not God's books? If you haven't a Bible, I durst imagine what you do have in that trunk." Isabel smiled. "Must be scandalous." The perfect rhythm of Isabel's spinning was mesmerizing. The warmth returned to the room. "Remember that I once was your age, child."

Ruth smiled. She was heading toward the handiroom for a book when the front door opened. In walked Daniel, his eyes purposely avoiding her. Daniel Osborne was a short, plump man with thin patches of gray hair around ears covered by quirky, wired spectacles. His shoulders rolled inward with the curve of hard years. His face, chiseled in deep, carved lines, yet ornate with stories that would never be told, was like his woodwork, and he looked a man whose occupation was his entire blood and body.

He removed his overcoat. "So this is our new Ruth."

"You must be Mr. Osborne. I'm pleased to meet you." Ruth walked to greet him and extended a hand, but he did not take it. It was the second time her handshake had been refused by a man since she'd come to this unforgiving place. She frowned. His hands were squeezed into black Spanish-leather gloves that he made no effort to remove, and she retracted her handshake at his resistance. "Thank you for taking me in, sir."

"I did not take you in. Isabel did." He shuffled toward the bedroom without removing his gloves. "See that you make better headway on that fence tomorrow. No mind the fuss you've stirred with the lieutenant general." He mumbled lower, "The fuss, all of it."

The bedroom door closed behind his words. The house lay still, thinned, hunched on a frail skeleton, with the two women not daring exchange words until the old walls settled again.

"Fear not, child," Isabel said. "He doesn't mean to be this way. The world hath not been kind to him. He hath buried four sons and a daughter. Hasn't been the same since our last boy shipped into the ground." Isabel looked to the window, out through the darkness. "The stones…" She quieted, and she missed her first beat.

Ruth clung to the sadness, but nothing more came. These stubborn, hard people were as gray as the land. Isabel retraced her wool and set it again, and Ruth took a seat near the fire, watching the bread rise slowly in the pan. The fire's crackle spoke for the passing time between them, marking its rhythm like a sputtering clock.

CHAPTER SEVENTH

An officer calls

Nothing strengthens authority
so much as silence.

—Leonardo da Vinci

By noon, Ruth had only lifted as many stones as the morning before, making less headway than she'd hoped. She hadn't even rounded the corner to the top of the field yet, let alone gone down the facing side. The sun was high but did not feel warm as the early spring chill rushed through her. She was marveling at how she could still see her breath at midday, when she kicked a lump of sod off a flat stone, and a sheet of loose dirt fell with it. She bent to the stone and flaked the rest of the dirt from the grooved surface. Words. Words in the grooves. A name. *Benjamin Osborne.* She flew back from the stone like it had burned her, dislodging another: *Andrew Osborne.* Her breath was stuck, her tongue blocking the flue, growing thicker in her throat. She looked away, wiped her hands, sweating, down her apron. She peeked back at the grave-stones, testing herself, then stared. There was no love in the plain lettering, but there was pain. Pain to be buried in a wall. She lifted the first gravestone into place, facedown and packed into the dirt, her fortitude packed in beneath it, and she could still feel the stone against her fingers after she'd released it. When Isabel called her for bread and ale, she nearly jumped and scrambled to the call as if she were climbing her way out of a pit. She went the long way around to ease herself, her heart frail and dry as blighted wheat.

"You will get parched, working out there all day," Isabel said, handing Ruth a tin cup of beer as she came through the door.

"That much ale will put me in the backhouse on the hour." Ruth took the cup, broke off a large chunk of bread, and swiped a sliver of tart behind Isabel's back. "Heavens spinning, I'm starved." She forced a smile, her chest still tight.

"You'll eat us out of house and home at that pace, dear. Do ration yourself."

Ruth sat and glanced at the open shutters toward the woods, just as the figure of a man crept closer to her stone fence. *James.* She stole her eyes away from the window and sneaked an extra piece of the tart beneath the table to take to him. Waiting until Isabel turned her back, Ruth bolted for the door, tart in hand.

When she approached the fence, the Indian was gone. She called out in the direction of the forest, "James! James! Are you still there? I brought you some tart." The reply was her pounding chest, the thrum in her ears as her breath caught up with her. "All right, I'll leave it here for you." She set the tart on a flat portion of the completed fence.

She moved away from the forest and toward the stone pile, then past it, its hauntedness, its names, her eyes traveling clear on to the harbor. There were no ships, only the gusting winds pressing waves into the docks. She longed to feel that seaspray rising from the hull again, splashing against her face. Turning back to the fence, she noticed that the tart was gone. Her pulse fluttered, and her eyes darted, frantic and impatient.

"James, are you there? I know somewhere you're eating your tart and realizing that I'm right. Come out, you jester. I won't hurt you." Then, she cocked her head, and there he was, where a moment before he had not been. "That *was* black magic! How did you do that?" Her question was met with no reply. "Do you like the tart?"

"Askook."

"You spoke!" Ruth blurted, her reaction so physical that she tripped over her own feet. "You can talk." But what had he said? "I didn't understand that at all."

"Askook." He pointed to himself.

"That's you? Your name? Askook. Well, it's more interesting than James. What language is it? What do you speak? Can I hear you say something else?" Her mind raced with fascination, her tongue hardly keeping pace. She swore she'd never talked so much or so fast in her entire life, but what if he disappeared again before she got it all out? "I find language so intriguing. I of recent began French, although I'm not supposed to tell anyone. Something tells me the secret is safe with you, though." She laughed, and Askook involuntarily smiled at her laughter. "A smile. Yes. Now we're getting somewhere."

"You talk great much, strange wonnux."

Ruth fell over onto the part of the stone fence she had been leaning against. She quickly righted herself, smoothing her dress, brushing the clumps of sod from the heels of her hands. "You knew what I said all this time and never said so? You let me go on like a prattling fool and couldn't interject that you knew English and not to call you James?" She quieted herself to take him in for a spell, appreciating him in an entirely new light. "You think I talk too much, do you? Well, maybe you talk too little?" She approached him a second time with her hand extended and stopped within inches of him. "Can we start over as friends?" *I need a friend*, she wanted to say, but finally held back. "I'm Ruth."

"Nuk, Ne-wohter. You say." Askook still wouldn't take her palm.

"It's customary to shake hands when one is presented to you."

"I know this cus-tom-ar-y. You Waunnuxuk not create shake-hand. No shake-hand with wonnux."

"Did you at least like the tart?"

"Tart." He rubbed a hand on his stomach. "Great much."

"But we're still not to be friends?"

"Wonnux build kepī'higàn`," he said, pointing at the stones gathered around Ruth's feet.

"The fence?" She mirrored his indication toward the pile of stones. "But I've not done a terrible job with it. It's my first fence, I confess, but I thought I was hooking it rather—"

"Fence, you say. No fence Musqáyuw Forest."

"Oh, you don't like the fence at all?"

"No Waunnuxuk ohke to make fence." He pointed at her and to the ground, the land, with wide gestures.

Ruth bunched her brows. "You mean it's not our land? But Isabel said the property line—"

"No prop-er-ty. Waunnuxuk word." Askook lifted his chest, unwavering. "You leave land. Free. Use, and bekedum kee to kee. Land to land."

Ruth understood enough. The land wasn't hers, and she shouldn't be fencing it in. She could use it, but she couldn't keep it. "Askook, building fences is what my people do. It defines a man's worth. Land is wealth. If you don't have a fence, you have no say whatsoforth in how anything is run around here. It's all dictated by property, by possession and wealth."

"This land no pos-ses-sion, you say, for fence."

"You mean it don't belong to us. Does it belong to you?"

"To Musqáyuw." He waved at the line of red maple trees and

anthracnosed black walnuts and tall river birches, multi-trunked with peeling bark that shed in layers in the loamy riparian soil.

Ruth looked from the trees back to Askook. "What if I purchase it from you? Can I do that? What is it worth? What do you want for it?"

"Pur-chase?"

Ruth made a motion of exchanging money, then put out her hand.

"You trade to sunjum?" Askook squished his face into one of confusion.

"If that would make it right. I haven't money, but I can get some materials for you. These are good people; they wouldn't like to think this land has not been purchased. I will talk to them." She pictured Gran's face, then blotted it out with Isabel's scorn for *men's talk*, and hoped the elder would listen to reason. "So how can I repay you? Will you accept a bargain?" Ruth smiled, but Askook's face grew grave.

"I make no shake-hand with wonnux."

Ruth kept her hand extended, despite his refusal. She smiled again, and he slowly raised his palm.

"Ac-cept bar-gain," he conceded.

She glanced over her shoulder toward the road to the center of town, each house, each small farmstead, then turned to see him still staring at her. A new revelation struck. "No one has ever purchased the land from you, have they. They just took it." Ruth still held firmly to his hand. From what she remembered of her old port town, they had always traded, but maybe she'd been wrong. Maybe they simply took the land, too. "Listen. I am making a plot of land by the marsh." She pointed past the Osborne property to her little parcel. "I'll build a house, and there will be space for you to visit. And I promise I won't build a fence." He pulled away, and she looked back across the field. "Askook... Askook?"

He was walking toward the forest, just as he'd done the time before.

"Don't go." She started after him, but he raised a hand.

"Ne-sookedung." He faced a tree and dropped the front of his breeches to his thighs, turning his back toward Ruth to relieve himself. She stifled a laugh and looked away. It didn't take her long to learn that word.

Ruth squeezed the fire tongs around the hot coals and lifted them one at a time into the warmed flatpan iron. She wrapped a cloth around the iron's hot handle and moved the flat edge swiftly against the dampened silk of her best dress before the coals lost potency. She hadn't ironed a dress for a man in all her life. It felt so frivolous. Her ironing was a slow protest before Isabel could button up the lace collar of the garment. Ruth seemed to have outgrown it, and she fussed with the buttons as she stared at missed spots on the kitchen floor she'd sanded. Outside the door, the wailing sounds of the councilor's servants' rudimentary wooden flutes and conch shells let the town know that it was time to leave for Second Meeting. Ruth was certain that if she complained about it, someone would find another stone fence for her to build.

"It took me hours to sand that floor," she said, as they left the house for The Road Congregational Church further up the Wequetequock. "I don't like the way he looks at me. Like he's measuring me."

"He is," Isabel said flatly.

"Like he's remarking property."

"He is."

"Property," Ruth murmured. "A Waunnuxuk word."

"What did you say?"

She sighed. "I spoke with a gentleman who said your land, the property you borrowed—"

"We borrowed no property," Isabel said loud enough for Daniel to take interest on the other side of her. "We own our land without loan or quit-rent."

"But Askook said—"

"Heavens alive, what sort of name be that?" Isabel glowered and pinched Ruth hard at the elbow, pulling her in close. "Ruth Miner! You've been—"

"—your property—"

"—is owned!"

"Enough racking," Daniel cut in. His eyes were as assessing as Samuel's. "You hens will nay make me late. Follow the path, not your tongues."

Ruth said, "But I desire—"

"Women's desires are not in accordance with God's Law," he said. "Seems Second Meeting will do you well."

To Ruth's surprise, Isabel nodded. The tightening collar buttons mimicked the stranglehold of their expectations, and she felt herself sweating. But she didn't want to be ostracized again, so she focused instead on the upland swells and swamps through town. The trading-house, the storehouse, the cooperage, the gunsmith shop, the guard-house: short of a stonewalled fort, the town felt unbearably cold and militaristic. The shipbuilding warehouses were a welcome change of backdrop, alive against the gray. The smell of felled oaks coated the air, green and thick, sticking to the bottom of the lungs.

The Road Church held the King's Court and was used as the upper meetinghouse for lesser gatherings, all under the care of Reverend James Noyes. The structure had been built on Agreement Hill on the Pequot Trail, the only road that existed through the area at the time of construction, running from the head of the Mystic River through the town plat to Kichemaug, Rhode Island. Ruth heard that Quakers lived in Rhode Island, which invariably made it someplace she never wanted to visit, least yet on a trail named for warring Indians.

The front door of the church near the back of the building led to a high mahogany circular pulpit supported by slender wooden pillars. Behind the pulpit swayed silk and damask curtains of deep crimson that looked too elegant to complement the room's simple design. A Bible rested on an excessive cushion sewn from the same red material with tassels hanging from the corners, taking up most of the space at the pulpit. The stand faced out over high pews that were gated and latched with small wooden buttons, painted white, and decorated with fine cherrywood railings. Each pew had been auctioned to the highest bidder, who was able to use it for ninety-nine years, but Daniel had managed to get Ruth squeezed into the Osborne gate as an inhabitant of the town—provided she followed the orders of the colony as the rest of the churchgoers were sworn to do—to the disgruntlement of some who had waited their turn and paid for their respective spots in heaven. Ruth understood the importance of this to Daniel and vowed not to undermine it.

The church had no heat or light, and she imagined that the winter winds howled viciously through the cracks in the walls. The décor was plain, save for the sweeping crimson curtains, and the aisle inclined slightly as it reached the back of the church. Entry doors opened to the right and left of the pulpit, and entering through them was a test of will, facing the entire congregation of starers, an intimidating experience for anyone, made worse for late arrivals. And the Osbornes were never, ever early.

Isabel conspiratorially whispered into Ruth's ear all the names and statures of the people in the town, whom they knew, who owned what property, whom they begat, and whom their begatted begat, rattling like a sentence lifted from Genesis. Isabel listed in no particular order as mentionables came to her, so Ruth got only bits and pieces of the town in stochastic manner: Thomas Parke, Jr., owned land. Mercy Palmer—who had her cap tipped to the leather tanner John Breed, who had just completed a mansion so lavish that it required fifty-one yards of carpet to cover the floors—who was the daughter of Ann Palmer, who was the daughter of Captain George Denison, who was a distinguished soldier in King Philip's War and had the property that began at the Chestnut Tree. John Mason, nearing thirteen, was the son of Samuell Mason, the justice of the peace. Mr. Davis of the homestead out near Osbrook Point, bless him. Ephraim and Hannah Miner, of the non-co-incidental Miners, who'd recently lost their boy, Thomas, bless them. Michael Lambert and Elizabeth Start, now Lambert, not married but a week and blissful, bless them.

They all went in one ear and out the other as they were blessed.

Ruth stared at the ceiling when focusing on the longwinded Noyes' sermon proved impossible, instead thinking of Shakespearean theaters with the same upswept aisles, and naming objects around the room she'd learned in French. She had heard that Noyes was considering founding a college focused on training Congregationalist ministers and lay leadership for Connecticut. She imagined that the school would never be a success with sermons as trialsome as his.

She lasted hour after hour, picking at a sliver of cherrywood from the pew in front of her, looking back at the repenting faces, how proud and statued they were, red-cheeked as the crimson curtains, until finally it was time to slink out, quickly, before the prying eyes of Samuel Whit-lock could find her.

Isabel opened the door to admit Samuel and to take from him the gift he had brought for Ruth: a small barrel of flour. Ruth thought of the books Owen had given her, musty-smelling from the sea, their bindings popping, cracking like the joints of an elderly hand when Ruth opened the covers. A barrel of flour dwarfed in comparison. An objectifying reminder of her womanly place. It irked her all the more that Isabel found the gift delightful.

As he entered, Samuel eyed Ruth's pale pink dress, too tight fitting now at the waist with a lace collar that draped lower than it should. The officer stood first speechless, then calculating, as if pricing her for the Boston marketplace like a head of livestock. He didn't notice that she'd sanded the kitchen floor.

"Hello, Lieutenant General Whitlock." Ruth curtsied.

"Samuel," he corrected. His voice was powerfully cold, but she could tell he was attempting an infusion of warmth into it.

"Might I call you Sam?"

"If it please you."

She stood taller. "You may address me as Lieutenant General Miner," she chuckled, but no one stirred. "That was a joke."

"I understood it to be." Samuel smiled, but it wasn't right for him, stretching his mouth tight, not showing teeth.

"You don't laugh much, do you?"

"Would you like me to?"

She creased her brow and looked at him closer now. He was sturdy, unbendable, his jerkin steam-pressed. *I ought to try*, she reasoned with herself. *He's trying*, she added, and thought of his wife in one of the coffins. She forced softness into her eyes and tugged at a sleeve of her dress. His wife before the last had died in childbirth, she knew, and though it sounded for all the world like a curse to her, she imagined how it must have torn him apart, to have wife and babe struck down in one swipe of heaven's hand. She smiled and hoped her face looked relaxed.

"No, I don't laugh much," he said quieter, and Ruth waved it off.

"You two go sit by the fire," Isabel said, shooing them from the kitchen. "There be corn for popping if you fancy."

Seated at the fire, Ruth watched the flames dance in quiet rhythm with Samuel's breathing. He had no interest in popping corn or in anything that might have made the time go faster. She had attempted a game, and it had been shunned. He was merely content with sitting, and Ruth held her knees tightly locked together to keep them from bouncing.

"What do you like to do, Sam?"

"Like to do?" The question appeared to repulse him. "I am a selectman of the town. I hunt. Command an army." He'd been appointed by the king of England to form brigades of reinforced companies each comprising two regiments of infantry, cavalry, and artillery, and to place qualified brigadier generals in charge of each brigade. He had in his command fully trained soldiers and bands of civilian militia at the ready for any call to arms. The town knew this, revered this, and Isabel reminded Ruth on every available occasion to do so.

"Do you read stories?" she asked. She thought maybe she could find the patience to read to him by the fire if it suited his mood.

"No."

"Do you like arithmetic?"

"Insofar as it keep my army provisioned."

"Writing?"

"As it aid in managing my affairs."

"The study of languages?"

"The king's English is sufficient."

She'd been avoiding his eyes, looking everywhere else in the room but at him. She memorized the ornately carved clothespress with inlaid bands of multicolored wood streaked down the edges, imagined French fleurs-de-lys adorning the plain-white porcelain pitcher atop it. She could taste the popped corn they weren't eating, so salty, and she finally drew her eyes up to Samuel. He was gazing straight back.

"I draw and study maps," he said.

"Ah, geography."

"Topography."

"Even better." Momentary excitement waned when it dawned on her that his creativity in the craft was probably driven by militaristic necessity. A means to an end. People had to die and relinquish property for his maps. A sudden flash of Askook caused a stubborn lump in her throat. It grew as she breathed around its constriction. She reached to undo a button at her collar, but as her eyes rested on the proud officer, she decided better of it and dropped her hand back to her lap like it were made of lead. He tried to smile again, and she found herself wishing he wouldn't do that.

"You are a curious girl," he said.

"Are you curious of nothing?" Askook's image remained in her mind, and she couldn't blot it. "Tell me about the Great Swamp Fight. I'd like to hear your side on why you fought Narragansett who'd only been peaceful—"

"I do not like these questions," Samuel said sharply. "I am not a man for chatter. My intentions are dutiful and forthright. I will not sit around reading books and…popping corn and…tittering in social engagements. And you should likewise not be inquisitive of military matter. That is not becoming of a lady."

A fire danced on her tongue, fueled by years of unchecked challenging without hesitation. But she stilled it, and the lump rose higher, nearing her mouth, her nose. She did not choke it down so gracefully as she would have liked.

He watched her cast her eyes away from him and down to her feet.

"I have some tenderness," he said, sounding embarrassed. "I play the violin."

Ruth made a stifled, choked pip and looked at his hands. Were they callused? *Turn them over*, her mind pleaded. Was there really tenderness there? A patient room of listeners gathered around his sitting chair applauded and nodded as he entertained them, and in her mind, she held his pages. Could he play slow songs? Yes, a slow hymn. She obsessed about which one. Which songs did he know? She raced through the pages of Gran's hymnal. Could he play from a tune book? She watched his long fingers and imagined them, too intimately, on a violin handcarved by Daniel. Of course it was handcarved by Daniel. She stared so at his hands that, when he lifted them, she jumped, and her only reaction to any of it was to laugh.

CHAPTER EIGHTH

A year in the making

Truth is ever to be found in simplicity,
and not in the multiplicity and confusion of things.

—Sir Isaac Newton

"It's not that simple," Ruth said to Helen, as the two women walked toward the woodshop, Ruth carrying a tuitkan of rum for Daniel's second helping of the morning. "How could God decree one religion of soundness if there is another that believes the same God, yet preaches different words? And what if there's more religions than we know, and they say another else entirely, yet still claim God? Which can be of soundness?"

Helen pondered. "We find out in heaven."

"That won't do. We'd have to know before we got there, or battles would continue in heaven that continue here, and what kind of heaven would that be?"

Helen Starks was a woman of Ruth's age, married to a farmer, Matthew Starks, and already a mother of two young boys. She found Ruth's talk of other worlds thrilling when few others did. The Starkses' church pew butted against the Osbornes', and the two women had become friends as the weeks passed. Ruth now had Helen believing in other planets—something most townfolk found mythical—and had pointed out Mars and another silvery one the name of which Ruth didn't yet know. She'd remember to ask Owen to bring her a book of the heavens when he visited. If he visited. This town was astoundingly brief of books, save one that could be found in abundance.

"Who taught you to have all these questions?" Helen sighed.

"My father told me tales, but mostly: books. I only ever saw the world through questions. It exists in my mind, on pages of someone else's stories, the places where the sea can reach, this Motherland of England we fight for, yet have never seen. We should only fight for land we know—"

"This is talk for men."

"Oh, don't give me that. Sam gives me that, the knave."

"He is right."

"God's teeth. That's hogwash." Fog rolled in from the harbor and covered the mounds near the edge of town that claimed the last of the coffins. She'd never seen this land, either, that she stood on. She'd never been anywhere but two places in all her life. She closed her eyes and thought of *Primrose*, somewhere nearby, returning from a trip to Maine, to the Quakers of Rhode Island, La Florida, all she'd never seen. Even this dreary port with its endless fog and hordes of mosquitoes seemed like a strange land to her still, after weeks of it. "Of all these things to know, I know nothing at all," she said. "Does that not bother you?"

"I don't think on it."

"That we are shackled to this dictation, this 'men's talk,' when there's other worlds out there." Ruth threw one hand to the sky, almost spilling the tuitkan. "Other worlds that do not know our shackles, so we must, in actuality, be so small within them." Her body tensed at the thought of her parents, their smallness. She could still hear her mother's voice, but she could no longer picture what her mother looked like. And she could not remember even her father's voice. She'd thought that was something that would never leave her, "But it does," she completed aloud.

"What does what?" Helen asked.

Ruth shrugged. "The frailty of thought against the obstinance of time. I wish…I wish I could hold it. But it goes before I can reach it."

Helen set her hand across Ruth's shoulder when they'd stopped before the door of the woodshop.

"We can't spend our lives wishing," Ruth sighed. "If we are small, then so are our wishes."

"Be careful with that talk here. You'll get lettered for blasphemy, and it wonnot be an insignificant thing." Helen fixed her friend's wool collar and tucked a strand of untamed auburn hair beneath Ruth's coif. "You are the strangest girl I've ever knowed, Ruth Miner." Helen chuckled, and both women smiled and nodded as Ruth alone entered the woodshop with Daniel's rum.

The days and weeks had passed, and Ruth had been in them, wrapped, whole, a part of their warmth and their storms. Stonington was not a staunchly puritanical town, but she trod lightly. Her land now had eight notched logs of a house frame, a tilled row of cabbages and maize mounds, and a bed of seeds that Askook had given her, having no idea what they'd yield; she didn't want to do or say anything to upset the fragile balance between swift tongue and swifter town. She taught Askook how to plant flax for linen and linseed oil, and the two of them tended the budding fibers together, unseen near the shelter of the trees. What didn't go to the tradinghouse or to the Osbornes, went to Askook for true payment of the land. She didn't build a fence. Samuel visited regularly, and she bore it—but he only ever came to the Osborne house; he didn't find it appropriate that a lady should own property, and she hesitated to broach the subject for fear he'd convince the magistrate that his mindset was the correct one. Three times a week, she helped Daniel in the shop to earn money for her land, cleaning the floor and shutter ledges, organizing the displays, talking with customers, sorting and sanding wood, running home to fill his sprouted tuitkan with beer or wine for his morning settler—then mid-morning cooler, afternoon bracer, mid-afternoon whettener, and early-evening stiffener before sitting down to beer at dinner, pretending to Isabel that the latter was his first drink of the day—and occasionally, whittling a tiny something with his tools and wood scraps. She made knife handles and overlong knitting needles, replacement spindles and children's spinning tops for the tradinghouse, carved miniscule beads for Askook.

She'd helped with a bow saw to cut cupboards to length; hewn plates and posts for house frames with a broad ax; and wielded a froe to pound the ends of quartered-sections of logs into split smaller sections for clapboards, shingles, fence pale, and lathe. She'd broken a dozen chintzy tool handles and filed as many metal and wooden wedges before she got the hang of the intricacies of careful construction, but the handling of the tools empowered her. These were her favorite days of the week, when she'd mingle with the townspeople and get to visit with her friend, Helen, who lived next door to the shop.

Ruth reached into her pocket and removed the tiny carving that hid there. Her knife scraped against it with strokes too careful, almost too gentle to dig into it. She imagined his face when he saw it, how he'd know each scrape was placed perfectly, how he'd see that she fretted and waited. The house might be built by then, a one-room rectangle without much room to add on, but it wouldn't be an excuse anymore. A short walk to the harbor. Once she had sheep to trade wool, she could consider the price for building a landing stage for the ship he'd someday have. She carved intricate lines through the hair and down the neck, until Daniel reminded her to do some real work.

Ruth admired Daniel's handiwork, the ease, patience that went into every cut. As he worked silently with his gloved hands, she'd wonder what the skin looked like beneath the leather, how his hands must have once been so supple and were now scarred, callused into hiding. When she thought of his hands, she thought of the stones of his sons, pounded out with such precision, how his grief slammed hammer to chisel, now buried deep in a wall where he'd never have to face them. She set down each dusted piece with gentle care, arranging furniture, utensils, tools, dolls, and dishes into works of art, all the while watching the town through the shuttered window cracks.

A woman entered the shop, shabbily dressed, nothing in her hands but time. Ruth had seen her before. Whenever something was amiss, this woman was somewhere nearby, perpetuating the problem, spreading gossip, pointing fingers. The visitor had not come to browse and could afford no custom work of Daniel's. She burst into the shop as if a hurricane had propelled her lunatic figure through the door.

"Mr. Osborne," the woman blurted, "I'd wish thee good day, but I hath nay good wishes for thee regarding that ward thou'rt harboring."

Daniel didn't look up from his woodwork. "Mrs. Crotchett, please do tell me when you have ever had good wishes for anyone?"

Crotchett. Ruth stared at the back of the woman's haggard frame. The famed Eunice Crotchett the town discussed at length behind closed doors. Eunice was clothed in rags full of holes and a cloak pulled over her wild head of tangled hair, which looked like Medusa's untamed snakes Ruth had seen in a picture book. Ruth bet that no one had ever durst tell Eunice that she needed to put on a bonnet. The woman's unpleasant eyes rolled into the cloak's hood like two waterlogged ships tossed upon abandoned seas, flickering above a snarling snaggletoothed pout bearing no signs of ever creasing into a smile. Around her lips were odd scars that might have been misconstrued for unflattering wrinkles, yet their presence inferred something more ominous.

"Dunnot thee take curt with me. Since that demon child—she be a demon child, I says!—hath showed itself, half the valuables in this town be goed missing. The ships complain of more losed baublry than ever at our'n docks. I heared just now! It be unholy, I says."

Daniel raised his hand, both bidding her be silent and indicating Ruth standing at the front of the store. "Anything you have to say to me," he calmly spoke, "at least have the temerity to say to the girl directly."

The disheveled woman spun around and sank her unnerving eyes into Ruth's skin like rattlesnake fangs. Eunice studied the young woman with intensity, disapproving of head to toe, then the shabby gossiper faced Daniel again and spoke in whispers, maybe tongues, that Ruth couldn't decipher. All Ruth could think about were the ships. What she wouldn't give. Reaching for another wooden dish to dust and display, she put her attention from the ornery patron back on the town through the parted shutters.

She felt she must have been daydreaming when she saw the familiar figure making his way in her direction from the harbor. Without a thought for the shop, she dropped the rag from her hands onto the floor and whipped open the door. With arms spread wide, she landed with a thud against Owen's chest.

"Ooof!" He held her in his embrace longer than he should. She smelled of salty flowers and fresh soil, and her ale-sweat was almost palpable. He wanted to bury his nose in her hair were it not for the public street. "Where'd all this muscle come from?"

"Lifting stones," she said breathlessly.

"Stones, God help us. You'll be a brute." He reluctantly let go and stood her back and straightened himself before her, brushing out the wrinkles she'd pressed in his jacket.

"And building a house and tilling my field and please say you're staying."

"Passing through. Back from Boston and the Graveyard for Pastors."

"Oooh, is it foggy in Salem this time of year? What book did you bring me from Boston?"

"I fear I've turned you quite to spoiled rot, that a man must buy your affection with books. I hope you know that's an odd courting convention." He pulled a small bundle from his pack and handed it to her.

She opened it eagerly to find two books, the first a scholar's book about the French language and how to speak it, with a glossary of common phrases. She smiled. The second: "The poetry of John Dryden," she read aloud and smiled wider.

"Ah, but look close." He flipped open the pages. "It's in French, so you can do the translations. I had to look a mite hard for that. Trouvaille."

She clutched them to her chest. "I shall treasure it and recite it when next you come. I will tell you: I finished *Venice Preserv'd*, and for all Isabel scolds me, she begged me to read the entire end to her as she was in tears at Belvidera's death—oh, sorry to spoil that for you. Belvidera does die at the end, apologies." Ruth couldn't keep from grinning. How she wanted to pummel against him again. "Do you know what I would like next?"

"Slow down, you tight acquirer."

"I heard that Thomas Miner—of the non-coincidental Miners, now, everyone says—has rows of lilacs that were brought over from England as a gift to his wife, and the sailors can see them from sea."

Owen nodded. "I saw them from Fishers Sound."

"You did? What color are they?"

"Light purple."

"Purple. Oh, what a color. Nothing here has color. I want so great a row of lilacs from England. Can you find me the seeds?" She clasped her hand over her heart, tapping her fingers against the book as if timing the response.

"I got no idea where to find purple-whatever seeds. I'm a sailor, not a green-thumb."

"Can you not find some woman to get them?"

"That is not usually the type of service I employ women for." He looked away quickly, and she punched him in the arm. "But I will see what I can do."

"This time I have something for you," Ruth remembered, reaching her hand into the pocket of her apron. She'd kept it there for almost two weeks, waiting, cutting new imperceptible details. "Close your eyes and hold out your hand. It's my first attempt." She placed a wooden figurine of a woman into his palm. "I should've started over when I saw I carved too deep, but I was determined to make it work. I'm learning the trade. You always said a woman's hands must be as useful as a man's."

He opened his eyes and stared at the little figure with amusement. "Uncanny likeness. I assume it's you." He couldn't keep the smirk from his face.

Her face reddened. "It was a token to remember me, but if you don't like it, you don't have to keep it." She reached to take back the figurine.

He clasped his fingers around it and withdrew his hand before she could grab it. "Are you kidding, you Indian giver? I like it." He tucked the carving inside his breast pocket and patted it twice.

"I implore you, don't use that effusion. It isn't kind."

He darkened. "When they stop sending their arrows into my crewmen's backs, I'll be kind. Look, you won't get me to bring purple flowers to savages, so skip to telling me how you're faring."

"Can you come into the shop? For a spell. I'm sure Daniel will have a tobacco leaf you can roll or a spot of flip to make it worth your while."

"No bribery can keep me long in Stonington. The docks here move with unfortunate efficiency." He cupped his hands around her head, down her hair. Damn the onlookers, or he'd kiss her. "I have to see that you're fair, or I'll madden." A pained expression paled his face, and the sky dulled grayer around him, snuffing the light, a visible darkening as if the clouds were in conspiracy. At once he knew in her expression that she'd set him free of his duties to protect her in this new land, that it wasn't required to see how she was faring, unless he meant it for good this time. He vowed to himself that next time he would mean it for good, but first—

"I've got friends now," Ruth said. "I got Helen. And Asko—" She stopped herself. "Although, if you've got some fresh fish, I can right do without our rotted cod barrel."

He grimaced. "You'll not have a lick of rotted fish again. I'll see to it." So, she did still need him. He brightened again, but it was short-lived.

"I'm building a house on some land."

"A house? Here, to stay?"

She nodded. "It's nothing yet, but soon."

"They let you buy land?"

"It's set me at odds with the women, which is why you must stay. I don't want this to be like Shrewsbury."

He looked at her sadly. He understood that, but— "I can't stay yet."

She forced a smile. "I'm scything marsh hay to sell to those with cattle, and it's been a fair trade, saving livestock buyers what get from the Palmers from needing import the hay, so I'm underselling you." She laughed. "I got a garden and vegetables and a cat what sits at the back of my field, and even a man calling on me." The instant she said it, she regretted the words that left her mouth.

"A man?" Owen shuffled his feet, ceased leaning so. "Calling on you?"

She watched everything in him change, fold closed like a paper fan. He crossed his arms, and she knew nothing would get in or out past them that wasn't made of iron. "Quite silly, huh?"

"Not at all silly. Alarming, aye, but not silly." He stood quiet, considered not saying a word. But it tumbled out. He had to know. In Shrewsbury, he'd never once had to worry about other prospects—but here? God, why had she come here? "Do you favor him?"

"God's teeth, no. He's old and coarse."

"Old?"

"Yes, and honestly, I've never seen anyone more in love with the English Crown, except maybe your father."

He instinctually hissed. "A royalist, then."

"Why, if I didn't know better, I'd say you're jealous." She hoped he'd laugh, but she knew she'd said too much. Why had she mentioned Samuel? She wanted to smack the books into her forehead for that slip.

"I'm not jealous," he said and slapped his knees. "Of course you have a man calling! You're probably the only unmarried woman in this town." Owen let out a mocking laugh.

"What's funny?"

He leaned in suddenly. "The thought of that man's face when he gets a look at those brands on your thighs. Surely you were planning on telling him? I hope you give him more courtesy than you gave me."

Ruth stood paralyzed. How he could cut. She felt him physically sag around her.

"I'm sorry for that," he said and scratched at a gnawing itch in his chest. "Of course I'm fucking jealous." He studied the sea over his shoulder, softening. "I shudder at the idea when I have naught to offer you and no idea how long you'll wait for me to have it. And it's not fair now to ask you to wait."

"Now?" she whispered. A pause yawned out between them. She knew this silence. She knew the sounds of chirping gulls and screeching insects where his voice should be. "There is something more."

"Ruth," he started strong, then simply nodded, ending with his chin at his chest. "There is something more, aye. Captain is expanding new trade routes through Lower South, past Virginia and Carolinas on down to Southern Devil Coast. It will be good for trade in uncharted waters for us, although it shall be…a while before I return."

"How long?" She cleaved to the somber hesitation that accompanied his words. He was holding back.

He looked past her, his voice quiet. "Since well you know Captain doesn't get all his merchandise from England as the Crown states he must, we've got to be careful with the cheaper products aboard. The spry news is we turn a profit. The bad: we'll be there negotiating good into winter."

"Winter! So long?" *That last bitter winter.*

He shook his head. "Come winter, it'll be too cold for *Primrose's* return to northern colonies, to this port, until spring."

"Spring!" Her jaw fell agape. She reached to his jacket to stabilize, grabbed cuffs, pockets, to steady herself. It was only spring now. "You are speaking of a year?"

He looked down at the ground, at the splotches of dirt on his holed boots and the torn cloth of his jacket, realizing the little he had to offer might not last her the year. He cupped his fingers over her hand clenched tightly onto his jacket sleeve, willing mettle. "Maybe longer."

"Longer? And what shall I do for a year or more? Don't you look down at your boots—look at me! Ask it now. All it takes is the town recorder. One trip. A quarter of an hour. I'm sure Mr. Stanton is in his chamber right now. I bought land! We could just—"

Her words were stopped by his fingers pressing into her wrists. "I got to do this. I'm already late. When the ship goes, I go." He thought about the longshot of Stanton Trading House at The Rock near the Pawcatuck perhaps ordering enough to make an autumn trip worth the haul now that shipbuilding was taking off at Stonington. He wished harder than he'd ever wished. "I'll write you a letter if I can come back sooner, but you have to understand that—"

She fell against his chest and threw her arms around his waist, burying her face into his breast pocket. He felt the tiny sobs rack her body, wrapped his arms around her gently, and rested his chin on top of her head.

"Don't dock me here. Not like this," he said. "I been saving for a small ketch. I'll sell my acreage in Fairfield. Wait for that, will you?"

She couldn't lift her eyes from the ground, but she pulled from him, at once aware of onlookers. *How happy she'd been to see him.* "Go, if you must."

"I must."

"Then you must. God speed you."

He turned before he changed his mind at the sight of her eyes amist, and she watched him walk back toward the harbor. Down the road, Miss Abigail Billings stepped from her door and curtsied to Owen as he walked past. He removed his hat and nodded to her politely, exchanging a quick word with the pretty young woman. Ruth groaned and clutched the books and turned.

When she pushed the shop door, the hinges swung back, and she faced Eunice Crotchett on the doorstep. Eunice's scrutiny bore through Ruth as the startled girl blinked hard. Without a word, Eunice brushed past her, slamming an elbow into Ruth's arm, nearly knocking the books to the dirt, then shuffling away as if demons were luring the wretched woman to follow them hence. Ruth gathered her wits and pushed open the door quietly, in hopes of avoiding Daniel's attention, but he sat glaring at her over his glasses.

"I caution you not to make a public spectacle of your amorousness for that young man while you be courted by Samuel Whitlock."

"I'm sorry, sir. I didn't think of it. He's..." She bowed her head. "He'll not be returning."

"Not returning?" The pitch of Daniel's voice rose.

"No, sir."

"Doth he not wish to offer for you?"

Daniel's sudden interest irked her. "I don't purport to know his wishes, sir. My apologies for leaving so abruptly." She lifted her rag off the floor and pressed it into a wooden dish and dusted it. Through the shutters, she could see *Primrose* preparing to leave the harbor, pulling in its moorings, lowering sails against the wind in ways Ruth would never understand, and she uneasily traced the shapes of the sails into the dust.

⌇

Lying on her stomach on the dirt floor within the notched-log base of her future home, Ruth opened a satchel of farming tools and pulled out two hammers on which Daniel had fitted buffed wooden handles to wrought-iron heads.

"This is all I've got for today. I can't take too much, or he'll notice." She closed the satchel and handed the tools to Askook.

He lay on his stomach next to her, *The New England Primer* folded open in his hands. Next to that was a glossary of French phrases. He followed his finger along with the words. "P. Pe-ter de- de-..."

"Denies. Peter denies."

"Peter denies His Lord, and c-ries." He looked at the illustration of a man praying to a rooster and glanced up at her. "What mean?"

"After Jesus was arrested, Peter denied knowing him three times. It's just a story."

Askook bunched his brow. "Q. Qu-een Es-ther—"

"Don't say 'thh' in that one. It's an odd word. Esther."

"Queen Esther comes in ro-yal state, to save the Jews from..."

"Dismal," Ruth said patiently.

"Dis-mal fate. R. Rachel doth mourn, for her first born."

Ruth scrunched her face and looked at the illustration of the woman holding a child suspended over a tiny coffin. She swallowed hard. "Well, that's morbid. Let's skip and try the catechism again today."

Askook turned to the back section and read aloud what he'd already learned, following with his finger. "*Spiritual Milk for Boston Babes in either England, Drawn out of the Breasts of both Testaments for their Souls' Nourishment, but may be of use to any Children.*" He paused and looked up, and she was thumbing through the pages in the French book to find translations for him. "Your debe sad." He tapped his forefinger against her sternum.

"Yes, I suppose so." With a faraway look, off to the peeling bark of the river birches that were thirsting for spring rain, she spoke as if in a dream state. "If I'd thought when I came here I should see a dear friend even less than I once did, I would have withstood all the anger of that town and stayed."

"This friend more than friend? Weektumun? Chauk?"

"I don't know. I thought. I know how long a winter is. This past one..." She picked at a chunk of daubing between the logs and shivered.

"He ahupanun from cuthannubbog." Askook made a sweeping motion with his arm, then brought it back in, returning to hug himself. "Keep his debe." He pressed his finger again to her sternum.

"What is that? His memory, you mean? His heart? His spirit."

"His spir-it, you say."

"Debe. Keep his spirit. I'll try. It'd be easier if my stomach felt better." She shifted off it. "I haven't been well these last days. I know it's these nerves, but I'm churning. All those stones made my body ache inconsistent, and now the marsh hay. I feel a new one every day. I fear I might be getting sick with something unknownst to me."

"Box?" Askook pointed to where the coffins had been.

"God's teeth, do not speak it."

"Pechog? Meyuggus?" He touched his abdomen.

She nodded, and he reached into his belt pouch and extracted a palmful of dried weeds or herbs of a brownish color. Crushing them between his fingers, he took hold of her hand and placed the fine dust in the center of her palm. He made a gesture for her to swallow the crushed plants. "Before dupkwoh." He made a motion of the sun going down from the sky.

"Night," Ruth said. "Dupkwoh, night."

"Night, you say. If pain." He patted her cupped hand.

"It smells dreadful. What is it?" She fanned her palm in front of her nose.

"Swamp kunx. Ac-cept bargain."

"Kunx? Like skunks? I trust you aren't poisoning me with dried skunks." She laughed, and Askook nodded as she stood and brushed herself off, careful not to drop the powder from her hand. She looked up at the sky, the sun melting downward. Then she looked at the forest and noticed cloth hammocking a wooden bucket beneath a spigot Askook had hammered into a tree trunk. "What are you doing?"

"Is inanadig. The blood, weeksubahgud, thick. Mmmmm." He made a sound of chewing something gooey and put his hands to his cheeks like it might be sweet or sour. "Like tart, you say."

"Sweet. Like the tarts I give you. This tree's blood—you really call it blood?—is sweet?" Intrigue overcame her sorrow. "You drink it?"

"Eat on bread."

"What does it taste like?"

"Inanadig." He smiled.

"Very specific." How lucky for her that he was picking up the Englishman's sarcasm. "Can I taste it?"

"Only gersubertoh." He pointed to the sun, but she didn't understand. He stood and took her hand and blew his breath into her palm.

"Hot," she said. "It has to be hot."

He nodded but made bigger motions.

"Hotter? You mean you must boil it."

"Bo-al, you say, is hot, you say?"

"Very hot." She made billowing motions with her hands and mouth. "Steaming."

He nodded. "Yes, bo-al it."

Ruth's smile grew. "Can I see it? Will you teach me?"

He nodded and waved her past the small pond into the first few rows of trees. "Ahupanun." He took her to the sugar maple tree that he was tapping. "Tree skin? Good tree." Indicating a red maple next to it and emphasizing the red color, he said, "Musqáyuw? Not as sweet, you say." Pointing to other trees around her, he gave the instructions for each type, shape, and size. He pointed to a pail attached to a tree and tapped his finger against it twice, until Ruth understood his word for bucket: "Woothuppeag. This tree: small, nis woothuppeag." He held up two fingers to indicate the number of buckets for a smaller tree. "This tree: thick, much blood. This: short, nuqut woothuppeag." He held up his index finger to indicate only one bucket for a shorter tree. "This tree: tall, schwi woothuppeag." The tallest trees received three fingers: three buckets. "See this skin: you say…broke.…"

"The bark is broken."

"Brok-en, no good." He touched his finger to a tap. "Smooth skin, in this." He made a gesture of about four inches with his thumb and forefinger to indicate how far to tap the spout, and Ruth nodded. "Watch." He pointed to the spout, dangling his finger off the end of it, up and down.

"Drip," Ruth added, eagerly, watching a single drip.

"Drip, you say. Nis days. Woothuppeag full. No keep."

"No keep? Don't save the blood?" Ruth mulled it over. "Ah, the blood will get rotted if not boiled straight away. Then what?" She was so excited to try it that she'd almost forgotten her turmoil. If it worked, she could sell it to the tradinghouse and have enough for more seeds for their garden.

"Boil thick, scrape bad wôpáyuw top, pour to…ah…cloth, you say." He made each gesture as he went along. "No bottom, make muttiano-moh." He emulated vomiting so well that she nearly did it, her stomach still queasy.

"Wô-páy-uw?"

He paused for a moment and pointed to a cloud.

"Cloud?"

He shook his head and sighed, raised his brows, and pointed to the skin on his arm. "You say, red." He then pointed to her skin. "We say, wôpáyuw."

"White." She flushed, and he nodded. "I'm sorry."

He pinched his lips together and shrugged.

"But what is the 'bad white top'?" She pictured boiling everything she knew to boil. What was white on top? "Foam?" That must be it, she reasoned. Filter it. Scrape the foam. Cool it. Leave the bottom settled layer, or it would make her sick. "And I can store this in a crock?"

"Pour hot, or will make sick, you say. Not steam-ing, no boil. Only hot."

"And I can spout all these trees?"

He nodded and waved his hands at the maples. "All this. Inanadig."

She smiled. "So, you need buckets and spouts from me."

He nodded again.

"I'll carve you some if I can have a few trees for my own."

Askook frowned. "Trees to woods, not Waunnuxuk."

"Right," she nodded. "I'll only borrow."

At the opposite side of the Osborne house, horse hooves pounded frantically past the guardhouse and down the erstwhile quiet street, and her heart leaped.

"Go!" she said. She squeezed her fist around the powder and shook the loose medicine into her apron pocket, then saw the colorful imported beads. "Askook!" She went back to him. "I took these from the dish at Goody Allen's mercantile counter." She situated the beads into Askook's hand and patted it affectionately. "This time tomorrow. Be safe in the woods. Byowhy." The hooves grew louder, and she trotted toward the Osbornes'. Halfway across the field, she glanced back, and he was gone. She smiled and turned to The Road.

At the house, she cocked her head around the corner. Horses used in this ragged-run manner meant only three things: soldiers, urgent messengers, or lawbreakers. Prisoners and dregs came by the shipful to the colonies to be removed from England's home soil. The French and Dutch had caught on and were following suit.

She looked to the harbor toward the sound of the hooves. A single rider galloped in her direction, kicking road dust into a whirlwind of offense to the resident mosquitoes. Coming close behind the lone rider were a half-dozen grouped riders, hot on his trail and clearly not his allies. She pegged the lone rider to be either a highway robber or someone fleeing treasonous or religious persecution, outnumbered and unable to keep his lead much longer. This last hill was his last hope. She thought of Owen, the French. Askook. Persecution.

As his horse approached her, she stepped out from behind the house's cover and waved her arm for him to follow around the corner. Impulsively, he pulled the reins toward her as she led him to the spot behind the house that couldn't be seen from the road. The rider huddled on his horse against the wooden siding, while Ruth peered around the edge at the troupe of chasers speeding down the road past her and on toward the woods in a flurry of shouting, dust, and confusion. The hooves died away, and for a moment there was quiet as she listened for them.

"Appears Fogcutter likes you," the young man said, startling Ruth when she realized she had been resting her hand against the horse's nuzzling muzzle. "Strange. She's usually jealous of beautiful women who steal my heart."

"Steal your heart?"

The rider dismounted and gallantly strode to her, his arrogant manner preceding him. He looked a few years older than she, filthy dirty from temple to boot with several days' hair growth around his chin and neck. Dark eyes peered out beneath a cocked tricorne most likely lifted from an unsuspecting—or dead—soldier. Adorning his frame was a high-collared coat of red velvet that must have been stolen from someone of considerable nobility, although the jacket was now quite worn, fitting snug where once it had been starched stiff. Around his neck, a red cotton and lace cloth was tied with the ends tucked into the collar of his shirt.

"I'm obviously a robber, so why would thee harbor me if not to steal my heart? I know thievery when I see it."

"The only thing obvious is that you were outnumbered and needed help."

"Not from a woman."

She scoffed. "Well, isn't that a merry thing to say to a woman."

"I've never had any women complain."

His smile turned cold, and he backed her against the house brusquely and looked her up and down, his mouth moving closer without warning. She took in a quick breath and stilled, ready to bring up her knee if he hurt her. She could cry out; Isabel would hear her. And do what? Get shot by the pistol peeking from the flap of his jacket? The odor of his unclean body wafted over her, and she tensed. He took a gloved hand to her chin and held it in place as he leaned his face into hers, kissing her unresponsive mouth. He pulled his lips from hers, a satisfied grin on his face, his stubble scraping along her chin. The sun was in his eyes, and she turned her head up sharply beneath his, hitting him in the brow with the stiff bill of her bonnet. He pushed her against the house with a grunt, touching his brow where she'd knocked him.

"You damn leftleggers," he cursed. "This is why I rob you."

Well, then. He wasn't Protestant. She assumed the worst. "I don't much care for Papists, myself."

"Mind your accusations," he said, placing a hand on the pistol butt at his side. "I may be many terrible things, but I'd sooner see grave dirt low'd o'er top me than be called Catholic." He rubbed his brow again and laughed, and it was neither full of mirth nor lacking it. "Do I at least get the pleasure of the woman's name whosoeth mocks me?"

She nodded toward the road. "They'll soon realize they're chasing air."

The highwayman knew she was right, that it was only a matter of time before Colonial Law doubled back on him, and he stepped away and slid one foot into the stirrup and pulled himself onto Fogcutter. "You can keep my stolen heart as a bauble. It's not worth much, but it's grand to know its whereabouts if I should require it someday."

He let out a strong hiya and kicked Fogcutter into a gallop back down the road toward the hill beyond the harbor. Ruth watched him go in a blur, wiping her sleeve across her mouth to dispel his wretched taste, dust left ground into her lip. She opened her cupped hand. Gold and silver coins mixed in with the crushed weeds. The robber may have stolen a kiss from her, but she stole something from his pocket in return. She had no use for an outlaw's heart, but his coins were as good as gold.

CHAPTER NINTH
The ocean's silent reply

The massive bulk of the earth does indeed
shrink to insignificance in comparison
with the size of the heavens.

—Nicolaus Copernicus

"You've muddled the spices enough," Isabel said from the morning table. "Now you're working anger into the flavor. Tell me what it is."

Ruth hadn't felt right for days. She thought of the coffins as she examined the cooling maple syrup and crushed dried spices and leaves. The spices had been flattened to sheer dust. Sprinkling the flakes onto a thin sheet of cloth, she took a chunk of honey wax and melted it with a candle over the top of the pile. The water boiled as she registered Isabel's words. "I don't know what's wrong with me." The way the nails had been so haphazardly hammered into the wood, no one wanting to linger too long next to death. She remembered how the coffins had sunk down into the ground at one end. It must have rained in the days before she'd arrived here, the ground too moist to carry them.

"I heard you at the bucket again this morning," Isabel said. "If you're sick, you must say it. We'll call a meeting, so it doesn't spread."

"Well, I feel sick, but I'm fine. Then I'm sick, then fine. I don't know. It will pass if I give it a moment." Ruth carefully pulled the corners of the cloth around the pile of spices and honey and poured boiling water over it into a tin cup. She brought the tea to the table and scraped a chair along the floor to join Isabel. "I certain hope—"

"Lift it. Don't drag."

"—it passes soon. Sorry I dragged it."

Isabel patted Ruth's hand. "Just rest, child. We're working you too hard."

"No, no, it isn't that. The pain is low, in my gut, and my chest feels tender. Here, and here." She touched her dress along the seams where her armpits met her chest.

Isabel hesitated. "Might I ask a rather personal question? When you go on walks with the lieutenant general, what do you do?"

"We walk, what else? We discuss dreadful boring things like military uniforms and cattle breeds." Ruth pictured her arm linked in his, how she'd memorized every stitch in the sleeve of his uniform but couldn't answer if asked the exact color of his hair.

"He's not touched you?"

"Touched me?" Her stomach churned. "You mean ungentleman-like?"

Isabel put her palms to the sky, then ticked off on her fingers. "You're sick in the morns. You have tenderness in your breasts. Your gut feels strange. You're eating like you're starving. Your moods bob like buoys. You've complained that your corset is getting tighter. You've outgrown your dress." Isabel paused and looked hard at Ruth. "Perhaps it's time we put these things together?"

"Surely you don't mean to imply that Sam—"

"I'm not making implications. Simply wondering his," she cleared her throat uncomfortably, "familiarity."

"Sam? He's a boring gentleman. He's tried nothing. No, no, not Sam, but..." Ruth's heart seized, and she looked back in fear at Isabel.

"But Owen."

Ruth averted her eyes, panic-stricken, toward her tea, letting the cloth soak too long, and she let out a sharp exhale. She swore she heard every grain of sand from the hourglass on the water bench.

"God help your sin, child."

Ruth stood from the table. Putting a hand to her abdomen, she fled to her bedding and sat herself on the edge of it in the unstirring dead air that choked all sense from her. Her mind raced, leagues a minute. Her eyes flitted about the room, landing on nothing. *What do I do now?* she thought, searching from the wool wheel to the ark to the wicker rolls peeking from the loft to the empty jeweler's box for an answer. *A year.* How could she wait for him? How could she find him? Her heart malleted against her breastbone. She could feel it now, a child growing inside her—this aberration. This, this perfect creation. *This sin.* Grabbing her cloak, she walked past Isabel's judgmental gaze and to the door, soundless, for no sound could reach her. Her head fair screamed with numbing static.

The harbor. To the harbor. The townspeople nodded and smiled, but she kept her eyes low as she approached the dock. They smiled now, but they'd shun her if they knew. When they knew. The Company of Merchants would withdraw her land claim. All the work she'd done to have a semblance of a life, to cobble it together—balancing precariously. The harbor was quiet, so different from the harbor she had known back in East Jersey. She neared the farthest point of the dock and stared out into the water, coated in a rich fog that strangled the wood and piles. A year. She breathed in deeply the ocean air, could taste the salt at the back of her throat, her lungs, all the way down to her abdomen, swollen with the sea.

The ocean dealt a roaring wave against the dock, and its anger left an answer to her unanswered question along the drenched hem of her dress, the soiled bottom where shame lies. An answer that didn't satisfy the soul but would satisfy society. An answer that didn't have to wait a year. She let out a ragged screech, a gull trapped inside her cords. Her stomach roiled against the very thought. As the sea calmed, its gray, lifeless waves retreated, furling back their banners. Her stomach eased, tension lifting. She scanned the horizon; it curved at the back, a visible roundness, an edge to other worlds. There were no ships. Tears stung her eyes. He wasn't coming.

"I've been seeking you, Mistress Miner."

The voice came from behind her, and for a moment her heart skipped, footing faltered. Then her heels dug into the dock, and she felt their weight bite in like filled coffins sinking into the moist earth.

"You know I've been patient," Samuel said gently, placing his hands on her shoulders. His voice betrayed the numerous times he'd already made this same proposition. "But might I know soon if my pursuit is fruitless? Might I get the honor of a reply?"

"What was the question?" Stalling. *Why?* It wouldn't bring a ship.

Samuel let out a slow breath. "If I may have you as my wife."

She peered over the ocean, searching. The tides roared once more, in answer, and she calculated the time it might take someone to track down the ship with a letter. Too long. She'd be showing. A tear rolled down her cheek. Her child rolled inside her like a wave. She sighed heavily, and her sigh was a burial. "Yes, Sam," she could only whisper it, "I consent to be your wife."

Unexpectedly, he wrapped his arms around her and pressed his lips to hers. She pictured that blasted highwayman! His scruffy chin and stolen clothing. How cheated she'd felt then, and how cheated she felt now. Another tear escaped, and she wondered if Samuel felt it wet their cheeks between them. She wondered what he'd say if she told him about the highwayman, about Owen. About the baby. She willed herself relaxation, praying that the violin had taught him something about the virtues of delicacy, but only came the thought of spoiled fish carcasses from the bottom of the cod barrel. She blocked it out, her heart thundering with the ocean, disgusted, tossed. Dashed as the waves upon the dock.

⌇

As the weeks of preparation passed, Ruth spent each available moment at the harbor, wishing for ships, and returning home to the house frame that would never be completed, the woodshop, the garden. A routine with no fruition. To Samuel waiting to stroll her from the Osbornes' down the main thoroughfare and back again, displaying. She quietly studied her French and traded new languages with Askook, whose friendship grounded her against her sullenness. She flocked to every vessel that landed, asked sailors, shamelessly, if they'd seen the fluyt *Primrose* or could plead for its immediate return to Stonington. It wasn't too late. She swore it wasn't. Each visiting captain was given a letter, should anyone see the ship at sail. Ruth counted the seconds, the waves, each mast in the distance, but she felt the insistence of the ocean's reply. Resilient and stridulous. Crashing in wave after wave of sardonic applause, but to her, silent as deafness.

Ruth thought of this as she knocked against Helen's door with the timidity of a churchmouse.

"Hello, Mistress Miner." Matthew Starks opened his door to invite Ruth inside. "Helen! It's Ruth," he called out toward the bedroom, tucking his shirt hurriedly, awkwardly, into his breeches. "I hope thee'll forgive my rudeness, but I was heading out. Already so late in getting to the beans today."

Ruth nodded politely, but her stomach churned as Matthew went out the door. Helen entered the room, her hair a mess of wild red, her cheeks flushed and dress untidy.

"Hope I didn't interrupt anything," Ruth said, curiously eying her friend's disheveled appearance.

"I made him so late," Helen giggled.

Ruth lifted a brow. She'd interrupted.

"Just batting the bed for mites, and I found one a mite hard to swat off." She made a brushing motion at the air. "Can I get you anything? Some fat?"

Ruth shook her head.

"So strange about the blacksmith's shop. Can you imagine? More than once!"

"More than once?"

"Yes, several times now someone's broke in at night and stoled tools and picks. I heard ax heads, buckets, even large kettles!" Helen went to the back of the house for the well pump and yelled through the opening, returning with a cup of water and a hunk of hog fat for Ruth.

The fat turned Ruth's stomach, and she cursed her morning sickening. "My, I hadn't heard about that." She put her hand to her belly, then down at her side quickly when she realized.

Helen spun around in a whirlwind of energy that made Ruth jealous. "Hadn't heard? Heavens, everyone's talking of it. Goodwife Crotchett can barely keep still about it."

"Yes, but what can that woman ever keep still about?"

Helen impulsively reached out for Ruth's hand, silently waiting, as if she'd expected that there was more to this visit. When nothing came, she said, "If you don't love him, don't wed him. There will be other men. You don't have to if you aren't certain."

"But it is a good match, no?"

Helen frowned.

Ruth looked down and noticed that Helen had freshly sanded her floor. "Isabel finds it a good match." She didn't know anymore if that were a lie or the truth. They'd hardly exchanged words for weeks. She took a bite of the fat, though her stomach groaned in protest, and she talked through the chewing. "What was Matthew like when you married him?"

"Exactly as he is now." Helen reached out for Ruth's cheeks and pushed them into a fish-face pucker, hoping for a smile. "I didn't wed a man I wanted to change."

Ruth winced. "He's not coming back." She studied the wooden chopping block at Helen's basin, knowing so well now Daniel's handiwork. The edges had grooves to dig fingernails into while holding it steady, and she was certain other woodworkers hadn't thought of that. "If God was to make it so easy as to hand out free anchors to a line of men, Owen would still avoid the line entirely."

"Do you not think him honorable enough to return when he can?"

"Honor," Ruth huffed edgily. "He's as loaded with it as he is with poppycock. Much good it does."

"Watch your profanity." Helen snapped to the shutters, glanced both ways down the street, and slammed them good and tight. "You'll get lettered and left out at The Rock. Or worse—" She leaned in to whisper. "You're like to have your lips sewed together in front of Sunday's congregation, what happened to Goodwife Crotchett."

Ruth's eyes met her friend's with a desperation that Helen could not understand, and the two young women hovered in a cloud of reticence. Stillness had entered the room between them, unnamed, unwanted. Ruth looked away, chewing the fat, then her bottom lip when she couldn't take any more of the taste. For the first time since sitting on her trunk at Stonington's port, Ruth felt truly alone, unable to tell Helen all that was true. How could Helen comprehend it? She'd not mean to, but she'd cast stones the same as all the rest if she knew. In the dawn of this new light, Ruth saw her for what she was: distance.

"I brought you something." Ruth dug around in her apron amidst stolen objects, trying not to let Helen see any of them. "It's even better than a woodcut this time." She pulled a tiny crock of maple syrup from her apron and placed it in her friend's hands. "The blood of the inanadig."

Helen eagerly grabbed for the gift. "You've been talking to that savage again, haven't you, with language like that."

"He's not savage. He's a friend, as close to me as you."

"Your foolhead has got me scared to death. You can't talk to that savage! It's unlawful."

Ruth felt the weight of the town—all that they stood for—behind those words, and she felt herself for what she was, an outcast. If there was justification in the stolen objects in her pocket, it was here—in the words that even her best friend could utter.

"Just try this. On warm corncakes if you can. I promise your life will never be the same." Ruth smiled, and the smile was deep and genuine, as if it would be the last exchange of happiness between them and they both knew it. But her mind went to Askook, and now, despite coming to confess, she held something back. "I must go to the shop before Daniel is too cross. You'll not judge me too harsh?"

"I'll not judge you at all. That is only for God to do. But I'll pray for you."

Ruth pondered the futility of this. "I hope one of those prayers gets through. I'm afraid God stopped keeping record." She closed the door behind her before Helen could scold and headed for the woodshop to carve as many sap spouts as she could get her hands on without being caught.

Chapter Tenth
A married woman's role

To every action,
there is always opposed an equal reaction.

—Sir Isaac Newton

"Bring her trunk into the main room. Rearrange to make space," Samuel addressed the townsmen who'd carried in Ruth's trunk, while he escorted her into their new home. "Woman. Clear out the clothespress in the hall for her belongings." A peculiar, rotund woman, dressed in a plain gray dress and well-worn blue apron, hustled to follow his instructions. "This is...um."

"Martha." She curtsied.

"Martha. She is now yours."

"Mine?" Ruth asked.

"Yes," Samuel said. "Your handmaiden, housekeep, whatever it is you women have."

"We don't *have*—"

His sweeping gesture indicated that it didn't matter. He marched on; he only ever marched, she realized.

Ruth looked at Martha, and the woman curtsied again. Her face was open and cheery, and when Martha smiled, Ruth imagined her mother, what she thought she might look like had she lived, from what Ruth made her in her mind. Martha must have been a mother; she had that maternal aura, and the house was filled with the scent of baking rolls. Her smile was the kindest light Ruth had seen in Stonington yet, thank the heavens. She smiled back wholeheartedly.

Samuel continued, "In the barn, the tawny stallion is yours as a wedding gift. It's mildly untamed, I'm afraid, but you will take away some valuable lessons in the breaking of it. The ostler care for the horses and livestock. Cleaning of the barn, that's Mereb. There are some inconsequential fielduns here and there, but you'll not remember the blackbirds' names any better than me. Don't mingle with them; it is unclean."

"Blackbirds, sir?"

"Yes," he replied, "the negro bondmen toilers in the field. Fielduns."

"Slaves? You have slaves...here?" How had she not known this? The Dutch held slaves in the colonies to the south, and tobacco plantations, further south than she'd ever been, received new shipments of slaves weekly. But Stonington was so far north, she thought. Were slaves coming in through Boston? Next time she saw him, she'd ask Owe— Her heart went cold.

Samuel laughed. "A man strives to own all that he can afford."

Blackbirds. She imagined them with dark wings and bird feet, pecking hooked beaks at the immovable soil. She swallowed. Helen's words came back: *I didn't wed a man I wanted to change.* Even Owen's hard-hearted father refused to carry slaves in his ship holds.

Samuel moved to the next room without a second thought of it, and she could only follow. She looked about the unnecessarily large post-and-beam timber frame erected on six two-story wall posts, complete with a judgment hall below and a chamber above. A steeply pitched roof covered a spacious attic over the chamber, standing the house nearly three floors at its highest gable. A massive fireplace with timber lintel spanned most of the west wall. Ruth shuddered at its flaming leviathan mouth and thought of her grandmother, bed-stricken, frozen—the warmth it would give that Ruth wouldn't receive from Samuel.

On the hooks near the fire hung a boring iron, branding iron, long iron peel, firepan, scoop-shaped fire shovel, tongs, several roasting hooks, and elegant, long-handled frying pans. The front of the main fireplace was surmounted with brass atop the iron to match the andirons and the accompanying bellows set. At the far left closest to the kitchen, its mouth flush with the back of the fireplace, a full-sized oven stood to waist height and closed with an iron door. Ruth paused to touch it.

Samuel pointed out various items in the rooms, what was hers and what was not. He showed her the partial stonewall cellar pit under part of the hall that was reached through a trapdoor in case of Indian attack or French soldier advancements, that doubled as a storage for the choice crockery ware and the pewter and silver brought from England. From this hidden passage, she surmised there had to be more secrets to King's Hall than she'd first imagined.

Up the center of the house, a stone chimney rose, bearing hooks with a burden of cured, salted ham, fetches of pork and venison, and pots big enough to soak the meat until it was edible all the way through, the novelty. The chimney was accessible on all two and a half floors, each floor having its own fireplace that circled around the entire bulk of the chimney, deep stone and iron caverns with the jamb and the back sitting at right angles to each other and to the hearth stones. The second level seemed to comprise meeting rooms for soldiers, governors, diplomats, trading merchants, the ilk. It served men only, and Ruth was instructed not to peruse its facilities, save to procure meats.

The upper levels were connected with a permanent staircase unlike any she'd ever seen, leading all the way up to the garret and decorated with handcarved balusters along a railing of pine. The wood was so fine, she could smell the pine from all other rooms of the house, even in the dark buttery off the kitchen that held shelves of jars, stone bottles, salt-glazed stoneware produced in the Rhineland, vinegar, mustard, boxes of aqua vitae in flat-sided bottles containing over a quart of liquor each, and wooden butts of wine and rum. The loft held the rest of the dried goods and materials, including barrels of ash collected for making lye; plaited and husked maize bundled with string that hung from nails in the garret; and peas, oats, corn, and wheat stored in arks solidly constructed of oak planks with removable lids to serve as kneading troughs when inverted.

The walls were wattled between the planks with a woven network of split wood and saplings that supported the clay daubing, keeping the house warmer in winter and cooler in summer, hugging the frames of real-glass windows that adorned the front and ends of the house all the way up the gables. Ruth was enamored of the furniture that adorned each room—trestle tables with turkey carpets; turned and rush-seated chairs; pine form benches; joined and boarded chests; clothespresses; cupboards; curios of war artifacts, fine pewter, and glass valuables; and curtained bedsteads—the wood of each finely planed and the decorative insets handcarved by European craftsmen. She nearly felt like royalty. A duchess. With…blackbirds landing on her shoulders, pecking, pecking. How awful. She squeezed her eyes shut.

"What is this nonsense?" Samuel's voice shook her free. He stood over her trunk.

"I'll plead with you not to call my possessions nonsense."

"Isaac Newton?" He flipped through the pages of a book. "Good Heaven, you understand these symbols?"

"*Philosophiæ Naturalis Principia Mathematica: De motu corporum*? Oh, heavens no, sir, not most of it. It's too advanced for me, but I've figured the very basic idea of motion's law. The first part you have open, there, talks of continuous motion in the absence of resistance. The ratios are complicated calculus that I cannot yet explain, but I understand most of the centripetal forces bit, and relating circular velocity and radius of path-curvature to radial forc—"

"I'm not interested in any laws but God's."

She stopped, and her face blanked. "That's frightfully shallow."

He took a sudden step toward her. "Did you call me shallow?"

"No. I said not wanting to know about the scientific world beyond the Bible is shallow, sir. There are laws—"

"There are no other laws but God's and mine," he said, mouth drawn back like a horse with a too-tight bit. His attention locked onto the townsmen in front of whom she'd made him look a fool. "Not a word of this," he said with eerie calmness. He gestured, then faced Ruth, squeezed her arm hard. "You are my wife now." He handed *Principia* to a Breed boy, who scowled. "Burn this."

"Don't burn it," Ruth pleaded.

"You'll mind me," Sam said, his hand twitching as Martha gasped behind him. He narrowed his eyes, went back to Ruth's trunk, and rummaged through her books. "This is in French!" This time he was loud.

Ruth tensed and swallowed hard. One she'd missed. How could she have missed one?

"Why do you have a book in French? What does it say? Can you read this?" He stood before her and fanned it open.

"It says, *Entretiens sur la pluralité des mondes*, Bernard le Bovier de Fontenelle."

"And you can read it?"

"Aye. Some of it. *Conversations on the Plurality of Worlds.* It explains Copernicus' heliocentric model of the univer—"

"Stop this." He pulled the book open to a page and pointed a finger to the French text. "What does this say?"

Ruth took the book from his hand and began to translate the French to English, filling in the parts she didn't know. She'd once read it in English, too, so it was easier than some. "Behold a universe so immense that I be lost in it. I no longer know where I am. I am just nothing at all. Our world is, um, terrifying in its insignificance."

"Enough blasphemy!" Samuel knocked the book from Ruth's hand and kicked at it as if it were a threatening snake, poised to strike. "Burn that. Burn it!" He turned back to her. "And you can speak it?"

She hesitated, then thought of the bow saw and the froe she'd handled. The stone fence. The brand that had marred her skin. The coffins of those who would never again speak their minds. Their smallness in the universe. Her face darkened. "Oui, monsieur, assez bien."

The back of Samuel's hand landed across her cheek. The townsmen stepped back, and one started to speak, but Samuel shushed him and lunged for Ruth. "That is the tongue of a traitor. That will get you hung for treason to the Crown, you stupid, curious girl." He gripped her, her arm, her dress, wherever he could find purchase. "This treason will be cored from your tongue with a hot iron. Are you loyal to the Crown?"

Her mouth didn't move.

"Answer me! Are you loyal to the Crown?"

She jerked away and put a hand to her tender jaw, steadying her shaking hands. She looked him in the eye but did not answer.

Samuel grabbed her by the arm and boomed, low and hard: "Out of here, all of you!" He punched the air where the townsmen had stood as they vacated, kicked a lockbox on the floor, and grabbed a curtain and tore it from the wall, a liberated hook following the curtain rod to the ground. He dragged Ruth through the house, knocking a lantern into the ewer and the ewer into a pewter tray that hummed, clanged to the wall, still humming. He slammed the bedroom door behind them.

"Now, you listen to me, wife," he growled, leaning in close to her, eyes dark specks of vitriol. "I'll not have you hung while wearing my name."

He gripped her harder, and she thought of the violin—these hard fingers clenched around the fingerboard, snapping it in half from upper bout to pegbox to fancy scroll carved by Daniel. She pictured the woodwork crumbling, tuning pegs popping off and flying. Samuel only knew English music, English hymns. The gathered crowd fled, their entertainment over.

"They are just books," she reasoned with a confidence she didn't feel, her shoulders trembling beneath him.

"They will be burned. Wife." Before she could protest, his mouth closed over hers, and he pushed her back onto the bedstead, swatting the bedcurtains aside like insects. She closed her eyes and held her breath as he pressed his body over hers.

&

Waiting until he was asleep in the dark—his breathing calmed and rhythmic, marching—Ruth slid slowly out of bed. She pulled on her stockings and boots and tiptoed through the house in her dressing gown, then removed from the bottom of her trunk the satchel of picks, nails, and sap-spouts that had thankfully not been found. And the remaining books. She would not see them burned. She knew it was risky to keep this regular rendezvous, but Samuel would go digging for the books in the morning, and she couldn't chance him stumbling upon anything else. She stood motionless, scarce breathing, and watched as the moon crept through the shutters and inched its way toward the faint line she had scratched lightly with a stick into the floor. Patiently, she waited until the streak of light muted with the line, then she unlatched the door wide enough to slip through the crack into the night.

The moon was a sliver, a needle of lightless light. She couldn't see Askook along the outline of the stone fence, but she made it to their hidden flax rows, retrieved the empty satchel he had left at the base of the chopping block, and replaced it with the full satchel she had been carrying. Words came to her of Helen, of Isabel, their hatred for *the savages*, the sorrow in Askook's eyes when she'd told him what the town thought of him, how careful they must be. She steeled herself with justification, and in the darkness, she found a thin scooping stone and dug a hole to bury the books. After digging, then observing the finished stone fence that Samuel had commissioned townsmen to complete for the Osbornes, and peeking into her maple syrup buckets to check the height of the sap, she had stalled all she could. She would have to wait to see Askook again.

Making her path around the field, she felt her way, lightless, to the rear entrance of the blacksmith shop, but as she reached with her lock pick for the door, she found it secured shut with two new, thick chains strung across the door, deadbolted to each side, and locked together with wrought-iron keylocks. She looked for another way inside, but the shutters were anchored tight, and the front was too parlous. She'd have to give up on it for the night and think of another plan come morning.

She sneaked along the side of the shop, then stealthily across the road where the trees could hide her movement. As she fled beneath the tree cover, she tripped over something large and landed with a thud on the ground. Looking back, she saw that she'd been tripped by heavy boots. Samuel's eyes flickered in the sliver, but he didn't make a sound. He hauled Ruth to her feet, yanked the empty satchel from her hand, and dragged her silently through the street back to their home. Closing the door discreetly behind them, he propelled her from him, and held up the satchel, examining.

"The blacksmith, the mercantile, the ships in the harbor, the missing crops in the fields. It's you."

Ruth appraised her boots. She expected him to flare like a prodded kraken, but he had that eerie calm about him that terrified her so. How had she reasoned she would tame that out of him?

"Look at you, in your dressing gown in the middle of the night. What on earth are you thinking? Where is this going?" He raised the satchel, dangling it like bait. "Who is getting it?"

She stood up straight. "I'm paying for the land that hasn't been purchased. It's been stole."

"So you're paying for stealing by stealing?"

Ruth flushed. It didn't sound as good when heard out loud.

"What land do you refer to? Surely you don't mean our land? I assure you this is proprietary land, granted me by the king. There is no higher authority than that, save for God, who has given us call to civilize this land he created for us. So, who are you paying for what land?"

"I can't tell you."

"You *will* tell me."

She shook her head. She knew he couldn't lose his temper in the middle of the night. He'd wake half the town. His desire for answers didn't outweigh his pride, and she watched that play out quickly across his face. His fists loosened around the empty satchel.

"You'll get back all you stole and return it to its rightful owners at dawn."

"I can't. I don't know where it is."

"Don't know where? Wife." He stared her down. "Where is it going?"

A rod threaded through her spine, and she stood straighter with it. "I cannot tell you."

His chest heaved in and out, but he steadied himself. "Have you completely forgotten God? Thou shalt not steal. What about that judgment? Your theft is a sin, and then you lie to your own husband about it. Have you forgotten all your teachings?"

"I have forgotten none of them, sir."

Sam boiled, yet Ruth looked like a baby bird, soft-winged and fragile in the light of one candle. He looked away, appeared to be counting to calm himself. "You will cease this" was all he could muster.

"You'll tell them?"

"No. God forgive me. Not this time, God forgive me, but you don't think of the position that puts me in. You must cease, or next time I'll take you to Council and lock you in stocks myself. Do you understand me, wife?"

"Aye, sir," she said quietly, looking down until she heard him sigh.

He pulled her face into his chest, wrapped his arms around her, and held her shivering body to him. Her breath pulsed through his shirt, warm and cold in rhythm, marching. "Come," he whispered. "We don't have to be like this. Come back to bed."

She squeezed her eyes shut, willed him away, opened them and studied the leafed table woodwork that wasn't Daniel's, and followed.

CHAPTER ELEVENTH
The inevitable conversation

And yet it moves.

—Galileo Galilei

Hop medic and thimbleweed and liverleaf and bearded beggarticks turned the passing weeks into spreads of pasture colors that Arrow kicked up under Ruth's command. She'd ride the horse to meet with Askook in secret at the far edge of the Red Forest where no one could see and never at the same hour, her truancy unpatterned. She memorized Samuel's military routine at the garrisons and learned when the selectmen were called to gather. She waited and she waited and she waited for him to come and go, to engage himself in his meetings in the secret parts of his secret rooms of his secret house. She lived her life in the quiet regimental cracks of his absences. There was nothing but time, and it could be clearly marked: There were nine months. And then there was a year.

But further down the road, a knock landed confidently on the door of Isabel Osborne's house, and the elderly woman opened it. Her breath caught.

"Hello, Mistress Osborne." Owen, fresh off the ship, grinning and smelling of salty sea air, bent to kiss her hand. He pulled out from under his arm a bundle of fresh fish wrapped in clean brown paper and twine.

She flushed, then fidgeted, her hands jittery against the folds of her dress, closed and quiet. "You're back so soon," she whimpered, taking the fish, but shrinking elsewise. "We hadn't expected..."

"I sent a letter. Things didn't go as Captain planned, but there's always next year. I can't say it sorrows me deep, as it frees me for other plans this year." His grin broadened. "I hear I have a house to finish building."

She nodded meekly.

"Is she here?"

"No, she's not here anymore."

His forehead scrunched, wrinkled down to his brow. "Anymore? Where is she?"

Isabel pointed across the street toward the last house on the right, a few doors down. "At King's Hall."

"Ah, someone else took her in, bless 'em." He clucked his tongue against the roof of his mouth. "I had something important to discuss with Daniel," he winked, "but I guess I won't need speak it with him, then."

"No, you wonnot." She toyed with her apron again, wringing her hands, smoothing the brown paper on the fish.

He couldn't ignore her frown. "Something wrong?"

"Many things."

He waited for her to divulge, pursed his lips, and pulled his soapstone from his pocket. "Well. I'll be down the road, should you need me." He leaned against the doorframe and lit his pipe away from the breeze. "Be there anything I can do for you while I'm here?"

She shook her head.

"Then I'll head off to find her. Where did you say she was?"

"The largest house. King's Hall. Whitlock."

"Whitlock?" He thought he'd been struck in the ribs. His focus grayed, and he held the doorframe to steady his momentary sway. "Samuel Whitlock?"

Isabel nodded, lowered her eyes, and backed inside the house.

Owen's soapstone hung off his lip, and he couldn't puff it. Air wouldn't move past the knot in his windpipe as he mustered the courage to knock on the door of the lieutenant general of the military that would fight against him, against *Primrose*. He stood before the towering house and kicked at the pebbles around his feet before approaching the entryway at the Christian door. With a less-confident knock, he tapped against the heavy, fine beech mahogany woodwork. Martha opened it, and Owen's mouth turned cotton.

"Hel–herm–Hello, Mrs. Whitlock. I'm look—"

"I'll go get ye Mrs. Whitlock," Martha interrupted, and moved to shut the door.

"No, I don't want Mrs. Whitlock." He stuck his foot inside the frame, marveling at the double set of winter doors that stood inside the first corridor to aid in keeping out the cold drafts. "I'm looking for Ruth Miner."

"Ye's looking for Ruth Whitlock," Martha corrected. "I'll go get Mrs. Whitlock."

He paled, and his pipe fell. As Martha closed the door, Owen missed his footing, nearly fell off the stairs, taking steps backward faster than his body could keep up. He kicked his pipe before he could bend to pick it up, to feel it with fingers that could feel. Realization was gray and horrifying, and it came over him in a wash, a rip current pressing him downward, under. He made for the road, approaching a run from the house back toward the ship. But he didn't get far before the familiar voice of Ruth called his name from the door. The siren song, shipwrecking him along jagged rocks. He halted and stared toward the harbor, afraid of what he would see if he turned to face her. What the sight would do to him.

Ruth stepped off the landing, everything colliding into her teeth, stopping anything audible from passing. She walked toward him, closed the gap between them, searched for her tongue and prayed her mind would follow it. "What are you doing here?" she said.

"I would ask you the same," Owen replied over his shoulder, still not turning to face her, his guts twisting into such tight knots that he thought he might heave. "But I fear I've already figured the answer, *Mrs. Whitlock.*"

"You said a year. How dare you come back here so early?" The words slammed against her brain. She didn't know if she were yelling or whispering or not speaking at all.

"How dare I come back early?" He spun around to her, his body crippled by the sight of the sun streaking across her face, mocking him. "I writ you a letter. Sent it direct on a ship bound for Stonington."

"Letter?"

His knees buckled, then he caught himself. "You. Married him?" God, that word.

"I begged you. Shameful, in the middle of the road." She flailed her arm toward where they'd once stood. "Everyone looking at us, I begged. It would have been but a walk to John Stanton's and a few minutes for the ink to dry."

"Is that how long it was with Whitlock? That's not the way it's done. This be the way it's done, standing here." He pointed to the ground in front of him. "I...prepared. I..." a gesture back down the road, "brought you fish." He paused at a new thought. "Have you bedded him?" She didn't reply, and he felt a kick from inside. "The brand on your thighs? Your—"

"He's not even removed my shift."

Owen laughed, desperately, through his nose. His palm skipped off his pants and at the windows, a pleading swing toward the door. "All those fancy dresses and real-glass windows and sterling-silver plates and trinkets. He bought you."

"Ça suffit! You know nothing about it." She clutched her apron to her like it was a child, folded onto her forearms, bunching it anxiously into the crooks.

"You made your choice, then." He shrugged, though not indifferently. "J'en ai fini avec toi." He turned, and, like that, walked away, silence trailing behind him.

She choked, like breathing around a chest wound. The words couldn't be unheard, and the space between them filled with distance as he walked on. She turned quickly toward the house, tears pushing at her eyes. There, she lumbered and wailed like an injured animal and closed the door behind her. Martha stepped back from the window and looked at Ruth as she entered. The servant rushed over, and Ruth, her turmoil consuming her, collapsed into Martha's arms, sniffing, keening. The matron rubbed Ruth's back.

"Breathe in deep, now," Martha began softly. "Let him go."

Ruth shook her head into Martha's shoulder and cried harder.

Martha peered around the corner of the kitchen to where the tip of Samuel's elbow poked out of a frameway two rooms over. "The master be still meeting with Sir Governor Andros," she said. "Ye got time to make yeself presentable."

Just then, the door burst open, hitting a birch hutch in its wild arc, and Owen strode in, his body thrumming, heaving—he'd been running. Ruth leaped back from Martha's grasp, and Owen's eyes, acute and ardent, fixed on her. She shook her head and pointed to the other room. But he didn't care. He knocked his hip into a table and swept his arm over a wooden bowl, sending it rattling to the floor, spinning, rocking to one side, then the other, then the other, as if to comfort itself. Ruth furrowed her brow and pulled her mouth into a *shhhh*. In one motion, he took the room, caught her in his arms, and cupped his mouth passionately over hers. Her heart thudded in her neck and her ears grew red and hot, the heat climbing her shoulders and chest in a rash. His embrace tightened around her, his hands burning forbidden marks into her skin.

Afraid to give in for too long with Samuel only two rooms away, she twisted from Owen's arms and pushed him back toward the door. Her head still shook, and her body mirrored. Tremors. Her knees jellied, and she thought she might drop right there. He reluctantly pulled back and took the steps that her pushing commanded. As she maneuvered him through the door, she closed it behind them and faced him on the front steps. An invisible line spanned their chests, and it pulled on them, like a halyard controlling a mast against a storm that blew such gales across the space that she didn't know how they were not both capsized in it.

"Can you not feel that?" he pleaded, again advancing toward her.

"I can feel it." It came out raspy, like dried ends of brittle straw.

"Why, then? Money, power, a bastard—"

Ruth's fists clenched at her side. Her jaw tightened, not subtle enough.

"So that's it." His nostrils flared. "You have his child."

"No, you fool." Tears rolled down her cheeks. "I have yours."

His chest seized. His thighs seized. He wasn't standing; he was floating, then drowning. He caught himself, a sharp breath reaching all the way to his gut, followed by another even sharper one. "Mine?" It didn't come out; he didn't whisper it. "Mine?" on the edge of the sharpest breath yet.

"You said a year."

"Mine?" he said. "And you told him my child is his?"

"He doesn't know there's a child."

Owen wobbled. His knees weren't just weak—they hurt—the whole of him hurt, felt crushed into the earth. "Would to God you'd waited. By God's Law—"

"Don't speak God's laws. Not to me! You don't know a woman's shame. The people here. What a town can do to a body. I've spared you."

"What have you spared me? This will haunt me all my days—how have I been spared? No shame could have come from a child with you. But now. My enemy will have my son?" He scratched at a beard that wasn't there. He'd freshly shaven for her. "I want to shake the hourglass—take us back there," he whispered and reached into his pocket and drew out a tiny bundled piece of cloth wrapped in a ribbon. "I wouldn't tell you no a second time." He took her hand, upturned it, and placed the bundle on her palm, then closed her fingers around it. His hand drew back quickly, the contact searing, and he stepped in the direction of the harbor, no further words, one audible choke. His shoulders hunched, yet tight with frustration, his clenched fists ground into his thighs. This couldn't be undone.

Ruth unfurled her fingers and looked at the tiny ribboned piece of cloth. Pulling the ribbon gingerly, she opened the handkerchief to reveal a small satchel of lilac seeds. Her fingers traced the embroidered O. W. T. on the handkerchief, and she pressed it against her face. It smelled of salt and his musty jacket, and she held her breath against it.

Chapter Twelfth

Bringing down the traitor

They that approve a private opinion, call it opinion;
but they that mislike it, heresy.

—Thomas Hobbes

Samuel stepped out the door to where Ruth stood in the road, Governor Andros following resolutely. The dust whirled as if horses had kicked it, and the spring sky dulled where a storm hung in the east, lines of dark augering into sallow chalk.

"What in God's Grace are you doing standing in the middle of the road?" Samuel took Ruth by the arm and conducted her toward the house. "Who was that boy?"

She loosened herself from him and arrested. "He is a…friend. Wishing me good in matrimony." A careless tremble played through her shoulders.

"You hold acquaintance with sailmen? I want his name, rank, and ship."

She contemplated consequences of these two worlds colliding, but—

"Name. Rank. Ship."

"Owen Townsend. First Mate of *Primrose*, sir."

Samuel's nostrils lifted as if by unseen strings drawn taut. "Jake Townsend's ship. This first mate, another Townsend. His son?"

"Aye, sir." The taste of ore, powdery, dry, entered her mouth from her cheeks. She swallowed and swallowed, but it stayed, a dysphagia thickening her tongue. This couldn't happen. These two couldn't collide. What had she done? She hadn't planned, curse it all; she thought she'd have a year before this. She thought it might start to make sense by then.

"This is the boy what bring you books, I presume."

She rooted in place, deep into the dirt. God, not that. Not the books.

"The French bindings. He bestowed those upon you?" He studied her silence. "He speaks French? Answer me."

"No," she lied.

"Does his father know he has acquired this literature?"

Ruth's head shook on its own, hooked to a sudden swivel. Rain fell far off, the heather curtain fusing into the heather ocean, seamlessly, without horizon.

"Jake Townsend is a known dissentient of the Navigation Acts and has refused to transport munitions for his Crown in our time of war. Has your 'friend' spoke of this? If I find proof that his cargo goes against the British East India Company, he's as good as strung up."

She planted herself firmly, although she knew opposing Samuel in front of Governor Edmund Andros would make her husband lose face. It was Samuel or Owen, and her heart was louder than her head. "This conversation sounds like 'men's talk' intended for Captain Townsend. I don't bear his messages."

He growled low. "Very well. I shall have a visit with the Townsends. Both of them."

Andros stepped forward and inhaled the audible breath that precedes a speech.

Samuel raised a hand and turned to him briefly. "You should return to Boston, Sir Andros. The Connecticut Colony has not forgotten your boundary disputes, that attempt of yours to take Saybrook. Your involvement with the Iroquois is a fresh wound." He waved it off like whisking a gnat from his cheek. "When news strikes of William's Revolution, there will come rebellion in the Bay Colony. Guard and supply Fort Mary with your all."

Ruth interjected. "*Primrose* has papers of safe conduct issued from this very colony."

"I am above those papers."

"You are not, sir."

"By grace invested in me, I am."

"They haven't the cannon needed to fend from pirates."

"You seem to know a great deal about it. But you wouldn't know anything about piracy, would you?" He reached for her elbow again.

She wrenched herself away and pivoted toward the road.

"Where are you headed?"

She didn't answer, didn't glance back.

⤸

Ruth all but threw her weight against Isabel's door. The skin of her knuckles seemed to stretch over too much painful nerve. Isabel opened it quickly.

"Where is the letter?" Ruth held out a throbbing hand.

"The letter?"

"Give it to me."

The pause in which Isabel hovered was absorbed in resolute blinking. "Very well." Another pause, and she walked to the shelf, then stopped as if she'd forgotten a purpose. Lifting the sugar block, she pulled from under it a letter with Ruth's name on the front, still folded and sealed with the wax insignia of *Primrose*, and she carried the thing back to the door, a brick of lead in spindled fingers.

"Why would you keep it from me?"

"It came your wedded day, child. It was for the best, at the time."

Ruth rocked, listless. It was still sealed. "Do you know what it says?"

"I do now." Isabel drew her eyes to the floor. "But you had made a promise, and you would have broke it."

"You're God-toothed right I would have broken it." There was no apology in her profanity. She dared the wind to carry it to neighboring homes, for anyone to pin a cloth of crimson to her chest. She'd wear the damn thing without shame. "Owen never wronged you. He trusted you to deliver it to me, and you betrayed him. Betrayed me. It was not yours to decide." A bevy of mosquitoes, brought in with the new damp, bombinated around her hair, bit her neck, and she smacked herself, shoulders and back, upper arms. When she came to rights, her lips were tight as a blasphemer's sheeted before a congregation.

Isabel gasped, and Ruth snatched the letter from her hand and slammed the door shut. She hastened toward the harbor, fighting the sting of tears and insects. Carefully lifting the wax seal, she read blotches too fuzzy to comprehend, and something violent seized her inside at the thought that she could now have been out to sea, drifting far from keeping the wrong promises.

✷

Owen pulled himself from the rowboat and up over the side of *Primrose* with a load of items from the dock. He addressed the men to grab wares and crates, as if nothing were amiss. But there was a sluggishness to his step, a rigid frown, that begged otherwise.

Captain Jacob Townsend's voice came from behind Owen's shoulder. "Did you see her in a grave?"

"She might as good have been in one, sir." He pulled a line around the old man's nosy intrusion. "Lordfellow, May: Give me a hand with these crates. Those two barrels go for Saybrook." He pointed to barrels and purposely spoke louder.

"So that's all I'm to get from you? That she might as good be dead? A whelp you'd turn tides for?"

Owen hardened.

"She turned you down."

He went back to the crates, touching boxes absently, the feel of their wood unregistering, weightless and meaningless. He reached again and again, mechanically, referring to his cargo plan that he'd drawn up to calculate the load line. He factored in the depths of different ports they'd visit, balancing the load to keep the ship sitting in the water evenly distributed below the marked line. Numbing work.

The captain asked, "Did she have a reason? Was it because of," he stopped himself abruptly, but Owen knew he was going to say, "Shrewsbury, the fire."

"She had a reason, sir." Numbing work, refocusing, graying. He'd said it louder than intended, and the crewmen standing around him turned to look in his direction. He breathed, steadied his mind, but everything in him would hate everything about this day for as long as he lived, and he didn't have to have lived it in its entirety to know it already. "Kingsley, grab that halyard. Ready yourselves for another load. The heavier crates will go in the lower larboard dry hold."

"Why doesn't ya tell your ol' da the rest of the story?" Kingsley's lip curled around slurry speech. The sailor hauled himself up the freight hole by the forearms, stepping his foot into the ropes of the block-and-tackle to come to the weatherdeck. The liquor on his breath was communicable by adjacency, and the men around him tottered.

Owen's spine hackled. "There is no rest of the story."

"Sure there be, mate. Tell your old man who the spiteful harlot married."

"Married?" the captain repeated.

Owen struck a finger to Kingsley's chest. "You hold your tongue, bootlicker, or I'll tear it out."

A heinous grin snaked across Kingsley's face. "We heard all about it at dock. Maked quite gossip from the pecking hens." He turned to the captain. "To spite this bloke," he thumbed, "the girl married Whitlock."

Owen took hold of Kingley's throat and slammed the sailor against the ship's railing. The old wood bowed and hissed, an eldritch dampened whining beneath the sailor's weight, inches from going overboard.

Owen gripped Kingsley's leg to flip him, but Thomas intervened, pushing the two men apart and dragging a howling Kingsley back to the crates by the scruff of the neck like an unwanted stray.

"Lieutenant General Samuel Whitlock?" the captain said.

"Yes, sir." Owen's reluctant reply came with a price. Blood rushed from his head to his chest and constricted each attempt at cohesion, balance, then back to his head again, hot and pounding. He swayed, light from his lunge at Kingsley. It took him a minute to believe he wasn't having a heart attack.

"By God, you'd better pray she hasn't spoke a word against us! How could you get involved with Whitlock's wife?"

Owen threw his hands up, loosed a line, didn't care how it crashed to the deck. But it was too late. The damage was done—its breath wreaked through the masts, creaking and brittle and visible.

"Don't look now, mates," Kingsley said, pointing to the shore, "but there be the trouble as we spake."

Ruth walked over the beach and toward the end of the dock, dazed and ghostlike. Owen tensed. The crew could see, coming across the shore, Samuel Whitlock striding after her with Governor Andros and several armed men behind him. Owen watched helplessly, a rifacimento of some Greek tragedy playing out before him in slow motion, in which he would no doubt be playing the lead role. On the end of the dock, Samuel caught her arm and spun her around to face him. The audience on deck remained eerily quiet, although they couldn't make out the exchange of words between the actors. When Samuel struck her across the face and knocked her to the dock, the chorus grew louder, and a stage bridge arced across the water and sky between dock and ship, and Owen flew its length without feet or reason, puppet strings animating him.

"God damn that son of a bitch." Owen flew and flew.

"Stop him!" the captain yelled, and a line of men stood between the rowboats and Owen, swords drawn and hunched into fighting positions. "You'll have every English militiaman in the colonies on our deck if you go after him."

Owen made eye contact with the line of men, each in turn, reaching into what souls they had, sizing them up. He pulled his dagger from his boot and rooted his feet steadily. "You better hope you kill me, because so help me, if I live, none of you will." As he prepared to advance, he felt a cold blade at his neck, its tip settling at the base of his throat. It drummed with his veins.

"Ease it, mate," Thomas whispered from behind Owen. "You can nay win this. Your father be in command, and you can nay fight them all."

"Et tu, Brute?"

"I's changing the ending, mate. Gimme your dagger."

Owen felt the flat of the blade press harder into his neck. Resignedly, he gave his knife to Thomas. In a tableau, crew and man and willpower, all were suspended until Thomas released his first mate from his grasp.

"Get that mutinous boy under control," the captain ordered.

Several of the men flocked around Owen and secured his arms.

"Sir, that nay be necessary," said Thomas. "He be a unarmed man."

The captain's face scarleted, a deep crabapple red, and Thomas shrank. Before Jacob could say anything further, the men's attention turned back to Samuel at the shore. The lieutenant general and his troupe had climbed into a rowboat and were headed toward *Primrose*. While the crew remained distracted by the rowboat, Thomas ferreted the dagger up his sleeve. The crew parted as Samuel, Andros, and the armed soldiers hoisted over the rail of the ship and advanced toward the captain.

"Captain Jake Townsend." Samuel's voice was preternaturally cheery. "We meet again. I trust your cargo is in standing with the Crown's Navigation Acts, good sir?"

"As ever it was, sir."

Samuel looked around the ship, seemingly inspecting for something that should or shouldn't be there. "I digress in these pleasantries. I have other business here, Jake, but have conviction that the munitions will keep for another discussion. You have aboard this ship, do you not, a son?"

Jacob was slow to answer, "I...do, sir."

"Only one?"

"Aboard this ship, aye." His voice warbled.

"How many other sons do you have?"

"Five, sir."

"Five, you rogue! Busy little man. Then perhaps you wouldn't mind giving up this one?" Before the captain could answer, Samuel called out, "First Mate Owen Townsend." He turned toward the crew and smiled, and it was a wicked smile. "I daresay I don't need to guess which one he is, as I estimate he's the one being held back from throttling me right now." He laughed.

The crewmen let go of Owen and pushed him to the middle of the deck. The two men eyed each other with contempt, squared their shoulders.

"You don't look happy to see me, First Mate Townsend."

"No, sir."

"You don't like me, then?"

"No, sir."

"I don't like you, either." His jaw tightened, and he ran his hand along the ship's railing until his glove snagged. "Don't you want to know why?"

"No, sir."

"Is that all you can say?" Samuel picked at the rough spot that snagged. "I don't like you because my wife does. Do you know my wife?"

Owen recoiled. That despicable word. "Aye, sir."

"Oh. There be some trepidation in that answer, there." Samuel stepped nearer to the sailor. "Did we strike a nerve? Have you tenderness for my wife?"

"No, sir." Not entirely a lie in the current state of things.

Samuel chuckled. "My wife has this infuriating little habit she garnered from somewhere, and she won't tell me its begetter. Can you venture what this infuriating habit is?"

"No, sir."

"Speaking French." Samuel's expression denoted how Owen didn't blanch. "My wager is you're the one who taught it to—"

"Stay your hand, sir," Owen said, eyes fanning from Samuel's face to his twitching fingers. "I would remind you as a respected general about the bad form of drawing your weapon on an unarmed man."

Samuel smiled. "I don't believe you are unarmed."

"He be, sir," the captain confirmed. "We disarmed him moments before you boarded."

Samuel raised his hands in applause of the crew. "Well done, men." He nodded in a round before settling his sights back on Owen. "Your crew doesn't seem to be on your side, either." His smile grew wickeder. "And why would they turn against you?"

"You'll have to ask them, sir. I don't speak for others."

"And when you do, how often is it in French?" Samuel moved his gaze to Thomas, who was visibly uncomfortable. "You. Step forward. Rank and name."

He stepped forward. "Second Mate Thomas Hewitt, sir."

"Ah, the navigator. A ship would be worthless without you." Samuel drew his court sword to the tune of the crewmen's gasps and brought it to Thomas' neck with practiced fluidity. "At the risk of my running you through with this sword should you fail to provide the answer I seek, Navigator, pray tell," Samuel indicated with his head toward Owen, "does this man speak French?"

"I'll nay implicate no member'a my crew, sir," Thomas replied.

Owen cringed.

"You'll risk death for a traitor?" Samuel asked.

"I'll risk death for my crew, sir. He'd do same for me."

"Let's see about that, shall we?" Samuel pierced the tip of the court sword into Thomas' neck, letting a ringlet of red until Thomas hissed through his teeth. Samuel repeated louder, "Does this man speak French?"

Owen ground his jaw. "Oui, Lieutenant-Général, je parle français." The ship stilled, and its collected ribcage hovered in place, its spine un-curving—no one breathed for its life, for its sails to flee. Owen exhaled. *So be it.*

Samuel flashed a ruthless grin and lowered the sword from Thomas' neck, a hint of disappointment in the act. The commander walked to Owen and studied the young sailor. Steps measured and calculated. "Unarmed, stupid…and loyal. Fool boy."

"Are you not blindly loyal to your Crown, sir?" Owen asked.

Samuel paced circles around the stationary seaman, looking him up and down, so much curiosity. "There is benefit to my loyalty. Where were you born, boy?"

"Shrewsbury, Province of East Jersey."

"Dutch country. Yet, you're not Dutch." Samuel laughed out his nose. "Or a Jersey Quaker. Or entirely English. Or entirely French? You're just complicating the fabric of our linen colonies." He called out across the deck, not taking his eyes from Owen, "Jake, harboring this boy on your ship constitutes treason. Are you willing to give up your son as a traitor to the Crown? Understanding, of course, that your refusal initiates the immediate seizure of your ship, cargo, and crew." Murmurings flew among the men, and Samuel chuckled coldly.

"If it be required, sir," Jacob hesitated, "then I have no choice but to do what I must for the safety of my ship and crew."

"No, Captain!" Thomas refuted, but Owen shushed him.

"Well, how about that!" Samuel laughed and applauded again. "Your own father just traded you in for a ship. And with no opposition from you?"

Owen didn't move.

"You expected it, then. There could be no clearer indication of a guilty man." Samuel looked back to Jacob. "We've got ourselves a deal, Jake, provided you break no other laws of the Crown and harbor no more treason on this ship. I can't think of how much it shall delight my wife to watch this treasonous bluejacket strung up."

"Strung up!" Thomas echoed, but the captain silenced him with a glare.

"Surely there will be a fair, impartial trial?" Jacob said.

"Surely." Samuel smirked. "Men, take the traitor. Gently, of course. We wouldn't want him to look a fright before the magistrate."

CHAPTER THIRTEENTH
Prison walls hold no allegiance

Necessity hath no law.

—Sir Oliver Cromwell

Through a crack in the stone wall, Owen saw the sun hanging low in the sky behind him. Its stretching fingers splayed across the ocean's silvery pall, the expanse so near yet unreachable. He'd been locked up for more than half the day, standing upright against iron bars and mildewed boards. Horizontal cross bars rested above and below his hands, ropes tied at the wrist around and through the iron and around and through again at the inside of the bars for good measure. It was a damn good knot, although with all the arounds and throughs, he couldn't tell which kind. He was stuck, unable to reach it with his fingertips or teeth without bars interfering, unable to sit down. A guard or two lurked through the passageway or waited outside, as well. He occasionally heard their coughing, their shuffling. Gnats circled his face, lit on his lips and nose, and the place smelled of feces and unclean flesh.

It appeared he was the solitary detainee of the place. He guessed that none of the jail's residents stayed long, nor did they return once they'd left. From the hallway came the sound of footsteps, a faint clodding on dirt; he imagined a guard at first, but the body was lightweight, and he knew. The ruffled tip of a dress crept into his view, then came to rest against his bars.

"What in Fiddler's Green are you doing here?"

Ruth's waist brushed his tied hands. She felt him pull back, unable to. "I come to help. I mean, to apologize." She looked older, sleep deprived. Her dress was bedraggled and her apron tied slipshod.

"Apologize? You?" He willed himself not to smile, yet he wished he could pull away from her.

"He found the Fontenelle. If it had been the Dryden, just poetry. Or Shakespeare. But all that talk about other worlds and laws. He's so…"

He looked at her hard. Her sorrow draped around her heavily. Across her cheek and upper lip laid the red markings of Samuel's palm, and

Owen winced. Bruises along her forearms bloomed purple and green.

"It's not your fault," he conceded. "Was my own French tongue landed me where I stand. Does your master know you're here?"

She shook her head, wrapped her fingers around the bars, algific and ungiving.

"Thought not."

Her hands gripped tighter, knuckles white in the waning light but spotted with red from the anger she'd taken out on Isabel's door. "They're going to hang you."

"Without a trial?" He twitched his face. "Itch my nose."

"They won't hang you on the Lord's Day, so it will be Monday." She scratched his nose and laid a hand on top of his. "Ne-quonwehige."

He couldn't move away from her touch. "What did you say?" Her touch, that touch. "Sounds like you been cavorting with Lenape."

"Pequot."

He turned his head too swiftly and hit his cheek on a bar. "There's no Pequot left around here. What the Pequot War nay wiped out, King Philip's War did." His nose itched again and so, too, a rash of lice bites along his neckline where his collar rubbed, but he didn't dare ask her to touch him again.

"I found the last of them."

"They're fugitives."

"I know."

"They're like to join the French. They'll burn down your town and trade you as an English slave. You'll fast find yourself on a slaver south, you isn't careful. Their name means *destroyer*, Ruth—remember that."

"Please. Hush this." Her face gallied.

"Aye, you're right. Let's talk more of hanging. Miracle I lasted this long, anyhow."

"It's not a miracle. It's mathematic chance." She trembled. How could he joke of this, the knave? "If I could get you out of here, I would go with you. Anywhere."

"I think I'll take my mathematic chances with the rope, thanks." But his fingers grasped at her, luring through the ropes, the fabric of her dress silkily running through his hands like liquid. He rested his head against the bars and spread open his bound fingers to touch the top of an imperceptible curve. "How is my son?"

"She's restless. Acting up, just like her father."

"She?" He looked like he'd licked a lime.

"Listen." She leaned in and whispered. "At the hour, Sam will have a guard around to check on you for the last of the evening, and then there will be no one for the rest of the night. He'll have another man stationed here between meetings morrow, so you'll have to go in the dark. I'll be back after the hour to open the gate."

"That won't be necessary."

"Tom will be waiting at the dock with the boat to—"

"Tom!" He wiggled his hands against the bars, but they didn't make the motion he wanted. "You got Tom involved? Are you trying to get my whole crew killed?"

"He'll sneak you back to *Primrose*. The ship is headed south, so you can hide until you get to Fairfield, or close to it. If Sam cares to find you, he will look for you on the ship, but he knows nothing of Fairfield, and we will be safe underway by the time he discovers that you are gone."

"*Primrose* is still here?"

"Tom said something about her being at a close port, London something."

"That's not so close. Tom stayed behind?"

"He did. There are rough winds."

Owen shook his head and glanced behind him at the wall cracks, a window too high up. He'd been watching those winds, the changing of the waves, for hours. "If those winds don't change, they'll put us in irons."

"You'll have to leave at first nightfall—"

"I was already planning on leaving at first nightfall."

"—and you'll have to— What? All on your own?" She looked around his cell, at his shirt, the floor. "How?"

"Just meet Tom at the dock and wait for me." He smiled and shifted his wrist, and two of her hairpins, perfect for picking locks, clasped the cuff of his sleeve.

Ruth's eyes creased, and a corner of her lip turned up. "You'll need this, too." She reached into her apron, drew out his dagger, and slipped it into his boot.

⋙

Owen inched his way along the outside wall of the jail in the dark. The fog hugged low against the beachgrass and sedge, the rocks like protruding heads and the cattails spindly swabs and hooks among fescue and cordgrass half disappeared in a veil. Creeping from the wall across the edge of the open shore, he could make out the faint silhouette of one of *Primrose*'s bateaux in the water, a British East India Company insignia on the side with the mark of the *Primrose* P. Thomas waved Owen forward, the motion jarring. The winds had picked up from the north now, to Owen's favor, as it would put them at a dead run through the Devil's Belt, instead of in irons. But they had to outrun whatever was lurking behind it, a false front invisible in the dark. He shivered and moved toward the boat. As he approached, he saw only one silhouette sitting low.

"Where is Ruth?" He leaned his head down to Thomas in the dinghy. "She's supposed to be here with you."

"I thunk she be with you."

He looked to the road behind him where nothing but night looked back. Only bullfrogs and crickets stirred. A thin wind whistling from the north. His heart pounded, lungs filled and held suspended there. "I've got to go back for her."

"What'matter with you? If she's nay here, she can't get here. She pro-lly couldna risk your safety. She woulda been first one here, elsewise."

"I know. That's what scares me. I won't leave until I know she's all right."

"Goddammit!"

Owen splayed his fingers, waving downward.

Thomas lowered the oars against the landing piles. A loud splash. "I willn't wait. This be our chance: Here, now. Take it or leave it."

"I've got to leave it."

"You'll hang. Dammit, you lickspittle, you'll bloody hang."

Owen breathed out, nodded, looked to the road, the bateau, back to the road. He was free now. He could leave. He looked back at Thomas and breathed again. In and out, and her touch found him behind the bars, and he blinked it away. "There's a shortcut to Winthrop area. Go to the Wequetequock around Elihu, and wait. We'll go through Chip'pachaug and the Nauyaug Points to the Nameaug dock—"

"Like hell. First of all," he lifted the oar and splashed again, "it's nay Nameaug no more. It be called New London now—"

"I refuse to call anything New London. One is bad enough."

"—Second, Fishers Island Sound will be unholy."

"It will."

"And the Devil's Stepping Stones...at night?"

"Aye."

"And you want me to wait at the Wequetequock? Mate." He laid the oars down on the piles and studied the thick swatches of quieting canvas around their spoons, the rusted ribbed oarlocks and button wearing thin, his gloved hands on the handles, fingers flexing in and out of fists to ease the muscles that had gripped too hard. "She's a married woman."

Owen looked at him. "Remember the code." He turned toward the road to the Whitlock house, the dark gnawing at him. The town lay otherwise still as his boots pounded against stones, and somewhere off, a tweed canid's howl rivaled the wind's. He pushed forward until the yellow glow of King's Hall washed over him. The house was alive with light, hemmed in a saffron wreath against the lowland fog.

His breath formed in mist against the window, and he pressed his fingers to it, thought of being able to afford real glass. Inside, Samuel paced back and forth, and it looked like he was talking to someone, although Owen couldn't see anyone else from his vantage point. On tiptoes, he finally made out the legs, then the arms, of Ruth, tied into a chair with her hands bound behind her back. Men's voices, indecipherable through the thick glass pane, rose and fell in tidal whispers like a following sea. While he assessed, his footing slipped, sending pebbles skittering against the house. Samuel's head snapped toward the window to see a shadow ducking beneath the freshly fogged pane.

Owen backed against the side of the house and peeked around the corner. The front door slammed at Samuel's exit, and the shuffling of feet brushed down the steps in a heightened trot. As Samuel neared, Owen leaped out and sent a fist into the general's nose. Samuel doubled back in unexpected pain, holding his face. Owen turned to run, but Samuel grabbed the back of the sailor's shirt and sent him tumbling to the ground.

"Get up, you worthless turncoat." Samuel blasted a spray of red from his mouth and lifted Owen from the dirt by the hair. "I should have known those ropes would never hold you." He drew his court sword, befogged by the pain in his nose, and pinned Owen against a tree with the tip of the blade at the sailor's chest.

Owen exhaled, cavitating his torso. As he regained his feet, he lifted his dagger from his boot. Samuel lunged forward with his brand, and the sailor swiveled, narrowly avoiding the blade, then lifted his own dagger and drove it forward beneath the lieutenant general's right shoulder. Half the length of the blade went clear out the back of Samuel's jerkin.

With a rush of adrenaline, Owen pushed Samuel against the side of the house as if the man were no heavier than a peacock-herl. Samuel's pained expression could be seen in the dark, haloed by the window's light and the blood down his lips and chin, and Owen twisted the dagger hard to one side. Samuel cried out and slumped forward. Owen brought the man's face upright again, between clenched fingers.

"No, Whitlock. I've untied knots all my life. Your ropes will never hold me." The sailor drew his boot up, pressed it into Samuel's gut, and yanked the dagger out of the bloody hole in the beaten man's shoulder.

Samuel screamed and blood left his mouth. He fell to his knees, clutching his bleeding breast. His breaths were labored, his eyes rolling unfettered in their sockets like loose marbles in his skull, and he couldn't get up. Owen loomed overhead, then raised a foot to Samuel's chest and nudged his body the rest of the way to the ground. The officer hit with a thud and lay still. Candles lit and flickered in the neighboring houses. The creaking door of King's Hall smacked open and shut and open and shut with the shuffling of boots and the cocking of guns, voices carried on the wind. A shot rang out, barely missing Owen's arm, and he turned toward its source.

Two men rushed at him, fumbling with their clumsy flintlocks, and Owen dropped his dagger and swooped for Samuel's fallen sword. He stepped toward the first man and dragged it, sharper than he'd expected, across the man's torso, slashing him from shoulder to hip, then brought it back to the man's neck and there was no sound save a *tst* like a whisper, and the man crumpled to the ground. Another shot popped, a small explosion following, and the smell of blackpowder filled the air, smoke playing around the gun. Owen wasn't sure where the bullet went, if it went, but it hadn't gone through him, and with a lunge he tackled the second militiaman, landing onto the body of the first, the sword loosed in the motion. The night lit up with candles around them, muttered voices closing in. Owen rolled with the soldier toward the house and grabbed a fistful of hair and smashed the man's face into a log. The soldier's head lolled, dazed, and Owen pried the gun from his fingers and brought the butt of it down onto the man's skull until his head lay sideways and still and silent.

Owen stood and stepped out of the light. He picked up his dagger, then sprang for the porch, taking the steps like he'd take a companionway, and he mounted the threshold, unhooked the latch, and threw his weight against the door. It creaked and swung inward, and men's voices rose inside the house. He spun around the door to confront the men, instead meeting the double set of winter doors that separated him from the anteroom. He'd forgotten about those. There'd be no surprise now; the men inside had surely heard his entrance. He put his ear to the winter door and listened, and the beech mahogany invaded his senses. He waited, curling a hand in and out of a fist, then he lifted the latch, so quietly. A shadow moved beneath the door, forward and back, then back again, and Owen threw the door open, snapping the shadow in the nose and sending the soldier reeling backward, through the anteroom and into the kitchen, where Ruth sat bound to the chair.

Owen's eyes sought hers, and she nodded to the next room, visibly disconcerted at the blood he wore. The man rose, and Owen sent him into the counter, the basin, flat-backed. The soldier kicked Owen in the gut, and the sailor reeled, his breath leaving him, then he kicked back, propelling the soldier away. He got to Ruth, but her bound hands required care. The rope split easily on the blade's sharp edge, but so, too, did Ruth's flesh, despite his best efforts. She seethed, breathed deeply through her nose, and the soldier regained ground and came back at them. She raised her legs and kicked at the man, entangling him in her skirts in the process. He tripped and yelled out for someone else. Owen turned his head toward the hallway. A militiaman from the next room left his post at the window and scrambled for the kitchen. He closed on Owen and struck him beneath the temple with the stock of his musket, then frantically fingered the trigger. Owen grabbed for the barrel, pushed it to the air. It discharged near his ear, an eruption, stinging and thrumming in a backfire, and the man screamed and dropped the gun to the floor along with pieces of his blown-off fingers. The man maintained his composure enough to grip Owen by the neck—one hand whole, one halved—and with the action returned in kind, the two turned circles.

Ruth stood, grappled with the remaining ropes, then lifted the chair with both hands, heaving it toward the Englishman ensnared with Owen. The chair cracked across the man's back, and he let loose his grasp on Owen's throat. The chair dropped to the floor, and the soldier staggered and fell backward over it, the air offering no handle for grasping. The back of his head slammed against the hickory floor and ruptured like a dropped bowl of ripe fruit. Owen blinked for only a second before thrusting his knife into the chest of the other stunned soldier who'd dragged himself up to the counter. The man rocked listlessly, then fell forward onto his fallen comrade, the two bodies colliding with a wet squish.

Ruth groaned and wrung her hands, and the time for thinking evaporated. Owen grabbed her wrist, and she pipped, sucked in quick air. He felt her skin slide unnaturally where he'd sliced her, but she didn't protest. Her hand was sticky, and his gut contorted, braided into knots, but he focused on the steps beneath him, the porch suddenly gone, the road a hemorrhage of gravel flying out behind him, and her flying out behind him, so near. He didn't know the thuds of his heart from his feet, but he was running and she was running, and nervous sweat blinded him. They couldn't stop until they reached some safety he was afraid they'd never find.

CHAPTER FOURTEENTH
Under cover of darkness

I am about to take my last voyage,
a great leap in the dark.

—Thomas Hobbes

Ruth was winded. The cold of spring's night shallowed her breaths. She ran through Owen's vapor, and the two jumped a wooden notched fence, skirted through mounds of maize, then cut through the Osborne yard toward Askook's flax field. Vestiges, murkiness through oiled linen, floated behind the Osborne windows, but she didn't stop to examine them. Owen glanced back, and the glow of a houselight made his eyes shine like coins, veiling him in a wash of amber over deep crimson. She prayed they could buy time with those coins.

"You're hurt," she said, slowing.

He looked down at himself. "It's not mine."

"God," she muttered. "God."

"I have a boat."

"God, God."

"Ruth." He turned, not so out of breath as she. "Stay bright. We have a ways to go." In the distance, he could make out the shadowy outline of the forest as they ran along the grass paths, parallel to the road. He imagined those onlookers with their candles finding the slumped bodies by now—time was scarce, its sands escaping.

"I thought you said you had a ship?"

"A boat, Ruth. Lordy, it's a boat. I do. I do have one. It's at the Wequetequock, and we'll go around the Wamphassuc Neck toward Nameaug." He led her away from the harbor and toward the woods.

"Nameaug?"

He grunted. "New London."

He tugged for her to move faster, but when they approached the forest, she halted. A silver-haired bat flew from a tree, dived at them, then away, and she jumped.

"We can't go in here," she said. "These are Indian woods. They don't belong to us."

"They don't belong to them, either. They're just woods."

"You don't understand." She removed her arm from his when her foot hit the edge of the Red Forest. "I know the woods. It is not safe."

"After what we just did, nowhere is safe."

Her insides sank and made the decision for her, as if she'd been possessed. *Nowhere was safe.* The woods had many Indian tribes that stretched into the north. Wild moose, black bears, boar, bobcats, foxes, and elk, especially new springtime mothers, were dangerously protective of their young. Ruth touched her belly. She understood that. She placed her hand back inside his grasp and followed him into the dark woods. Her heart slapped against her ribcage, a pace unbearable, and the echoing of the thumps pounded into her brain. A wolf howled. A dove coo-cooed from somewhere, out of place. Each sound in the distance was heard with the acuteness of the blind—twig crack, leaf rustle—and backlit by the faint small-hour horizon glow, she swore she saw the shadowed outline of Indians.

"Owen—"

"I know." He'd heard the wolves.

Ruth followed so closely behind him that she stepped on his boot heels. Her eyes were on her feet, but when she looked up, her fears swarmed around her, armed to the teeth. Owen halted abruptly, and she slammed into his back and squeaked. They stood still. Something rustled. Another howl. Closer now. She stared into the dark, willing shapes that weren't there.

"Move," Owen whispered, and he took up her hand again, dragged her onward.

They tore through the woods toward the cove, the moist ground clumping to their shoes, still hearing what they could now discern as footsteps behind them. Seeing outlines against the forest edge. Hearing a wolf bay, then snarl, whine and snarl, then squeal and go quiet. Approaching the dirt path before the bend in the Wequetequock, Owen halted again, and she crashed against him once more.

Three men on horseback cut off the path to The Road and headed toward the runaways. With the forest surrounding the couple so newly that branches still stuck to them, the maple scent lingering, the only way to the cove was through the approaching men. Ruth backed up against the trees. At the first, she thought the mounted men were Samuel's militia, that the whole town might soon be upon them, but a closer look gave her pause. She tensed.

"Where are we headed at this hour?" The leader shifted his horse alongside Owen and lifted a boot to the sailor's shoulder.

Ruth recognized the scarlet velvet coattails and the unkempt face wedged between a blood-red kerchief and a stolen tricorne. The man's horse turned to her, sniffed at her, let out a low *sssppphhh* into a pulsating nicker, and the rider followed the flare of the large nostrils to eye her curiously.

Owen shrugged his shoulder out from under the rider's boot. "Who's asking?"

The rider pulled back his overcoat and revealed a flintlock pistol butt, glinting as the moonlight passed through the clouds.

Ruth realized then how many clouds yawned above them. Light was scarce and getting scarcer. What clouds she could distinguish brooded from the blanket—pillars of thunderheads. She was thankful it masked the blood that bathed them. "They're highwaymen. Just thieves." No sooner had she said the words than she regretted them, her voice eliciting an inhale from the rider that could only imply recognition.

He studied her, and Fogcutter pranced, one eye on the thunderheads, one eye on Ruth. "So we meet again, my pretty thing. Those lips. Those precious pickpocketing fingers."

Owen whipped around and glowered. "Lips?"

The rider chuckled.

"I received a better kiss from your horse," Ruth said.

"Kiss?" Owen's mouth drew to creased lines, his jaw rigid iron to his shoulders, and he reached down, itching for the feel of his dagger. He grabbed Ruth by the wrist, her skin still sticky, and yanked her in line behind him. "We haven't anything on us."

"Then you shouldn't be using our road. We've a toll here."

"What's your toll?" Not that he had a damn thing on him. The prison guards had emptied his pockets on his way into the cell.

"That pretty thing you've got there. Women sell real nice upriver."

"I'll not be your toll," Ruth said, too loud, and Owen shushed her. She shushed him back and turned to the highwayman. "That's how you'd repay me for helping you?"

"Helping him?" Owen said.

"As I recall," the rider said, "when you 'helped me,' you rather helped yourself to something of mine, and I reckon you'll get plucked plenty for it on the road upriver." He moved Fogcutter closer to Ruth, brushing her shoulder, but Owen drew his knife and came between them, pushing her back, putting space between them all. The outlaw chortled and placed a hand on his gun. "Judging by the way you's sneaking at this hour, I'll wager someone would pay a few shiny shillings for you, eh? So how about a little bribery?"

"How about a little fight, you son of a bitch."

"I'm not a son of a bitch," the rider countered casually. "I'm the son of a fine lady what sleeps above King's Arms and Blue Anchor servicing Boston's finest sailors—as yourself, I can tell—with your gray balls the size of great gray whales. Perhaps you've seen her? Can't be but thirty-odd years. Bet she still looks the part. Hell, you've probably put it to her yourself. For all we knows, bluejacket, my bastard brother here could be your brat, making us damn related."

"Ça suffit!" Ruth said. "You'll have to catch us. Owen, run!"

Ruth's challenge sent the highwaymen into a charge at her, and all three closed in. Owen pulled her back, back, until they'd stepped into the woods. She started running. He held up his dagger. When the rider drew his flintlock in triad, a wailing banshee tongue-warble howled from the forest. The rider glanced up. Indian warriors swarmed from the woods and encircled the runaways with slings, axes, and arrows. Ruth stopped abruptly, her heart racing. A few colonial muskets caught the light, and the three highwaymen, their horses skidding across the dust, rearing and beating, fled the circle and doubled back to the west, toward the Pequot Trail. Owen pulled Ruth to follow, but the circle closed. Their eyes adjusted to the new figures. Clubs, sharp stone objects at the ends of sticks, bows with feathered arrows pointed at them in the dark. Ruth tried to make out the faces of the ambushers. Owen held out his dagger with one hand, clutching Ruth against him with the other. A voice arose in the dark that she recognized.

"Askook?" She could see his gleaming eye whites by the moonlight, and he walked up to her, looked closely into her dilated stare.

"Canakisheun?" Askook asked. "Bad woods. Bad stones."

"Aque. Ne wohter. Ne sewortum," Ruth said. She wiped her sticky hands on her dress. "We must get to Wequetequock Cove."

Owen gazed, astounded. Her language was a death sentence any-where else but at this moment, and he was anxious to move from it. He looked to Askook. "Please, can you tell them to lower their weapons?"

"Chunche bekedum bunnedwong, nepattuhquonk, do tugging. Pa-kodjiteau," Askook said to his men, then turned to Owen. "Bekedum bunnedwong." He made a motion for Owen to lower the dagger.

Owen lowered it, flipped it, and held the handle out for Askook to disarm him. Askook waved it off. Owen breathed easier and extended a hand in a gesture of peace. Askook did not take his hand.

"Go to nuppe." He pointed. "Askuwheteau. Safe."

"Tahbut ne." Ruth nodded. "You are a godsend."

"Go to cove!" Askook pointed and muttered some words to his men, and the Pequots dropped back. He lifted his hand toward the woods, and the men were gone as they'd come, on feet of fog and canvas, without further word to dilute the night.

Ruth stared after them. No matter how many times she'd seen him vanish into woods that swallowed him forthwith, it was always too abrupt for her. Owen turned her away, dust settling on The Road. As they moved along, they heard the rustling of leaves now and again, sometimes caught shadows ghosting at the tree line, but this time it felt reassuring instead of frightening. Far off now, there were still the sounds of horse hooves, and subtle ululations echoed in patches throughout the forest, moving as the two moved.

Arriving at the bank of the Wequetequock, Owen listened for the shallow-draft bateau listing against the shore. "I'm sorry about your hands."

She harrumphed and lifted her skirts as they negotiated the swampy shoreline. Images flashed, maybe real for a moment—she was without end or beginning—the swamps of Shrewsbury, Kees Karelszoon with his stick. She stood straighter.

They approached the boat, its rocking quiet against the rocks, and Owen looked around. Where was Thomas? Footprints led back and forth across the mud where the hawser had been roped around a tree. Panic struck him at the thought of the Pequots and their weapons. He scanned the footprints for sign of a struggle, a fight, any blood.

Ruth considered the silhouette rocking in the tide before her. "That's going to take us along the shoals?" She gestured at the old dinghy. "Am I to call this battered piece of wood a boat?"

"She's one-ten-thousandth the size of my fluyt, so aye. A boat." He held out his hand and lifted her into the shallow, and she steadied herself against the side. He looked around again for Thomas. Nothing stirred significantly now, and a lump came to his throat. He had to wait. He couldn't wait.

"Surely we must abide until morn? How will you get through these waters?"

"With savoir-faire, my doxy. And moonlight." Owen pushed one leg against the shore, setting the boat adrift in the cove. "And a little luck."

"And a good navigator." Thomas came out of the sedge grasses, tying the front of his breeches.

Owen breathed out, calmed himself, straddling, digging an oar into the shoreline. Both men dragged their weight into the boat and situated, and Owen pushed off the rocks.

"And oars." Thomas lifted them and put them deep into the water, their canvas heavy, and he watched the figures of the two passengers in the darkness. Bloody, shivering.

In the moonlight, the crimson crown of Owen's dagger shone as he wiped it on his breeches to slide back into his boot. Thomas breathed through his nose, but the men were otherwise quiet, and after a time, Owen took over the oars, and Thomas looked out at the shore, reading the landscape, mulling. A bog lemming darted into a moist hole, and beaver splashed into the water along the shoreline. Owen watched Ruth as she sat shivering, and it wrenched him that he'd planted fear in her. Her hands trembled against the wood of the boat bench and rattled the oarlocks. Time passed, and Thomas took over the oars again. It went on this way.

"Be very still," Owen whispered. "I need to listen to the rapids for overfalls."

Ruth asked, "Overfalls?" then cupped her mouth.

"There are overfalls and races along the sea surface through here where peculiarities in the sea bottom can propel water with deadly force." He saw her lips quaking as she pinched them together in the dropping temperature. Her fingers shook in her lap, and her billowy blouse rippled as if the wind went right through it. Of course she was cold. How had he not thought to grab a shawl for her? They'd had to flee so quickly. "Are you cold?"

She shook her head.

"Come over here. There's no escaping the late gales she's bringing with her." He nodded to the clouds and scooted back on the bench seat, spread his knees, and patted the space between his legs.

Ruth moved to his bench, leaned her back against his chest, and he clasped her in his thighs. His body was warm against her back. He took the oars from Thomas, each stroke like a slow machine. How little effort he required to lift and quiet the bulky oars, how regular his heartbeats against her ear. She rested her head on his collarbone and listened exclusively to his unruffled heart. She could have slept, had sleep not abandoned her to fear.

Into the soundless journey, the rapids shifted one way and the next, and the boat rocked from side to side. Through it all, the men remained rhythmic. The volatility of the water increased as they rowed and drifted along the rocky shoreline past Wamphassuc Neck.

Owen spoke softly to her, "Once we get past this unsteady patch, we'll hit Nameaug Harbor."

"New London Harbor, ya twit," Thomas said. "*Primrose* rests right of the bend, east of port." He spat over the boat side. "They rename towns, y'know."

Owen grimaced, an action that Ruth could feel against the side of her face. "What plan have you got for boarding?"

"Nay a bloody good one, mate. We got be lookin' for a signal from Lordfellow. He's waiting on weather. You ought'n address one other thing." Thomas took over the oars and nodded at her. "Captain knows she's Whitlock's wife."

The blood ran even colder through Ruth's body at the mention of the name. Owen looked at her, too, the side of her face all that his eyes could reach.

"You's both unwanted here. He finds neither of you, you'll be whipped and keelhauled as flouters."

Owen chuckled. He'd heard that threat before. He could picture the captain saying it. "You'd not look so pretty with barnacle cuts and missing limbs, doxy." He nuzzled his nose into her hair. "Just stay quiet wherever Tom puts you. The captain will have to go through me first."

"It's the stable again for us, then?" she said.

"I's afeared this time you'll getted even more of what you deserve," Thomas said. "Her jockeys be fulled up on wild Indian horses traded from Hudson, so you getted yourselves a comfy hound crate." Owen made a moue, and Thomas laughed the laugh that always made Ruth question his motives. "No barking, you mangy curs."

They neared the bend past the last cove, and Ruth made out the gallant outline of *Primrose*, nested in the harbor of what she assumed must be New London. The cove was quiet in the dark, a few lit hang-lanterns along the shore too dim to be but fuzzy spots from where the bateau listed. The sobs of the leopard bullfrogs and the yawning snores of pickerels chorused among a screech of crickets and spring peepers.

Thomas lifted the oars from the water and laid them across the boat, leaving the three isolated passengers to drift. "The waves be steady right here, so we's to wait for a signal if we can see from this distance. Keep quiet; the sea carries voices for a league."

Ruth couldn't imagine anyone hearing them over the croaks of the frogs. She blew into her cupped hands, then tucked them under her armpits. The boat turned lazy circles, and the same shore rolled by again and again, its two or three landmarks dizzying.

"What is taking so long?" Ruth said. Dew had formed on her shoulders and hair. The wetness soaked through to her skin, and Owen's breath against her head, hot then cold, reminded her that she was chilled to the bone. "Where is this phantom signal?"

Thomas squinted toward the ship. "Mayhaps we's too far out for Lordfellow to see the tender. That storm'ts coming be making the cove unsteady. I can't risk idling closer. We have to wait 'til he see us. I'll wager it willn't be but a few."

"I don't do well with waiting," Ruth said.

"No kidding," Owen muttered.

She reached into her pocket and pulled out the mirror she had kept there since she'd stolen it from *Primrose*'s cargo hold over three months back. She'd learned this from Askook: Lifting it into the moonlight, she twisted the glass toward the light several times as reflections cut across the water in bright illuminating streaks. Moments later, a tiny sliver of light reflected back from the docked ship and then another in the opposite direction, splitting the night in blades of white across the water's surface.

"I'll take that as a signal," Owen said, noting how she no longer looked so fearful. He set the oars back in the water and rowed to the ship. His balance was admirable in the rocking tender. He moved from end to end, attaching the hoisting ropes without a wobble, while Ruth held on for life. He reached for the dagger in his boot and lifted her to his side, then grabbed hold of a pull rope dangling from the ratlines and sliced it with his knife as far up over his head as he could reach. He wrapped the rope around her and secured her to his back. "I won't risk you climbing up alone, so hold on to me." He tugged the rope to send the signal up to Lordfellow that they were at the ladder.

"You can't intend to carry me all the way up the side." She put an impulsive hand to her belly. "You'll surely drop me."

"Do you really think I can't carry a hundredweight?" He shook his head. "I should keelhaul you myself for that offense." He yanked the rope tighter around her. "If I dropped you, I assure, it would be for pure jolly sport."

Ruth snapped her mouth shut and held on to him, while Thomas climbed up behind them at the ratlines. As they reached the top of the rope ladder, Lordfellow cut Ruth's bindings and hoisted her over the rail. The three sailors turned the hefty windlass to lift the rowboat up the side of *Primrose*, securing it temporarily near boat deck until it could be handled with its davits less quietly in the dawn. The ship was asleep. The few men on shortwatch looked the other way, seemingly in cahoots. Owen wondered how many wages that had cost Thomas. A midshipman paced in a boatcloak next to the officer of the watch, and the sailing master gazed outward over the cove, watching the few lanterns on land, his wool cap low over his ears and his speaking trumpet in his hand. The old oak filled Ruth's senses again, and she imagined the crossing, how light it had been by comparison. His face without all that added tension.

Lordfellow turned to Owen and handed him a small bundle of papers he'd held for safekeeping, and Owen looked down at them sadly, thumbing the broken wax, nodding absently. Thomas waved Lordfellow along the deck to keep watch and turned back.

"Go down below," he said. "You know wheres. Don't let no one see neither of yous until Fairfield, or we's all be keelhauled."

Owen eyed the front moving in, visible even in the dark. "Looks like you could use me back on weather before night deck."

"Aye, but I willn't do it, mate. Get below."

"Aye, sir," Owen replied and nudged Ruth. "He's first mate now." The words felt empty in his mouth, but he swallowed it.

She scowled. "Aye, sir."

Thomas smiled greasily. He stood at least a head taller than she, looming over her. "The rank positioning be nay up to me, girl. This be a ship, and she, her captain, and he be sayin' what goes. Enjoy the hound crate." With an unbecoming guttural groan, he skulked across the deck, conflicted, though mostly tired.

"Be cautious with him, Ruth."

"I did nothing."

"You scowled."

"Is scowling a keelhauling offense, too?"

"He's torn between loyalty to the master and loyalty to the dog."

"He knew all along what your father was going to do to you!"

"My entire crew knew. It's not personal. Tom was doing his job. I'm sure most of them know I'm here now and haven't said a word. It swivels back around. Ain't none of us like each other. I happen to like Tom because we've both been at this so long we're near brothers now, and maybe for no other reason." He looked out over the unsettled ocean, gauging the distance and changing direction of the coming front, still thumbing the letters. "This storm will turn us inside out. I can't stay below."

"You have to. Your father."

He reached for her arm and led her down the companionway and a series of ladders to an enclosure at the back of the cargo hold, barely wide enough for standing up or lying down, empty except for a pile of blankets Thomas had thrown into the corner in preparation for her arrival. A wooden floor sloped toward the familiar grates at the back, and the oak reeked of piss and flea powder. The kicked-up powder left a chalky mist that rendered the air hard to breathe, and she could taste the thickness.

"Not quite big enough for a romp in the trough, is it?" Ruth ducked her head at the ceiling as her sigh petered out. She was exhausted, her lower back aflame.

"That's a good thing."

"Well, a little romp wouldn't hurt. It's not like it'll put me with child." Her chuckle rang hollow.

He looked at her hard, and for the first time, the thought of his child—a human life relying on him for survival—really and vividly crossed his mind, followed by the thought that this might not work, that he might die for a child he may never see, never hold. "I wasn't ready for this. To do it all this way. The thought of you and a baby and me stuck in the middle of it…bloody scares me to death. What if I can't…"

She approached him when he left it hanging, realizing herself the gravity of the situation in a way she had not yet comprehended. There was a child. It was real, and it was coming. He turned to see the look of fear back upon her face, and her uncertainty tore at his composure. He held out the stack of a half-dozen letters that she recognized—each penned on the parchment he'd given her, in her own hand with impatiently placed words, the wax seal of Daniel's woodshop; each asking for the return of *Primrose* to Stonington Harbor. Unceremoniously, he tossed them on the pile of blankets in the corner of the crate.

"I've got no books." He took a breath, studied the cuts on her hand that she'd loosely wrapped with her apron, and paused. Breathed slowly. "I came fast as I could; you must believe I did. Turned the whole ship around, Captain be damned, heaved us out of irons by hawser, to get to you. Would to God I'd never left you there at all." Without being able to face her fearful eyes, he ducked through the crate door, sealing it behind him and leaving her to stare at the letters scattered like unanswered prayers among the piss and powder.

CHAPTER FIFTEENTH
The gales of the Nor'easter

For as the nature of foul weather
lieth not in a shower or two of rain,
but in an inclination thereto of many days together:
so the nature of war consisteth not in actual fighting,
but in the known disposition thereto
during all the time there is no assurance to the contrary.

—Thomas Hobbes

Rain beat heavy on the ship's deck, the dark of it tangled with the dark of the sky forming a seamless sheet, black and fast. Owen positioned himself at the portside railing, soaked through his clothing, his wool cap droopy over his head, russet neckerchief wrapped around his neck, marrow cold, and he lifted the scupper stopper to widen the drainage hole. The deck's floodwaters emptied through the grates in the railing each time the fluyt thrust forcibly to one side. He waded in water up over his ankles, and his boots filled. When the ship rocked back to starboard, he let go and slid with the momentum toward *Primrose*'s center, stopping himself against the foremast, reaching for the rigging to furl the sails before the wind grew wilder.

The storm was big, and the crew was small; what men not on deck were bailing water from leaking bulkheads inside the hull. The sails snapped back and forth like whips, and the foretopgallant sail had torn along the port leech, cloth stripping further from the buntline rigging with the passing seconds. Several of the clewlines and garnets that were attached to the edges of the sails had snapped, become ensnared, loosened in the wind, proving it difficult to utilize rigging lines to furl the feet of the sails up to the overhead yardarms. Some of the furling would have to be done semi-manually.

His footing remained secure among the rocking waves, but he was already fatigued. He grabbed hold of the ratlines to the foretopsail rigging and hauled himself to the lowest spar, above the course sail, pressing back against the wind to release the first clew sheet where it had unattached from its clewline. He grounded himself firmly against the two-hundredweight sail before the wind changed, so he could hold tight enough to the port clew to slide in along the lower yard and release the center sheet. The sail snapped back on the released corner, nearly knocking him off the yardarm, but he held on to the flapping topsail and climbed the rope ladder with the clew tucked beneath his arm.

He made his way up the ladder with his legs wrapped so tightly around the ratlines that the muscles cramped. He ignored the pain, approached the fixed yard at the head of the topsail, and struggled to secure the portion of the sail that he'd released from the sheets. With half of the sail handed, he swung out again for the rope ladder. The wind whipped it out of reach before he finally claimed it, and he lowered himself to the bottom spar to repeat the process, releasing the topsail's last sheet before climbing back up to the head and hauling on the remaining secured buntlines, completing the furling.

Back on the deck beneath the sail, spent, he looked up at the ripped topgallant, even higher still than the foretopsail and blowing wilder— its rhythm a clapping heartbeat for the storm. Bitterly, he exhaled and thought, *Dieu aie pitié*. As he placed a hand, pruning and fatted with moisture, onto the rope ladder to drag himself to the next tallest sail, he heard the murky voice of Thomas calling across the deck. Help had arrived. Seemed God had a modicum of mercy left after all.

Thomas ducked beneath the cover of the main course, his wide-billed hat filling with rain and sagging down around his face, limp as a bonnet. "Great Poseidon of Atlantis! This be incredible." He watched the wind flip Owen's rope ladder like a child's toy in the jaws of an invisible dog. "You sure as a fiddler shouldna be on deck." He glanced up, rain pelting his eyes. "You getted the broke forecourse and top down yourself? Sixteen stones apiece?"

Owen nodded, but he looked it.

Thomas swung up the ratlines toward the starboard topgallant clew. "You's a beast, mate. Sleep at all?"

Before Owen could shake his head, the deck filled with crewmen sliding across the rainwater of the slicked oak planks toward the masts. Thomas yelled for the men to hand the sails, and the two men helped each other down from the ratlines.

"We shouldna be in this cove," Thomas said. "It's spitting them waves right back at us. If the storm takes a anchor, we be broached."

"The old lady's deck is taking on water faster than I can drain it, and she's leaking below."

"I patched the worst of it, but."

"But." Owen arched a brow. "I sealed the passenger deadlights, but I fear she'll stave the hull and pin them inside." His message hit Thomas with the urgency intended, but it was no longer Owen's decision to make. He waited, feeling the weight of the water root him to the planks.

"Sails first."

"Aye, sails. But I'm at the scupper. She's listing over the side at full tilt, and the next rogue's coming right there, starboard rail. Brace your footing, mate, or God keep you if the rail doesn't."

Thomas rocked, faced the wave, unready. Owen slung a rope around the first mate's waist, and his sailors-hitch secured Thomas to the mainmast in seconds. The ship came around, rolled with the waves until her horizon matched the earth's horizon, and water battered one side until she was nearly flat. The knot yanked Thomas around his middle, but it held fast, and he gripped it to stabilize his footing. As the great ship tilted, Thomas stayed put at the mainmast, but Owen slid with it toward the scupper to drain the deck water.

He landed hard against the railing and caught hold of the scupper rope, opening the large grate to its widest. As *Primrose* fought to right herself with the outgoing burst, he saw another incoming wave at portside, about to force the ship back in the other direction. He ducked beneath the meager protection of the railing as the wave crashed above his head and sprayed over the deck, an endlessness of dark fog obliging him only long enough to return to his feet before the water climbed his torso. Chest-high in floodwater, he gripped the rail and his service rope and waited until the ship's deck reached a sufficiently steep angle, then he lifted the grate release to unleash the overflow from the deck. The torrent pulled him against the scupper, smacking him into wood, and the rope holding it open snapped from his hand. The bulky iron gate crashed down on his foot, pinning him to the deck and rail.

Owen howled and grappled for the rope that had slipped out of reach. He caught it and haled the iron scupper gate from his foot just as the next wave sent the vessel careening back to starboard. He was propelled on his side across the flooded oak planking, landing ribcage-first across the bottom of the mainmast next to Thomas.

Owen drew himself up, rubbing his ribs, his diaphragm leapfrogging for air. Something might have been broken inside. "That didn't go as planned." His numb fingers groped for the mast.

"Aye, I'll bet not." Thomas nodded. "But you successfully drained half the deck."

"And half the feeling from my leg." He could see the danger in which the restricting harbor had put them, the waves sucking in and spitting back. They were too far from land to reach it, but too close to avoid the waves that returned from it. "She's going to uproot our anchors." It was a whisper lost to the sails' frantic snapping. Fragmentary in the wind. "If she severs even one… The weather and bridge decks might succumb, so the leaks… The passengers will have to be secured, and—"

"And Ruth?"

"Will have to wait it out like the rest of us." Owen looked away.

"She's far below the water line."

Owen fidgeted with his buttons, wished for his pipe, visualized it filling with rain, leadening, too heavy for lips to lift, soggy ash in his collar. He stiffened. He pictured her terrified, locked in there. Pictured the captain leaving her to the fate of passengers heavy with yellow fever.

"Can't believe I's pleading for her," Thomas said, "but the wench be in the lowest belly of the beast. We take on water down there, she'll be drowned with no secured deadlights or locked runners."

"And if we seal her in that tiny crate, she'll run out of air." Owen considered the options. "We'll get the door runners up on her, too."

"Substantial effort."

"Passengers don't die on my watch."

"I give the orders now," Thomas reminded.

"I'm not your crew, mate," Owen said, fatigue testing his patience. Why had he been so impulsive as to get back on the ship? He should have taken Ruth and run with her through the wilderness. Just run. With the baby, she might not have made it far, though. There would have been nothing for days and days, maybe weeks, but eventually there'd be a settlement. As quickly as he'd imagined a warm cabin, a hearth, a fresh deer kill, he imagined Whitlock's men, much faster on horseback, heading them off, surrounding them, beating them to it. Had Thomas not been involved, Owen could have kept rowing the shallow, further south, all through the night and morning, until his hands bled from oar slivers and his shoulders stiffened immobile. But it hadn't gone down that way. Here was here, and so be it. There were worse places; at least the ship was home, and he knew every crevice inside and out. When the storm passed, he'd take Ruth, and they'd get off the ship with the morning crates at Nameaug—no, he'd call it New London now, to blend in—and head inland. But for now, she needed sleep. Hell, he needed sleep. He sighed and lowered his head. "I'll take responsibility for her deadlights and runners, with your permission, sir."

A spark of purple-black rose like a cobra from a woven basket of purpler-black, and the horizon melted from itself and into itself until a continuous sheet of upswell came hurling high, over the bow to twist the ship, to upend her, to strain her anchors and snap her lines, threatening her bearing to the ocean's bottom. The black loomed tall over the rail as if standing, as if the wave could walk—its feet dependable, and the ship a mere pebble in its path.

"Grab that halyard!" Owen shoved Thomas against the mast and sloshed toward the crewmen mounting the storm-torn deck. It should have been dawn, but there was no light to it. A stern lantern crashed to the deck behind the men, but the rain doused it instantly. "Help me secure the lower deck seams and staved bulkheads! Lock the runners on all the holds, jockeys, the crates!" He neared the crew, steadied himself upright against the rail while the craft stabilized her hull, braced herself.

"What bloody hell be him doin' here?" Kingsley spat, dipping for cover near the bridge deck's breezeway. "That cuntson near got us kilt! We take no orders from traitors."

"Kingsley," Thomas shouted, his voice nearly lost, "it's my command."

No more could be said. The rogue swell walked over *Primrose* and sent the crewmen plunging against the railing. As the mighty fluyt righted herself in the aftermath, her mouth filling with seaweed and fish and dead birds, and purging itself of rainwater, only one man had kept his footing on the deck. The swarm of depleted men looked at Owen standing in place like a statue. If they were to stay alive through the breakers that ricocheted through the cove, then they'd need to heed the statue. He pointed. They followed.

The sky opened with strips of lightning, and the rain pelted Owen in the chest, the face. He withstood the wet shrapnel, his grip sturdy on the rail above the scupper. When the ship pitched back, he again let his body roll with it, sliding to the opposite scupper to release more water back into the furious ocean. He was fast losing the deck, but a lull was coming. The lulls were as terrifying as the brunt of the storm, the darkness shielding from view whatever would come after them.

The keel leveled momentarily, and Thomas came alongside Owen at the starboard rail, trajectory erratic as a fly's. "Don't look now, but you's wracked. Best git."

Owen turned. Captain Jacob Townsend, his sleeves torn nearly off from patching planks below, made his way up the stairs of the companionway dragging behind him the reluctant, struggling Ruth, red gashes pocking her arms, her dress soaked through, clinging like static.

Owen drew in a breath through his nose. "There goes the trouble of locking the runners." He could run now. The captain hadn't seen him. He could hide. But in all likelihood, the captain might throw her overboard. Owen waded across the planks toward them, kicking the splattering water away from his calves.

Jacob flung Ruth from his grasp, and she slammed hard into the rail. Her balance gave way, and she collapsed like a ragdoll. The motion spun through her, down to her belly. Her vision whirled, images trailing in spots like the butts of lightning bugs, and she vomited. Rain washed it away instantly.

"Captain!" Owen yelled. "Careful of her."

Jacob jerked to the noise. His face when he saw Owen held first the tiniest glimmer of relief, followed quickly by surprise, then melted into righteous fury. "You." He couldn't say more, but it didn't matter. The venom in that one word was poison enough.

"She's got no legs for this." Owen ignored the captain and lifted Ruth from the planks, propped her easily against the railing. "This deck is no place for her. Your anger is with me." He pressed one hand into the middle of her back to keep her at the rail and yelled for Thomas to get her below with the other passengers.

"She was in a crate! Whitlock's wife, you hobsop son of mine!"

Owen banked his hand at the stormfront, his brows raised as a cockalorum. There wasn't time for this now. "The windlass fair near snapped. Capstan is allowing us nothing against this resistance, and the devil's claw is buckling. Unstowed shallows are too full of water to hale to boat deck, and look there—land's two leagues away. Not the strongest among us could swim or row it. I bid you open your eyes, Captain, 'cause there's your deck report."

Jacob tore at a piece of cloth dangling from his ripped sleeve. "Dump them both overboard. Remove her witchery from my oak." He grabbed Ruth, and the wind absorbed her protest.

She tore her arm free and stepped back.

Owen said, "We don't throw women overboard on a civilized ship, sir."

Winds rattled through the lookout, howling like wild dogs against the thudding of metal on wood. Rain pelted his eyelids until he could scarce lift them, but he stared down the captain, the wedge driven between them as thick as the oak planking. There would be no returning from this moment. The ship knew it as Owen knew it, answering with creaky overheads and shaking yardarms, swinging in ways their joints weren't meant to bend. Ruth spoke, but no words left her, and the men watched her lips move, a tiny mute ventriloquist puppet cast between them. The captain gave another command that the wind swallowed, and Owen stepped closer.

"Leave her be and stop groping for her," Owen said, then hesitated. "She is...she is with child."

"That be nay your concern."

Owen's gaze fell to the deck. His brows bunched, and his discomfort was admission. Jacob's cheeks appled and twitched, his nostrils flaring like a cornered horse. A fragment of thunder crept through the clouds, reaching them late. Everything that had been so carefully balanced had tipped. Waves ripped across the deck, and the ship lurched, but the men clawed the rails, each other. The caulking burst between the plank seams, and the hull took on more leaks. Jacob balled his fists.

"I rue the day you was born, son."

"Do not call me son. You are not my father, nor have you ever been one to me."

Jacob stilled.

"Aye, I know all about how Mother came to you. Your passenger with a bastard inside her she'd discovered too late. You wifed her before you figured the bastard out. But this son—" he looked at Ruth; wind whisked her hair into whips that scourged her cheeks and neck, her skirts tangled around both their legs in swirls, and his heart raced, "—this son is mine."

Jacob stiffened, but Thomas stepped in, his eyes gentler on Ruth now that he knew her state, and said, "I'll deal with them on the morrow, Captain." He threw a withering glance at Owen, urging the restless sailor to keep still—noted his tightened jaw. They'd all felt the new shifting beneath them. "This lull willn't last."

"You could use another set of hands," Ruth said.

"No," Owen said and looked at Thomas. "Not on deck."

"Down below," Ruth reasoned. "Put me to work, sir."

Thomas grinned wryly. "The sails is drawn; we's done all we can on the weatherdeck. We got to get everyone below. I believe it be in God's hands now." Thomas shooed Owen before the captain could grab Ruth again. "I have her. Scuppers."

"Aye, sir." Owen pinched his lips together and held himself up along the rails, moving toward the scupper with the ship's cradled weaving. A fist formed in his lungs, and breaths were strikes at the dawn dark, no light yet creeping.

Thomas ushered Ruth toward the companionway stairs. "Just do what you can, lass." Then they heard Jacob call across the deck, away from them.

"I'll see that you never again sail on an English ship!"

Owen turned toward him. "I would sooner string a noose around my own neck than sail beneath an English flag again."

A burst of wind and seaspray tore across the weatherdeck, lashing the crewmen with stinging saltwater. Faces turned, eyes shielded, bands of red-burn across leather cheeks. The deck was lost. The wind threw *Primrose* back to larboard.

Owen's urgency rang out through the deluge: "The starboard anchor is giving way!"

A link in the massive, anchored chain tore apart. The chain snapped back toward Owen like an unwieldy tentacle, riding a corkscrew wave over the edge of the deck, and smacking the foremast so forcefully that the mast split the length of one side with a clangorous crack.

"Get away from the masts! Get down below!" The vessel jolted astern, and the chain followed gravity's arc toward the panicked sailor running to warn the men along the railing. "Move from the rail!"

The iron cable plunged, slung downward, ripping out a section of the starboard railing and the bowsprit, sending the deck's water in a rush toward the opening, and funneling John and Kingsley over the side. The entirety of the foredeck seemed to wash overboard, unsecured items submerged and swallowed. The two men landed in a flooded rowboat below, barely attached at boat-deck height by broken davits and Carrick-bent ropes. The water poured atop the tiny boat, and it rocked, spilled over, and dragged the two waterlogged men over the sides, holding on to the ropes and slippery wood.

The funneling rush hit Owen at the back of the knees and knocked

him sliding into the draining water. He kicked his leg out to the same
wrought-iron scupper gate that had previously smashed his toes, and he
dropped it again to halt his fall, pinning him between the pelting water
and the railing. He dangled there, the weight crushing. Over the edge,
John and Kingsley held on, and the water poured from the upper deck
onto the men without mercy. As the mighty ship retreated from the
next advancing wave, Owen fought to release his leg from the scupper
and slid once again to *Primrose*'s center, stopping himself against the
mainmast and thinking about how many men at sea died this close to
shore. The air had gone from his chest, and it heaved in and out ineffec-
tively. No more time for thought. He grabbed hold of loose rigging and
tied a Carrick bend around the mainmast and around another rope at
his waist. Leftover rope was wrapped around his forearms and secured
in easy knots. He had gotten a feel for the rhythm of the erratic rocking,
and he waited for the next opportune movement.

Thomas corralled the men toward the stairs to safety below deck and
looked over to Owen crouching into position. Realization anchored.
"Damn you, no!" He ran toward Owen. "I order you to stop!"

Both men then felt the movement of the ship turning with them,
and Owen took a firm hold of the rope at his middle. Planting his boots
into the oak planks, he surveyed Thomas, then leaned back. Owen's feet
slid down the slanting deck with the ship's tilting, sending him backward
over the edge of the broken railing in a funnel of drainage. Thomas
yelled, tried to grope for a jacket sleeve before Owen could slip over the
side, but it was too late. Owen landed on his back across the benches of
the hanging bateau, while tides drained down over all three overboard
men.

He shook the pain, the new fire in his backside, then removed the
ropes wound about his forearm, securing them in knots around John,
strapping the downed sailor to his back. Owen grasped the slippery
rope, dug his boots into the side of the ship, and climbed. Inch by inch,
he pulled them both toward the deck, the fatigue finally hitting him
halfway up.

Thomas came to the railing. Another lull had settled over them, and
he reached for the rope to lift them before the next swell knocked the
climbers off balance. Thomas released John's arms from around Ow-
en's neck and loosened the rope as they reached the deck. When John
was secure, Thomas extended a hand back over the edge, but Owen
pulled away, dangling. There was still one more man overboard. He

exhaled and let go of the railing with the ship's next tilt, dropping again into the tender below.

Kingsley clung to the side of the rowboat, and the knots that secured the rickety thing were fraying. Owen lowered an arm, but Kingsley, from fear and exhaustion, wouldn't move to grasp it. Bracing himself against the side of the boat, Owen seized him by the back of the shirt and hauled him over the lip of the dinghy. The expenditure collapsed both men in a heap. They lay there panting. Owen knew by the tremors beneath him that the next wave was coming, and he was so crazed from lassitude that lemon dots sprinkled a far horizon, and he imagined an end, spinning hallucinatory through the black. He hauled himself to his feet—his head high as if on tobacco leaves or skunked drink—and he steadied his balance.

He looked up at Thomas, and exhaustion looked back. The men were spent. Neither had the stamina now to haul up the weight of two men. Owen nodded toward the boat ties, and Thomas' expression indicated that he already knew. The ties could not withstand a cranking of the windlass without snapping. Owen thought of his life—what he had that was worth saving. Ruth. Their child. He looked at Kingsley, lolling around like a beached porpoise. What did he have? *Fucking nothing.* But he wouldn't survive in the water. Owen was the stronger of the two. He looked back up, blinked rain out of his eyes, and stretched a hand into his boot.

"What's you doing?" Thomas yelled down. "Damn you, don't be a fool!"

Owen withdrew his dagger and severed his own rope. He tied it with hitches around Kingsley's thighs and lower back, like a sling for the mostly lifeless body. "Pull him up! Godspeed. There's no time."

Thomas battled with the rope, but the slippery threads cut into his chapped hands. Frankie heard the call and rushed to take hold of the rope behind Thomas. Her burst of fortitude permitted Kingsley to asylum in good time.

"Untie him quick. We's got to get this rope back down," Thomas said, taking hold of the knots, counting seconds between swells. "Damn fool cut his hoist." He turned to Kingsley, who lay across the deck panting like a rabid mutt in its last throes, and kicked him. "You hear that? Better man than you down there."

Thomas looked over the edge. His fingers stopped working at the rope. Time was gone. He stared. Owen's inferior boat, held in place by mere threads, was fifty feet from being overturned by a leviathan, moving at a speed too rapid for thought. Thomas yanked Frankie back toward the fluyt's center, then secured them both to the mainmast with butterfly loops in the bight of the course sail's sheeting.

Down below, Owen braced himself for the wave, as it surely would pull the last threads of the dinghy loose and send him plummeting to the sea. He reached for the boat ties above the fraying section and held on as the water rose. But a serpent bladed the sky, looming dark on dark, yet backlit with flickers like tiny streaks of dawn's light across shutter slats: the wrought-iron anchor chain had been dredged up and was thrashing once more across the sky, his rowboat its intended prey.

The iron bonds landed across the tender, splitting the frail dinghy down the center, physically halving it. Owen felt himself falling as a tremendous pain tore through an arm and leg. He held his breath. Black water poured over him, pinning him against the ship's side, and he could see nothing but darkness. As he slid down the remaining half of the dangling, bisected boat, the knot around his waist found purchase on the oarlock. His fall stopped abruptly, juddering his torso. He felt he had snapped in two, just as the boat had.

When at last the wave rolled back to the sea, Owen was still suspended from the shallow by the waist, and he could newly see the source of his pain. The chain had wrapped itself around the severed boat, and it banded his left arm and leg within the embrace of the iron and wood. The anchor links lacerated his skin and sent blood down his limbs. The saltwater stung the wounds like a swarm of wasps. He could not dislodge himself. Then, the boat ties. He felt more than saw that the weight of the chain was tearing through the weakened ties, each splitting thread a jolt.

The ship shifted her weight, and Thomas made it to the top of the rail to look down at Owen. "We's gettin' a rope! Hang on!"

"There's no time!" In Owen's free hand, he still clutched his dagger, his knuckles rigored white. He had to rid himself of the boat and get distance from it if he were to keep from being pulled beneath it when the last threads snapped. He contemplated the seabed, how far he could get from the boat, whether it would be enough to make a difference. He pictured Ruth's face and closed his eyes.

"Please, mate, hold on!" Thomas sounded far away.

Owen drew his dagger to the knotted rope around his waist and sliced it through, releasing his body from its bonds. As if a cog in a rhythmic machine, gravity twisted him one way, then sharply back the other, and he slid down the boat, spinning out of the grasp of the tangled chain, landing feet-first into the murky ocean water. Within seconds, the last remaining tie snapped, and the cleft dinghy plunged, along with the anchor chain, into a whirl where Owen had descended. Violent waves claimed the wreckage, body and all, the spits of white foam clouding visibility, ghosting bubbles, shadows dwarfed by bigger shadows.

Chapter Sixteenth
Captains are made not born

In the reproof of chance
lies the true proof of men.

—William Shakespeare

"Damn ya, bull'eaded screw," Frankie muttered, approaching Thomas at the rail.

He scanned the sea's rough surface. "He's already so fatigued. I don't…" His voice trailed or was lost.

Most of the crew had gone below deck with the last swell, but now there was a lull, and the quieter spaces lasted longer and became more frequent, signifying passing. Thomas and Frankie manned the rail, eyes sweeping.

The captain joined them, his face blank. "Jonah's lift, I say," and then he turned away.

Frankie wrinkled her nose at him. A minute passed with no sign. Two minutes. Three. Four, then Frankie's voice rang out. "A'oy there! At the lines!" She pointed. "'e's climbin' up th'fore sta'buhd 'ull!"

Thomas strained to see. Owen's head, then his shoulders, popped from the water, clutching for the tangled rope ladder to heave himself up, his arms shaking, muscles useless.

"Throw th' net down!" Frankie shouted, and she ran toward the crew. "C'mon! Get th' bloody nets!"

The crew looked at her, considered, then went on.

"'aul-in, 'aul-two, 'aul-belay!" she called. "I bloody good know Fuhst Mate 'ewitt give ya 'is own gold coins t'get Owen t' Fairfield. Ya took'd th' coins, damnya, so you'll get 'im 'ere, bygod, or ya' ovuhboard next!"

The crew scattered for the windlass as if God had commanded it, and chorused, "Haul-in, haul-two, haul-belaaaay!"

The net dropped near Owen in the water. Letting go of the ratlines, he rolled into it like a hammock, wrapping it around and around him.

The men sang out, "Haul-in, haul-two, haul-belaaaay! Bosun's pipe-two, haul-belaaaay! Haul-up, haul-two, haul the haaaay!" and gave a jerk and pulled out the handspecs and inserted them again, again, again into the windlass gears, pulling out and putting in, each man praying it wouldn't snap. "Bosun's pipe-two, haul-belaaaay! Stamp and go, stamp and go—Bosun's pipe again to blow! Haul-in, haul-two, haul-belaaaay!" in unison, and they turned the netting windlass, the resistance disheartening, and they lifted his battered body over the starboard rail of the fluyt before the ship's tilt could leave their favor. They laid him on the deck. He shook, achieving only shallow breaths. Each time he struggled to stand, the men pushed him back to the deck.

"Infirmary," Thomas said, and Frankie was first to grab an arm.

The lower deck was mostly dry, but large sections took on leaks through the seams. Men with barrels and rags caught the water, bailed it, and plugged the holes in advance of further damage. The hammering of reinforcement boards echoed through the hull. Passengers heaved sick from the rocking of the ship, and Owen heard their cries as he passed. Yellow fever came back to him. Ruth in the hold. His baby. He grasped at the hands holding him, but his strength was tiny, and he caught nothing. The sailors carried him by the gun deck and the ship's sail room to a lowered hideabed in the infirmary alongside John and Kingsley, then departed for warm, dry blankets, presently in scarce supply.

Ruth, sent to the infirmary to help with the wounded, drew in a breath when Owen entered the room and was laid out on the bed. A charcoal taste rose in her throat and her chest fluttered numb from top to bottom, her heart dropping down from its casing to someplace useless below. She hurried to him. His flesh was cold, clammy to the touch, his wet clothes stuck to him like a second skin, but when he saw her, he reached for her, only half aware, yet calmer. She went to the table, quickly prepared a wrought-iron flatbox with saltwater and set it atop some makeshift slats and a heating pan.

"Have you tallow?" she called to one of the sailors.

He nodded. "We better'n tallow, lass. We barrels of whale oil and sperm wax."

Her brows arched. "I'll need whatever you can spare to warm the water: oil, wax, fire. Any dry clothing can be parted with. And clean rags."

"No clean rags left."

"Owen has been lacerated, John's got severe roping, and Kingsley's got a splinter in his calf as long as the plank that imparted it. I beg you, find some rags." She looked away from him and rubbed her hands together for warmth, then prepared a needle and thread.

Owen shook, the pallor of his lips belonging to a ghost. "Turning into a regular jacktar, shouting orders like that." He fumbled for his buttons.

A midshipman returned, and Ruth poured the thick, waxy whale oil into the pan and tipped the candle to light it, allowing the flame to warm the water in the flatbox. She left it to heat and turned to Owen, his eyes fixed upon her, and she approached with a wetted rag, threaded needle.

"Lay back."

"I'm fine. Help the others."

"You're bleeding. Lay." She tapped the flock beneath him and leaned in.

One of the men shoved by. "Git them wet clothes off him!" then, "Hell if I wonnot git my gold pieces," he mumbled.

The sailors reached over one another for his boots, jacket, hose, buttons, while Ruth readied her needle to stitch his wounds with weak sewing thread. She prayed it held. As a crewman untied Owen's breeches and shook them down his legs, she chuckled nervously, about to witness him splayed out naked as a Roman table centerpiece. He grinned and watched her. She laid the warm cloth across his forehead to bring some color back into his peaked face, his persed lips, and the crewmen swaddled him in dry blankets and rubbed the circulation back into his fingers and toes. The sailors moved on to tend to John and Kingsley. Ruth pressed the needle into Owen's arm and dragged the thread through the cut with a series of pops.

"Why didn't you tell me he wasn't your father?"

He studied each of her deliberate stitches, how perfectly pulled, carefully placed each one sat, strung through his skin like a piece of art. He sought eye contact, but she looked down, brushed his hand from hers, and went on with the stitching, wiping seeping blood away with a glycerin of oil and lye on a dampened salt rag. He winced at the sting. "Words unspoken are not necessarily secrets. It wouldn't have excused me."

"I forgave you a long time ago. You have to forgive yourself. I can't do that for you."

She pulled back the blanket to clean the wounds. Her touch along his naked thigh sent a rush of blood through him, but he was too tired for more than the thought of it. He laid his head back onto the hard slab and stared at the leaks in the ceiling planks and stringpieces, contemplating how much damage one storm could do, and how he now found himself tossed in the middle of two.

Time passed quietly between them, until Ruth released a sigh that she'd held for too long. Something new flickered in the corner of her eyes. "When you," she started slowly, then paused.

"...killed your parents."

She choked thinly. The boat heaved and creaked.

"Say the words, Ruth. Face them like I have to."

She had faced them. She waited for his eyes to meet hers. He'd dropped a torch on her family's barn, goddamn him. It killed their stock; the Miner fields went up in flame. She starved for a year with crops that wouldn't budge in the hole he'd left, that singed ground, the same where she'd buried her parents. But it was an accident. One slip of the hand. None of them could have imagined in one moment what would come of it, how far it would spread, how fast, what all it would destroy. How deep the sorrow would go. But none of that mattered now; it was buried in Shrewsbury with her parents and Gran and a dead horse. He'd only been a boy, careless as boys are, and she, the laughing girl who'd chased him while he held fire. They couldn't have known then what they knew now.

Owen lifted a hand to her cheek. He could see it all playing out on her face, again and again. "He despised Mother when he learned about the lie I was, and that ruined all of us: her, my brothers. I've scarce touched a thing I didn't ruin." His eyes turned misty. "Hell, I ruined our baby. I couldn't even do that right." He looked away.

Her face contorted with hurt as she knotted the last of his stitches. "You set it right." She thought of what Samuel must have looked like in the morning light, dead in a slump it had been too dark for her to see. She was glad for that—she had enough visions of Stonington's dead. She tried to picture her father instead, but he was gone. Rosalie's face when Owen was around, however, she could picture perfectly; he could never have ruined his mother. Her joy in her sons was transcendent of all destruction. Ruth imagined that so, too, would be Rosalie's joy in her coming granddaughter. She put a hand to her belly, and then picked up his and did the same. "It's made all right now. Nothing can replace what was lost from our childhood, but her childhood has not yet been ruined."

"His," he smiled, but his eyes were still wet. He moved to say something, a concession perhaps, when a crack of splitting wood came from the main deck above them. It rattled the walls of the ship from stern to bow, threatening the collapse of planks around them.

"What in Triton's name was that?" one of the men yelled.

Owen bolted upright in his blankets. "The foremast!" Pain followed the motion, and he winced.

The remaining men pushed for the companionway to get to the weatherdeck.

"Quick, Ruth. Help me into some clothes."

"God's teeth." She took a deep breath, then helped him to his feet and over to the table. "They abandoned you. Let them rot."

"Thomas did not abandon me. Nor Frankie. They're up there. I will die on that deck for them should it be God's will. It's a code I can't break."

"If it be God's will, I shall trust nothing to that lout again."

Owen dropped his blankets to the floor and stood naked as he was born, rummaging through the pile of clothes the men had laid out on the table. Ruth looked away from his body quickly, out of reflexive convention more than shock, and waited for him to pull up his cotton hose. She only peeked once, but it was enough to remember the trough.

He came toward her, turning under the cuffs of the shirt he'd taken from the pile. "There now, I've nothing more to hide from you. You've seen me stripped as I was birthed."

"Shame I didn't see it before I left Stonington. I'd have stayed behind."

She took hold of his shirt, straightened out the underturned collar, and smoothed the fabric down over his chest, biting on her lower lip to keep from protesting. If he was going, he'd go, no matter what she said. She admired him for that, as she loathed it.

"Kiss me, doxy," he whispered.

Their lips met, and the storm lifted until the sounds of wet, leather boot soles clobbered the companionway steps to the gun deck like horse hooves. Owen jerked his boots over his swollen feet and strapped the tops to his belt ties, adjusted his carriage, checked that his dagger was still properly sheathed after a plunge into the sea, and faced his attention toward the commotion at the stairs.

"Get them men down below," Thomas called, and half a dozen drenched, injured men were rushed into the infirmary in the hammocked arms of spent crewmen. "Owen!" Thomas yelled as if over the storm, despite his proximity. "The staved foremast felled and teared through larboardside. A yardarm impaled the captain! Munroe, Stark, and Lordfellow be down, and we's lost half our railing."

Several more sailors broke through the infirmary door carrying wounded men, among them the bloodied body of the captain.

"Lay him out quick," Owen said, and as Ruth witnessed his confliction, she went to Jacob's side with a warm cloth, implements of repair, blankets, rag bandages. Blood seeped through Owen's breeches, but it didn't faze him.

Thomas' voice fair erupted, "The captain be indisposed, and I nay know what to do next. I be too exhausted." He bent, put a hand on his knee to prop himself, and put the other hand on Owen's arm. "Lead us as captain, for godsake."

Owen nodded, certainty standing him straighter. The men shook hands.

"Deck report, Captain." Thomas stood upright, clicked his boot heels together. "We's taking water over the broked rails faster'n can be drained. The foremast be broached and lodged across the bridge-deck access, and the mizzen might not hold out much longer. We be down to one anchor berthed. Water be seeping in the hull down to cargo. I can nay longer secure weatherdeck, Captain."

"Forget the deck," Owen ordered. "Get all the men below before they're thrown boardwise and lock everyone in with runners and dead-lights. Only men with specific assignments are to be on weather. If we lost the rails, then we lost the deck. Any part of the ship that can't be secured gets cut off. We're all tired, but this storm will not wait for us to get our strength back. Stay stalwart; drink clean water, not beer; keep focused. She doesn't have to look pretty, but we have to keep her afloat, mates." He made his assignments swiftly and confidently, and the men dispersed.

Stillwell and May dropped a new larboard anchor. Leaming and Richardson locked down the lower portside hold where the fore had fallen through. They reinforced it, stopped any leaking with passengers' clothing articles and pitch, and secured everything possible with leather straps. Crawford and Fenwick scoured the lower deck for damage, reinforced holes, patched them up. Whalers and Taylor managed the same with the cargo hold leaks, then tended to the terrified horses in jockey and drained their stalls by hand with buckets. Penn and Leonard rolled all heavy cargo to the edges of the ship and tied it down, compensating more weight on the larboard cargo to make up for the lack of anchor. Davis and Spicer calmed the passengers, brought them food if they hadn't eaten, but rationed everything carefully. They snuffed out any candles the passengers had and made apologies for the darkness, then stuffed rags into holes in the living cargo hold and instructed all persons to yell immediately if a leak were spotted. Frankie went into the crate holds and storerooms in search of fresh supplies. Edmund and Ruth tended to the injured men, and Owen made the infirmary his temporary captain's quarters until he was more rested. Thomas oversaw every station, and fear of facing Owen come dry deck made all the men work without protest.

Thomas returned for regular briefings, and the men sank back into a harmony that had existed before a fateful spring day had tested it. On his way out the door this time, he turned to Owen and said, "It's a honor to sail under you, Captain Townsend." The two men exchanged nods, and Thomas left.

With the worst of it ending and the loss mostly accepted, Owen shifted his attention to Ruth as she patiently cleaned and dressed Jacob's wounds, her eyes flitting about like a spritely dragonfly, despite the distress. Owen didn't dare ask how he was. He wasn't sure he wanted to know—what his reaction would be to either answer. "I need you to take care of the men with Ed. Keep them alive." He looked at Jacob. "All of them."

She faced him with a smile tugging at the fringes of her mouth. "Aye, Captain."

"You don't have to call me that."

"Aye, Captain."

Owen fought a grin, but it was nigh on impossible as he looked down into Ruth's beaming face. He was finally a captain.

CHAPTER SEVENTEENTH
The last sunrise

Of all the things visible,
the highest is the heaven of the fixed stars.

—Nicolaus Copernicus

The sky creased with a stain of pink in the distance, above the horizon. Clear ocean heavens rolled into a low fog that seemed to form over the ship and blanket into the shore, nearly swallowing it. The rain and wind had stopped by morning, and the damage to *Primrose*, though extensive, had not been terminal. She managed to stay afloat and unbroached without crew fatality. Marveling at how the great fluyt had come to rest in the cove, righting herself above the gentled waves, Owen took the flatbroom to the deck, squeegeeing the remaining water and debris over the edge of the broken railing. Quiet work for a quiet morning. His muscles pleaded bankruptcy. Gulls circled overhead, in and out of the fog, reappearing; they mocked his condition with walloping laughs. He had hardly slept, his motions mechanical, as he slid his gaze across the irreparably damaged deck, then onward to the open sea. He could almost believe that life was that calm, that he wasn't a treasonous, murdering fugitive about to jump ship with what was left of the crates, an unwed pregnant woman in tow, to run off and dissolve into the wildernesses surrounding New London, and maybe never look back at the ship that had sired him.

"What sirens are calling for you now?" Ruth's voice pealed like a song.

Owen jumped and turned to her standing behind him on the deck, haloed in fog, still wearing soggy clothing, her hair in damp strands about her shoulders. "You didn't sleep?"

"I was ordered by my captain to take care of injured men."

"I didn't think I had to order you to take care of yourself, as well. Have you ate?"

"I may have depleted significantly your rations of hardtack, yes, Captain."

"Don't make my son fat." He grinned.

"I don't think it works that way, Captain."

He yawned and scratched at the beard forming at his chin. "How is…" He paused, searching for a civil word.

"He's leveled somewhat, sleeping now. The yardarm missed anything of importance in him, if there is anything of importance in him."

She walked to the rail beside Owen and stared out over the water. Plumes of yellow split the sky's abdomen around puffed columns that looked as though St. Peter had opened a carriageway to the Gates. The clouds threw navy shadow spots over the water, the spots moving as the clouds moved. Ruth took it in with sailor's eyes, with his eyes, seeing the allure of the sea's rich trove of sparkling rhinestones. She swore she heard music, sea shanties floating over the calm, but soft and without chore. She appealed to her mind to solicit the notes, to memorize every one.

"You should be out of those wet clothes," Owen said. "You'll catch a chill."

"I have no others, Captain."

Each time she addressed him as such, his heart grew heavy. On the heels of his momentary liberation came a thought that veiled his face. He drifted back to the sorrow of the aftermath, littered with impatience to escape it or to accept it fully. He kept his eyes on the horizon, the fog at his back like a lurking memory, ready to shroud him in darkness. "Watch the sunrise with me. There's a perfect dawn after every storm. This is my favorite sky." He took hold of her wrist, still swollen and bandaged from being cut loose, and led her in front of him, pinned her gently between the rail and his chest, and rested his arms on the railing around her. "Shrewsbury. That last time I ran to your cottage, we went through a storm to the south, and there was a sunrise like this what followed. Dark purples and yellows like war cannon discharging. It felt like the beginning and end of everything. Then, I saw the grave—oh, God, the grave. I thought it yours. I thought they'd killed you right where you slept. I imagined all manner of terrible things, that you'd cursed every last one of them, and they'd hunted you down like a dog and left your frozen body to thaw out for wild beasts to devour. I cried there, I did. At that unmarked stone, over your body. Over horse bones in the stable. Tears I'd not shed since I was a boy. When I first seen you aboard *Primrose*, I thought you was a ghost I'd never be rid of, come to haunt me for abandoning you to the cursed winter."

Footsteps sloshed through the puddles on the deck. "Doesn't you never sleep, Captain?" Thomas asked, joining the couple against the rail.

"Not of late."

"By God, that be a beautiful sunrise. Like 'at storm never even happened."

"I'd agree if I wasn't looking past you at a disintegrated ship." Owen's face hung like an unhinged door as he took in her haggard form with dolor. Her fallen mast would make the crew's journey back to Fairfield a slow go. It solidified his nerve to abandon. He ought to tell Ruth. He thought of telling Thomas, but that much nerve wasn't in him now. *Primrose*, his mother's namesake, her battered planks, his home.

"Aye, the old gal was tied to the whipping post." The wind slower, gentler. Thomas studied the shattered railing, downed mainmast, splintered bowsprit, listing mizzenmast, unshipped and torn sails, severed anchor chains, leaking plank seams. He smacked Owen on the back with an assuaged grin. "You can have this whole mess. She be all your problem, Captain." He lifted the broom to push the remaining deck water through the scuppers on his way to the aft portside. "I will, of course, expect to remain your first mate," he said, back turned.

"And who could I ever replace you with, huh? Kingsley?"

The two men exchanged an uneasy laugh that trailed across the deck, and Owen looped back to Ruth at the rail. Her face was flusher than the sunrise, and he looked away. The ship wouldn't be his—or hers—but she still beamed aboard it.

"Oh, stop it," he said.

"Aye, Captain. Whatever you say, Captain."

He muttered to himself, "C'est ma chance."

"Oui. Saisis-la!"

Her words impressed him, and his heart thumped into his ribs, though the two of them unwittingly spoke of different chances. He tilted her chin upward with his forefinger and moved his mouth toward hers, and he would have moved tide and shore to have stayed in this moment, but the alarming sound of the watchman's voice caught fire in his ear and propelled him back abruptly, turning the couple's attention to portside.

"Intruders! Larboard! All hands on deck!" The words were a gunshot across the planks, shouted through the speaker trumpet.

Under the insufficient watch of fatigued men, privateers rowed briskly from the shore at the shortest distance, cloaked in fog, and were mounting the ratlines portside. Owen looked to the rail to see five pirates, armed with cut-and-thrusts and civilian rapiers, crouched at larboard with swords drawn. Over the rail, more heads popped up, and the men advanced swiftly, several toward Thomas and the sailing master. Before Ruth knew what was happening, Owen had his dagger unsheathed.

"Bring me Égard!" he said, grabbing her by the arm and dragging her from the invaders' line of sight. "Warn the men of attack!" He prodded her in the direction of the companionway, and he turned to face the fray with his dagger glinting in the sun like a beacon.

He leaped onto the fallen foremast and felt the throb in his thigh, then swooped from above with his dagger downward, driving it between a pirate's shoulderblades. The pirate went down without seeing what had hit him. Owen retracted the blade and swiped it across the neck of the next advancing attacker, before stepping to the side of the man's descending sword, leaving the falling edge to lodge itself into the planks of the deck. The opponent fell forward, his throat opening like a sluice gate, a stream of crimson onto the floorboards. Owen kicked the body aside and drew the wedged sword from the wood. This was not the sword of a pirate. No, the side-sword he retrieved from beneath the dead man belonged to the British military brigades under colonial command. *Militiamen.*

Half a dozen more climbed over the rails from the rope ladders below, emerging from the fog, and he strained to see them, their boats, how many there were. "Cut the ratlines!" He made his way toward Thomas and slid the appropriated sword along the deck to his first mate. "Behind you, Tom! They aren't bloody pirates. They're English militia." His crew filled the decks, sleepily, unready, utilizing whatever weapons they could find, and he knew they would be outnumbered within moments. There would be a price to be paid for their exhaustion.

He heard the cry of a female behind him, unmeshing with the assemblage of masculine shouts. He turned, and Ruth stood before him, shielded beneath the bridge-deck breezeway, extending before her the scabbard of Égard, hilt-first toward him. Her crested poise paralleled a sea goddess of fables, cheeks scarlet from the sun's torment. He wrapped his knuckles around the waisted grip, slipped his forefinger through the ricasso, and felt her hold on. He drew the saber from the scabbard with one hand, the forged blade sliding effortlessly along the oiled-fur lining, as if the sheath's throat had spit her from its mouth.

"Hide!" he said. "Go below, anywhere you cannot be found." She shook her head, and he turned back around. "Then get a weapon!"

He met his blade with that of an advancing militiaman. Owen's body was overcome by instinct: exhaustion laid waste. He matched the man's steel and sidestepped dispatched swings with catlike grace. A distracting shout came over the rail, and the Englishman turned his head. Owen thrust the tip of his sword through the Englishman's heart, then breathed in the heavy affirmation that comes with the pulsation of a dying man's organ impaled at the foible. Before he could dislodge the blade, the edge of a side-sword cascaded toward his left side. He raised the dagger in his left hand and parried the slinging sword away from him, a rippling shake traveling up to his shoulder, buying enough time to draw Égard from the dead man and slash her across the advancing attacker's stomach. Égard cut a clean slice through the man's gut without effort, as if parting whipped mascarpone. The Englishman was still lucid when he witnessed himself spilling upon the deck, a stench of bile and excrement that made Owen's mouth go sour. The sailor delivered a mercy blow with his dagger into the man's heart, although he wasn't sure his opponent's senses had lasted long enough to appreciate the pardon.

On the deck, Lordfellow and Thomas stood back to back, fighting outward, and Owen made his way toward Frankie, near the larboard rail with a sword she'd picked up from the deck, to protect against the overwhelming number of militiamen forcing her backward. Before Owen could reach her, an Englishman stood ready to bring his sword, raised high above the head, down across the top of her shoulders.

"Frankie!"

Owen dived forward with Égard's flatback to deflect the sword edge falling toward her and parried it aside in time for her to stab the attacker in the ribs. Catching hold of the parried sword, Owen lifted its dull back between the forte and the foible and half-sworded another militiaman in the chest, then sidled back to back with Frankie, each providing mutual coverage for the other's blind side. More militiamen climbed over the starboard rail, and the crew fell back or fell down all around him. His eyes lit on Kingsley and May, Davis and Stillwell, then back to Thomas, outnumbered. Owen couldn't get to him. If he tried, it meant leaving Frankie open, and she was small and inexperienced and not a Jonah to militiamen as she would have been to pirates. She moved her head to dodge an incoming jab, and the sword sailed inches past her face and into the back of Owen's shoulder. The pain struck him as quickly as the blade. He struggled to focus on the adversary in front of him, but he could feel the blade pushing through his shoulder from behind, ripping muscle and flesh, the sound like tightening a saddle cinch. With a grunt, the Englishman yanked the blade out of the captain's back. Owen felt the tip withdrawing from his shoulder, the hole that it left. The pain of the exit was worse than that of the entrance, full and hot, and he yelled.

He whipped his saber around, disoriented, sending his metallic-gold-and-red sword knot into a frenzy of distraction. The ploy succeeded, and the Englishman failed to block the incoming strike. A slash through the man's wrist severed his swordhand from his arm and sent it to the deck, still clutching the impotent court sword. The man fell away in agony, and before Owen could deliver a coup de grâce, another side-sword came at him.

He raised both his saber and his dagger in an X above his head to block the incoming sword, but the power of the blow propelled him backward and left the lower half of his body exposed to another fighter attempting to flank the sailor. Falling to the ground, Owen parried the first side-sword away while rolling under it along the planks, causing the unbalanced men to plunge downward toward him. Extending Égard out before him, he raised the tip toward the two plummeting assailants and impaled the first through the gut, sending the second onto the out-stretched sword of the first. The combined deadweight pressed Égard's hilt back against him, crushing his abdomen with the pommel, and he groaned loudly.

Winded and pushing himself out from under the two men, he slid his blade clear and rolled to his knees, only to find himself at the mercy of another man's weapon. Owen halted, kneeling, his face inches from the point of a militiaman's side-sword, but the Englishman made no motion. Owen followed the length of the stilled sword to the tip of the civilian rapier protruding through the man's chest, holding him in place, a grotesque statue. As the corpse dropped to the ground before him, the shaking figure of Ruth stood in its stead, clutching the accountable rapier in a white-knuckled grip. She was unable to utter a sound for the revolution of it, but she stood bold. Stunned, he fixated on her. She dropped the rapier from her hand and looked at him, begging instruction. Blood ran down his right arm. His eyes glazed over. The shock crept up him like a poison.

"Hold on to that sword," he managed, "and get out of here. This is nothing for you to see. Hide! Hide yourself aw—"

A pain struck him near the heart so intense that he was certain it must be death. His blood rushed to his chest. The warming sensation numbed him. His body was going limp, went limp, came back. Went limp. He looked down to see the point of a sword at his other shoulder, mirroring his previous wound. He felt the intruder behind him, pushing the blade forward and upward. The agony was shiny, an orb of light, many lights, stars, then graying. He instinctually grabbed hold of the blade, praying it stop driving through him. Blood creased between his clenched fingers.

Ruth raised her sword again and rammed the attacker and screamed, but Owen couldn't hear it. He shooed her but made no motion, willed her to flee, but not a man went after her. She swung her sword, and they stepped back, and she swiped at air, and they stepped back again, out of range, waiting. But the man behind him fell; she'd gotten him. Owen tried to breathe, but each gasp hurt. Took concentration. Then, wouldn't come at all. He would soon follow the man behind him to the deck, he knew. He shook it, shook the thought. Shook it as his body shook.

He rested his dagger across his knees. The blade ran red, and the red dripped around his kneecap. Ruth knelt and drew the blade from his back, and he watched the tip at the front of his chest. It slid out as it had entered, leaving an impressive hole, and she let the blade drop to the deck behind him. It wouldn't be long before another militiaman picked it up, but Owen hadn't the strength to turn for it. He struggled to get to his feet, but the damage was too great—waited for the miséricorde, but knew it would not be granted. His was to be a slow death at the hands of the militia.

Fiery sunspots. An ocean rising up. A fog with fingers tore at his clothes, his skin, his chest. Hot, fevering. He focused again on Ruth, tears streaming down her cheeks, unreachable now. She was surrounded. They were surrounded.

"General!" a nearby voice yelled past Owen's ear from one of the advancing men, and he heard it again, again, echoic as thunder.

At the sound of it, a rush of strength came over him. He wiped the blade of his dagger across his breeches and sheathed it in his boot. Somehow—some ungodly how—he managed to lift himself to his feet. Clenching both hands around Égard's hilt, he raised her into an alber position, readying himself. Blood streaked down both arms. His shirt sleeves were soiled in a bourn of claret that reddened the sharkskin grip and dripped off the blade's tip. The sailor released a cry like an eidolon, appearing as if a reincarnation of himself with all his power anew.

He wielded his sword against the blows. He felt nothing but the motion of his blade, until a blast pealed through the air, and Égard was stricken from his hand, his flesh stinging, not by another sword, but by the ricocheting *plink-plink* of a bullet sparking off the blade at his fingers. He struggled for the recall of the sword knot as the handle spun from his grasp. The battle had changed. Owen turned toward the shot, and his body convulsed. On the other end of the drawn flintlock stood the foreboding figure of Lieutenant General Samuel Whitlock, his right arm dressed in a sling, and his left holding outstretched the still-smoking gun.

"Seize that traitor!" Samuel yelled. Sweat dripped down his forehead.

The militiamen within earshot followed the point of Samuel's flint-lock toward Owen. The sailor found himself surrounded by five, then seven, then a dozen swords and clubs drawn to his chest, and through the din, someone handed Samuel a freshly loaded gun.

"Take him alive. I want to watch him hang."

"I went willingly once. This time you'll have to kill me." Owen blocked fists and jabs that came at him, until eventuality took its course.

"There's better sport to be had." Samuel turned to the men standing near him. "Kill every last man." He looked at Owen. "And torch this whole Godforsaken ship."

Owen's eyes went wide, and he heard the screams around him. Fists grabbed him, his jacket. His saber was knocked to the deck and his sword knot sliced from his bloodied hand. He could only stare as the militiamen sparked gunpowdered torches that lit up like Greek Fire. Damp though she was, *Primrose*'s old wood burst into a flourishing or-ange haze around the crew, and Owen watched, stricken, as the blaze swept toward the companionway.

"There are pass...passengers below. Injured men. Horses. Gunpow-der...in the hold. You'll blow your own men apart."

Samuel took calculated strides toward Owen, the click. click. click. speaking for him. He slid his gun into its chest loop and paused in front of the sailor. "I warned your father not to defy me with a traitor aboard this ship. It appears I didn't make myself clear enough. You defy me, you will burn. Where is your father, First. Mate. Townsend?"

"I am not first mate." A sharp thwack of a pommel into his ribs doubled him over.

"I will ask you again. Where is your father?"

Owen was quiet, twitching in pain.

Samuel motioned for one of his men to fetch a captured member of *Primrose*'s crew. Owen looked up to see the unfortunate person of Lordfellow driven to his knees next to Samuel. The lieutenant general took hold of Lordfellow's hair and pulled his head back, but Samuel's glare never left Owen.

"Where is your father?"

"Holding open your pew in hell," Owen spat. "Sir."

Without warning, Samuel unsheathed his sword and drew the blade across Lordfellow's throat and threw the body to the deck. A gurgle, then stillness. Owen gagged, his insides plunging, and Samuel motioned for a militiaman to retrieve another captive.

"Do we need to do this again, boy?" Samuel forced *Primrose* pilot Edgar Stillwell to his knees next to Lordfellow's dead body. "Where is your father?"

Owen looked at Stillwell's frightened face and muttered, "Infirmary. Injured during the storm." The sailor scanned the calamitous landscape of his ship, her damaged rails blazing yellow and orange, the plumes of smoke rushing to the sky in fruitless signals. He calculated the depth to the gunpowder, when she'd go and they'd all go with her.

"Unfortunate for him." Samuel turned and drove his sword through Stillwell's chest. The impaled sailor let out a difficult whimper before slumping to the deck next to Lordfellow.

Owen looked away.

The lieutenant general sheathed the court sword. "A captain goes down with his boat, Owen. A little legend of the sea you might have learned h—"

"I am the captain of this ship, and she is *not a boat*! A boat is how you got onto my ship!"

Samuel's eyes lit with new life. "This coffin will burn before I'll see it sailed beneath a French flag. Take him hence."

As Samuel turned from Owen, the sailor writhed impotently in the grasp of the militiamen. His own men fell in numbers around him. At the portside rail, Frankie—and an advancing militiaman struck her through the gut with a court sword. Owen sank. He watched her slump to the deck as he slumped. His eyes, of their own, traced the deck for

Ruth and found her beneath the breezeway near the aftcastle, tending fruitlessly to a fallen crewman. Who was it?—he could not tell. *Ruth*. At the sight of her, he fought against the soldiers. The trail of the fire moved toward her like it was summoned, soon to pin her against the bridge-deck wall. She would be trapped and burned alive with the rest of the crew and passengers. He refused the image.

At Owen's commotion, Samuel faced him. "Silence that traitor. You got some mutiny in you still, boy?"

Owen's face met with knuckles on his nose and mouth. Blood left his split lip and septum, cracked. His vision blurred. When his mouth opened in feigned reply, his teeth were no longer seashell, but the spotted red of winterberries, a string of torn mouthflesh dangling across them. As the Englishman moved to thrash his pommel into the sailor's face again, the action was stopped short by Samuel.

"Do you not yield, boy?"

"I do not yield." Owen twisted free and got one knee under him, rose on it.

Samuel marched to him, drew the flintlock from its holster, and slowly, deliberately, began the process of loading it with one hand while Owen watched. Samuel blew some remaining powder from the exterior and touched the barrel to Owen's forehead as if all routine. "Let me persuade you otherwise." He lowered the gun swiftly from Owen's head and fired a shot through the sailor's right foot. The bullet rived through leather, skin, bone, vessel, and wood, and the splashback of blood and tissue erupted across Owen's face and up to Samuel's epaulets.

Owen screamed and hunched over his foot, trying to catch the blood spilling between his fingertips as it fountained from the hole in his boot. His tongue twilled and wefted to the roof of his mouth. He looked up at Samuel, delirious haze surrounding them both, all, and he could only muster, "Ruth."

"What was that, boy?"

"Save her." He pointed to her near the bridge deck where fires swarmed.

Samuel followed the head nod and outstretched finger. "Ah, wouldn't that be your final appeal? The harlot. Save the girl. How noble. Tsk-tsk, I fear you and I haven't reached an understanding." He gripped Owen's hair and wrenched his head back. "My duty here is not to retrieve my wife; it is to watch you suffer. So tell me, boy: what if I don't save her?"

Owen lost his balance on his knee, swayed. "She is with child."

"Oh yes, I know she carries my son. And after her, another woman will. Save her? No, boy. You will watch her burn." He twisted Owen's head toward her, then released him, and the sailor's head snapped forward.

Owen hung it over his foot, the firelike sensation creeping further into his kneecap and thigh and abdomen like a smoldering cloak. Gray-red fog. His sight, going. Ruth, going. Burning leather and singed flesh coated his nostrils; the stench intoxicated him in a haze of fumes. His throat, so parched and stripped that he could no longer speak, allowed a final breath too sharp to withstand, and he closed his eyes against it and slumped over, thudding on the deck. The militiamen took hold of his clothing and hauled him to the rail.

Samuel watched until the body had gone over portside, then turned away. He looked to the raging deck fire and past it toward the morning sunrise. Without notice of the painted skies, he barked across the deck like a rabid dog, "Burn this coffin!"

CHAPTER EIGHTEENTH
With trial; without benefit

I can calculate the motion of heavenly bodies,
but not the madness of people.

—Sir Isaac Newton

"Welcome back to the Stonington gaol." Samuel Whitlock ran his pistol along the bars of Owen's cell. "Mon-si-eur Townsend."

The sailor was back in the same hold, extra pains taken to ensure there would be no escaping it. Iron chains held his wrists behind his back, and stock encasements bound his ankles. No tender had stitched his lacerated shoulders nor dressed his shattered midfoot. Instead, a solid-iron ball was shackled around his wounded leg, resting against his disintegrated arch, severed muscles and tissue. A brown puddle collected in sawdust beneath his body. Crusted maroon transuded his clothing around his shoulders and armpits, at his shirt collar where it caught drips from his split face.

Samuel extracted a white handkerchief from the breast pocket of his jerkin and held the delicate linen to the bars. "What is this?"

"A kerchief." Owen's speech was slurred, unrecognizable.

"Yes, a kerchief. O-W-T." Samuel read the embroidered initials as if learning to spell from a child's hornbook. "Seems an interesting coincidence, does it not, Mr. Owen Ward Townsend?"

"That's *Captain* Owen Ward Townsend."

Samuel laughed, then held up the handkerchief again, shifting from foot to foot. "You dare tell me this is not yours?"

"If you dare tell me you let her burn."

Samuel smirked. "Let me say this another way. Did you bed my wife in my own bed where this was found beneath her pillow?"

Owen wished he could admit to the alluring deed. He imagined her hands beneath the pillow, soft as they once had been when they touched him, caressing the cloth while she lay there, cursing his return. "Any man or woman along this coast could have the same initials. Ornate majuscule is quite the fashion. For all I know, it come from the very pocket of an *Obsessive War Tyrant.*"

"I've hung men for far less significant coincidences."

"Congratulations, sir." He slurred it. "Initials on cloth be pretty insignificant."

He wadded it in his fist. "Did you bed my wife, you worthless brigand?"

"Does a trough count for a bed?"

Samuel flexed his chest so hard he popped a button that had been loosely clinging to its line. His shirt was too tight, the fabric shrunken from rain or heavy washing; Owen saw that now. How lofty the man thought he was, in outgrown clothes. The brass plinked on the floor, and the button rocked like a dreidel. Samuel raised his gun toward Owen. The sailor narrowed the one eye that would move.

"I committed no adultery with your wife. Can you sleep peaceful now?"

"As peaceful as your men at the bottom of the sea."

Owen's gut seized, a gripe low inside him. He'd heard the explosion. It had rocked him from deep unconsciousness and struck him like a club. He had known then as he knew now: his men were at the bottom of the sea. "They were good English men. You aim to wound me, but you killed your own. Expect no honor from that."

"They were traitors. You traitors will meet the noose or Davy Jones, I don't care which, but you will not walk free on the Dominion of New England."

"There is no Dominion. Open your eyes. You have a new king. The Dominion is abolished. I'll see Fiddler's Green before I'll see another Dominion."

Samuel slammed his pistol against the bars and tried to grasp hold of the iron with his slung arm. "I'll core that traitor tongue with a bodkin! Your men disobeyed me. Your father disobeyed me."

Owen grinned sadly. "You can't bear to lose something you own."

Samuel squeezed the trigger and fired a shot from his flintlock past Owen's head and into the cell wall. The sailor felt the ball breeze by, flutter his hair, but he kept his eyes locked on Samuel. Half a dozen guards appeared near the cell door, lined beside the lieutenant general. He unlocked the double chain around the bars slowly and tossed the handkerchief to the floor at the prisoner's feet.

Samuel stepped back as the men entered. "Keep him breathing."

❦

Two hours crept by on a snail's belly as the lower-Stonington meetinghouse filled with eager faces of the town. Ruth sat in the pew, fingering some chipped paint, an empty seat on either side. She knew this well, this alienation. History flooded over her, and the scene squirmed in ugly familiarity as it unfolded before her. They'd come to burn the witch.

The setting was farcical. The head councilor and selectmen hadn't even seen fit to hold the trial in the upper King's Court or to take it to the magistrates in Mystic. The lower meetinghouse was situated closer to the gallows and closer to the councilor's home, so it was preferable on all accounts for a case already decided. Traveling distance, taking all that time away from a day's work for a foregone conclusion, would not have been a popular choice for a Monday.

Ruth sat to the left of the council pulpit where she had been ushered. To her left, the meetinghouse filled with the shop owners and farmers she'd come to know. She found Isabel and Daniel Osborne in the crowd, tears spotting Isabel's downturned face, Daniel's gloved hands folded before him in prayer as he kneeled by his wife. Seeing them instilled a wound. Ruth's shame rose from her like a scent, permeated the air around her, and she sat in it. She wondered if Isabel would be called to speak against Owen, if the elderly woman would be pressed to reveal their secret to the room. She caught Isabel's eye, and the two women exchanged a nod.

Across the room, Helen Starks sat with Matthew and their boys but could not meet Ruth's glance. Ruth bowed her head, unable to withstand any more. She counted the seconds until she would see Owen crucified before her. All the secrets her heart had interred and intended to keep buried would be dragged out in chains and beaten in the center of the room like a blackbird. She thought of the word, of Samuel. Her secret was also his blackbird, owned, a price on it if it tore loose. She squeezed her eyes shut, willed herself to breathe, afraid to open her eyes again in case the terrible anticipation of Owen's suffering might turn her composure to dust sprinkled at the floor of the pew. The wrought-iron poker branding her skin again. She was in the midst of God's self-proclaimed. Their judgment was hot and permanent.

Mid-thought, a brush against her skin jolted her back into the church. Now sitting in the pew to her right was Helen. Ruth faced away. Helen reached out and took her hand, pressing it calmly, void of moral verdict. The room grew stuffy with body odors, and Ruth noticed the rancid smells, focused on them. Unclean men who reeked of the animals they husbanded, and women too long in their same shifts without washing. The closed doors and shuttered windows squeezed both scrutiny and bodies inside like a stuffed doublet ready to burst through its seams.

"I know," Ruth whispered. "I should have waited. I deserve this."

"No woman deserves this." She lifted an arm around Ruth and held her, rocked her. Helen pulled a face at a farmer who looked at them disapprovingly.

When it seemed all air had been sucked from the room, the door blew open. Not a spectator in the room could break fixation from the entranceway and the commotion there. It took three strong men to drag Owen through the aperture. Two more had to join to get him up to the stand beside the pulpit. His body was unable to move of its own accord, his head slumped forward with blood draining from his mouth and nose. His eyes were swollen shut. A wash of smeared crimson wove along the floor behind his trailing boots like an extravagant red carpet rolled out for the benefit of the King's Council that would follow.

Ruth's ribs collapsed at the sight of him. His face and broken body were not his. He looked like he should be dead, like he'd died several times over. Helen gripped Ruth's fingers as the townsmen positioned him into a chair at the side of the council's pulpit.

Still chained at the wrists and ankles, he held up his head with considerable effort and scanned the crowd. They were struck mute at his beaten state; a pause hung in the air that begged to remain, and the most self-righteous among them would not have wished his predicament on a mosquito in the thick of summer. His eyes came to rest on Ruth. He exhaled, and it hurt. *She was alive.*

Ruth's lips had been split by Samuel's fist. Puffy purple bruises and red blotches of dried blood decorated her cheekbones: a warning sign for Owen to watch his conduct. He knew that she had paid a price to leave Stonington with him, and the guilt hardened him. The meeting-house door swung open, letting in a bout of fresh air on the heels of two silhouetted figures striding into the room. The townfolk turned to watch the entrance of Lieutenant General Samuel Whitlock. Ruth looked at Owen, and his face appeared vanquished. Samuel shook hands with Councilor Burke, and Owen's eyes closed.

Councilor Burke was a regal if dowdy man, dressed in brown doe-skin breeches with a white trim sewn the length of the outer seam and a matched jerkin buttoned over a clean ivory linen shirt, starched collar rising to his earlobes. He adjusted his powdered English wig and approached the pulpit before a Bible, a piece of parchment, and an ink-well. The congregation rose as he seated himself. Except Owen, whose desire to stand was even slighter than his ability to do so. With eyes cast to the floor, he saw two polished boots come to a halt before the stand, heels clicked together militarily.

"Disrespectful boy, you will stand for Councilor Burke," Samuel said.

Without looking up, Owen slurred, "I can't stand. You put a ball through my foot." His speech was slower than usual, dysarthriatic and unclear—at length, incomprehensible—but he was primarily lucid.

Samuel clutched the boy's jacket and heaved him upright. A sour smell came from Samuel's slung arm. Owen's weight was forced over his shattered foot, and he let escape a moan. Gasps from the room. Some townswomen gripped the pewbacks in front of them. Samuel let go of Owen's collar. The sailor collapsed back to the seat. It had taken most of his energy to manage that much, and he was winded.

Ruth buried her face in her hands and mumbled. She was struck quiet by the procession of the council and Helen's embrace wrapping her shoulders tighter.

"It is my understanding," Councilor Burke began at the pulpit, "that we be collected to determine if this young man is a traitor to the Crown in our time of war. Judging by his uncourtly state, it is evident he has already been determined thus so." He glared at Samuel. "Therefore, I declare this trial expedient, so we may be dismissed in time for an early dinner." He turned his attention back to Samuel. "You all know Lieutenant General Samuel Whitlock, selectman of this town, appointed by the king to represent the English Crown on this, the Crown's soil." Burke next nodded to the sailor. "Boy, state yourself."

"Owen Townsend, Captain of *Primrose*, defunct." He struggled to make words, but they were heard well enough to proceed.

"A captain with a defunct ship is a captain of nothing. Hapless occupation." He gestured. "Lieutenant General, the floor."

"Your Council," Samuel nodded, "I'll be ad rem at once. This widdiful boy is French, if not a spy for Louis' Alliance or the Viceroyalty. He speaks the tongue as well as any native and airs it freely. He has murdered the Crown's men, injured me thus"—He flapped his sling like a bird wing and winced. The smell came again, and even Councilor Burke physically recoiled—"and sailed as captain on a ship that refused to carry munitions from Boston to our allied garrisons in the fight against New France. Under the king's rulings in these matters, I move for this boy to be convicted of treason, a crime punishable by de—"

"I attacked only after being attacked," Owen interrupted. "My men acted in kind when attacked first by your men."

"Are you calling me a liar?"

"I was not captain of *Primrose* when the ship was proposed with munitions. That was under the command of late Jacob Townsend, an English royalist, who I succeeded only in brief, and who...who be now dead by your command. It is unjust I should stand accused of his crime. Seems to me he paid it."

"This very man turned you in to me as a traitor."

"Aye, to save his crew after you threatened him if he nay did so. To be expected considering what a target you were willing to make his ship to privateers, without regard for his papers of safe conduct. We had safe conducts, Your Council."

"Where be those papers?" Burke asked.

Owen smirked. "Check his pockets."

"Privateers, did you say?" Whitlock deflected. "You mean others of your kind, Townsend?"

"It's Captain Townsend."

"Captain of what ship?"

"The one you burned, sir. With passengers and crew aboard."

The townfolk gasped and murmured, and Samuel reddened. "You kidnapped my pregnant wife. I shudder to think of the deeds you committed on that pirate ship. Taught her your dastardly French tongue. Gave her French books to poison her English mind." He mimed flipping the pages of a book, then crunched the phantom object in his fists.

Owen grinned. "The real reason I'm here."

"Lieutenant General," Burke said, "your wife is not on trial here. Keep to task."

"On the contrary," Owen said. "She is on trial, poor creature. You can attack my character, my background, my name, but there is no proof of anything here. It all comes down to me," he pointed to himself, "knowing her." He pointed to Ruth, and the stares of the room followed his finger.

"And how do you know her?" Samuel asked.

"That nay be the story for this court."

"Tell me."

Owen hesitated and breathed hard. "At eleven years of age, I murdered her parents in a fire. The deaths were an accident; the fire—" He looked hard at Ruth. "—was...was just play. Is that what this room wants to hear? I orphaned her and she took the blame for it, and I let her. I will plea to that a thousand times, and I'll hang humble for that crime as I shoulda hung then. But I'll never plea to being a traitor in your war over conquered land I want no part of."

"You'd have us believe your only guilt stems from the acts of a child? Come now, boy; we demand justice." Samuel approached him and knocked his slung arm into the sailor's shoulder. The odor that wafted from it had a pungency of damp cargo holds. "You did this to my arm."

"And you did this to me!" Owen's anger fell hard, swiftly from his mouth, unchecked. "Look at your arm? Look at *me*. You shot a hole through my foot. Broke my nose and ribs with mattocks while I was bound. Unarmed. Your men run swords through my back. You murdered my captain, my crew." He breathed heavily, and his anguish was palpable, stupefying to the onlookers. "You set fire to my ship carrying thousands of pounds of food and supplies that could have garnished your entire town for a year, no doubt burning alive thirty-two passengers and twelve beautiful horses with it. You took the woman I love, abused her, destroyed what little joy she had left, forced her to become your wife who should have been mine, then stole my unborn child!"

Ruth's chest constricted. The room fell quiet, without breaths. *There it was.* Her cheeks flushed the color of French wine, and she felt the heat rising up her neck, strangling her bootless throat. She lowered her eyes when she heard the sigh that escaped Helen. Ruth figured her friend would withdraw tenderness at the new admission, but Helen clutched her hand tighter and hugged in closer. Ruth had been wrong: Helen was not distance.

"Child?" Samuel recovered. "My child?"

"*My* child." Owen thumbed his chest the best he could. "You speak of truth and justice as if you could define either one. The truth is worse for you than any false witness. The truth is that her child is mine."

"Yours." Samuel curled his lips at the word.

"The truth is that you shoulda just let me leave the harbor."

Samuel mounted the rail near Owen's stand, grabbed the sailor by the hair, and yanked the boy from the chair across the railing. "You adulterous traitor!"

He struggled to move his head out of the maddening grasp. "We committed none."

Councilor Burke waved for townsmen to pull Samuel from the incapacitated boy. "Lieutenant General, this tribunal is not about your wife."

"It is all about my wife!" Samuel threw from his shoulders the townsmen who tried to control him. "You, Townsend, are a liar. An adulterer, a traitor, a murderer, a…kidnapper, a pirate, and a scoundrel!"

"And you, Lieutenant General, are a torturer, a murderer, an arsonist, a tyrant, a lousy commander, and a narcissist." Owen tongued the inside of his mouth where Samuel's fist had landed, then spit a loosened tooth out at the general in a spray of red. "And last I knew, there was no law against being a scoundrel."

Ruth peeped, and Samuel turned to face her. "You scorned your husband," he questioned, "by bedding this man?"

"No, sir," she replied quickly. If the truth was being told, then so be it. She wouldn't let Owen dangle alone. "Never with you as my husband."

"But. If not as your husband, then…" He blinked rapidly several times. "I took you for a chaste bride."

"No more chaste than you, sir."

He stiffened and flung himself toward the pulpit like a child in the midst of a tantrum. His sling followed his movement like an attached ragdoll, and his voice cracked. "This woman's vows mean nothing. She has nullified our union, and I renounce her as my wife."

"Control yourself, Lieutenant General, or this court will be adjourned with no verdicts issued." Burke pounded a mallet onto the pulpit so loudly that half the room started. "You don't get to renounce your wife and release her in disavowal. You took her before God."

"She lied before God."

"Then perhaps you should have courted her longer before you wed a girl half your age. One fresh off the boat, no less." Burke cast a look toward Owen. "Or in this case, not terribly fresh."

"But that is not her only secret revealed to me after—after!—I wed her, Your Council. She conveniently forgot to mention that she is a witch."

The room choked in collective disapproval of the word. Superstitious goodwives knelt in prayer at the thought a witch could be in assembly among them, making great show of their faith. Audible chants went up from a pocket of the room. The mere mention sent them into seated panic, stirring and shuffling feet, whispering to neighbors, some of them finding something to throw to defend themselves when it came to it. Ruth gripped the railing in front of her. *That word.*

"That is quite an accusation. You've seen her commit dark craft, Sam?" Burke said, formalities laid to waste.

"No, I confess I have not witnessed it, but she is marked. Upon her flesh where no man could miss it, she is twice branded." He bounded toward her, seized her arm, and peeled her from her seat.

She struggled to break from his grasp as he battled with her petticoat with his one working arm. "No! Sam, stop. I beg you," she cried.

But he corralled her against the pew, lifted her skirt, and squeezed hold of her flesh, revealing plainly to the room two branded W's burned deep within her inner thighs. Instantly, the voices rose louder from the crowd, whispers to shouts, and she wriggled to free herself. Helen, appalled, clambered to release Ruth's skirts from Samuel's hold, but he slammed the woman back into her seat, her elbow hitting the wood, her head striking the banister.

"Have decency, Whitlock!" Owen yelled. He tried in vain to pull himself up on his shattered foot to get to Ruth.

Matthew Starks jolted from his pew. "Do nay lay a hand on my wife, you claybrained boar tit!" He jumped over the pew's railing to get between Samuel and Helen. "Show humility while my boys be watching." Over the threshold, three men of the court dragged Matthew back across the railing and pushed him down in his seat. He thrashed, but one of the men cuffed him.

Burke joined in: "Release your wife at once. Your wife is not on trial here."

"Enough!" A new voice broke through the din that quelled the room in a rippling effect as each head turned. Daniel Osborne rose from his pew. "Not another word against this girl. You should be ashamed of your conduct to her. She is headstrong, aye, wayward. She lacks discipline. But she is no more a witch than you or me. Her punishment has been handed for a cause that is not brought before this court today, and she will bear that price for eternity. It is not ours to cast this judgment a second time. If she is to be blamed for brands she carries, then let us all be blamed for our own, as well."

"Daniel." Isabel tugged on his sleeve.

He brushed her fingers aside and removed his gloves, tossed them to the pew, and held out his hands in prospect of the room, flipping them from front to back for a full view of each side. There, burned into the backs and palms of both hands, were the time-faded, yet clearly visible, marks of a searing bodkin that had been laid across his skin until the flesh had singed away—a secret from another town, another life.

"We didn't come to this tribunal to speak of adultery or bastards or witchcraft or to see a poor orphaned girl slandered so," he said. "Here I stand before you, a man who's carved your furniture for over twenty years. A man you've trusted and welcomed into this town, this meeting hall, your church, your homes. A man you thought you knew, whose past you don't know at all. We all have brands—some show; some don't. But we all wear them. It is not ours to judge these transgressions of others while we wear our own." He raised his hands to some unseen light. "Let he among us without sin be the first to cast that stone. You know the passage well, but you do not practice it."

Reticence laid over the room such that a person could hear every other person's thoughts as plainly as if spoken. A stunned Samuel had released Ruth in the midst of this deliverance, and she hid herself behind the cover of the pew's railing. Helen, her hand to her own head, bent toward Ruth and wrapped her skirts around her to hide her.

Burke cleared his throat. "Well. That was…certainly an unexpected plea for Mrs. Whitlock. Those are wise words, Mr. Osborne; let us heed them and cast no further judgment." Burke lifted his gavel and made to lower it.

"But. The traitor." Samuel pointed at Owen.

"Ah." Burke rested his forehead in his hands and massaged his temples. When he reopened his eyes, he seemed surprised to see that he still had a room of people staring at him. "Boy, I've half a mind to let you go after what you've been through, but I'd be hanged myself for cowardice. Answer me plain, if you will: do you speak French?"

"Aye, sir," Owen said.

"You can say, 'I am the captain of a ship,' in French?"

"Je suis le capitaine d'un navire. En français." He looked at Ruth, and she smiled thinly.

"And you can read French?"

"Aye, sir."

"And your ancestry is French?"

"Aye, sir."

Samuel interjected, "His father is—was—English."

"Incorrect, sir. Both of my parents are French and alive." Owen glowered at Samuel. "You see, Lieutenant General, I am not a turncoat, as you accuse. Just a bastard with no English blood in me standing on the wrong soil."

Burke reclaimed control of the questioning before Samuel could respond. "A bastard. As so, too, will your child be. That is the legacy you leave."

"It appears so, Your Council," Owen said.

"And you admit that freely, knowing you'll hang for going against the king and his appointed men in a time of war? You admit to knowing with full consciousness that your crime is treason?"

"I'm afraid so, Your Council."

Councilor Burke furrowed his brow, wrinkled his nose at the disheveled sailor. "Rather foolish, don't you think?"

"I prefer to call it honorable, sir. I have not lied on this stand, and I am not ashamed of being French."

"Very well," Burke concluded. "It is England's ruling that you shall hang for high treason as a traitor to the Crown. In addition, a fine is imposed that you shall pay ten pounds to the King's Court for putting this girl with child."

"No!" Ruth blurted, bolting to her feet and clinging to the rail before her.

Samuel turned toward her and snarled, "You would petition for this traitor, even now? Do you wish to be strung up beside him?"

"By God, I'll go to death beside him, child and all, if you've no mercy." Her body folded with weakness, but she found herself able to muster a strength that all her common sense told her to tamp down. "Look at him. Has he not suffered more than any man ought? He cannot even stand. He'll have scars that cloak him in shame forever. Surely that is punishment enough. God in Heaven, Sam, show that you are capable of mercy."

"Do not take the Lord's name in vain in my court, young lady," Burke fumed. "Only God can decide now if there is mercy for a traitor to the Crown, for the boy will find none in the King's Court. The sailor will hang. But I decree that it shall be come noon tomorrow, as today's excitement has already postponed my dinner long enough." Burke eked out a pip of anticipation for his dinner. "I would like to get to it before the pot boils dry. We've dragged this out ad infinitum. We've damaged reputations of some of this town's most respected people, and we've unduly slandered those of lesser standing. We should not be proud of the events that transpired today, but we shall learn from them how to be better guided by the Lord's hand on the Righteous path. Just be relieved your neck won't be strung alongside his, Mrs. Whitlock, and I'd advise you to watch which man you plead for. I need not remind that you're only married to one of them. I hope you'll recollect that come noon morrow at the gallows."

"But, Your Council," Samuel said, approaching the pulpit. "I must object. The boy's already escaped the gaol once. We can't risk—"

"Don't let your little, uh," Burke waved his hand, "obsessions cloud your judgment, General. The boy cannot even support his own weight, let alone flee."

"But, sir, do not let him fool you. Mark my words: you lock him in that cell, and he won't be at the gallows come noon tomorrow."

"Very well, then, the pillory for him. He shall stand if he's able, poor son, at the pillory until he hangs at noon."

"The pillory!" Ruth cried. "Why would you choose the pillory, Councilor, and not the stocks? Is it possible you have even less mercy in you than Sam?" She balled her fists against the pew railing.

"You will not speak to me that way. Your penchant for mercy toward the wicked is winning you no favor." Burke directed his attention back to Samuel. "And not another word out of your mouth about the sailor, General, or I shall like to take pity on the boy instead. In all future proceedings, mark me, you'll mind your conduct in a more honorable way when bringing men before me. Traitors or no, I expect them to be able to stand on their own. God's court will provide judgment, not English brigades."

"I understand, sir," Samuel conceded, "but what of her? Is she to get away clean in all of this? After how she wronged me?" He raised his finger against Ruth.

"You want to see your own wife punished?"

"Your Council, as I'm now forced to rear a half-breed bastard, and as I cannot believe a convicted traitor that my marriage bed has remained unsoiled given this evidence, she must be publicly marked for adultery and dishonor to her husband. And you might well mark blasphemy and false witness, too."

"You are aware that most men plead for their wives *not* to be punished, yes?"

"Sir, she has been warned." He pierced Ruth with a glare that nailed her to her seat. "More than once. She must learn her place."

"Very well." Councilor Burke turned disinterested eyes toward Ruth, who sat now in stillness, awaiting, her face blank, hands folded in her lap. "Mrs. Whitlock, what is the Third Commandment?"

Without blanching, she replied, "Thou shalt nay take the name of the Lord, thy God, in vain."

"And the Seventh?"

"Thou shalt nay commit adultery."

"And the Ninth?"

"Thou shalt nay bear false witness against thy neighbor."

"And do you know the words of Peter 3:1?" Burke paused for a minute to take in her hollowed stare. "'Likewise, wives, be subject to your own husbands, so that even if some do not obey the Word, they may be won without a word by the conduct of their wives, when they see your respect and pure conduct. For this is how the holy women who hoped in God adorned themselves, by submitting to their own husbands.'"

"Aye, sir." She knew the damned passage. She'd lived it.

"And the words of Colossians 3:18, 'Wives, submit to your husbands, as is fitting in the Lord.' And Proverbs 12:4, 'An excellent wife is the crown of her husband, but she who brings shame is like rottenness in his bones.' Shall I go on?"

"No need, Your Council." She didn't break eye contact as she listened to her judgment handed down from the alliance of self-righteous men. She thought of Kees Karelszoon. Apprentice Crawford and Reverend Morgan and Captain Jacob Townsend. What was one more?

Councilor Burke continued with what he deemed to be God's certainty, "Nowhere does the Lord sayeth to bed a sailor who is not your wedded. Your husband seems to think your disobedience to the Seventh Commandment is the worst offense, and no doubt, you've acted as a fallen woman, whether in or out of wedlock. But since I deem your treatment of the Third Commandment, the blaspheming of all that is Holy in His name, to be your worst offense, I shall combine their numbered order to bestow upon you—this very evening, since we might well get on with it—ten lashings upon the back at the whipping post."

A murmur traveled through the crowd, and a thunk of the pew, and Daniel Osborne stood, looked from Samuel Whitlock to Councilor Burke, shook his head on a burdensome sigh, and walked out. An impatient stillness followed him into the light of day, and the people slowly turned back to Councilor Burke, much quieter now, disturbed.

"Let the scars be a reminder of your dishonor and disloyalty to your husband, vows, and vestal virtue. And let them be a reminder, as well, to Lieutenant General Whitlock, as to all men of this town, that if he is to request punishment of his wife at another man's trial where she does not even stand accused, then that punishment shall not be light, but induce physical defect, a blemish which he shall see each night in his bed henceforth. The child in question, once born, shall not bear the Whitlock name and, once weaned and able, will become bound to the lieutenant general's house or stable of choosing for indentured servitude of a time no less than twenty years. Six weeks after the child is born, Mrs. Whitlock shall be cloaked in a clean white sheet and made to stand publicly before The Road Congregation on two consecutive Sabbath days, and likewise for one day at the general court. Mr. Matthew Starks, you are to pay a half-crown for your profanity in this courtroom; and General Whitlock, you are to pay a full crown for yours, as well. The boy's sentence stands as previously stated. You should all be ashamed of your conduct here today. My sentence is passed. Mr. John Stanton shall record it; sealed in the presence of a witness, Mr. William Hewlitt, attesting; under the care of the justice of the peace, Mr. Samuell Mason; and in the name of the Connecticut Colony governor, Mr. Robert Treat, not present. It is done, and I am hungry. Now, leave this room, the lot of you, before my judgment and my hunger worsen one and the same."

Dead, still air that had filled the room was replaced by a breeze as the townspeople, funereally quiet, shuffled out around Ruth. Daniel's gloves still sat in the pew he'd vacated; she could see them now, was taken by them. She couldn't register fear or sorrow, remorse or anger. Nothing stirred inside. Tears did not fall, and her hands did not shake. Samuel strode over and stood before her with his stiff shoulders pulled back like the heavens were tugging on strings attached to his chest. He looked down at her, and she studied his deep-set eyes. His fox eyes. How far they went back into his skull, a portal to superiority. His will had been served, and it was expected for life to continue as if little of consequence had happened this day.

Under Samuel's victorious leer, two young townsmen approached Ruth and lifted her gently by the arms, removing her from Helen's embrace. Ruth knew the two men: Two of the Breed boys of her own age whom she had come to find witty, John and another Samuel, that unfortunate name. She thought how John was the wittier of the two, a wasteful thought to have now. The young men held her arms loosely, possibly half hoping she would escape. They were hesitant in the post they'd been assigned as selectmen. But Ruth felt relieved that two such men had been handed the punisher's whip, as perhaps they would make it gentler.

"I do not blame you," she said quietly to John Breed.

He spoke not, but the look on his face stated he would blame himself enough for the both of them. Samuel cleared his throat, and his omniscience pulled Ruth back into her dark reality. Not of the sentence handed down to her, but of a sentence worse. One that remained long after the whip had done its damage: she'd still have to live with the man she'd married.

"Oui, la justice est la vôtre," she whispered to him, without caring any longer what he could do to her. "Mais pas pour toujours."

He raised his hand, but the Breed boys puffed their chests and ushered her away. She watched the selectmen gather around Owen to carry him off to his own fate. As she was taken through the door into the awakening light of day, she looked back into the shadowed room over her shoulder, and mouthed—too quietly for Samuel to hear, but too obvious for him to miss—a parting curse: "Dieu n'a pas de pitié."

Chapter Nineteenth
With a little help from friends

A desperate disease
requires a dangerous remedy.

—Guy Fawkes

She stood at the kitchen counter of King's Hall. Her fingers traced the lining of the glass window as she looked toward the lower meetinghouse at the far end of the street. She breathed shallowly into the cloth bandages beneath her corset that bound her from shoulder to waist. The cuts throbbed. Around the corner of the meeting hall, less than seventy rods away, the elongated shadows of Owen at the pillory stretched beyond the lighted candles that had been placed in the dirt around him.

The moon was a dark slice out of the sky. Not a moon at all, but a straining on the threads of the night's fabric. She pulled from her apron pocket a wrapped cheesecloth. Her hand quivered as she placed it on the counter, never taking her eyes from the window, consumed with Owen's broken silhouette on the horizon, willing motion to animate the shadow. Her body continued moving, leaving her mind behind. When she looked down at the cheesecloth in her hand, she couldn't comprehend it as an object. She opened it mechanically, shook the thin, powdery dust onto another sheer cloth, and shuffled to the stove for the burning kettle. She hurt, each step a reminder. From the hearthroom, the tubby sounds of an awkwardly held violin vibrated through the top plate and out the F-hole and into Ruth's mind numbingly.

Pouring the hot water into a pewter cup, she soaked the cloth of powdered mixture into the water and stirred the cloudy liquid around with a spoon. She peered once more out the window, then back to the cup. The herbal aroma of paralyzing calamus and valerian, crushed with sage, lavender, chamomile, linden, harvest mite, and rose hips, filled her nostrils and retrieved her attention. Once she'd allowed the water to cool slightly so as not to boil out the toxicity, she shook the tiniest amount of musquash root into the cloth and replaced it in the cup, careful not to touch it or to get her nose too close to the steam. This tea would do more than relax the nerves. She turned away from the window and realized her hands were shaking around the lip of the cup. A bit splashed on the floor, and she steadied herself.

"What is it ye be making there, child?" Martha whispered behind her.

Ruth jumped and covered a hand over the concoction, brushing the remaining leaves into a jar near the water basin and pricking her finger on a thorn. "Just tea." She held a hand to her heart and murmured something.

"Child, ye's distant."

"I am," she said hastily, then slower, "I am."

"Come, lay ye down."

"Martha?" she asked without urgency. "Do you ever dream?"

She paused. "All God's creatures do."

"Surely you didn't dream of being a servant all your days?"

"No. But come, it's nay so awful." Martha moved to place a hand on Ruth's back and stopped it midair. She stepped instead toward the jar. "Oh, deary."

Ruth capped it quickly and slid it to the back of the counter. She placed a hand against a windowpane and thought of Martha dreaming, the stories she'd told, how back in England, she'd lost her husband to the pox, and her only son had been accused of a crime. Ruth never learned if Martha's son committed it, but they were poor, so it didn't matter why or how or whether he'd done anything at all. Martha sold the two of them into servitude for twelve years to pay for their passages to the New World so he wouldn't be put to death. Ruth imagined the nine weeks that crossing was, and how Martha must have counted them as Ruth had counted days for the ships. The fourth day on the ocean, her son caught a fever. Two days later, his skin was yellow; blood came from his eyes and mouth. A week after that, he was dead. Put to death another way, less humane than the first. And here, Martha—a binding contract signed by Lieutenant General Samuel Whitlock who had been charitable enough not to bid her serve both sentences of servitude consecutively in her son's absence, though that was well within his right. Ruth counted again in her mind, as she always seemed to count. This was nine and one quarter years ago, leaving Martha with two and three quarters left until she was free. She had lifted her hands when she'd told the story, showcased the room, and said, "Free to be a stranger in a land that is nay my own, while my only child be gone. Freedom doesn't seem so important now."

"Martha," Ruth whispered, remembering it as she looked out the window, "you must never give up hope that the day will come when your freedom becomes important again."

The servant looked down and brushed absently at her sleeve as if something were stuck to it, and Ruth studied her. Though being anything at all was not for the borel, Martha had wanted to be a painter. Her uncle was far wealthier from the making of locks and hinges than was Martha's family from the making of nothing. He'd come down from Ashton-le-Willows in the hundred-of-West-Derbyshire for her tenth birthday and brought her a gift of paints. She'd used up every last drop of that paint and stretched it out as far as she could for as long as she could, and even then she'd added water to the colors until there was no more color. Ruth thought of Martha's words now: "When the colors are gone, ye're left with some muddied water, and naught else. Then ye spend the rest of your life wishing for more paints, settling for muddied water." But Ruth witnessed a spark flash in the corner of Martha's eyes that showed colors reclaimed and told Ruth that freedom was, indeed, something far more desirable than ever before imagined.

Martha looked at Ruth's tea, curiously, the aroma odd. "Might I have a taste?"

She waved Martha away. "This is for Sam."

Martha narrowed her eyes, but Ruth shooed her out and back down the hall, following behind, dazed again when she saw Samuel, the violin pressed to his neck like a second chin. She'd once thought of how tender that sight could be, but now the wooden object appeared a growth, and around it the layered wrinkles of his neck betrayed his age. He held it too low to accommodate his sling and only plucked the few strings he could reach—not even a melody surfaced from it. He didn't play to entertain; he only ever played when he couldn't think of the proper way to phrase a letter he was penning. Once there had been a kind of poetry in that; now it was echoic annoyance harmonized with dangerous hatred. His powerful hands did not look soft or romantic against the fingerboard or the bow. Instead, they looked meek.

Ruth shuffled toward the flickering candlelight of the hall where sat an elegantly carved wooden-and-stoneware inkbox and quill on his elegantly carved desk next to an inelegant petition to executives in Boston. It didn't mesh with the grandeur of the great house, but everything Samuel touched seemed to turn inelegant. The petition was a plea for the release of the deposed governor, Sir Edmund Andros, who Ruth recently learned had been captured in a revolt against his upholding of the Dominion and his support for the Church of England and the Navigation Acts. The capture was a significant blow to Samuel who had been counting on Andros' alliance in an organized English takeover of New France's frontier to the west. She loomed over the letter, remarking the laid, imported paper upon which each word was messily scripted with his unslung left hand—not his writing hand, to the misfortune of the addressee—with the sharpest quill tip. She wondered if he'd ever had to write with the flat birch bark and dull quills she'd known all her life or what he'd do if she followed her urge to dip her finger into the liquid seal wax and press it into her cheeks, like she'd seen Askook do.

"You've had a successful day," she said.

He started and set aside the violin quickly and moved to the desk to lay a hand over his papers, smearing the still-wet ink. An unfresh odor wafted from his arm when he moved, and Ruth stepped back at the smell of it. A dark stain seeped through the cloth sling. The underside of it was yellowed with saturated sweat. Ruth bunched her nose and set the cup down on his desk. She could no longer smell the tea for the air surrounding him.

He took a wealthy sip from the cup. "Mind your tongue to me, wife."

"I'll silence it completely, sir." Her voice was unnaturally calmed.

"You knew he was going to hang. That should not have come as a surprise."

She arched a brow. It was the first time he'd spoken on the subject since she'd been whipped at his command hours prior. All she'd seen as it had happened was Owen's face, swollen and pussed with crimson. She faced away from Samuel to return to needlework at the edge of the fire. Her hands shook again. He looked long and hard at her, but she refused to turn her head in his direction, though she watched from the corner of her eye. He slid his knees back around under his desk and lifted the pewter cup for another long drink. Within a few moments, he appeared sleepy, then exhausted, and his head seemed to waver as if it had come undone.

Ruth approached him slowly as he laid his cheek onto his desk, then she prodded him several times to make sure the tea had truly taken hold. He didn't respond. She tiptoed down the hall to the servants' quarters, where Martha was busy ripping out the seams from one of Samuel's old uniforms. Martha's instructions had been to lay the pattern pieces over some new material to create a tidy-looking brigade for the fight against New France.

"Martha." Ruth walked into the room. "The master is tired after his long day. He has requested not to be disturbed at his desk. I would ask that you stay in your room until he wishes to be relieved."

"Oh yes, Mrs. Whitlock."

That name.

"I willna tarry," Martha said. "I'll be up all the night with these uniforms to suit his deadlines as is. Man's never sewed a thing in his life. Has no idea the time it takes. Forgive me."

"No forgiveness needed." Ruth turned.

"Oh, Mrs. Whitlock?"

She stilled. She was afraid to turn around, for fear Martha knew something was afoot. "Aye?" Ruth cocked only her head in Martha's direction.

"Perhaps ye could proffer your opinion? What would the master approve more for his militia, the plain or the subtle plaid?" She held out a swatch of plain fabric and a swatch of plaid with the tartan bands so tightly woven that they looked solid from a distance. Both were in the Royal King's colors.

"Plain. He's only ever plain." The two women exchanged curt nods, and as Ruth headed back for the door, any remnants of whimsy faded. She held her breath.

"Mrs. Whitlock?" It hung there, not connected to anything.

Ruth paused, breathed, but nothing came. She stepped forward as if crossing a battle line, a toe barely setting down. Still nothing came. Behind her, she heard Martha pick up her needles and shuffle some fabric, crinkle the pattern print. Ruth swallowed. *Martha knew.* Ruth closed her eyes and crossed the threshold.

Sneaking through the hall toward Samuel, she walked as if dragged. His outline shaped and slumped monsterlike over the desk. The hallway smelled of his uncleanliness, and he was backlit by the hearth like a devil asleep in hellfire. Her hand mechanically patted Owen's dagger tied at her waist. They'd taken it off him at the jail, and John Breed had quietly returned it to her. She prodded Samuel, then reached down to his thigh and removed his flintlock from his belt. With her hand shaking against the wood, she stared at the piece, and it rattled. Her breaths were erratic; she calmed them and raised the gun and aimed it at his head and blinked through a mist that clouded her eyes. She took a step like she could walk through it, and when tears fell at the quiet click like an oil lamp catching, she unclicked quickly and lowered. To murder a man—any man—was the worst crime. She swallowed. And to kill him this way meant she, too, would die. Her child. He wasn't worth her child. And none of it would save Owen. Owen, who needed her now. No more time to stall. She brushed past Samuel and out the door without thinking to remove her apron or to put on her nightcloak. Her balletlike tiptoes hardly grazed the front steps as she ducked below Martha's window in the direction of the lower meetinghouse, no heavier than a shoreline mist. Her back thrummed, but she ignored it.

A few footsteps onto the road, she halted before the far-off silhouette of Owen's body, trapped with neck and arms locked in the pillory, unmoving in the chilly night. In her hasty planning, only then did it strike her that he was too weak to escape on his own legs, and with no way to lift him herself and nowhere to hide him even if she could lift him, the whole effort was for naught. So intent on freeing him, she'd neglected that there would be a step two, and three and four. She thought of the stable. Mereb would help, but how far that would be to drag the body, just the two of them. Martha would be too clumsy, bless her, and Robert's servitude was nearly up, so he would undoubtedly tell Samuel first chance he got. No, getting the househelp involved would be too risky. She'd need a different plan, one that required even more nerve than the first.

She turned to the Red Forest, the trees' darkness harboring the only people she knew who might—*might*—help her. The muted moonlight proved little help in guiding her to the edge of the trees, but she knew the way so well. As she stepped inside the forest's mouth, darkness encapsulated her, and fear lodged in her windpipe like a creosoted flue. An eastern screech owl tremoloed above her, his whinnying trill intertwining with his long purr, a nocturne that echoed to her as mournfully as Samuel's violin. Holding one hand outstretched and the gun in the other, she identified the maple trees with spigots and buckets and walked sightlessly from those familiar markers in the direction that Askook had often pointed.

Her fear rose into her throat, tightened. Her back throbbed, each step sending a thrill through it, but she kept steady. She wished that she had a candle, that she knew how to fire a gun, that she'd grabbed a cloak or a shawl. How hasty she'd been. She wished she'd killed him— that she could do it, that the hardness of that were in her bones. Her thoughts flew, but she scarce drew a breath, in case it would be too loud. Her feet padded softly, and focus ran careless. The repeated flashing memory of Owen's silhouette slumped in the pillory reminded her how little time remained. She listened for any recognizable sounds or voices, hearing amplified, pupils widened. A fire's glow or messenger torch might catch her eye, she prayed, before she was caught by someone—or something—else's.

Her heart hammered in her ears, all through her jaw, her teeth, when an uncarefully placed step landed on a rolling log, and she squeaked and lost her balance. She twisted her body and recovered her footing before she slipped to the muddy bedrock. She pressed her hand over her mouth and froze. She'd lost her bearings. The wind burst around her and whistled its mockery into the trees. She tuned in to the sound and prayed for her eyes to adjust in the dark, for direction to come to her. Anything familiar at all.

Suddenly, the night spurted limbs. A masculine arm, sculpted with a history of war, seized her from behind as effortlessly as if she'd been air. A palm clasped over her mouth, and another arm locked securely around her waist, pressing her injured back into a barreled, naked chest. Her back tore open inside its bandages, but she twisted to break free, reaching for the knife that was out of her grasp. His embrace tightened. She gripped her pistol but couldn't sense what was happening around her. Multiple voices belonging to multiple men spoke—to the left, behind—a language too fast to recognize.

The man holding her waist let up his grip, and she seized the opportunity to throw back her elbow. He yowled and lost his hold against her slippery dress fabric. She drew her pistol and cocked it, backing away, unsure in which direction any of the men were standing. She could hear their footsteps congregating around her—to the right this time. She spun. Nothing. To the left—she turned circles to evade each sound. Then she smacked into one of the men. Her chin hit against his bare chest, a tooth into her lip, and he apprehended her. She wrestled to break away from him, but his arm circled around her ribs and cupped her breast. The motion surprised her, and she fumbled with the pistol, squeezing the trigger prematurely. The shot cracked like a thunderclap, reverberated through her tight jaw, and the bullet whizzed through the canopy of trees overhead. She was sure the townfolk had heard it, but who would know what it meant? Several more men approached, and she felt their hands reach to her body and half-drag, half-lift her to her feet, never removing a hand from her mouth. She kicked and fought and dug her nails into flesh all through the woods, but her captors didn't let up until they neared an encampment.

Ahead of her shone the sparks of a fire, only slivers of which could be seen between cracks in the bivouac lining. The encampment had been covered on all sides by tall, strung-together animal hides suspended from the tops of trees by wooden poles and leather ropes. Lifting the bottom of the hides, the men accompanied Ruth into the center ring and flung her loose, not bothering to relieve her of her pistol or knife. The men backed away, leaving her to stand alone in the circle. Everything around her came to a halt. Her face burned hot and sweaty.

The grounds were simple, as if the Indians were unsettled. It appeared to Ruth that there were not very many of them. She counted but seventeen figures, all men, standing around the fire, looking back at her. They were clad in breechclouts and leggings of footless buckskin pantlegs tied and tucked into belts, donning moccasins, earrings, and headbands of intricate patterns adorned with crane and egret feathers. The fiercest of the warriors among them stood out in mohawks and scalplocks and were outfitted in breeches, ammunition belts, and Dutch boots she hadn't seen since Shrewsbury.

The weapons were many, though primitive and gruesome: bows and arrows, pikes, clubs, pronged spears, animal horns and tusks, nets, sharpened wood and stone and bonehooks. The men glistened with sweat as if they'd been dancing or fighting, and not a one of them looked pleased to see a white woman before him. She was thankful, at least, to be standing untouched for the moment, to collect herself. She ventured a guess that she was not among the cannibalistic Iroquois or among the Pennacook or Abenaki who would sell her into captivity in New France. In the light of the red flames, she could make out several makeshift woven stick and birchbark arched-roof domes, and little else.

A tall man walked toward her. He wore no shirt; his chiseled chest heaved and beaded with sweat. Everyone fixated on him, awaiting what Ruth imagined was his command. Below his bare chest, he wore colonial tie-front breeches, stockings, and calf-length softened-leather English boots. He sported a ceremonious wooden and beaded neckpiece around his throat that hung halfway down his pectorals and spread like a stiff fan across his chest; a bow and quiver slung around his back like a baldric; and an impressive mohawk with bright red feathers woven throughout. His face was painted with dark shades of red and black that made the whites of his eyes glow in the flames. The paint terrified Ruth, as she was quite sure it was intended to.

She raised her pistol to him, a timid plea more than a warning, but he didn't break his stride. His disciplined people took his cue. None stirred. He stopped fifteen feet from her, sizing her up with hard eyes the way Samuel had done while remarking property.

"Are you in charge here?" she asked, feigning confidence, hoping he understood her.

"Machk." He thumbed his chest, and the beaded necklace shook. "Pequot sunjum. I believe you misspeak sa-chem." He sounded the word out phonetically, his English practiced, a necessity to survive in woods now sandwiched between English colonies. "Warrior chief," he added as an afterthought.

She lowered her gun and smiled but received no smile in return. She extended her hand in a handshake, but as she took a step toward Machk, he raised his palm for her to stop. "You said you are Pequot," she said. "I'm looking for Askook, if he's here. I understand I might not be in the right place, but I mean you no harm. Please, I need his help if you know where to find him. There is an innocent man who is going to hang, and I need to set the prisoner free to—"

"We don't help your kind."

"My kind? You mean English?" She looked down at her dress, her apron. "Or woman?"

"English. Woman…eh." He shrugged and looked at the fire. "We burned alive in our beds. Children were cut down to hide from your people. Those who run was shot."

"I was not there." She knew what he meant. The massacre. She hadn't yet been born, but it was legendary now. She hesitated, toed the dirt. "What about French? Would it matter if I said he's French?"

Machk narrowed his eyes at her. "French soldier?"

Ruth could lie, but she could also be sold to New France. She shook her head. It was clear now with whom the Pequot had allied themselves, and it came as little surprise after their treatment by the English in the Pequot War. "Not a soldier," she replied, "but he can help you. He's a French ship captain. He knows how to sail, how to fight, and he can supply you with goods. He can gain whatever access you'd need to the harbors—my God, I can't believe I'm saying this. He can thieve and scavenge materials to repay you, and—"

"Not our concern."

Tears threatened, and the fire broke out more beads of sweat along her hairline. "I am not deceiving you." At her despair, a familiar figure walked into the fire's glow. "Askook? Aque! Ahupanun!"

Machk's eyes blazed into the side of Askook's face hotter than the fire, angered that the feckless warrior had mingled with the English and taught this woman their native tongue. Askook's expression returned his disappointment. He stood before her, his face straight, his usual relaxed scalplock now standing in a mohawk as tall as Machk's, with woven red feathers and leather holding it in place. He appeared to be preparing for war.

"Ruth, why here in night do kiyo wetun? Wishbium!"

"You know this woman?" Machk spoke in English when he wanted Ruth to understand his displeasure plainly.

"Nuk, Sunjum." Askook lowered his head at the admission. "She is juni shquaaw. Meezum goods, sweet, tarts, muneesh, weyout light sticks, tuggung with wood." He demonstrated gripping the handle of an invisible ax. "Pays, buys the land, ohke of jocqueen. Returns keeg to keeg." He was reluctant to say more, humiliated in his trial, but his silence was as crippling as his admission had been.

Machk grabbed hold of Askook's arm and swung the unmindful warrior to face him. The ruling was quiet, but clearly final. "Mudder, nekânis." He gripped Askook's arm tighter. "Mudder. Nenequdder." His eyes leveled the lesser-ranked warrior.

Askook nodded in subjugation.

"Please," Ruth said. "Askook. Please tell your sunjum I need help, that you trust that this is not a trick. They're going to hang him. My debe, remember?" She touched her sternum, just as he had shown her. "I can free him myself, but I can't lift him or hide him or heal what they've broken in him. Please, there's no time left." She advanced toward Askook, but before she could reach him, Machk stepped in between.

"We will not help you."

"She not matwan," Askook reasoned. "Will wōtĭʼně."

"No. She is enemy, and I see no way she can help us. She is one of the Big Knives, one of them: a chokquog. Do not forget this. I will help allow her live if she leaves now. Go, woman!"

"I am not one of them, *knives*—I am not," she shouted. "I've taken nothing from you, only gave."

Machk stood his ground against her defiance, unmoved. Askook looked to the dirt, torn between obeying orders and helping the desperate girl he was now so fond of. When the final decision was made, he would have to stand by his tribe.

"Fine, then." Tears finally wetted her eyelashes, and she wiped them with her sleeve. "I thought you were different from the *savages* I'd been taught to fear. I thought you, Askook, might know what it's like to be on the wrong side of this town's logic. But go ahead and draw your weapons on this town and watch all your remaining people get slaughtered in the street like hogs. I'll not cry for you." She moved quickly toward the hides, wondering if she would be shot in the back. The hollowness of her words sounded back to her; she would weep for them. She would. Just not tonight.

"You cannot get through woods alone," Machk called.

"I'll find my way; don't you worry yourselves. He won't hang for me. He will not."

"You will never make it." Machk laughed at her, ignoring Askook's distressed look. "You not go right way."

Ruth stopped at the wall of hides and thought about which way to go. It all looked the same. She aimed to the right and started walking out.

"No, not right."

Without looking at him, she headed back to the far left.

"Still no," he said, and this time he was laughing outright, and the tribe joined in, save Askook.

She spun and impulsively raised the pistol toward Machk. In half a second, he had unslung his bow from his shoulder, notched an arrow from the quiver at his back, and trained the sharpened point at her. His hand was drawn back against his cheek, his eye steady.

She yelled and shook, frantic, "You'll have militiamen from here to Boston tearing apart your camp if you kill a white woman."

"It's fool to put gun on man who has allowed you live." Machk kept his hands still, the arrow trained.

She cocked her pistol.

The camp of men drew arrows as quickly as Machk had and surrounded her, ready to loose them at their leader's command. Every man, except one. Machk took his eye from Ruth to glance sideways at Askook, who made no effort to draw on her. Askook dropped his weapon to the ground.

"Undi, wemooni," Machk spoke to the insubordinate warrior through clenched teeth.

Askook drew a hard breath. "Ruth, do not do this."

"I don't want to do this. I came for help, not for this."

"Ruth, pŭnŭm boshkeag." Askook motioned for her to lower her gun. He sensed that she couldn't understand that the sachem would have no qualms with sending an arrow through her chest if she did not comply.

Machk saw this, more than he wanted to see. He translated, his eyes on her heart: "He said lay down your gun."

Askook gestured around them. "If bushkwa, n'shuh. Ge mŭchŭnŭ."

"He said if you shoot, then you perish."

"Ge papoose mŭchŭnŭ."

Machk sighed and looked down at Ruth's belly. Discomfort shifted his stance. He redirected his arrow tip to aim to the right of her heart. The release would wholly miss her body. "Towwigoh?"

"Nuk," Askook nodded.

Another couple seconds, and Machk groaned and lowered his bow altogether and motioned for the other warriors to do the same. He looked down to the ground, then back up at Ruth, then directed a nod behind him. "That way." He pointed his thumb over his shoulder. "It's faster to go out woods to the road. How is your night eye?"

She lowered her pistol and remained in place. "Very poor, sir." She nodded hesitantly and headed in the direction of his pointing, but as she neared the wall of hides—

"Woman. There are lightfeet in these woods, not us, not friendly to Waunnuxuk. You need some men."

Askook turned to his leader, surprised. "I go." He pointed to others. "Teecommewaas, Kitchi, ahupanun."

"But, woman, before you go," Machk turned to her, "these are conditions. Things we need."

"I will do whatever I can," she said too quickly.

He pulled a folded piece of parchment from the pocket of his breeches and handed it to her. She opened the paper slowly, unsure of what she might be handling. It was a list. A list of items needed by the Indians. But not just the Indians; there had been some other collaborators.

"Most of this is in French," she whispered. "All of this is going to New France? Paper cartridges, poudre, muskets, tallow, axes, hammers, spears, bows, charcoal, sulfur, powderhorns, shot molds, arrows." She paused for a moment. "This is for the French soldiers…for war, isn't it? War against my town, my colony, my people. You want me to supply your war against my own town?"

Machk did not reply.

"Boots, bouilloires, flintlocks, swords...*women?* I am to bring women to serve the camps of French men?" She glared at Machk, who didn't flinch.

"The man is one of them, you say. You say supplies. Help him: help them all."

She whispered, "And if I refuse?"

He smirked, glanced down her quickly. "Then your child's sire does not live, and you not go free."

"And I become one of the women to make good on your barter."

"And your child is cut from you."

Her hand went to her belly. "That is a cold bargain. You are using me."

"You are not here to use me?"

She sighed. Of course there were demands. The Indians and the colonists had expected returned favors from each other for two hundred years. "I can't find all of these materials. It's not possible, but I will do what I can." She looked again at the list. "What is nietsissimoŭ?"

He made a gesture of smoking.

"And minshkudawâpû?" She sounded it out, as had whoever'd written it.

"Firewater."

"Firewater? You want hundreds of barrels of whiskey?"

He grinned. "Morale."

"Tobacco, loose women, and whiskey for morale," she scoffed. "Nothing like a war between gentlemen."

"You have word if we have yours."

For the first time since she'd exchanged either pleasantries or misdeeds with the Pequot, one was extending his hand to her unbidden. She saw how it was done. He would shake if the bargain entered into his favor—he'd been too many times betrayed to do otherwise. She reached out her trembling fingers and accepted his palm. His harsh grip dwarfed her own as it clasped in concordance.

"My word be yours," she said.

"You'll still need more men. Matchitehew, Bear Son, Matunaaga, go with them." He turned to Askook with a warning that sounded endearing, "Joyquish."

Askook nodded. "Wombunseyon, nekânis, kuttabotomish."

Ruth watched as the two men shook hands and parted ways, under-standing little but the consequences of this employment. "What did he say to you?" she asked Machk.

He looked down at her, hesitant in her knowledge of a language that had been a capital offense to speak in the Connecticut Colony for fifty years, and nodded his head toward the road. "Go."

She knew Machk would not forgive her if Askook did not return, no matter how many barrels of whiskey or gunpowder she could obtain to meet their bargain. Machk shooed her, and the enlisted men started toward the back entrance with a single lighted torch, small weapons, and supplies for medicinal aid. Askook stopped before her and nodded, as if he knew what she wanted to say, but he didn't want to hear it. His lifted palm led the way and ushered her once more into the dark woods.

Chapter Twentieth
Considered a victory

In my end is the beginning.

—Mary, Queen of Scots

Traveling with the Pequot, Ruth admired how effortlessly she reached the road. They skirted through yards and grassy patches, footfalls of mist, their feet skimming as if padded. The silhouette of the pillory near the other end of town came into view against the backdrop of candlelight. They neared the wooden structure, and Askook motioned for the others to fall back to allow Ruth to investigate. She wished again for a cloak as her skin prickled. She tentatively walked into the light but stopped after a few steps, paralyzed by the stillness of the tableau. The confidence she'd gained in making good time on the road disappeared at the sight of the unmoving body slumped in the candle glow.

"Owen?" she whispered, but sound didn't leave her.

His head hung down, and his neck supported the weight of his body that his legs could no longer hold. Blood gathered beneath him, so thick on the ground that it was still wet. She choked on a glottal wail that hung in her throat, approached him cautiously, and touched his face, but the action provoked no response.

"Owen?" she whispered again, smoothing his matted black hair behind his ears and positioning her face close to his mouth for signs of breath.

She examined closer his broken frame. The lower half of him was saturated. She traced the drips back to his midsection, drawing away his jacket lapel. She pressed her hand to the wetness and almost screamed as the candlelight revealed the red that coated her fingers. She threw her wet hand over her mouth and tasted the bitter acidity, the lick of cast iron on her lips, and she wiped it off with her apron.

Her touch triggered a reaction from him, and Ruth low-cooed at his movement. She crouched before him as he struggled to hold up his head. He opened one eye slightly, the other swollen shut. The brow above it had been split by lashings with pistol butts and pommels.

Glistening scarlet drops dangled off the tips of his eyelashes. As he lifted his face from the shadows, Ruth saw a rope cutting through his mouth, his cheeks pulled taut enough to expose gums, holding a rag in place between his teeth.

"Dear God." She pulled his dagger from her waist. Drawing back his hair from his cheeks, she sliced through the rope, and removed the cloth from his mouth, easing the tension in his jaw, then removed her hairpin from her bun and reached for the lock at the end of the pillory.

"Can't stand," he managed, his breaths shallow, gasping against the pillory's pressure on his neck. He watched her hair cascade around her shoulders. "Legs." He indicated, and she saw them, bent contrary to nature, their crook at an impossible angle.

"I have help to carry you from here." She motioned to the Pequot warriors in the shadows. "We'll take you to safety in the woods."

She examined his wet clothing, his stomach dripping a red trail down his broken legs. She blinked. Her vision clouded. She grabbed hold of the lock and jammed her hairpin into it until the lock gave way. The top clamp of the pillory creaked in protest against her lifting, much heavier wood than she'd imagined it to be. Once it lifted, she moved to hold him up, but he fell, groaning at the abrupt movement against his shifting bones. Ruth dropped to his side. The candlelight stretched across his stomach like an open mouth swallowing him. His abdomen had been shredded, a red band around his middle where he had been slashed with small, innumerable cuts—slow bleedout. She faced away, feeling about to vomit. Shifting him had ripped cuts afresh, and the blood discharged again. He held up his palm and shook his head when Askook and the warriors emerged to help, kneeling by Owen's mouth with animal horns of whiskey. Ruth removed her apron and wrapped it around his stomach as he took slow drinks of the whiskey, swallowing scarce any of the numbing liquid.

"He whipped you." He reached for her, pushing the horn away, unaware if he felt what his fingers touched. "Are you hurt?"

"I suspect it will hurt much more tomorrow." She bunched her brows. The maroon at his ribs was already coming through the cloth as she finished knotting the strips around his middle.

"Reach my pipe?" He nodded toward his pocket, the one they hadn't bothered to empty.

She removed his soapstone and a pouch of crushed tobacco leaves and peat, packed the pipe with her forefinger, and lit the tobacco and moss with the flame of a candle near his head. She put the pipe to his lips and held it as he took shallow puffs. Askook unfolded a blanket, and the men worked to ease the blanket beneath Owen, side to side, afraid to shake him into shock.

"Just hold on." She tied another strip of cloth around his ribcage with one hand, holding the pipe at his lips with the other.

He took the soapstone in his mouth and watched her hands close over his wounds. Slurring, he spoke around the stem of the pipe. "Aye, there, that's perfect. I'll be good as new in no time." He reached his hand to hers to still her futile restoration. "Ah, but do…make sure… you don't miss that." He nodded toward his right leg.

A gasp escaped Ruth. In all the rush, she had missed it completely; blood seeped out around the opening where the tibia had broken through his skin and clothes. "Oh, God's teeth. Oh, mercy be thine."

"Looks like you'll need another apron."

She reached to touch the shinbone, to remove the locked chain from around his legs. His body convulsed erratically as the spastic nerves twitched, and he sucked in air through clenched teeth. She lifted his head into her lap, ran her fingers down his cheeks, and fumbled to hold his hand in hers.

"What do I do?" Her tears landed against his eyes, lips, dripped down into his ear.

"You let me go—"

"No."

"—and leave me here, so those tyrants see I won." He chuckled, gagged. "I'll consider this a victory." He watched Askook wrap the destroyed leg.

"You won't die," Ruth hushed him. It didn't seem like any victory to her, and she wouldn't hear it. She lifted his dagger from the ground beside him and reached to sheathe it in his boot.

"Keep it." He pushed her hand away.

"You'll need it."

"Not where I'm going. But listen: she's my messenger, my limb."

She studied it closely for the first time. The tip, so sharp, the handle worn with imprints of his hand. "And what have you named this one?"

"That dies with me. You'll find your own name."

Ruth held the dagger, wiping the blood that now adorned the tip. "He will be a he. If he is to be my messenger, then I shall name him Triton."

Owen smiled. "Messenger of the sea. Good name." He touched the dagger. "Go for weak skin…unprotected. Hands and arms. Throat. Keep Triton with you. You must…must never…be unarmed." He tried to touch her cheek but couldn't reach.

She raised Samuel's pistol from the ground. "I'm not."

He managed a chuckle, but the attempt made him convulse, cough uncomfortably. "Do you know…how to fire it?"

She fingered it. "Only accidentally."

He twisted the corner of his split lip into a half-smile and looked at her gun. "That's the pistol what took my foot." He watched her expression change, as if the firearm had sprouted spikes that pierced her hand. It smelled of gunpowder. "It went off recently. Did you fire it?"

"A warning shot."

He snorted. "You don't get warning shots. Can…can you reload?" He didn't wait for her to shake her head. "Okay. Watch."

He held up the miniature satchel wrapped around the grip, loosened it, and placed it in his hand. His sticky fingers felt for the patch. Words came slowly, laboriously out of the side of his mouth, as he clenched his lips over his pipe, lifted a ball wrapped in a paper patch, and backed it with blackpowder.

"Goes in here. Keep off hands."

She already knew that if it got on her, she could light up with it. He filled the flash pan with blackpowder, directed it toward the vent, and closed the trap to keep it in the pan. He pushed the ball in the end of the barrel and stabbed it down with the rammer, then backed it with more powder.

"Don't load all three." He pointed to the three barrels and symbolized explosion with his hands and puffed cheeks, and she remembered Samuel telling one of his men that the design was unstable, but that the sear on the tumbler at half-cock should prevent accidental discharge. Owen pointed to the barrels that Ruth should use.

"Two barrels: two shots. Fourteen seconds…to load, or you…you're dead. No warning shot." He cocked it back, aimed at nothing. "Ground yourself. Don't fear sparks. Get close. If you can't…load in thirty, get…get a second pistol. Use two hands. Aim for chest." The rush of words took what strength he had left, and he gasped for air between sentences. "Practice. Shoot me through the heart."

"No! No, sir, I won't." She shook her head vigorously. "You'll suffer every minute with me, by God's teeth."

He looked at her, and his vision left him and his eyes were someone else's and he felt himself floating above himself, looking down over the scene, over her. There was a pain, immense, then nothing, then more and more, and it were as if flowers bloomed in thick vines in his gut. He spit the pipe from his mouth and choked on his own tongue. He finally grunted, "Oh, Godddd, take me. Christhell."

Ruth lifted the pipe from the ground, dumped the tobacco, and watched helplessly as his body shook before he let out a stabilizing sigh and struggled to finger his own breast pocket. She brushed his hand away from his chest and reached into his pocket, replacing the pipe and extracting from his jacket a piece of cloth wrapped around a blood-stained letter that, when uncovered, was marked *Mrs. Rosalie Townsend; Fairfield, Connecticut Colony*, and sealed with the wax stamp insignia of *Primrose*. She ran her fingertip over the seal. She would never see it again. She wished—God, if only for one solitary minute—she could stand with him at the rails, untouched by suffering, feeling the seaspray in her hair and his chin resting on her shoulder while he repeated some vulgar sailor's fish tale.

"Post it to her. Promise."

"If it should come to that, then I shall take it to her myself, but—"

Her words were interrupted with his sudden coughing, a deep-chest choking that made him writhe. A trickle of red ran down his lower lip, followed by another cough that sent a rivulet down his chin. He spit it from his mouth. "Like sucking goddamn musketballs."

"It's not supposed to be like this," she sobbed and broke apart. She ached to hold him together in one piece, to keep him with her, memorizing every moment, so fleeting. "You can't do this."

He reached his shaky fingers to her belly and laid his hand across the curve, leaving a handprint of red upon her dress. "You must…tell my son that I—"

His body once again shook, and Ruth took hold of his head in her arms to steady his convulsing. His open, unswollen eye lost focus, and his grasp loosened in hers.

She spoke in a whisper so light, sure each breath would end him, "Does it hurt?"

He shook his head. Nonetheless, a tear left his eye. "I…I expect him to…load a gun…. No warning shot." He struggled to keep his eyes open.

A violent heave spewed forth enough blood from his mouth that

Ruth had to glance away. She looked hard at his lips, hoping for words, as he worked to move them, and he uncupped his fist inside her open hand. She spread his opening fingers and lifted from his hand the cloth that had wrapped the letter. As the powder and shot spilled to the ground, she saw what she grasped: his once-white handkerchief, embroidered with his initials and soaked in what remained of him. She held his head to her breast as he made a last strive at a breath. Crimson dripped from his tongue and lips, and his head pressed back into her arm as the resistance left him. The motionlessness that followed paralyzed her.

"Owen." She tapped his cheek, but there was no response. "No, Owen. Please. I forbid this." She struck him harder on the face but received nothing in return. Placing her head to his chest, she still felt what she prayed was the faintest heartbeat in her ear. She turned to Askook. "His heart…I know it is…. It must still be beating. Please. Owen! Please, Askook, tell me it's beating! Hold on, by God's teeth, please, hold on. Owen." She shook him fiercely, but his still body didn't respond. She couldn't wake him no matter how she shook him.

Askook watched her prodding the body for countless minutes and then took hold of her wrist to stop her. The warrior lifted the sailor from her lap and laid Owen back respectfully onto the blanket, drawing Ruth's hands away from the motionless body. Reaching to Owen's eyes, Askook gently closed the still lids and held a palm over them, murmuring a throaty, quiet song that stretched into the night as if carried by common nighthawks and poorwills and nightjars.

Ruth cupped her hands around Owen's cheeks and pressed her lips against his, feeling his blood, its warm wetness on her mouth, tasting dried rind and mudclay wash across her tongue. Askook pulled on her shoulders, took her by the arms, lifted her to her feet. She resisted, then pounded her fists into the patient Pequot's chest, unable to make any sounds but the low guttural moans of the mourning.

"Let him go," Askook's gentle voice spoke into her ear, and he gave the signal over her shoulder for the men to carry Owen in the blanket back to the woods where his body could not be defiled by angered colonists. "Keep his debe." He touched her sternum, pulled his finger back, and it hovered in the air too long before dropping.

"Nuxquatch," Ruth whispered.

He held her and ran his hands briskly up and down her arms. "Ne sewortum, mits chauk." He kissed her forehead and sang throatily into her hair.

Ruth turned to see the warriors lifting the lifeless figure, each grabbing an edge of the blanket. Askook held her in place against the sanc-
tuary of his chest until he was certain the body was far enough away
that she wouldn't try to run to it. Once his tribesmen sank into the
shadow of the woods, he released her, patting back her hair, and then
backing away from her into the dark night, chanting a low song. It was
the sonancy of farewell, a bereft cadence, the lilt and rhythm of lone-
some pines swaying into each other, then forever apart. It would be the
last time she'd see Askook, and it was in his nocturne, in the drumbeat
of his steps. Machk's reprimanding had made sure of that.

As she watched him back away, she had never known such fright. His
silhouette smaller and smaller until it disappeared into the woods, leaving Ruth standing at the pillory in a stain of Owen's blood, mesmerized
by the flickering candles' glow and stilled in emotional shock.

Owen was gone.

ACT III

Measure for Measure

CHAPTER TWENTY-FIRST
A light before dawn

In so many and such important ways, then,
do the planets bear witness to the earth's mobility.

—Nicolaus Copernicus

Ruth hardly drew breath, dragging foot behind foot along the stone road by the light of a candlelamp that had been placed at the pillory. She felt she'd made it much farther than she had. Every few steps, she paused to face the empty structure behind her, taking in the remaining candles casting an eerie glow over the dark stain on the ground. The night was all buzzing and stillness. Insects swarmed her candle, and she didn't feel their pricks and flutters. When she turned back toward King's Hall, she could still see the stains inside her eyelids.

Soft lights shone through oiled-linen windows, through shutter cracks along the thoroughfare. Her feet tripped on uneven rocks. Her thoughts. Elsewhere. Short bursts, screaming curses. Her mind was leaving her. Screaming as it left, an unquiet exit. And every few steps, she cast her eyes back to the pillory, praying it had all been a heat-dream from backwhipped fever. Praying his silhouette would be there when next she looked. Where was it?

Approaching the house, knots grew and thickened in her stomach, clenching the child within; she did not know what would be waiting on the other side of the door. Through the window to the servants' quarters, Martha sat at the wheel, rocking gently with the rhythm of a foot moving on the treadle as if music played somewhere off. The servant looked up, stilled, and noticed Ruth first, drawing nearer the house with a lit candle illuminating her, too stunned to think of extinguishing the flame. Ruth halted on the steps—a pistol, a dagger, a handkerchief, a letter, a lit candle, all encircled in her arms, cradled like a child she fretted she might drop. Her numbed brain unable to think on how to lift the latch. As if by miracle—no, by witchcraft—the door opened itself, and Martha reached out to pull Ruth into the house.

Samuel was still out cold at his desk. Martha eyed him, eyed Ruth, then led her on tiptoes down the hall toward the servants' room. Ruth hugged close to the opposite wall when she passed Samuel. As Martha dragged her into the light cast from hallway candles, a gasp sneaked from the handmaid's lips. Blood covered Ruth from mouth to boots, the hem of her dress, down to the footprints littering the hall. Martha pulled herself upright.

"I think I should draw ye a bath." She led Ruth to the bathing room.

What a small room it was. Closed-in, claustrophobic. The walls fell against Ruth until she was swallowed in them, and the ceiling turned mealy and shrank and sank around her head and she shrunk under it.

"Just a bath will do a deed for thee, ye'll see." Martha removed the candle from Ruth's shaking fingers and placed it on the stand near the door, wordlessly.

Ruth didn't move. She might never move again. Shrinking into the walls. Her cheekbones sank beneath the weight of soggy lower lids, her bones nearly peeking through gaunt, translucent skin, weakened thin as wet tissue paper.

"Don't leave from this spot, child." Martha went back to the servants' room across the hall to set a cauldron of water over the fire. Returning with a damp cloth, she blotted the splotches of blood from Ruth's face. "I must go fetch the yoke and yield some more water for the basin. Please, don't move. Oh, deary." She patted her cheek. "Please."

In the time that Ruth was left alone, she felt herself growing numb, first at her toes, fingers, in from the limbs toward the center, where came forth a dreamlike state, from her chest up to her neck, crawling esophageal through to her skull, her mind, unsure of what was real, what was fantasy, where those lines blurred. And how they blurred. She didn't feel like Ruth: Who was Ruth? What defined this being? A new identity swept through her bones with rigor, and she felt them calcify, as if her whole self—whatever it was—had turned bone-thick and could push back against the shrinking walls. She scratched at a crawling sensation inside her veins but couldn't reach it. The room moved around her. Blurred spatters fell from the walls, crimson, rusty, as if once attached to décor, now like autumn leaves quickening in oncoming cyclonic winds, crunching as they whirled.

Martha returned and filled the basin with the near-to-boiling water one bucket at a time, each time walking back into the bathing room to find Ruth in the same spot, a statue, unbreathing beneath the marbled veneer, clutching the pistol, the dagger, the letter, a bloody cloth, immortalized in stone. One by one, the handmaid removed the items from Ruth's hands and set each down on the stand, making a show of it. Then she left for more water, nervously.

Ruth looked down, her hands empty but still curved as if holding. His red handprint across her belly. She laid her hand on top of it, moving her fingers in between the spaces his fingers had left, and squeezing the fabric like she could hold tight to his flesh again. His child moved inside her, and the room set back to spinning. She took hold of her thin dress fabric and tore out the swatch of his handprint.

Martha returned to find Ruth as before, minus a swatch of cloth. Martha snatched it from Ruth's hands and set it aside. "Let's get these soiled things off now." She mechanically untied each cord of Ruth's dress, front and back and corset beneath, and swooped the heap from the floor to discard before Ruth could look down. Martha hoped that with the bloody clothes stricken from view, Ruth would step back into her senses, fill in the shell she stood in. Having returned, Martha lifted the shift over Ruth's head and shimmied the pettied undergarments to the floor, relieved to see that, except for reopened back lacerations freshly seeping through cloth bandages, the blood had not come from the naked body standing before the washbasin. Martha removed the soiled bandages, her stomach lurching as it had when she'd first wrapped the shredded back, the folds of skin hanging in tatters like yarn loosened from skeins.

Ruth stepped into the basin against Martha's warnings that the water would still be too hot. She climbed all the way in and sat down, leaning her back against the basin's edge, neither the heat nor the torn flesh of any consequence. The numbness seeped back in with the heat. Martha poured another bucket of water into the tub and lathered a cloth with a pine-tar lye soap. The harsh cleanser sent the prickling of nettles through the cuts, but Ruth remained still.

"You'd like an explanation," Ruth said, after she'd washed the blood from her face, nails, and hair.

"It be nay my place to demand explanations when the mistress of the house is covered in blood, holding two weapons, silent as a graveyard." Martha considered the pinkish water and thought of changing it. "If it was the master, I'd assume some poor chap lost his life, bless the boy. But when it's you—" She squatted near the tub to fetch the soap that slipped from Ruth's fingers over the edge of the basin.

"Morrow at half before noon, they will gather around the gallows to watch a man hang. Eager, they will. But they won't see him. And they won't see me, either." She stared at the soap.

Martha remained calm, listening between the lines. "What happened to the boy?"

From the walls that had swallowed her, Ruth heard his last breaths and his last words, and they were her breaths, and she felt them again. She cupped water into her palm and dragged it along her arm where he had lain, feeling him cradled there, the convulsions that had pushed his head back and back and back into the cushioning crook of her elbow. She'd held him, and she held him still.

Martha sighed. "We should wake the master." She could only whisper it, after glancing twice at the door. "Better for he not to think ye responsible."

"You'll need salts. Pine needles. He'll be hard to wake if he wakes at all."

"I'll fetch pine." Martha looked around the room. Panic had taken her good sense, and she ran inventory of the cleanliness, what objects needed removing to have the place in order. "Ye knows this is a terrible idea, child, yes? Ye'll still be his wife, no matter where ye go. Take heed of some convention. He'll find ye and punish ye." Her eyes fell to the bloody objects on the stand near the door. "We's got to get rid of these things. Your dress is soaking in hot lye in the quarters. When it's clean and dry, I'll patch the missing fabric with a sash, so—"

"Martha."

"Oh, deary." Martha lifted a bucket and set it down again, fidgeting, then picked up the blood-slicked dagger and handkerchief. "I'll go rinse these straight away."

"No," Ruth said too quickly. "Leave them be." The young woman stood in the tub, feeling unrefreshed, but with something more vital pulsing through her. "Please."

Martha looked down at the soaked spots of red, and then back up at Ruth, who appeared to be rising from mist.

"Those are the paints. Remember? Once the colors are gone, you're only left with muddied memories. Please, leave it. I'll need you to fetch for me the carrier I borrowed from Sam."

Martha laid the items down with newfound care for their significance. As Ruth stepped out over the side of the basin, Martha hastened to her with a dry cloth, patting carefully against her raw back flesh, where strips hung like birchbark. Martha winced, dried quietly, then left to fetch Ruth's nightclothes and the requested carrier bag.

The dagger rested on the table atop the handkerchief, the blood of one mingling with the blood of the other. La liberté sera mienne, she swore to herself. She took in the stiletto's crimson crest, the stained shagreen grip. Et le tien.

Martha returned with a fresh bedgown of a safe mulberry shade, in case any remaining blood should leak through. She laid the gown on the edge of the stand and rotated Ruth to wrap the wounds in clean bandages. Martha slid the gown over Ruth's head and tied the threads loosely, then pulled strands of damp hair into a bun at the base of Ruth's neck.

Gathering each item on the end table, Ruth enveloped the dagger inside the handkerchief and placed it with the letter and the swatch of bloody dress fabric inside the top of the leather carrier bag. "Before I waken Sam, I'll require a piece of his leather, heavy gut, and a stiff needle." She wanted to leave now, to run out and away before Samuel awoke, but she couldn't. Arrow was not safe at night and neither was the dark countryside. She needed the landmarks, the ocean to her left. "Instruct Robert to prepare Arrow's saddlebags before dawn with imperishable provisions and two warm blankets. Bury Sam's coin purse far to the bottom."

"Oh, I wish ye wouldn't."

"We haven't the luxury of wishes. I'd like a few moments alone."

"Ruth—"

"I'll not have you held accountable for my actions." She turned toward the hall, away from Martha's misted eyes. "Then we'll pack my trunk."

"Ye'll not share his bed tonight?"

"I'd rather take the stable," she muttered as she exited the room and didn't return, trusting Martha would have a few moments of patience before her curiosity set in.

When Ruth had finished packing and walked to the kitchen, she noted how the footprints of blood and dirt had been scrubbed from the wooden floor, their wet spots shiny. She procured the salt of hartshorn from the buttery and loomed over Samuel, curling a lip. Uncapping the hartshorn, she held the capsule beneath his nose. Nothing happened. The thought of touching him drilled a numbness into her fingertips, but she reached for his shoulder, took hold of an epaulet, and shook the epaulet like a hot handle on a pan. She held the vial to his nose until he brought himself to his slow senses, and she retracted the capsule quickly into her palm, then up her sleeve. She lifted the cold cup of tea from his desk before his eyes refocused, then she disappeared around the corner of the hallway to discard the concoction into a chamber pot, before slipping into the buttery to replace the jar of hartshorn as if it had never been moved. A hair to the left, and it lined up with a ring of settled dust that she wouldn't point out to Martha.

"How long have I slept? It isn't like me to sleep away half an evening," Samuel said. He shook his head and pressed some feeling into his hands, fingers to palm, palm to fingers, then tried to stand.

Ruth didn't answer. She didn't want to hear his voice. She watched him wobbling, steps unbalanced as a toddler—*building a Virginia fence*, so Gran had always said. She moved about the kitchen, tidying up odd things for such a late hour, touching the sugar block twice, a canister over and over, setting the jar far back out of reach, then furiously scrubbing his pewter cup with a mixture of rough sand, a task usually left to the servants. He watched her closely, her movements suspect, but when he came toward her, she brushed by him briskly, the smell of his unclean arm surrounding her again, and on into the hearthroom.

There, she stopped. Like an unwound clock, all of her stopped. She glanced back to the kitchen, her face shuttered as a house in winter, and she looked down in front of her and touched a hand to the bridge of the violin. He'd taken what she loved. What right did he have to music, to serenades and hymns? With one more glance over her shoulder, she lifted Daniel's beautiful mahogany woodwork and threw it into the fire, a whining, slow-release hiss melting from the strings.

Samuel came from the kitchen, dazed, and she stood in front of the fire to block his view. He reached for her, then stopped. Something had left her eyes. They were hollowed like cored fruit, and they looked right at him and saw nothing, and she could see that he saw this now and felt it wholly. She chuckled a thin sound. A sound that lingered, then struck against the chimney, the cabinets, the shelves, and clung there, organic to it all, owned now by the house where it would echo onward.

Samuel's face deepened into a ravine, the lines cavernous and sinking at the sides of his mouth. His mouth that moved but said nothing. Then only: "Ruth."

Then silence from both.

"Ruth."

"Sam."

Clatter came from the servants' quarters that pulled his attention, the smell of lye at this hour, and he slinked back from the hearth like the dying rooster in a cockfight. When his attention came back to her, she paraded past him wordlessly, hurriedly, unwilling to share the same hallway with his marching steps. Behind her, the violin crackled, its polished veneer fizzling, and she felt his eyes shift to it as she walked away.

Chapter Twenty-Second

Born for the mission

I pray you, Master Lieutenant, see me safe up,
and my coming down let me shift for myself.

—Sir Thomas More

Ruth awakened, prepared. She sat on her trunk in the servants' quarters, where at some midpoint in the night, she'd joined a cramped mattress with Martha, who hadn't handled well the thought of her curled into a ball alone in the stable where Mereb snored. Ruth had been up for most of the night, packing, pacing. What little sleep she achieved was restless and seeped out of her in sweat. Now, she waited for Arrow to be prepped and prayed for speed before the house and town came to life.

Keeping one eye on the window, she practiced. Her hands busied themselves with mindlessly muzzleloading the barrels of the flintlock until she could do so without pause between the steps. She had shorn down the leather ties and shortened the length of an old saber frogbelt of Samuel's that she found hanging in the livery shed. It fit snug enough around her waist, now free of the discomfort of a corset against her lacerated back and burgeoning belly. She'd tossed the thing in the shed, its ribbed cage resembling bones of a dead fish washed ashore.

In the reflection of the window, she drew the pistol on herself, going through the motions of cocking, aiming, squeezing, grounding her feet for kickback before re-aiming, envisioning a black cloud of pungent smoke enveloping her eyes and nostrils. Two shots. She drew the gun from the frog. Faster. Then she'd pull a drawstring satchel, with compartments of loose powder, paper wadding, and solid lead balls, from around her belt in a one-two grasp that ended where she could pack it all in with the ramrod. She counted the seconds. And waited. Watched the window and waited.

As she drew the gun again on her reflection, her eyes settled on her opposite hip, remembering his words. Two pistols. Use two hands. Ruth slid the flintlock into the belt and drew it with her left, her fingers fumbling and heavy, like sponges fatted with water. So many extra seconds. Her weaker thumb couldn't cock the tight lock. I'm dead, was her thought, and she repeated the motion and died again.

She once more drew the pistol, switched the gun back and forth between hands, cocked, aimed, made a muffled explosion sound in puffed cheeks, reached for the balls and rod in one pass, and counted the seconds for reloading. She smiled a little, though she didn't feel it. Throughout the night and morning, she'd gotten it down from five clumsy minutes to thirty-seven seconds. She looked at her image in the glass, with her loaded gun aimed at her own mirrored face, and ignored the alarm that rose in her chest, pleading with her to fear her own absence of fear. Her eyes lit again on her empty hip, and her mind heard the refrain of his caution.

Then the morning was shattered by the scream that Ruth had dreaded. Someone had seen the blood, the empty pillory. Someone had an eighth of a mile to get to the Whitlocks' door and to pick up every curious, enraged, righteous onlooker and selectman on the way. She'd hoped to be gone by now, but she counted the seconds again, this time for a different purpose. She gripped the gun. Ready or not, it was time.

Lifting the latch to her packed trunk, she withdrew the dagger, still encrusted with brown remnants of dried blood, and she sheathed it in her boot where she had sewn a lopsided but functional encasement from a scrap of Samuel's leather. She'd dulled two needles with the work and had callused her fingers, but the mouth fit Triton like fur to a beast's back. The cold handle pressed into her stocking, leaving the faintest outline. The panicked voices doubled, then tripled, finally enough to wake Samuel. How she loathed the sounds of his waking.

Robert's shouts clamored down the hall and mixed with the fray. That meant Arrow was finally ready. Ruth closed her eyes. Rustling sounds came from the bedroom. Samuel struggled to dress himself around his uncooperative sling, and Ruth heard his grunting from two rooms away. She imagined him cursing her for not being there to dress him. The pounding of angered fists made it to the front door before anyone else could.

"Woman!"

He'd meant Martha, not Ruth.

"Robert! Good heavens, what on earth are you good for, if not to open the door?" Samuel yelled from the bedroom. "Must I do everything? Galleysod!—where is my pistol?"

Scurrying feet pattered down the hall—Martha. Followed by a

lumbering shuffle—Robert. Ruth stood silent in the servants' room. When heavy boot thunks stomped past to join the commotion, Ruth slipped the other direction down the hall to Samuel's secret meeting room, about which she was not supposed to know but, in fact, knew entirely. She was ready for the fancy imported English padlock, and she entered the locked door with ease, its hidden entrance covered behind a dull tapestry of rams that looked to be of Oriental persuasion, drawing no suspicion of passersby. She couldn't even recall anyone admiring the tapestry in earnest.

She inched into the secret passage. A room no bigger than a closet, windowless, dark, and musty. The unassuming cabinet at the far end was where she was sure Samuel's choice firearms were housed. She skirted stores of powder barrels and opened the set of doors. The smell of gunpowder flooded her nostrils. She lifted from the middle shelf a dark-wood, triple-barreled flintlock, a replica of the one at her right hip, excepting the darker grain of the wood. Some kind of mahogany, she guessed. Samuel did enjoy his mahogany things.

She tucked the pistol into her belt at her left side, chafing the gashes on her lower back, and took in a breath, willing the belt to melt into her hips. She next emptied as much of Samuel's stash of bullets and supplies as she could comfortably carry in her apron without noticeable sag, and she reached for a full powderhorn hanging on the wall.

Mid-reach she saw, mounted on a hook like some kind of trophy, the gleaming metal and sweeping hilt of Égard. Her heart slowed like the end floes of lava over rocks, but her mind sped. Samuel had taken the sword from the decks of *Primrose*. To adorn the wall of his secret war room like a souvenir, gloating over the remains of the dead. She walked to the sword in a trance and lifted it from its hook, stricken by its presence. It would never be his. Clutching Égard, she headed for the door.

The voices down the hall rose and kept rising, and she guessed that half the town stood between the kitchen and the front steps, caterwauling their woes to Samuel, their savior, in such a crazed, incoherent frenzy that he must be only now piecing the story together. As she stepped toward the exit, her eye hooked on a stack of papers on a table near the door. A pile of what appeared to be maps, detailed maneuvers. War plans. Ruth moved closer to take a look at the measurements, pathways, inventories, the hidden tunnels, the marked X's revealing Samuel's secret munitions stockpiles. Waterway routes, militia hideaways, allied involvement names and locations, French intelligence interceptions.

Plans to destroy parts of the forest to burn out the Indians, build protective barriers around specific sites, and conquer entire areas along the waterways of New France while the unaware slept in their beds. She rifled through the pages, mesmerized.

Her heart pounded as loud as gun cocks, and it took her precious seconds to realize it wasn't her heart that click, click, clicked. Marching down the hall in her direction came Samuel's boots. Precise steps laid as to the rhythm of war drums. She picked up the stack of papers and folded them into her boot, then froze behind the tapestry as Samuel's footsteps neared. Feet, then inches away. He stomped into each room, yelling her name louder and louder every time he had to say it. She silently watched his shadow rushing back and forth in front of the tapestry, until he paused outside the passageway. Ruth held her breath. It would take one miniscule noise, one shift of a shadow, for her to be noticed. She willed roots grow from her feet and the skin of a chameleon she'd seen in books. Only a turn of his head, and he'd see her outline silhouetted through the thin cloth barrier. He turned back toward the front door.

He marched, marched to the red-faced and howling crowd in his kitchen, and Ruth ducked through the tapestry and pulled the secret door quietly shut behind her, watching his back as he walked away from her. She tiptoed across the hall to the servants' room and placed Égard into the top of her trunk, delicate as an heirloom, and snatched her longest cloak to cover the pistol and powderhorn at her side, her drooping apron pockets full of lead balls and paper wrappings. She turned the hallway corner to face the madding crowd.

"What! What!" she called back. "I'm right here. What is all this commotion? Are we in such a hurry to advance the time to high noon?"

"Seems we've no need for high noon," Samuel said.

"Certainly the tide disagrees."

He turned to face her. "The prisoner has escaped. Someone freed him." His cold look, those fox eyes, hazel irises thinned, chiseled to tiny pinpricks—he could have torn a hole through her with just that look.

"Is that so?"

"Yes." He drew his mouth tight. "That is so."

"With help from she!" A voice rose from the group, recognizable as belonging to the effectual Eunice Crotchett, her wild hair whipping through the air like the knotted thongs of a cat o' nine tails.

"You'll charge my wife of no such thing, Goodwife," Samuel said.

"No, Sam," Ruth said. "Do let her go on. I'm interested to hear how I helped him escape when I was with you all eve-last, making you tea, sewing uniforms, darning your socks by the fireside whilst you penned at your desk. Sleeping by your side."

He looked up at her then, and he stared good and hard, and she stared back. Her jaw was set firmly in her tight chin, tight cheeks. She tried not to feel violently ill when she looked at him. Still, she knew he hesitated to push. He wouldn't get to the bottom of anything in a crowd of frothing animals.

"What proof has us o' this?" Eunice shrilled, scrunching her mouth into a pout that showcased the scars of once-sewn lips. "I doesn't believe nay a word of it. Thee've been scarce but troublesome since thee come to this port, and not one word what leaves a slick mouth be God's Word." She pointed with a finger bent by age and idleness. "Inn't no truth in her."

"It is the truth." Samuel brought his hand forth to still Eunice's frenzy. "She was with me all eve-last, Goodwife. She was with me night on into the morn. You have my word, and surely you can believe that my word is God's Word, no?"

"She released him with her mind, then. Witchery! She's witched as oak." Eunice writhed in gyrations that inspired pain in Ruth's back. "Thouest seed the brands clear as God's Light. Thaumaturge!"

"Be still," Samuel said.

"Why would I go against my own husband, Mrs. Crotchett?" Ruth said. "Have I desire to be whipped at the post whilst you throw rocks and rotted fruit again?"

"There was tracks to the woods," the woman fumed, still whirring about the room in frenetic hysterics, then down on a knee, hands raised high as if conjuring. "The devil's woods. Thee freed the traitor and leaded him straight unto the devil."

"And how did I free him, pray tell? The only one who had the key to the pillory lock was Councilor Burke." Ruth spun around and pointed a finger at one of the most powerful men in town. "Perhaps you should blame him?"

"Me?" Burke said, as the crowd turned toward him with suspicion— these simple minds so easily diverted. "I did nothing. It was my rule what locked him there."

Before Burke could go on, Ruth turned to the man beside him.

"How would I have made that blood? He'd have to have bled for hours to leave that stain. How could I have done it quick without the expertise of a butcher, huh, Mr. Badcock? Do tell us in your beast-carving experience," she felt her throat rise into her head at this, "how long that would've took me to achieve. Or how long it would take you." She went to the next man. "Or mayhaps it required the skill of a swordman like yourself, Mr. Leonard?" To the next: "And Mr. Potts, how would I have carried him when this whole town witnessed that it took five men to drag him to the council chair? Surely that feat would stand in need of a man of your strength, Mr. Potts, no?" Her finger flew out from her, to the next and next.

"Nay listen to her!" Eunice screeched. "She'll steal all thy souls."

"I don't want your souls, what worthless things. The lot of you. Look at you. Falling over one another to reach the blame. Why not take a closer look at yourselves? It could be any one of you casting stones. Tracks into the woods, did you say, Mrs. Crotchett? Perhaps it was *savages?*"

Gasps and sideways glances.

"They are joining with the French, you know?" she continued. "Or maybe you hadn't thought of the Pequot War, Metacomet's War, how there would be such consequences? There are consequences for taking land, for massacring. Face them, you fools! Which brings us to the French."

Samuel cleared his throat.

"You do know they are encouraging, nay, *endowing* raids on our settlements headed by Indians and the New French, no? Blame them. If he were indeed a traitor, then likely his own soldiers of New France freed him."

More sideways glances. Yet, this time, none durst speak, all their mouths tightened as if bolted shut.

Ruth went on, "Perhaps he cavorted with highwaymen? Pirates? Some of his crew who survived?" She glanced coldly at Samuel. "His family of five brothers, as able as him." She spun again, finger forward. "Or you, Mrs. Crotchett, in your desire to see me burn for it. You want truth? The truth is you don't know. Not one of you know. And I won't bear more of your unfounded blame without proof. Unless you're daring call my husband a liar, then you can all leave here assured that I was at home eve-last."

The townspeople backed away slowly, receding like oozing molasses, through the door and down the steps without further opposition. Ruth stood firmly entrenched until the last person was out of sight, then she turned to walk past Samuel with nary an acknowledgment.

His outstretched arm stopped her. "You and I both know there is a period of time eve-last during which I cannot account for your where-abouts."

"Say what you are meaning to say, General."

"How did you know there was a pool of blood?" He expected a flinch but received none. "How did you know that the lock was lifted and not broke?"

"Lucky guesses, General."

"Stop calling me that! It is not commanded."

Martha's frightened voice trembled from the doorway, "It be true, Master Whitlock, sir," and both parties turned to look at her. "I know I has no right to speak up to ye, master, but I can attest to she being home all eve-last."

The servant held up an armful of sewn uniforms that accounted for more than could have been finished in her regular hours. Ruth knew then that Martha had stayed awake into the small hours preparing for this alibi.

Martha said, "She didn't want to disturb ye by the fire after ye had nod off, so she come into my quarters to sew with me. We stitched per ye's request to have thine men outfitted neatlike. Then I give the mistress a bath to clean and nurse her—" the pause was quick, "—self, after which I dressed her, and she awaked you. That was the whole eve, sir, start to close." She gave a nod, then her eyes went to the floor.

"Thank you, woman," Samuel said.

"Her name is Martha," Ruth said. She smote her hands together. "Then, there you have it. You won't believe me, but you'll believe a servant whose name you can't remember." She laughed coldly. "You may thank me later for getting half the town out of your kitchen with-out bloodshed." She walked past him and lipped her thanks to Martha, kissed the woman on the forehead slowly, calmly, and squeezed her shoulder lovingly, then yelled down the hall, "Robert!" Heads swiveled. "Please assist Samson in carrying my trunk over to the Osborne home, and have Mereb bring Arrow around. Don't let Mistress Osborne refuse you. Tell her I'll follow hastelike."

Samuel bolted down the hall and blurted, "What do you mean by all this? You're my wife."

She looked in his direction without looking at him. "I'll still be your wife from across the road."

"Do you want the entire town to know about—"

"What this town knows," she interrupted, "came from your mouth, not from mine. I no longer care what this town knows or thinks it knows or doesn't know or has to say about any of it. I'll be at the Osbornes'. You can find me there, but I won't stay here with you and let you make a servant of my daughter."

Samuel's fists tightened at his sides, threatened a swing. "You don't get to walk out," he said.

She looked up at him. "I'm taking Arrow."

"Arrow? The stallion?"

"Aye. He's mine as he was gifted. I'm keeping him." Over the past month, she'd spent her free time breaking the young stallion that Samuel had acquired as a gift for her from a raid against a nearby New French encampment. She'd grown fond of the sleek, responsive animal, and she shuddered to think of its decline if left in Samuel's care. "He'll need a new nickel bit the next time you're in Boston." She leaned in. "I'd advise you whilst there to stay away from the punch at The Blue Anchor, or I hear you'll end up with the French disease by nightfall."

Samuel breathed heavily through his nose like a dehydrated horse.

She pulled her cloak tight to conceal her firearms, and she brushed past him where he stood stunned. She headed to the door, turning to him with one last request: "Buy Martha some paints. Good ones, from Boston. The most vibrant colors you can find."

"Martha? Is that the woman? Paints from Boston for a servant?"

"She'll need brushes and some heavy linen canvas cloth, too."

"All right, wife. If I do these things you ask, you're still leaving?" She didn't answer, and he stepped to the side, allowing her the exit. "I'll pray this works itself out in time."

"You'd might better pray there's still a god willing to hear your prayers." She walked out the door and crossed the road to where Robert tied Arrow at the shutter of the Osbornes', a few houses over. She didn't look back. She'd never look back again.

Isabel stood at the door, wiping her hands with the edge of her apron. "Blessed child." She took Ruth by the shoulders and led her into the house. "I hope you know the consequences of this. There be much idle talk today. I don't know what story to believe."

Ruth took in the familiar room, the home that had briefly been hers, the floor she'd thrice sanded for a man who never noticed. "Don't believe all that you think. You'll not find truth in beliefs."

"I want to believe he escaped into the woods." It came out almost too low to discern. Isabel was unable to meet Ruth's eyes.

Ruth turned and put her hand on Isabel's slumped shoulder. The elder reached out and took hold of Ruth's fingers, urging her to say something, but Ruth didn't. She broke away and went to her trunk; time was precious, and she'd already gotten off to such a poor start. She retrieved from the trunk her leather carrier bag containing Owen's letter to his mother and some travel necessities for the road. She didn't know what the letter said—she could open it or keep it or read it before delivering it—but she'd sworn this to him, this promise. She'd learned the weight of those—how important to keep the right ones.

Isabel got a glimpse, then, of the glistening, polished wood butt and iron trim of the pistols around Ruth's hips. "Heavens. What be you planning?" She went to Ruth's side.

"There is something I must do."

"It requires those?" Ruth didn't respond. "Will you return?"

Ruth thought carefully about her reply. She lifted his blood-spotted handkerchief and tucked it between the cuff buttons along the ruffled cloth underside of her wrist. His sword felt light as she clutched it and headed for the door. She'd made another promise to Machk, to Askook. If she didn't make good on that one, then they, too, could find her wherever she went, just as Samuel could. And she loved Askook, like family, like a brother she'd lost and continued to lose. She paused, left Isabel's question hanging in the air, and stepped through the door.

She approached Arrow, the four-year-old Spanish Mustang with a muscular coat of tawny leather, a shiny black mane and tail, gray patches on the tips of his nose and legs, a symmetrical white namesake arrow patch pointed down his forehead. He was smart and fast. Strong and adaptable and a sure-stepper. She strapped the scabbard onto his back—running her hand along the smooth dock that yielded no distinguishing superstitious brands. Untied him from the shutter. Stepped her foot into the stirrup and swung up onto Arrow's back as if she had always belonged there. If there was one thing she'd learned during her solitary existence back in Shrewsbury, it was how to handle a horse. Arrow was born for this mission, and the beast seemed to know it. He pawed at the earth like he could move it.

Chapter Twenty-Third
A long day's journey into night

The human mind cannot be absolutely
destroyed with the body, but
there remains of it something which is eternal.

—Benedict de Spinoza

Fairfield was two days away at a good clip. Ruth knew her body and strength would rebel, but she rode Arrow along the edge of Stonington Harbor, then north around Quanaduck Cove as fast as the animal could go. She'd be able to slow him around the well-populated towns, but only there and then, if she wished to remain safe. The path lay mostly open, coastal, but go too far to the west, and a horse could lose its way in thicket.

The roads, necessary though they were, meant highwaymen: the dregs of England's society who had evaded jails and capital punishment by coming to the English Colonies to practice the deeds they knew best. The woods meant Indians, and fewer and fewer of them were friendly to encroaching colonists. War garrisons littered the way with soldiers stationed on both sides of the war, the French if she hugged too close to the west and the English if she huddled too close to the eastern towns and shoreline. Wild boar with javelin tusks and wolves that took down resting horses at campsites were equally as frightening, and Mother Nature scattered fog, swamps, coves, insects, and early-summer rains across the trail. Arrow moved uneasily beneath Ruth, a lunging mountain of uncertain flesh, both target and compass.

With the water in sight, she followed the curve of Fishers Island Sound toward the Devil's Belt, where she would find Fairfield. She prayed something would let her know when she got there. She would pass fourteen, sixteen other settlements along the way, all looking more or less identical to one another, their rows of farms and crude log, stone, and brick homes depicting the class of the inhabitants.

Behind her, she could make out Stonington as a set of tiny dots, much the same way she'd first seen it from the ship. Arrow galloped along the road toward Quiambog Cove, and Ruth's thighs and buttbone burned at the continuous jarring motion. A clatter arose from behind the trees that frightened the stallion, and Ruth turned her head to see a single rider heading toward her at a full gallop, his pistol high in the sun. She called for Arrow to run and squeezed his flanks between her sore thighs.

The rider came in tight along her side, and she recognized the tricorne, coat of red velvet, the neckerchief concealing half a familiar face. The highwayman. Beneath the stolen saddle and doeskins was Fogcutter, the beautiful dark mare now challenging Arrow. Ruth's eyes darted to the robber's pistol, then back to his face, and she could tell that he had identified her, in turn. She called again for Arrow to ride faster, faster, putting the highwayman behind her, but the rider remained on her tail, determined.

As her horse galloped down the dirt path, the horses of three other bandits appeared with such startling speed that Arrow twisted his curple, reared, and threw Ruth to the ground. A gun went off. The three new highwaymen circled her as the fourth familiar one cantered up behind. She rolled on the ground into a sitting position, her hand across her belly—her legs and back tingly from the fall. Her tailbone already felt bruised.

She called out, "Haven't anything better to do than snag on me again? God's teeth! There's more of you every time I see you, you tight blackguards."

The red-velveted highwayman stopped his horse in her line of view. He smirked, casting a wanton eye toward her mustang. "That be a fine stallion you's got there. Nice breeding, by the look of him. Would go for a Neapolitan price 'round here. A Red in these parts'll skin you alive for that 'stang. From whence'd you steal a looker like that?"

"I didn't steal him," Ruth said. "He's mine."

"Yours?" The rider smiled. "Mhm, and I'm King William."

"Well, Your Highness, he's mine. Are you just going to sit there on your throne, or are you going to be a gentleman and dismount?"

The highwayman looked at her curiously but remained atop his horse. "I'm no gentleman. You still owe me coin, so you'd better hope your king doesn't decide to impose interest."

He watched her struggle to her feet. A scorch streak ran down her thigh; it was her gun that had misfired in her belt. Drops of blood peeked through the back of her dress, and her hands gripped her pistols.

"It's unwise to go for your guns, lady." He contemplated the blood. It wasn't from the fall. "Besides, you're already hurt."

She knew Arrow would flee if anyone but she tried to mount or rope him, and she was equally sure they would all chase the horse if he was to run, nor would they catch him. She was of no value so long as Arrow stood next to her. Staring from one man's eyes to the next, waiting for one of them to make a move, she seized her opportunity and smacked Arrow on the dock with a hiya. When he took off, she turned to run the other direction, willing to take her chances in the woods as the men fruitlessly went after Arrow.

The three unfamiliar riders instinctually hightailed after the mustang as Ruth had hoped, but the velvet-coated leader aimed Fogcutter's muzzle toward her. He dismounted midstride, catching her waist and dragging her down to the ground beneath him. She landed hard on her chest, and her cheek skidded into the dirt, her eyelid taking in some dust that stung. The highwayman straddled her and pinned her arms.

"Do your worst." She spat dirt from her mouth and blinked the dust from her eyes.

"My worst, huh?" He held her down, watching the red seep through her clothing, then he moved his fingers to the cords that untied her dress back. "All right, my worst." He stripped the cord out of its loops and parted her dress to the bloodstained bandages, newly ripped open in her fall from Arrow. "What offense?"

She shifted to remove his weight from her tender midsection.

He strung her dress cord back through the loops like he'd done it a hundred times. When his task was complete, he put his mouth to her ear, exhaling hard. "I *should* do my worst. Teach you a lesson. Not wearing a corset be good as consent out here. You'd better hope my riders find that pretty stallion of yours, or you'll have to come up with another way to pay us." He ran his fingers suggestively through her tangled hair, ensnaring some knots against his knuckles. "But I'm sure you'll think of something." The highwayman reached around to her front, untied her frogbelt, and removed it from her waist. "Get up." He pushed himself from her and grabbed her arm and lifted her to her feet to face him.

The three robbers rode back with Fogcutter but without the prized mustang. Spitting the dirt from her mouth onto the highwayman's jacket, Ruth grinned at the riders' inability to catch Arrow. The velvet-coated robber watched her satisfaction.

"Think you're pretty clever." A corner of his mouth lifted. "You're not getting far on foot."

"You'll release me?"

He let up his grip on her wrist. She had nothing else on her. Her horse was gone.

"My pistols?"

He stood there, staring. The thought gnawed at him like a creature on the bones of the dead. There was something. The gash marks across her back. The cheeks bruised from wrath. She'd done something, the weight of which escaped him. Then, the scrapes from a fall off a horse—she must surely be hurting still from that, but she'd been versed in hiding it well. With a grunt, he handed the belt back to her. She took it and strapped it around her waist.

"You ninnywit!" one of the other men called down to him. "We could get good exchanges for them."

"Shut your mouth, Angel," the leader said, not taking his eyes from the curious woman. "I'll na' leave her unarmed to get scalped in this territory. I'm not so much of a lowbrow barbarian boor." He stepped from her and mounted Fogcutter, his eyes still transfixed. "But in good faith, don't shoot me in the back, lady." Leading Fogcutter in a diagonal four-beat, facing nearly backward toward Ruth, the robber's body language gave him away. He didn't think she'd survive. He was giving her the chance to change her mind.

As the men segued from a four-beat into a slow trot, she watched them until she was sure they were out of sight, then let out a high-pitched whistle. The four riders, not as far advanced as she'd figured, halted to look back, and there, exiting the woods at a canter, came Arrow in a beeline toward Ruth. On approach, the stallion slowed, stopped, turned his flank to Ruth for mounting. Kicking her foot into the stirrup and lifting herself onto his back, she directed him toward the woods away from the highwaymen.

The riders wheeled their horses around and took off after her. They held the advantage of familiarity with the surroundings, but she had speed and a head start. Her stallion could not be outmatched by the four riders, and that was exactly the desire Arrow stirred in them. But Ruth hadn't bargained on their agility in the woods. They knew the dirt trails, the sections of clearing, the fastest routes, their cardinal bearings. Accordingly, they split in different directions to head her off at each turn, already knowing her path before she'd determined it.

One of the men came fast on her left and shoved her from her saddle into another rider who'd sneaked up on her right. The righthand rider caught her and slowed to a trot, then eased her to the ground from the horse as they came to a halt. She would not be getting away. She was too fatigued and sore. The youngest rider aimed his pistol at her head. The men closed in around her.

"I warned you that you'd have to pay us," the lead rider said, panting slightly as he dismounted and walked up to her. "We're interested in the horse. And this time, the pistols. You only get my charity once." He looked hard at her, expecting her to spit, but a tear ran down her cheek. Then, exhausted tears that Ruth, herself, didn't understand. "Well, now. What be this?" He let go of her arms.

"I won't make it to Fairfield." She blinked her eyes, willing them to cease watering, but she was emptied of resolution.

He grabbed her by the shoulders and shook her. "Come out of it."

He reached to her leather belt straps to remove her pistols, and her tears stopped when his knuckles brushed against her belly, sending a jolt through her. She pushed his hands away from her belt.

"I don't bargain twice for the same bargain," he said. "I didn't want to take your pistols, but now it's the principle of the thing. I let you keep them once—my mistake. This time, it's your mistake. You should have shot me in the back."

"I have valuable things."

"Oh, I'm sure you do," he chuckled. "But you also have some mischief what's bound to drive us men to bits, so we just want the stolen horse."

"He's not stolen," she replied. "Yours is stolen. And she's a broodmare, so keep her away from my stallion. He'll injure himself, and I don't want him mixed up with your bad breeding."

He grabbed hold of her mouth with one hand. "I've had quite the pleasure of your sharp tongue. Might I also have the pleasure of your name?"

"I'll give you no pleasure."

"Obvious enough." He let go of her cheeks. "Name?"

"Only if I can keep my pistols."

"Your pistols are yours. Name?"

She took the frogbelt and looked him in the eyes. "You first."

"I said I'm not interested in bargaining." He sighed. "Val."

"What kind of name is that? Short for something?"

"I don't want conversation. Give me your name." The sound of his own simpering made him wince. "Valentine."

Ruth laughed. "What kind of masculine Protestant name is Valentine?"

"You already know I'm not a leftlegger, you baiter. I'm a Friend."

She pursed her lips and squeezed her brow to a point.

"I see. You prefer *Quaker*. Charming."

"Quaker?" Ruth stepped back.

"Not laughing now, are you."

"Who's Quaker around here?"

"I'm not from around here." He cooled, everything about him now swam in ice water. "Why are you going to Fairfield? Why are you on the other side of Stonington on a stallion that will get you killed?"

"I'm to deliver a message to someone."

One of the other highwaymen spoke: "Val, let's go. Get on your horse. Rob her, take her down, or forget her, but we got to move."

Before Ruth could protest, Val was reaching for Arrow's reins. She jerked her arm away and drew both of her pistols. One pointed at Val's gut, the other at his crotch. The three mounted riders drew their guns and aimed them at Ruth, in kind.

"One of these guns will not miss."

Val cleared his throat.

"I'll not be your prisoner," she said. "You'll take me safe as you can toward Fairfield, or I'll remove your bawdies right now. Tell your minions to lower their locks."

"All right, calm yourself. Calm yourself." Val snorted.

"One of her guns inn't loaded," Angel said, his eyes on the black-powder on her dress.

Val wasn't chancing it. "You want to go to Fairfield? Fine, I'll take you to Fairfield. But threatening to make me less of a man be not the polite way to ask, lady. So maybe let's try this again, eh?"

He put the tips of his fingers against her guns and aimed the barrels to the ground before inching his hands over hers to uncock the sear from the tumbler's safety notch. When the guns were uncocked, Val turned away, mounted his horse, and sat back, ready. He reached out and snatched Arrow's reins, wrapping them securely around his palm, despite the horse's tugging.

"But let me make something clear to you, lady," he continued. "This be my rabble, and you get no say about the hierarchy. I'll take you to Fairfield, but I'll nay be your prisoner, neither. If those pistols point my way again, I'll dump you without your horse by the side of the road to be mauled by a bigger bear than me. You'll be like to find yourself dancing naked 'round Thomas Morton's pagan maypole drunk, unchaining the naughties for the merry, merry, merry boys. Now, frog and mount."

Ruth holstered her guns. She mounted the stallion with impressive quickness. When Val pulled on Arrow's reins, however, the stallion wouldn't budge. He narrowed his eyes at Ruth.

She smirked. "He doesn't like Quakers."

"My, isn't everyone quick to judge." He threw the reins in Ruth's face and watched her closely as she paraded Arrow past him.

The five of them rode along at a decent canter, quiet, until Val picked up the small talk. "You know, lady, you footed your laughs in, but I never got your name."

Ruth glanced at him.

"Everyone calls me Val. Only my mother called me Valentine."

"Oh, I shall call you Valentine. Make no mistake of that."

He grunted. "I'll call you filly."

"You will not."

"Tart?"

"No."

"Darling?"

"No."

"Naughty wench?"

She reluctantly chuckled and doubted he'd stop on his own. "Ruth."

"Ruth," he echoed. "Ruthless Ruth. That was hard-won, that."

"Valentine what?"

He glanced at her with the measured look that his face wore so well. Hell, she'd drag it from him at some point, he knew. "Mason." He lifted his tricorne and swept her a half bow from his horse. "Valentine Lewis Mason, in the flesh."

By nightfall, the group was down to four from five. One of the highwaymen had doubled back to case the road for new unsuspecting victims hours prior, seeing how the current journey was not affording him any profits. Val wouldn't take the chance in robbing anyone with Ruth in tow. He looked over at her, and she was riding much slower, despite her determination to keep up. Grief and stress, loss of sleep showed in the slouching lilt of her body in the saddle. Her thighs threatened cramping, needing to be stretched. Her eyelids grew heavy.

"Draw up," Val called. "Time to stop for the night."

"Thought we were heading straight through," Angel said. "To make good time while we have the darkness, remember?"

Val nodded toward Ruth. "She can't make it."

"I don't care about her."

"I can so," Ruth said, picking up her speed. "If you can do it, I can do it."

"I admire your vinegar, but you're no good to anyone if you fall off your horse. Let's hole up behind that tree cover while we're in a quiet lull. If we go farther, we'll lose the trees."

The four riders trotted over to a nearby copse, dismounted, and tied their horses to low-hanging branches. When Ruth stood, her legs jellied, and she nearly sat without intending to. Her mind was pulled back to the copse by the swarm of mosquitoes that found her as she waited, draining her of blood she didn't have to spare. An eight-note call came from a barred owl in a yew tree hole, and when Arrow nickered, a flapping and flashing of brown-gray and white swooshed past and away. Ruth listened harder. The call came again, far off, then rustling.

"I'll gather some leaves and sticks for a fire," Val said, once they'd settled. "Angel and Stefen'll get you cozy, Ruth, but don't expect too much talk out of them. These boys be lousy company."

Val's voice petered as he disappeared into the darkness, leaving Ruth with the other two robbers. They ignored her.

"You don't talk much, do you?" she asked Angel.

"What do you want to know?" He cleared out a pit for the fire, then he spoke again abruptly, "I'm not Val. Not friendly. Not Quaker."

She watched him working on the hole. "Might I help you?"

"No." He turned his back, and the three stood awkwardly avoiding words and eye contact for several minutes. "You're slowing us down. This is now a lost day for me, and I have no desire to go back to Fairfield."

She smiled, despite him. "You've been there before?"

"Yes."

"So you'll know it when you see it?"

"Of course."

"I find that comforting."

"I'm very glad." The conversation, with that, was over.

Ruth turned to Stefen, who hadn't said a word for the entire crossing. "Have you been to Fairfield, too?"

Stefen looked back at her, eyes wide as that barred owl's, but didn't reply.

Angel turned to her. "We've all been to Fairfield. Val'll get you there. Lay it rest."

She turned back to Stefen. "Shall I assume you feel the same?"

Stefen shrugged his shoulders indifferently.

Angel came back around and took hold of Ruth's arm. "Leave it be."

"Easy. Let's not kill each other just yet," Val said, as he came back into view with an armful of dry leaves and sticks and plopped them into the patch of dirt that Angel had cleared. "Have we all been getting better acquainted?" He chuckled.

Angel released Ruth's arm and tossed Val the powderhorn.

Ruth rubbed at the spot he'd squeezed. "We were talking about Fairfield."

"I know," Val said. "I heard every word. Every Narragansett lurking in the woods knows we're headed to Fairfield. And what, pray tell, was Angel's reaction to that?" Val flashed a sly grin to Angel and dumped the tiniest amount of blackpowder onto the dry leaves, stroking a chunk of sharp rock against a steel striker. "Stand back," he instructed, and a small muffled explosion popped the tiny spark into a heady flame in seconds. "Welcome to the marauder's fire. Twice the blaze in half the time. Now…" Val turned to face them with his hands clasped together. "Fairfield?"

"That's not funny," Angel replied.

"Are you a castout there?" Ruth asked.

He ignored her, stood by his horse, and dug into his saddlebag for any scrap of food he might've missed.

"There's food in mine. Onions, carrots, corn, cucumbers, squash, bread," Ruth said, and he moseyed over to her saddlebag at the peace offering. "Grab one of the brown jars, and use that on your bread. It's sweet. You've never tasted a thing like it, and by this I'll swear a psalm. I've got turnips, parsnips, pumps, jumbles with dried fruits—"

"At least you're good for something," Angel said. "Regular traveling pantry. Not to mention enough ammunition in here to supply a trainband." As he dug further into her saddlebag, he removed the stack of folded war plans that she'd stolen from Samuel's desk. Angel looked through them curiously before she could see him. "What are these?" He waved the papers in the air.

Ruth bolted upright from where she'd taken a seat, sore thighs be damned, rushed toward him, and tore the papers from his grasp. She'd meant to leave them at Isabel's, hidden under the flock, but in her haste to get Owen's message to Fairfield before it should travel there another way, she'd left them in her boot and had to tuck them dangerously away. The fire warmed at her back, and she grimaced, too close to it.

"What are you planning, girl?" He grabbed her by the forearm. "With those pistols, I should have guessed. No girl got pistols like those. You're some kind of spy. Who sent you?" He gripped hard and rattled her as if answers would fall from her pockets like shaken coins.

"Enough!" Val said. "Whatever her business be, it doesn't matter. You know we don't ask questions of others. You're free to go toward Boston, and I'll catch up later, if you don't want to head home."

"Home?" Ruth said, her face brightening. "You live in Fairfield?"

Angel shot an agitated glance at Val then let go of her hard, the motion sending her backward. "Whatever your occupation of contrition is there, it doesn't concern me. You're on your own." His hand twitched on his pistol.

"Whoa. Whoa, whoa, whoa." Val stomped between them. "No hands on pistols, chopstraws. Are we going to shoot each other, gathered 'round a fire?"

He pushed them apart. Angel sat in a huff on the far side of the fire and dipped his hat low over his eyes, ignoring both of them and dozing off in a matter of minutes. Val hrmphed and sat beside the fire to warm some bread. He tapped the ground next to him, and Ruth sat down. The fire made her ache, and the last thing she needed was to think of her utterly emptying ache. Stefen leaned against a tree trunk, away from the fire, hardly looking to be breathing, but transfixed by Val's newfound association with Ruth.

"What's his story?" she whispered.

Val raised his eyes to gloar back at Stefen, sensing the onlooker's disapproval. "Why don't you ask him?" Val said loudly, then picked up a pebble and threw it at Stefen. "What's the matter, bastard? Mouser get your tongue?" Val turned his attention to finding a stick to scrape against the plaque on his teeth. "Meh, you'll get nothing from him. Good-enough kid—just shy." He leaned back and rested his head against a knapsack, chewing the bread he'd stuffed whole in his mouth, looking up at the warmish night, before lowering his tricorne over his face.

With everyone nodding off, Ruth's hearing tuned to the woods, listening again for that owl, and her heart raced. Images came to her mind, and she shuttered them. Ghosts of men carrying something into the woods. A stretcher. A blanket. It vanished too quickly. She couldn't reach it. "Valentine?" she spoke softly.

After a few seconds, he murmured an acknowledgment beneath his hat.

"Are you ever afraid of the dark woods?"

He removed his tricorne and stirred, pulling off his jacket and laying it out on the ground next to him, far enough away to remain uncharacteristically gentlemanly. "Sometimes," he confessed, an undertone of reassurance that he wasn't afraid now. "I'm more afraid of open spaces." He leaned back and put his hat over his face once more, patting his jacket on the ground for her to forget about the woods and to catch some sleep.

She lay down beside him on the soft and still-warm velvet coat. "Thank you for the jacket, Valentine."

The tenderness in her voice made him lift his hat and look at her face while she situated herself on the ground. He hadn't thought of her as tender, of possessing tenderness—this was new, and he didn't like that he had thought it. She removed her frogbelt and propped it beneath the collar of the jacket for head support. Val could at once smell her skin.

"Why do you smell of flowers?"

She lifted her cheek to find that he was propped up on one arm, watching her. She was unsure if his watchkeeping made her feel more or less safe than the rustling of the woods. "I crush them on me, dried flowers and herbs," she said. "It was something my mother always did."

"It's lavender."

"Aye." She dropped her cheek back on the velvet, surprised he could pinpoint the scent.

"Do you feel safe with me at all?" The question was accidental but couldn't be retrieved. Val had softened.

Ruth glanced at the other two men, then thought about the consequences of her answer. "Given my options." She nodded across the fire to the sleeping lump of anger that was Angel.

Val laughed. "Pffff, ignore him. He's an unbreeched babe. He's near four winters the younger. Bad as we was all reared, I think his was loneliest."

Ruth knew Val meant it for Angel, but he stared at Stefen as if the comment were directed at him, and his gaze at Stefen turned almost compassionate until the younger boy looked away. Val was a talker. Too long in the woods, on the solitude of horseback, he spilled himself easily for the sake of conversation, companionship. In this solitude, Ruth felt a kinship with Val that she didn't understand. She thought of how she'd first done that with Askook, rattled off just to hear a voice. She pictured the Indian the last time she'd seen him, sinking back into the woods, his mourning chant, and this is what played in her mind as Val talked of his mother, a sailors' lady—which made Ruth bristle—he hadn't seen for years, not since he'd picked up Stefen. She was in Boston somewhere now, near the Black Sea of Bendell's Cove. Fish Street or Ship Street, he thought now, before saying that she'd never gotten over his father. Ruth imagined his father as an older version of Val, maybe able to grow a beard instead of boyish stubble.

Ruth picked at a loose string on the velvet coat. The sleeve was tearing. She gave it two months before it was clean off. "What happened to your father?"

"You don't like Quakers," Val replied coldly.

"I don't know any Quakers, except you." There had been Quakers in East Jersey, pushing Shrewsbury out from the West, but they weren't in her Dutch settlement. The town had feared them, though. It was a capital offense for a Protestant to bear a half-Quaker child. "All I know of Quakers is they wouldn't be approving of your velvet coat and wouldn't be aiming pistols at anyone."

"That's very limited knowledge."

"I know Quakers don't believe in the Sacraments or baptism or communion or heaven and hell."

"I believe in heaven, but not hell. Do you believe in hell?"

"Look around," she whispered.

He paused for the time it took to study her face, how it hung like a hound's into a frown, merely habited. Then he told her what she didn't know. It was true he had no theology of heaven or hell and didn't believe in the outward Sacraments. But her knowledge of it was prejudicial, and they didn't call themselves Quakers, and he didn't kindly like her saying it to him, frank of the matter. He said the Society of

Friends was a gentle lot that didn't believe in the punishments other religions imposed or that ministry was preordained by God, but rather that God existed inside everyone at all times. Ruth smiled at this, that their concern was with life in this world rather than in the next, and it made her again question the very idea of heaven, of the order of the universe. Quakers—*Friends*—didn't have to hear sermons or go to loud churches to find Him or to boast of their meetinghouse attendance as a way to measure piety; Val said they only had to better themselves daily.

"Admittedly something I nay do well," he laughed. "But I try sometimes—I do." Friends didn't believe in war or self-defense or violence. They didn't preach, and when they prayed, it was silent, and then he listed off the luxuries that were forbidden: the gun he carried, art and the written word, poetry, the pleasure he took from company, outward affection, displays of romantic whimsy, holding hands in public, and then huskiness when he said: "The lavender crushed on your skin is most definitely forbidden."

She faced away from him, not entirely sure how she felt about any of it. Forty miles ago, she had him held at gunpoint. Still. She tensed. "I'm sure stealing and coveting the goods of others is forbidden, as well," then immediately she reddened, thankful she faced away.

"As it is a commandment, yes." He threw himself back on the hard ground, handling her judgment vulnerably.

She heard him shifting in the dirt, pawing like a hog, removing lumps and rocks from beneath him. The sounds traveled over her as a rumor would, an eavesdropper to his discomfort. She petted the thick velvet that he'd sacrificed.

"I know my Bible as good as any God-fearing soul," he mumbled, "but a man must survive. I don't ask God for much of nothing. Keep me on my horse, and for that, I'll keep out of His way."

She turned back toward him, and he looked miserable, that face like a boy told he wouldn't be inheriting the farm. "Your father."

"All right, my father." He hesitated, then propped himself back up on an elbow. Blood left the propping limb, and he shifted it, but no comfort would come for either of them. They weren't meant for comfort in this life, or apparently, the next.

Val's father was a missionary Friend, a follower of George Fox, who'd come up from the Carolinas. He spread his word along the way in small groups he found, then had the misfortune of landing in Massachusetts Bay, an unkind place to the Society. He hadn't planned on staying, but then he hadn't planned on meeting Val's mother, pure and fair, practicing the faith accordingly. They fell in love and married and kept their pleasure private, and Val came along and was cherished. But his father had loved the faith even more than his own family, and he left them to spread his word.

"They promised they'd pray each night together in separate places at the same time to feel connected through the Spirit and all that other horseshit." Val picked a clump of grass and tossed it aside. "He never come back. My mother maddened. The more I grew to look like him, the more she come to despise me. My guess is my father's pacifism met a few leftlegger Prods like yourself," his eyes lit on her, then past her, "who wasn't interested in spreading his version of the Word. But I doubt I'll ever know what come of him."

Her heart kicked then. The pain in him. Was losing a father to the unknown any better than watching one burn alive? Did they hurt equally? She imagined maybe so, if pain could be equaled one to another. She resisted pressing him further. "We are as cruel to our own, you know." She waited. The night had folded in on itself and wrapped her up in it and folded and folded until it was small enough to place in a box, her folded inside it. Her body, bent such as that. "I am branded a W upon both thighs."

His eyebrows rose, more out of shock that she'd admitted it than shock that it happened, his gaze otherwise constant. "That is a cruel trick, isn't it. For witchery, then, I can figure. Punished for a crime no man could prove in a place no man could miss." Val smiled tightly. "I know you want me to be astounded, but I'm not the least bit surprised that a woman like you is branded a witch." He bit his lower lip and squinted his eyes, contemplating, fidgeting. Even in the dark he could see green stains on his fingers where he'd plucked at grass. "You're safe here with us. We all know it—that shame." He looked back over to Stefen, who still stared silently in return. "Isn't that right, Stefen? Tell her your story." Val kept his eyes glued to the quiet boy for a few seconds. "Not in the mood for talking, kid?" he chuckled, throwing another pebble at him, as the younger boy deflected it without any change in expression. "All right, then, I'll tell it."

Stefen drew his shoulders back against the tree. A frown dripped from his face and disappeared into the shadows of his neck like black liquid.

"Stefen's my brother by half. Our mother's son from a Friend she taked up with and married after my father."

Ruth studied Stefen as Val spoke of the boy's father trying to raise him after their mother had renounced her faith and abandoned them, sold herself up the river to a brothel. But Stefen's father wasn't one of the lucky ones: Caught the first time, he lost an ear and a hand and was banished from Massachusetts at the end of a triple-knotted cord. The second offense, they held Stefen's eyes open to watch his father stripped naked, abacinated, then beheaded by the descendants of colonial magistrates Richard Bellingham's and John Endecott's endeavors to exterminate the Quakers from Massachusetts. Stefen recoiled at the telling of the story, his face now all black liquid, drawn solemnly under his hat. Ruth opened her mouth to say something to him, but Val stopped her.

"You'll get no word out of him. They bore out his tongue with a hot iron. He was scarce five years old, and they shoved the bodkin so far down his throat, it seared shut. He means no disrespect, but he can't utter a word. You know…they don't always kill you. Sometimes they just toy with you like a ol' barncat to a mouse. Sometimes your fate is worse than death: you have to live with it."

Val reached up to his neckerchief, untied the knot at his chin, and pulled the bandana from around his neck, exposing, deeply engraved into his neck, the brand of a heretic, a solid letter H, to the right of his Adam's apple. Ruth could only imagine how gruesome it would appear were he to remove the neckerchief in the bright light of day. Black and menacing. Scar tissue swollen and rehealed in ugly bunches around it, like the rings of a cutaway oak trunk telling its age. She was thankful her own brands were so hidden before guilt took her over for the thought. Val let her take in his vulnerability for a moment, his neck tensing, his Adam's apple suspended as if he didn't dare swallow past it, lest it cast the light more unfavorably on his marring. His skin crawled with the gooseflesh of humiliation. He searched her eyes for signs that she would think his marking hideous or unsightly, worse yet, deserved. But her face was calm and considerate, and her gaze held no judgment.

He finally swallowed and said quietly, "Why don't you tell me about the child you're carrying?"

Ruth felt the blood drain from her face and the hand that propped her. Air stopped flowing in her nose, and her eyes stung like burweed marsh-elder spores had blown into them. She thought on all she'd said.

Her words certainly hadn't betrayed her secret—she'd kept it so close inside her breast, an encasement for her heart. She didn't reply. She stared into the woods, deep as if really looking, but looking at nothing. Listened for the barred owl, and heard instead a crackle of leaves, insect wings that hissed like untuned instruments, the wind, a ghost.

He noted her silence but kept his.

She shifted from him completely and laid her head down and faced away from him so he couldn't see the stream of tears that clung fast and stubbornly to her cheeks, collecting along the lining of his velvet jacket where the secret so close to her breast might thereafter be held so close to his. She had no release, nowhere to escape, and she couldn't let it out, beat her head and fists against the hard ground, throw herself onto the fire. Her only choice was to allow it to consume her slowly until the pain ran its course and made way for the exhaustion that would finally bring sleep.

"It shall remain your secret," Val accepted. "But should you need something, you could do a lot worse than me for a friend."

CHAPTER TWENTY-FOURTH
Fairfield

I keep the subject of my inquiry constantly before me,
and wait till the first dawning opens gradually,
by little and little, into a full and clear light.

—Sir Isaac Newton

A shuffling jolted Ruth from sleep. She shot her hand out until it caught purchase on something solid, and she gripped it, and aimed it at the noise. Opening her eyes so quickly caused the dry nerves to throb, and she was briefly blinded by the irritation.

"Quick on the draw there, girl," Angel said. He ignored Val's gun that she held extended, and he kicked Val in the side. "Come on, get up. We're in the open. Time to move."

Ruth caught her breath. She blinked until the dryness receded, and drops formed at the creases of her lids. "I could have shot you."

"Not with that gun you couldn't." Angel smirked. "It isn't loaded."

"Not loaded?" She turned to the waking Val as he sat up slowly, and he jerked the gun from her hand and tucked it in his belt sash. She screwed her mouth tight. Damn hypocritical Quaker.

Angel yanked the knapsack out from under Val's neck and threw it over Fogcutter, and Val's head slammed back into the hard ground. "Easy. What's the hurry? It's barely dawn." Val stood and meandered toward the trees behind the horses for morning relief.

"You know the hurry," Angel called over his shoulder, glowering at Ruth. "We're packed. Let's go."

Ruth stared after the men emptying themselves in the woods, envious, her discomfort catching up with her again. In the night she'd sneaked off quietly; in the day, privacy was something to be desired but never had. She pulled herself to her feet, dusting off her dress and stretching out, feeling the severe ache in her back from the combination of whip lashes, pregnancy, and the hard ground, and she walked toward the woods.

"Where are you going?" Angel called.

"Ne-sookedung." She disappeared into the woods.

"The hell'd she say?" Val said, returning, and Angel shrugged. Val extinguished what was left of the fire, kicked dirt up over it, and tied the leather cords of his trousers.

"How long is it to Fairfield?" Ruth asked when she'd returned. She handed Val his velvet jacket. His neckerchief had slipped down, and she saw the brand more clearly. Hardened tissue, purpled around the edges of it. The H was deep and prominent and black. Sloppy work, sliding off the protrusion of his Adam's apple so that it had been pressed in twice, echoing itself like a shadow captured in flesh. He caught her looking and yanked the bandana back into place.

"We made good time," he said, glancing past her. "A few more towns, a few more hours. We'll be there before nightfall."

He removed a horn of flip from his saddlebag and mounted his mare alongside the saddled Angel and Stefen. Ruth climbed up onto Arrow, and the four set out for Fairfield with an agitated Angel leading the way. The countryside coiled into watercourse gutters and bowed back up into arched hills. Rocks eased into more rocks at the east and then into plains at the west, and in between was pocked and craggy flintstone covered in sedge grasses, lapidarian to the hoof, uneven. The horses protested. They swiped their long necks at redtop bentgrass and big-bluestem, sneezed the field-meadow foxtails from their flaring nostrils, and swatted their tails at the waterflies and bullstangs that the herring gulls dipped after, blue-gray headspots and yellow beaks bobbing in and out of gray wings.

Val filled in the quiet when they'd slowed their pace around the third or fourth town. "What is so important in Fairfield to warrant this?"

"I have a letter to deliver to someone," she said.

"A letter?" He handed her the horn of apple brandy. "All this for a letter? Couldn't send by sea?"

"No. It's too important. There was a promise of personal delivery."

"I make a lot of those promises and never make good on a single one."

"This is different." She held the brandy horn to her lips and took a welcome swig. The liquid dripped slow and waxy down her throat, but it couldn't reach what ached. The ocean pulled at her face. The air hollowed around her, like her head was stuck in a pocket of empty sky, and she gagged. Pain, then.

"Do you need to rest?"

"No." Her fingers tensed around the reins, drew too hard on the halter. She felt nothing of the stripped leather, and Arrow's jaw clicked in discontent. She let up and took another chug from the horn.

"Do you know where to find the recipient of said letter?" he asked.

"No."

She saw the look on his face before he buried it. Damn women and their fool heads. If she encountered the wrong people it would be but hours, minutes for her to end up in chains on a slaver to Barbados—as was the fate of hundreds of orphaned or captured boys, women, and Indians.

"What's the name on your letter?" he said.

She bit her lower lip and surveyed the land to her left. There sat the ocean, peaceful in its wildness. She'd been hearing it for miles, but now she could see it. With brevity it stilled her. She pulled up on Arrow's reins, and the horse stopped, threw back his crest, lengthened his poll, and shook himself like a wet dog. "Townsend."

Angel yanked on his reins, hard and thoughtless. His horse let out a sharp whinny, and he crossed his stallion in front of Ruth's, blocking her path forward. "Say it again."

"Townsend."

Angel exchanged a curious look with the other riders. "What business have you with them?" he said. He maneuvered his horse opposite hers, facing her in his saddle. "Answer the question." His horse pranced, kicked forward its fetlocks nervously.

"I told you I have a letter."

"Addressed for who?"

She hesitated. "For Rose."

"No one calls her Rose."

"I have always called her Rose."

"No one calls my mother Rose."

She drew a sharp breath, sliding in the saddle. Lightheadedness glossed her, perhaps from the heightened voices, perhaps dehydration. "You are a Townsend? But. Rose has no son named Angel, so who are you?"

"More concerned with who you are."

"I know you are not Owen. You're not old enough to be Ash. Your eyes aren't dark enough to be Elias. You've all your front teeth, so not Avery. That leaves Ethan and Gabriel." She stared at Angel, and he stared back in disbelief. "I spent half my childhood remembering the names of the six Townsend boys, and the other half running from them, so which one is—"

"Gabriel," he said quietly.

She didn't recognize him. It had been a decade since she'd last seen him as a child of five. "Angel Gabriel. I should have figured that. But we always called you The Baby."

"Don't call me no Baby now. Who are you to me?"

"I used to read to you as a child, taught you majuscule, Bible stories."

"Ruth," he paused, squinted, "Miner?" At her acknowledgment, new alarm struck him. His face dropped from an astonished oval to a tight, apprehensive pucker. "What letter do you have for my mother? Why are you here?"

She could not answer him. This had been a speech she'd practiced and practiced, but the words didn't find her now. Her throat seized like muslin lining had been shoved into it.

"Owen," he muttered to himself. His eyes widened. "Where's Owen?" He grabbed hold of her wrist. "What happened to him?"

She jerked her arm from him, but in his grasp, he popped her cuff button, and something came from her sleeve. They watched as the handkerchief drifted and landed on the ground, against weeds, the initials O. W. T. peeking through splotches of dried blood. Gabriel stared at it, a muted patch of cloth beating like an extracted heart in the wind, fluttering with the shafts of fringed brome, keeping it alive.

Ruth alighted and took up the limp cloth. Tears came, and she felt that red puffiness that her eyes had been for days, alternating between too dry and too wet. She hadn't answered a word when fire calcined in Gabriel's gaze, cauterizing wide pupils to the edges of the irises. He grabbed her and shook her.

"You lie!" he seethed.

"God's teeth," she spat.

Val dismounted Fogcutter and stood between them. "Gabe, control yourself. She come all this way to tell your mother this. Listen to her."

Ruth righted herself and pulled away. "He was…put to death for treason to the Crown, suspected of being a spy for New France. And your father…your father was murdered, too, for harboring a traitor. *Primrose* is gone."

"My father?" He paled. "What do you mean gone?"

"*Primrose* was burned by the English militia. Owen was captured, but your father—" Damned cotton tongue. The fires flew up in front of her, the red and orange and screams of men who fell around her. She felt the heat of it and stepped back as if the heat emanated from Gabriel. "Burned. Burned with his ship."

His eyes met Ruth's as another memory flashed between them, a long-ago one—one he was almost too young to remember, but the glimmer of it hung there, sparks and ashes, between them. He looked away as she told them all she knew. The torture, the burning, the whipping, even the Indians. Everything but Samuel, for she couldn't bear to speak his name, to admit how close she was to it all, the real fire that sparked every blaze to follow. She stammered, then cried, and when she was done, she looked back to the ocean. There were no ships.

Retaliatory urges welled up in Val when she mentioned the whipping. He blessed that they were far from a stand of trees for all he wanted to punch something. He kicked at the fringe brome as it waved merrily.

Gabriel said to her, "You held him when he died?"

She nodded.

"Small mercies, then." He turned, pulled himself into his saddle, and waited wordlessly for the others to follow suit.

Ruth rooted into the craggy bedrock of an upland swell at the head of a marsh where it oozed off to the east. Her plumbean feet refused to step away despite necessity, and her mind recoiled with the thought of Fairfield, how he might have taken her there, in different times. How these mercury and baneberry, yarrow and sweet flags and wild mustard might have speckled their home field, and to the south, a light streamed in across the ocean and threw the rest of the lands into blues and grays to the west. Arrow nudged her, and somewhere off, the creak of wagon wheels rolled down a path to intersect them at some unknown juncture. She broke her reverie and turned to her horse. The train of distraught riders traveled again, this time toward a much melancholier destination.

"You're going to break my mother's heart," Gabriel finally said. "Owen was her favorite."

⁓

The four rode for the better part of the day. Ruth saw that the closer they got to Fairfield the more Gabriel's composure weakened. As he slouched, so, too, did she. His pace slowed when they entered the town, and the train of riders slowed with him, feeling it, as if they could change the past if they could only halt the future.

Fairfield's homes were aligned in clunky rows, leadlights illuminated, diamond-paned glass windows. Extra garrets for the rich folks. The

harbor was more bustling than Stonington's, with modest shipyards and
a wharf built sturdily on pilings with an extended platform for ships
to moor up to. Ruth imagined this is what Stonington's harbor would
behave like soon, with the booming shipbuilding warehouses lining the
walk to The Road Church, but she blotched the thought from her mind
when King's Hall seeped into the image.

In the distance stood a bowery, apart from all, stubbornly fastened
to a hillside of rolling grains. A large, reddish-colored home of many
rooms and a steeply pitched saltbox roof surrounded by acres of farm-
land, just as Owen had described to her. Gabriel broke into a gallop,
guiding his horse toward the farm. Ruth, Val, and Stefen picked up and
followed, kicking dust along the main road like a swell. Ruth figured this
was Gabriel's way of making an entrance.

She was at once terrified where relief had momentarily been. The
farm loomed tall as a bank of dark clouds in a coldfront. Ruth lifted
the leather carrier from her saddlebag to her breast and dismounted,
hiding behind Arrow until Val came seeking her. He held out his hand
to hers, and she gave it to him. She was surprised to learn that his hand
also trembled. Stefen alighted and took hold of the horses, gathering
their leads, walking them to the tie post without haste. He'd stay outside
with the animals. Gabriel had already entered the door, and Ruth could
see two figures running across the field toward the house. She made her
way inside, hearing scolding coming through the door.

"Gabriel Martin!" Rosalie Townsend's voice rose on the air like hissing violins, a hymn played backward. "Where have you been? You can't
just run off without so much as a say-so."

Gabriel withstood it and waved his hand for Ruth to enter. She
stepped down the four or five feet into the sunken structure onto the
vestiges of what once was a white-pine floor showing through in scuffs
and burn marks and dirt, jutted against a colombage wall with French
pierrotage stones and daubing between posts that intersected other
posts at cross angles. Val followed and stepped to the side near Gabriel.
Rosalie's head swiveled toward the young woman. No further introduc-
tion was necessary.

"Ruth Miner. My little Ruth. Look at you. Grown up."

Ruth curtsied politely and took in the room, the house that had been
his. Indecorous with exposed beams overhead draped with dozens of
herbs, skins, strips of drying meat, onions, carrot petioles and grip-
ping-barbs and radish heads. Some hung down so low the boys had to

duck and weave through them, and if the soft herbs weren't enough to dodge, it was worse to miss ducking beneath one of the dozen cast-iron lamps Rosalie had hanging from the same beams, intertwined and camouflaged among the meats and greens. A small sea-green cupboard stood shin-high near the entrance, a keyhole in it leading to nowhere while a makeshift wooden latch did the real work, the top waterstained in the shape of a ewer ring and paint-peeled and covered poorly with old, sheer French lace. Beneath it collected a wealth of lint flakes and dust—Rosalie's trifling concern for housewifery. Next to a wide hearth, the Townsends had a modest, rectangular brick oven fitted with a sheet-iron plate that spanned the width of the top surface. A stack of almanacs and chapbooks sat shambolic at the edge of the kitchen table. Ruth fixated on them before noticing that through the doorway beyond the stairs, a billiards table took up most of the next room, what she could see of the tip of a spinning wheel taking up the rest.

"Don't you look like your mother. Spitting image, bless her rest." Rosalie's thick accent enveloped Ruth even tighter than her embrace. Rosalie smelled of fresh bread, and on her breath sour goat milk, which was somehow not unkind to her. "It's no wonder that boy of mine hasn't shut his mouth about you, getting to see all this pretty-pretty-pretty," she lifted bunches of Ruth's hair, "while we've been missing it all these years. Surprised he's not here now, peddling you off as his *wife*." She raised her forehead into that face mothers make when they know secrets. "Don't you blush; we know how these things go. He mentioned autumn-last about bringing you here to visit. But ah! I get you to myself this day."

Ruth cleared her throat, but nothing came. This damnable litany of welcome.

Rosalie bounced lithely around the room that was also cramped now by the riders and two more of the Townsend boys. "Hello, dear." She curtsied before Val. "You must be one of Gabe's naughty friends, keeping him up to no good, I presume." She scolded them both with a finger that wagged in time with her head to unheard music.

"Val Mason." He removed his hat and bowed, a full head of wavy, dark-brown hair tripping over itself into his eyes. Mid-bow, he took Rosalie's hand and placed a kiss on her palm, cupping her fingers closed to trap the kiss inside. "It's all my pleasure to see you, Mrs. Townsend. I've heard so many good relishes from your charming, respectful son. He dotes on you most fairly."

Rosalie grunted, followed by Gabriel's matching one that sounded inherited. She cocked her head and drew her lips to a playful moue. "Teach him to do that thing you just did, and he'll make out all right."

Ruth mustered, "Mrs. Townsend—"

"Please, child, don't you start to Mrs. Townsending me. You always called me Rose."

Gabriel grunted again.

"I loved the way you said it. Made me swear I had petals. But how rude of me! Can I get you anything? You've ridden so long; are you thirsty? Ethan, go fetch our guests some brews, darling." She turned to Val and Gabriel and put the back of her hand to her mouth. "He's the good son, that one." Then back to Ruth: "Did you come all the way from Shrewsbury? How is your dear grandmother?"

Ruth's lip quivered, and the door burst open, and the two figures came in from the field, heavily panting, squeezing into the tiny kitchen and routinely ducking beneath the herbs and hocks.

The shorter one yelled, "Goddammit, Gabe. I've had to pull your damn onions on the lower quarter for days."

"Gowkthropples, the lot of you." Rosalie spun to fix the incoming boys. "Avery. Mind that tongue before it goes the way of your teeth. We have guests."

But as the tallest one entered the door, silhouetted by the outside light, Ruth's heart accelerated. "Owen?" she said too soon, as he stepped toward her.

"No, mistress, but the confusion be made every day, rest assured. Ash Townsend, happy to serve a pretty lady as yourself." He picked up her hand, kissed it politely, and then raised his gaze to hers. "The pleasure is mine, Miss —?"

Ruth didn't answer. His features. His eyes the same powder blue. His black hair hanging shaggily around his ears and neck, matching the same patchy day's growth at his chin and jawline. His cheekbones prominently set, the same pointed French nose, same easy smile that both Owen and Ash had been bequeathed by their mother. He had grown into Owen, into Rosalie.

Ruth whispered, "You look just like him."

"So it has been my misfortune to be mistaken for the scoundrel my whole life."

Rosalie said, "Do you not recognize her? It's Ruth Miner, from Shrewsbury. Huzzah!"

"Ah, so it is." He smiled, but he dropped her hands quick as a poisoned hemlock root and stepped back. "So many years. Have you brought the blackguard with you, then? Or rather, has he brought you? Are we to celebrate a joining? Shall I fetch a hog?"

"No," Ruth managed to squeak out when she glanced to the solemn faces of Val and Gabriel. They were humorless statues, but their silence made plain that the message was hers to deliver, not theirs. "I regret with the heaviest heart that this is not a social visit." She studied a tapestry that Jacob Townsend had surely brought up from the Devil Coast, a tobacco pipe from a Southern plantation hanging near the water bowl, anything but the faces that turned so suddenly serious. "There is nothing to celebrate." Quiet blanketed them. It seemed to suck the air from the room, and Ruth was certain everyone would start gasping for what remained.

Rosalie steeled and said, "Come now, boys, queue up. Give her space."

The brothers filed to one side of the room and stood in a line, an approximation of military attention. Ruth took in their grown faces with an unnamed ache: The spitfired young Gabriel. Her knees shook, and she thought the floor would fall away from her feet. Quiet Ethan. One of her hands had been tightened into a fist for so long it had cramped that way. The toothless grin of scrapper Avery. The unnaturally dark eyes of Elias. She couldn't look, wouldn't look. The haunting likeness of Ash. Mirroring what was missing.

"What is the news you bring?" Rosalie asked. "Is it my son? My firstborn baby?" The longing in her voice, God.

Ruth's fingers shook when she pulled the letter from inside her carrier bag and handed it to Rosalie. The confused mother took the letter. Hesitated. The stones in the colombage seemed to roll out of place and toward her, bringing the walls down with them. Ruth felt it crumbling, this façade of shelter, of safety.

"It does not say anything good, does it," Rosalie said.

Ruth had visualized this moment with Rosalie, but she had not imagined their shared pain would be on display for the entirety of the Townsend family to witness. "I know not what it says, Rose. The seal is unbroken. But given what I do know, it cannot say anything good, no."

Rosalie clutched the letter to her chest. For the moment, ignorance was her happier ruler. She knew her beloved son's handwriting. She thumbed the parchment, then handed it instead to Ash. He sucked air

through clamped teeth. Dried blood adorned the edges, and as he slid
the seal open beneath his thumbnail, his eyes scanned, and his chest
collapsed. Ruth whimpered, uncontained, and Rosalie looked up to the
ceiling, past it, past the dangling radishes, her lips moving, murmuring
something to God.

Ash read, "Dear R., If you are reading this, then I am dead and so
is Jake."

Rosalie wailed one long moan. The sound that fled her was beastly
and guttural, and she folded at the midsection as if on a hinge. Elias and
Avery rushed to her side to aid her into a chair.

Ash continued, "We leave you what little we ha—have. Please know
I go to…to death…for what makes a man honorable without shame: a
woman, a country, a ship, and an unborn son. Yours still in death, and
ever, O."

Ruth felt the room collectively turn to her, their stares red hot and
drumming. She closed her eyes. What space did those words leave for
secrets? The fire of *Primrose*'s decks raged around her, and she stood in
it, her eyes stinging from smoke. When she opened them, Ash's gaze
bore through her.

He flicked the letter against his palm, his mouth hawming. "Unborn
son?"

Rosalie stood from the chair, walked toward Ruth as if her feet never
lit on the ground, and took the young woman's hands in her own. "You
are carrying his child?"

Ruth lifted her head, the heavy burdensome thing, and she nodded.
Rosalie enveloped and cradled the girl, kissing the waves of auburn hair
softly.

Ruth stayed in the embrace, pressed her head in further. "I'm so
sorry. I'm so. God, Rose."

"Please, baby, my girl, my girl I never had. Call me Mother. My
grandchild you carry makes you my daughter, no matter how paper tells
it." She pulled Ruth away enough to cup her cheeks and read plainly
there how no paper told it. "For my beloved son, we both shall mourn."

"I have brought you his sword, Égard," Ruth said, feeling embarrassed at the insufficiency of the offering, but Rosalie knew instantly
the significance of this, and her eyes freshly glassed.

From behind the two women, Ash stepped forth from the queue
and stood before Ruth. He tugged at his pantlegs, rolled one of the ties
around on his fingers, weaving in and out of each digit. He didn't look

at her when he spoke. "If it is needed, I will look after the care of my brother's child and give him the Townsend name. I do not have much." He extended his arms as if to demonstrate. "But I can build a home, and I can farm, and I've forty-six acres of land less than three-hundred rods from here, to provide a life for the child. I can turn over my brother's land, too." He paused, hands tugging on his pant ties again. "And for you, Ruth, of course. You, too. To live modestly." He paused again, and he thought he might be able to look at her, but his stomach churned, and he couldn't. "Shit," he cursed at the wall. "Pardon." He pinked. "If it is needed."

Ruth couldn't reply fast enough. "It's not needed!" She peeked at Rosalie, chagrined, and collected herself. "Forgive me. Thank you, Ash. It will not be needed."

"Thank all the might of Christ!" Ash released the tension in his shoulders, and his stomach settled.

Ruth and Rosalie chuckled at him, despite it all. "My sweet daughter. I'll send word to your grandmo—"

"She's gone."

"Oh. Oh, oh. Dear."

"May we stay for the night—and perhaps Val and Stefen shall need rest, too?" she motioned to Val, who bowed, and Rosalie nodded. "I made a promise, so there's something I must do elsewhere, but it would have been Owen's request for you to see her, to know his child. Son amour pour vous était aussi grand que le monde."

Ash gasped. "Please. You can't speak that here."

Rosalie smiled, venerated. "Ma chère fille, je te remercie," she whispered, and kissed Ruth upon the cheek while ushering the young woman toward the loft above the billiards table, that strange luxury.

"Mother," Ash said. "Don't encourage."

"What is a woman's purpose, son, but to encourage the wicked ways of another woman against all of man's laws and conventions?" Rosalie laughed fully in the midst of her heartbreak, and her laughter replaced in the room a new lightness, her pain numbed for a time, the numbness numbed. They felt everything and nothing, and smiled and cried, and Ash scowled, his head shaking.

CHAPTER TWENTY-FIFTH
Promises made

In trust, I have found treason.

—Queen Elizabeth I

After three days of riding, Ruth neared a stand of turkey oaks, their leaves fanned like tom feathers, barbellate cups cradling large acorns, and she saw Stonington Harbor over the backbone of Wolf Neck, the bend of Quanaduck Cove. Val and Stefen had escorted her as far as they could, but the men had to drop out at the last haven of sycamores before Wolf Neck. Glumes of wheat waved in a tiny toy field, bent thirstily toward the earth, awaiting bange. A man in a meadow tugged at stubborn roots, and she imagined his bloody hands, how he'd later twist the stems out of the crabapple daulks from the orchard behind him, preparing the tart things for a market barrel. She directed Arrow through town without pausing, kept her head low to avoid recognition. *The back way into the woods.* The Pequots had shown it to her once, and she could find it again with some effort. She hurried past the townspeople, the grist mill, the leather tanner, the lower meetinghouse, Daniel's woodshop, King's Hall. Her gut seized.

When Arrow approached the woods, he snorted and pawed at muddy ground. She squeezed her feet against his barrel, then harder on his stifle, but he only stepped forward once and stopped. She patted him and gave him the moment, but the hesitation sped her heart. The town lay behind her. She watched it, then tapped him on the croup, squeezed him harder, and he moved forward. As she steered him into the woods, she couldn't see any paths or campfire or hanging hides. Nothing seemed familiar, as if gloaming had settled over the daylight and darkened the woods. She reached into her saddlebag, retrieved the maps and documents, and slid them deep into her calf-high boots. She patted the pistols at her side and pushed on, five minutes, ten minutes, the wood darkening before her as she deepened into it.

Then, Arrow skidded, mud slinging beneath his hooves, and Ruth stopped abruptly. Soldiers in blue and white coats rode toward her on horseback. She hauled on Arrow's reins, but he was too green to tell her intended direction. The dense woods offered few outlets and little maneuverability. The Pequot campfire did not present itself, and in her haste the soldiers surrounded her. She couldn't fight them if she'd wanted to; her flintlocks held but three balls between them, and the soldiers counted over a dozen. *God's teeth.*

A man pulled ahead of the crowd to stare her down. He was curved in his saddle like a scythe, beard unkempt, pistol drawn. He held himself with that pompous demeanor that men of position have, despite his tired curve. His beard grayed around his mouth and seemed to gray further as he sat there. His black tricorne—adorned with an unnecessarily garish cockade and excessive red and white feathers—sat upon his head too big, cascaded over his eyes. It gave him the distinctive features of an awkward exotic bird, the curve lending to a heroned neck. The commander's blue coat with high shoulders and gaudy braided epaulets would have been a match of Val's had it been red, with its brassy buttons trailing to mid-chest and linsey-woolsey fabric curtailed down the abdomen to rest over the top of both a horse saddle and baggy doeskin culottes buckled about the knee.

"Parlez-vous français?" The accent clearly native.

Of course. The coat did look like what she imagined Louis XIV might wear. "Français, oui," Ruth said, "and English."

He squinted, cocked his gun, and aimed it at her. A head nod indicated that she was to follow him. Then he shouted some orders to his men in French, and they circled in behind her. She moved along with them, and they rode deep into the woods. They stopped at a crude camp of soldiers gathered around a fire. With English colonists too terrified to enter the woods, this thick brake of red maples provided cover for French forces only seven-hundred rods from the heart of town. The French, with their myriad other idiosyncrasies, were not superstitious of woods, and by the looks of it, they'd newly arrived. Her particular town had likely become a target because of a certain outspoken, militant lieutenant general residing there. If they found out her connection to this certain unmentionable lieutenant general, she'd find herself at the end of a bayonet.

Some of the soldiers dressed in fine blue coats and some wore plain clothes of unclear distinction, but all donned weapons, from pistols to muskets to rapiers to longbows. They sharpened hangers, cleaned gun barrels, shaped metal objects in the fire. Some of them must have been reformed loyalists, some may have lost out in the Glorious Revolution, and others were probably Papists of New France or Old World France. The French stood out like cardinals in a snowdrift, their crests and plumes high atop their tricornered caps and their rapiers polished, brandished, showcasing decorated pommels and intricate swept hilts of high-quality design.

No one paid attention to Ruth as the men escorted her within the confines of the encampment. But they turned a covetous eye to Arrow. The Spanish Mustang pranced like he knew it. His legs were built for speed, his coat sleek and shiny, his manner wild but ready. As the riders halted, the gray-bearded bluecoat made a rude head gesture for Ruth to alight.

A younger gentleman, overdressed as intemperately as the first, went to the graybeard, and the two men looked in Ruth's direction while they spoke in quiet French. She dismounted. The younger man approached her, eying her stallion intently from beneath his tricorne, which tilted to the left for clearance of the bayoneted musket he held against his shoulder. By the time he settled his austere gaze on her, it had already traversed the rest of the encampment from side to side and back again. The men who had brought her into the camp vanished on their horses into the woods at the command of the graybeard, and she was left to the devices of the younger soldier.

"Where did you get this horse?" the officer asked in carefully articulated English, coated with the thick accent of a French National.

"Arrow was a gift to me."

"Arrow? A Spanish Mustang stallion of breeding is not a girl's gift." He laughed mirthlessly and drew a rope from a leather carrier beside the fire. "Who are you, why are you in these woods, and where did you get this horse?"

"Don't concern yourself with my horse." She squared her shoulders.

The soldier shoved her toward a small maple, thrust her spine against it, wrenched her arms around behind her, and tied them with a rope around the trunk. He leaned to her face. "He's not your horse anymore." He propped his bayonet under her chin. "Let us try this again, oui? Who are you, and why are you here?"

She didn't answer.

"Do you know where you are?"

She shook her head.

"Do you know who we are?"

"Aye," she muttered.

"Française ou Anglaise, et où avez-vous trouvé ce cheval?"

"I take neither side." She groaned at the tight grip of the rope on her wrist. "And with all due respect, sir, where I got my horse is none of your concern."

"You do understand français, then."

"Enough to get by."

"Who taught you?"

"I am widowed, if that is what you're asking."

"It's not what I asked. Was your husband French?"

She looked down at the ground.

He decided it didn't matter and swiped at the air. "You speak it, as well? Dîtes-moi à quoi vous pensez en français."

She stayed quiet, kept looking down.

"Do it."

"Votre plumes rouges sont ridicules."

He fleered unexpectedly and breathed hard through his nose. He put one arm on the maple over her head and leaned into it. "I don't like the red feathers, either." With the other hand, he adjusted the bayonet at her throat. "But one must be well dressed for war."

"I suppose it is necessary to flash a feather or two." She glanced up at his hat. "Or five. Impracticality be damned."

"It's not so clever to be smart with me. I could make your stay here short. Or quite long."

"You're not going to release me. You can't very well release an Englishwoman who speaks French and knows the position of your battalion."

"You think I'm going to kill you?" He contemplated and shrugged. "Maybe I will; maybe I won't." He tapped the bayonet situated under her chin. "I do not make a habit of killing pretty girls, but I might leave you tied to this tree as we move out of this camp tonight. The wolves won't care if you're a tasteless leftlegger."

"Sure they wouldn't rather eat a froglegger?" She smirked.

With a grunt, the officer pulled his bayonet from under Ruth's chin and turned away from her. He put his attention to Arrow and reached for the bridle. The mustang jerked his head out of reach, and the soldier attempted a second time. Grabbing the reins, he tugged the horse toward him, but the stallion stood immoveable.

A clatter of hooves from the eastern side of the forest indicated the arrival of newcomers to the camp. They entered around the columns of waxed tick mattresses rolled out under open air and soap-rubbed canvas sheeting propped up on sticks for low tents. Ruth could smell the apple peel in the soap weatherproofing from where she stood. As the soldier turned away from the horse, Ruth raised her boot up the tree trunk and laboriously worked the concealed dagger from the sheath with her bound hands, then tucked it away between the ropes. A dark horse galloped into the camp carrying a rider. Ruth had to look twice.

"Machk," she yelled impulsively, then snapped her mouth shut as Machk dismounted.

The Frenchman spun around. "You two know each other?"

"You two know each other." Ruth sucked on her lower lip. "God's teeth."

"Pourquoi est-elle ici, Capitaine Lavoisier?" Machk asked, with French as developed as his English, glancing at Ruth, unmoved.

"Careful. She speaks the language," the captain said, but Machk looked as if he already knew.

"Machk, please," Ruth pleaded. "Tell him to release me. I was coming to find Askook. I've got something for you."

"Askook?" Captain Lavoisier said. "She's looking for one of your Redmen?"

"Weshãgunsh," Machk muttered at Lavoisier and bristled. "They trust each other. He foolishly freed her Frenchman for bargain."

Lavoisier eyed Ruth with new curiosity. "Frenchman?"

"That tortured sailor. But do not trust white witch." Machk spit on the ground. "I learn she wears the name Whitlock."

Ruth's heart bucked against her ribs. Her hunger made the echoing hollower, painful, and her heart beat fully against her emptiness.

The soldier turned slowly. He marched up to her. "A widow? Very clever, Mrs. Whitlock."

"All right, Capitaine Lavoisier," she conceded, "we both know each other's identity. What of it?"

"You know what of it."

"Whitlock will pay you more to dispose of me than he'd ever give for my return." After having chiseled away carefully at the threads until her hands were loosened, Ruth gripped the dagger behind the tree but remained in position, waiting for the right moment to present itself. It occurred to her that this man was no less barbarically militaristic than Samuel, but she'd made her promise to Askook. And she'd keep her promise to Askook. Now, whatever happened, it would have to be for her. The child. Her own well-being. She'd done everyone else's bidding; it was time now for her own. "Are you and this Pequot tribe allied?"

"Don't concern yourself with our allies," Lavoisier mimicked.

"If you are united, then the information I've got for Askook, for Machk," she took a deep breath at the admission, "is for you, too. I made my bargain."

"What side are you on, Mrs. Whitlock?" He walked to her with his chest roostered.

"My own."

"What you are speaking is treason. We are marching on your town, on your own husband's forces, within the fortnight, and now that you know, you are right: I cannot let you go alive."

"Nous avons un ennemi commun. I can help you catch him. *But*. But there are good people there."

"Keep quiet."

"Sir."

"I cannot trust you to—"

She brought her knee to his groin, whipped her hands from behind the tree, and extended her dagger out in front of her. He threw his hand over his crotch, and hot breath left him in spurts. Her arms felt torn at the elbows, but she tightened them.

"Now hear this, Captain. The French are not my enemies. It is my turn to make the bargain. I believe that is how it is done; the one who holds the knife makes the demands."

At this, Lavoisier raised his bayonet toward her.

She stepped back. "God's teeth, listen! I will give you the locations of Whitlock's munitions, the underground tunnel and communication system, supplies of blackpowder, detailed inventory, schedules for shipments, names of associated parties, specific breakdowns of their fighting strategies and what they know of yours. I've got all this. I will give you this. But you must promise me something in return: Naught else in my town gets touched. My friends, my home, the Osbornes, the Starkses, my harbor—you don't put a finger to any of it. You want Whitlock, you take Whitlock—I will serve him to you on pristine pewter. But then get out of here. Don't touch the rest if you be an honorable man. Do we have a deal?"

Lavoisier lowered his bayonet and turned to Machk, who had re-mained unmoved through the exchange, amused, nodding. Ruth kept her dagger pointed at Lavoisier and pulled from her dress pocket the list that Machk had given her. She handed it, folded open, to Lavoisier, being sure Machk saw it in the transition. The Indian stood still as the surrounding maples, watching intently.

"I believe this might be your script, Captain," Ruth said.

He didn't look at the list of materials. He didn't need to. "This was your bargain, then, for a Frenchman convicted of treason."

Ruth's chest fell. What difference had it made? She'd lost him anyway. The bargain was only the hollowed remains of what could have been. She turned to Machk. "I fulfill my half of the bargain as I swore I would. I honor it for Askook—my friend, your warrior—and I'll consider this a deal." She cautiously reached to her calf, taking the folded stack of maps and strategic plans from her boot. She handed the papers to Machk, and in continuum, he handed them to Lavoisier without a glance. "I will not make a trade of women. We're slave enough already. For that, you are on your own. We are even now. Honor your deal." She backed toward Arrow with her dagger still drawn on Lavoisier.

"Now, wait," Lavoisier said, eying her. "Where do you think you're going?"

He lunged toward her as she kicked a foot into her stirrup and swung herself into the saddle, swiping down with her dagger toward his tricorne and slicing through the excessive feathers, sending the red tufts through the air like flapping birds.

She smirked. "Much better." She knocked his shoulder away from Arrow with a dismissive kick and turned her horse to gallop toward what she hoped was The Road, still hearing their voices.

Lavoisier yelled, "Stop her!"

Machk raised a palm to keep everyone in place. "Let her go. She is more valuable to us out there."

She looked back only briefly to see the Pequot nodding toward the documents she had given them. The two men exchanged a glance. The treason of a general's wife was worth the weight in gold of all the gunpowder kegs they'd just been handed.

Chapter Twenty-Sixth

The avengers

And where the offense is,
let the great ax fall.

—William Shakespeare

Ruth lifted off the reeds like she'd been propelled. Wetness had seeped through the back of her dress from the marsh, and the space was dark around her. Her dry eyes throbbed from their sudden opening. The middle of the night. Muffled voices. Commotion in the street beyond the small, half-built frame of her house where she'd been sleeping, tucked under a canopy of sticks and leaves for a roof. The sky past it rimmed with orange. She reached for her shawl, then pulled on her boots, half untied. She rummaged beneath the reedtails for her dagger. The smell of—what?—smoke? God. Lavoisier had the maps. The men stationed in the woods, so close. Flashes in her mind: The troops rolling through the streets, ransacking the fields, people, livestock. Leveling the homes with torches. Breaking their bargain. Stealing whatever guns and horses they found.

The commotion increased. More voices now. Horse hooves, although not many. Not yet an army. There was still time. She considered an evacuation plan for Isabel, Daniel, Martha, and Helen's family. Sneaking through the back acres toward the Starkses' well, taking enough hogsfat to make it through the fields and up into the inland swells beyond the church. Horse tracks would be too obvious. They'd have to run—and wide apart, less traceable. They could catch the Pequot Trail and take it northeast to Westerly, be there by the next nightfall—although, that was Rhode Island, full of Quakers. Not that she feared them now, but the others would. Days northwest, they could make Norwich, but Ruth had only heard its name and had no bearings for it. She considered this while she strapped her frogbelt across her waist and filled her pockets with paper cartridges.

She climbed over the frame that only came to her waist, then ran toward the center of town. Coming up from behind the Osbornes' home and stepping into the unusually bright street, she saw it. Samuel's house—the beautiful King's Hall—ablaze. The wood chewed by the mouths of sparks and spit into the clouds, licking the night sky like barbed snakes' tongues and branching out like chaffs of grain. The fire spread quickly. People stirred to waking, a fleeing body or two, running from or toward the blaze, gawking, running, helping, gawking. The culprits on horseback, fewer than she'd imagined, lit and placed new torches. She had expected the French—where were the French? The figures she saw gathered there instead—avenging the deaths of their fallen, repaying the burned planks of *Primrose* in kind—were the Townsend boys.

Ruth rushed to the house. Samuel's outcome didn't enter her mind. Nor the fiery fate befalling the handcarved banisters and full iron stove, but there were innocents here. "Martha!" Ruth searched the flames for any semblance of an entrance. The main entryways had been lit first, and the flames ate them entirely. From atop his horse, Gabriel blocked her attempt before he realized who she was, nearly knocking her off her feet. "What in mercy's name have you done here?" she said. "You'll bring the militia against your whole family."

Gabriel looked down at her. "Let them come." He pulled his horse back to throw another torch. "We'll be ready."

"Is he inside?" She nodded toward the inferno.

"Yes. With Lieutenant Governor Nicholson and what's left of the cursed Dominion. We'll burn them out."

Ruth caught a glimpse of Avery and Elias behind the house dragging a man out to the field with pistols drawn. She turned from Gabriel. "Dear God. Robert!" she yelled when she neared the brothers, waving her arms fanatically. "Please, stop. Don't hurt him."

The two boys turned to look at her with pistols half-drawn in her direction. She reached them quickly and pulled Samuel's servant from their grasp.

"Leave him." She took hold of Robert by the shoulders. "He did nothing."

She faced him, the poor man disoriented and burned on his arms and face. Bubbles rose along his cheekbones, his eyelids—the eyes they circled didn't look at anything, just through it. Glazed and burned.

"Are you all right?" Tears pushed at her lower lids. "Where is Martha?" Robert nodded toward the stable, and Ruth turned him in the direction he was pointing. "Go to the barns, and get her out of here.

Get the ostlers and hands as far from here as you can, and don't look back. You are free to go. Release the slaves, and take them with you. Show them the way. Robert, you hear me!" She shook him again. "Release them, and get them from here. Go north, and keep going north." The boys raised their pistols at his fleeing back, and she shoved the outstretched barrels toward the ground and slapped Avery across the ear. "If you hurt them, any of them, I'll see you punished, so help me, I don't care what name you wear. They are innocent."

"Innocent people die in war," Avery replied. "My brother's death should have taught you that."

"This is not war." She gestured around her. "*This*. Is not war."

She turned away from the brothers. There was something new. Something else. The hairs along her spine stood to ends. In the street behind the house, thundering like a storm approaching. Horse hooves. From the Eastern Road near the forest, and she could hear them so plainly now. Could no one else hear them?

"Run, Avery. Go!"

She pushed him and ran toward the road, toward the advancing noise. She was winded from her careless sprint by the time she rounded the corner, and she almost crashed into two horses. Ash Townsend and, to her surprise, Val Mason, both sat mounted on their horses, fueling the blaze with more fire. She looked back and forth between the two men.

"Go home," Ash commanded, already impatient. "You're not needed in this."

The pounding of horse hooves grew closer, closer, replicating, and she heard someone scream. The words followed, yelling, that the munitions bunkers had been robbed. As she turned to run, there they were. At least thirty advancing French soldiers, and she faced them head-on, in their blues, whites, golds, and grays, as they charged into the town toward the blaze of King's Hall. *The town*. Her throat hardened. It would be ashes by morning. What had she done?

Amongst the soldiers, she recognized Captain Lavoisier. He stampeded past, then drew up on the reins and tugged his horse around to face her. The stallion reared, and Lavoisier managed it back down. He nodded to her and pointed candidly up to the five red, uncut feathers adorning his tricorne. She furrowed her brow, expecting him to march through town, setting fields and homes aflame. But he turned back toward King's Hall. *The pristine pewter*. It was then so clear to her. Her people might be spared destruction from the French soldiers, but Samuel would not. So be it. He'd killed one of theirs, and they were coming for him. The hooves pounded, and she stood to the side of them.

Intermingled among the French soldiers were their Indian warrior allies. A handful of Pequot faces Ruth recognized. The troops gathered around the fire, lined up sloppily, untrained. They were perplexed. They had anticipated a surprise attack, but it had been upstaged by the arrival of the Townsend brothers. Fire already tore through what the Frenchmen had come to burn. The grounds blazed around them, and they stared at it. And then a shot rang out through the dark from the Western Road. A Frenchman let out a cry. Ruth turned toward the sound in time to see the man who'd uttered it fall from his horse. The air sparked with red spray, pieces of rib bone in it. Attention turned from him and toward the Western Road. *The English were coming.*

The two sides to meet right where Ruth stood. She watched it in her mind already. The bodies falling from horses. Some to defend, some to destroy, but all to fall. Amidst the clattering of hooves, the volleys beginning, another sound cut through the night. Ruth looked back. The debris-laden silhouettes of Samuel and the Dominion Honor Guard fought fiery wooden beams to emerge through the engulfed doorway of King's Hall. Ruth gasped. As the English brigades, both trained British military and simple militia rabble alike, reached King's Hall from the southwestern garrison, the French charged into them—horses and men on foot, Indians—and the two warring sides met. But Ruth's eyes were on Samuel. Unbreathable smoke, the smell of dampened musk and scorched sod. So many shots fired that her ears rang with them as if her head were inside a gigantic muted bell, some phantom tipping it from one side to the other, one ear to the other. Samuel raised his court sword high and headed for the French and Pequot, then disappeared among them into the smoky darkness of the frenzy.

Shouts, musketballs ripped into the night in all directions. Elias Townsend's horse ran toward the field without a rider. God, the Townsend brothers—what of them in all this? She made out the subtle outline of Val riding toward her, just barely. Then nothing; then he reappeared, riding with a torch in one hand and fending off an English militia rider with the other. The soldier gripped Val's jacket as the men fought, clutching and releasing each other's clothing, hair, until the militiaman abruptly jerked Val sideways. The gesture knocked Val into his own torch and then to the ground in a rupture of flames that quickly spread over his jacket, flammable hose, and greasy hair.

Ruth screamed.

She ran to him, smothering the flames on his body with her shawl and rolling him through the dirt. Mud and grass clung to him and choked out the flare. He lay on his back, smoke coming from him like an old stack furnace, and he groaned and whimpered and caught his wits in the smell of slag and ash, his fingers black as scoria pressing against her softness. She crawled over him with her shawl and held his shaking body, and then the English soldier loomed above her, his silhouetted gun raised, a nimbus of fire haloing. Val pulled Ruth against him, lifted his pistol, and fired a shot into the chest of the advancing soldier. The Englishman's body exploded outward in red, then slumped to the dirt with a thud, bucking, then still. Val lowered his head back to the ground and dropped the gun from his grasp, still clutching Ruth to his chest. She stared at the gun, disbelieving.

"Yes," he said, "it's always been loaded."

He coughed and shuffled, and she saw then that burns covered his chest, arms, and neck. His clothes melted into his flesh, bloodied and blackened. She studied this in glassiness, the blackness of it wetted into the landscape that sat like a hole, a canyon that began at the edge of where they were. Then, an explosion cleaved the night and halved two sheets of darkness with a brilliant orange-white light. Barrels' worth of blackpowder from Samuel's munitions room blew the roof off the back of the house next to Val and Ruth. A series of gunpowder explosions followed one after another, pops and roars, and Val rolled his body over the top of hers, shielding her pregnant belly and covering her ears and face with his hands. Fiery debris showered over his back, spidering down the sky like skeletal fingers. Another loud explosion went off next to his head, sending a ringing through his ears and coating him in a cloud of black fumes. He choked down deep, painful breaths of smoke and spent powder, and cupped his hand over his right ear, watching her mouth move. She was surely shouting, but he did not hear a word. One long, high note stayed against his eardrums, and beyond it was the milkiness of nothing.

He lifted Ruth to her feet, but a war raged on all sides, and there was nowhere to go. From out of the darkness, then, Gabriel rode up, dragging along the reins of the retrieved Fogcutter. Val mounted the mare swiftly, reaching a hand down to help Ruth into the pillion behind the saddle, but as she extended her hand to his, another shot rang out, and it startled the horse. Fogcutter lurched forward, and Ruth misstepped. The bullet pierced Gabriel's back. Both horses reared in the panic.

Ruth cried out to Gabriel and ran toward his horse with her pistol drawn, firing a shot in the direction of the first projectile, but he had been struck by a stray that found the youngest Townsend standing in its way. Before she could reach him, his horse took flight, and he slumped over in his saddle. His stallion tore across the field into the smog of gunfire, and she lost him. Fogcutter, too, had been spooked into a run, and Val was caught in a struggle to control the mare, twisting out of sight.

Ruth spun back to see the French fighting in the blaze against the English. *Now this was war.* She had to get to Arrow. She had to get out of there. Her feet led her absently away from the fire and in the direction of the Osborne home, but a mounted militiaman cut off her path on a horse so dark, it looked like the rider sat only on the night sky.

He spit on her and swung his sword at her torso. "I'll cut that sinful child out of you, ya cunt."

She stepped clear of his blade and raised her pistol before he could take another swing. She cocked the flintlock and fired. The kickback sent her to the ground, and the ball clipped him in the arm, tore through, and exited the backside of his shoulder. He screamed and cursed and pulled back, letting go of his raised sword and dropping the blade. Ruth groped for her other pistol, but the militiaman had already retreated, howling curses over his destroyed shoulder.

Ruth scanned the field for Val, but instead she saw a cluster of familiar Pequot standing near the Eastern Road, engaged in combat with militia. At the front of the group, the surefooted Machk stood a head taller than the rest, his warpaint rivaling the frightfulness of the flames. Ruth pocketed her spent pistol and held the loaded one in her outstretched hand as she moved toward him, hoping to find Askook. Machk's eyes flicked to hers across the front yard of the burning house, and he held out his hand to her. He drove the English brigades back while Ruth carefully picked out a safe path to reach him.

But as she got closer, she heard an awful cry, a bellowed then keening ululation—the wail of a white man emulating what he called savage. She looked up toward Machk in time to witness it. A court sword entered through his torso from behind. Ruth's feet planted into the low goutweed she stood in, and she felt herself sink all the way to the slave tilth. She thought she moved, but she stood there, her hands out before her as if to reach it, to reach him, to catch him.

The Englishman drew the sword out from Machk's back, and as the Indian slumped forward, Ruth saw the killer plain then. The blood splashed upon him. The uniform in the king's colors she'd sewn. A sling about one arm. And there, firelight glinted off Samuel's shiny buttons, little reflections of evil spirits glistering about his figure. He couldn't even face a man in war; he had to stab cowardly in the back. He reached down to grab hold of Machk's lifeless body by the head, to lift the Indian's hair toward the sword's blade.

Ruth screamed, and it tapered into a mournful lament that coursed across chaffs and pods as if to lay them flat. Three-toothed cinquefoil and barren strawberry and golden ragwort leveled into nothing around her, the night only darkness surrounding this illumination. Samuel dragged his sword across Machk's head and scalped the dead Indian before turning his gloar to Ruth. He met her eyes and recognized the pistols, the saber frog at her side. For the first time, in that moment, he saw her, truly, what she'd been capable of, what she'd done. What she'd done to him. How she'd led them straight to him. Her stomach convulsed into tight knots at the sight of Samuel's fist clenched around Machk's bloody scalp, and she bent over and vomited on the ground before her. The reaction was unexpected, and she reeled and vomited a second time.

The lieutenant general walked toward his treasonous wife—his court sword drawn in one hand and Machk's bloody scalp dangling in the other. It was then she saw how fatigued he was, how sickly, his gait slow and erratic. She righted herself and raised her pistol toward him, but her aim was poor through her watery eyes and the smoky haze of the fire and blackpowder. She regretted wasting those two shots in her first pistol. How she needed them now. Two barrels: two shots.

She aimed for his heart, but the pistol didn't comply. It released a wild ball that whizzed past Samuel's hip and off into the crowd of English militia behind him. His lips twisted more. He laughed at her. All the while, he steadily advanced as if it were a game. She took aim for the second shot. But this time, the barrel was too high, and the lead ball vanished into black air above him. And that was it. The two bullets had been fired, and they hadn't struck his heart.

She reached for her ammunition satchel, fumbling for a paper cartridge with shaky fingers and counting the seconds in her head. One. She became so acutely aware of the surrounding universe. Two. Aware of panic in the scents of swamp rose, then the shadblow with its small

apple-fruits that disappeared so fast, spicebrush and staghorn and blad-
dernut. Three. Samuel stepped closer, dropping the scalp, unflinching,
and Ruth had barely started to reload. Seven, eight. The ocean, full-
mouthed and moiling—she heard it now where it bruised the dock,
that swale it butted into, that muskeg along the edge of her land—she
could smell the leatherleaf now, trailing. Eleven. Then, Samuel was
close enough to reach her, and she smacked the gun across his jaw and
turned to run.

He lashed out and caught her dress, and she tripped. The ground
came up to meet her, and she knelt into it, then rolled away beneath
Samuel and turned and threw the half-loaded flintlock at him, the ramrod sticking him as he deflected the gun against his sword and clasped
her about the belt, pulling her back toward him. His fingers shook, and
he sweat as if fevered. She squirmed loose and got to her knees, but he
caught her and dragged her to him.

"What trouble you've wrought me," he hissed. "You want to mourn
for a Redskin, then you'll die like one." He slid his arm from the sling,
a seething sound through teeth, grabbed hold of her hair and pulled it
back and brought his sword toward her forehead.

She kicked out and twisted, but he held fast, though his apparent
sickness made him unquick. His hand slipped on her oily strands, and
he recaught. When his body brushed against her swollen belly, new life,
new tenor came to her thrashing. She wriggled free enough to draw her
dagger from her boot, and the grasp was at last hers. Triton's blade shim-
mered in the dartling flames. She could reach little, but as he brought
his blade against her head, she heaved back and cut his forearm. Samuel
jerked, and his blade nicked her, then slipped and swiped across the
bunched hair he held in his fist. Her head wrenched free of the severed
strands, releasing his hold on her. He held in his fist a clump of her
unattached hair. He stared at it like a foreign thing, and in his stupefied
moment, she swiveled around and drove Triton into Samuel's throat,
twisting it so fiercely that it nearly severed his head from his body. A
spurt of red coated her blade, face, and dress, and Samuel's eyes were
opened wide, his mouth still in an O that stuck there, claiming his last
sound. His body dropped to the ground, his head hanging by sinewy
threads indistinguishable in the red. She stood over him and closed her
eyes, feeling the soft, worn leather grip, feeling Owen's hand laid across
her belly. How she'd wept then. How she didn't weep now.

Ruth looked to Machk's body, dazed. Askook's vision of hope for

the restoration of the Pequots' future appeared shattered as their warrior sachem lay defiled on English ground. The summer wind whipped
across the open field, and Ruth could no longer feel her hair blowing
in the breeze, could smell nothing of the sedges and sweet crabapples
now, could not hear the ocean. A hand absently at the back of her
head—hers maybe, she wasn't sure—stroked short ends of hair like
dried straw, cropped jaggedly along her scalp. It was the hair of her
youth, now lying across Samuel's bloody neck. The new locks to be
reborn in their place would be her own, untouched and unsullied by his
dirty hands. He could never hurt anything she loved again.

Shouting came. Still a battle. It hadn't stopped because she had
stopped. Snapping-to, she heard Val as he stampeded toward her. He'd
regained control of Fogcutter. He pulled the horse alongside her and
lowered his arm, surveying her and the corpse beside her.

"Come, now." Val pulled her onto the pillion and aimed Fogcutter
for the relative haven of the woods.

She put her arms around him and held to his jacket. He felt her
breaths against his right ear, but he couldn't hear her breathing, any
words she may have uttered. It was the first he'd realized his ear was
truly dead to him. He scrunched his face, choked it back. They neared
a copse of bitternuts and pignuts beyond the clearing, tall hickories that
looked ominous in the false dawn, a black on black with a thin ambient
meridian passing through its base. Val halted, feeling Ruth still seething
at his back. Her breath fell on his neck, and her hands were tucked
inside his half-buttoned, singed jacket, gripping into his burned chest.

"I killed a man," he finally breathed out carefully.

"You came here to kill a man."

"Yes."

He kicked his leg over the side of Fogcutter and slid down, reaching
up to catch Ruth. He pulled her into him and held her there, and they
trembled together. Her cropped hair ran snagless through his fingers as
he drew her face to his shoulder.

"Are you hurt?" she asked.

"Aye, I'm on fire."

"Not still?"

"Still."

Ruth pulled back and looked at the side of his face and hair, his
burned arms and neck. A seared bandana half-covered half his neck.
The rest was covered in red, white, and brown bubbly burns like an old

man's warts or the popped liquidy blisters that had appeared on her toes after the frostbite. His brand was erased. She put her hand to her belly. It was this exact moment she saw on Val's face that he knew nothing could replace a ghost. Everything else was in shadow, and she only saw it in this shadow. She, herself, was in shadow, her vision, her line of sight, all she sought.

He gestured back to the yellow halation. "I'll wager you wasn't seen in any way anyone could prove."

"Proof has never been of consequence."

"Blame me, if it come to it. They won't catch me. Go home, Ruth Miner. Sleep off that anger before it poisons your child."

"You're going? But."

"No buts."

"I'll not find you again." She'd meant it to be a question.

"You'll find me if you want to find me." Val pulled himself up in the saddle where he could see the flames in the distance. "If ever you should desire a man still in the land of the living," he laughed without mirth, "bring your fine mustang and your bastard child and find me. I may prove worth finding."

He reached down from his horse, nearly unrecognizable from their first encounter, and he took her hand to his lips, placed a kiss on her palm, and closed her fingers around it. He looked older, sorrowful, a youthful glow gone from him, and Ruth lamented that she'd snuffed out one more light. But it was her penance to lose it, to watch it all gutter as punishment for the haste from which she could never seem to learn, never seem to untangle from her nature. Val pulled away quickly, aimed Fogcutter's muzzle to The Road and charged away from Ruth. Smaller and smaller along the winding path, a tenor to him that singled him out against the maples like a lodestar, until he disappeared around a landmark she did not know.

❧

The fire crackled on at dawn. Ruth walked among the men still working to extinguish what endured. To her relief, no one paid heed to her as she slinked through town. She stood out with cropped hair, sprayed in blood, yet stood out not at all.

The population gathered. John and Prudence Hallam brought buckets. Thomas Wheeler shoveled dirt onto the low flames, while his wife, Mary, fetched more water. John Randell, Aaron Stark, Goodman John Fish, Peter Blatchfield, Joshua Hempstead—they were there with their hands at the ready. She knew them all by name, yet she knew no one.

She thought of Val, off somewhere, sleeping under some brush. Was he in pain? Would he have to cover more of himself now? She imagined him finding an abandoned byre near Wolf Neck, one with a sturdy partition to separate Fogcutter and Val into different rooms under the same roof, and he'd live there, reclusive, farming patches of tough soil only when dusk settled. Then her thoughts drifted to Owen, sleeping under a dirt mound somewhere in the Red Forest. She looked toward it, and in the dawn, with the sun slipping through its flooring like fingers pointing upward, the red bark looked to be on fire. She craved him, his laugh and sharp tongue, and she was lost among the crowd of familiar strangers. Could she live in the land of the living? No, she didn't think so. Not here. Not this land that took the living from her. She came through the back of the group of onlookers to view the remnants, to hear their gossip of the forty, fifty, hundred, five hundred French soldiers with guns, swords, and torches tearing through the town on a violent rampage that left King's Hall in ruins, Samuel slain at its doorstep, a town loudly in fear. There couldn't have been but thirty, she remembered. There was no talk of highwaymen. No word of the uncredited Townsend brothers. No mention of Ruth. With their savior gone, they'd forgotten her.

Word was of the French soldiers, Captain Lavoisier, who might have been dead in her field, the English militia, men of Stonington's garrisons following her husband's command. All the dead left behind sorrowful wives and needy children, widowed and fatherless. More wooden coffins to fill the streets. Her sorrow, however, sat most with the Indians, for the now-leaderless and diminished Pequot. For Askook, whose body might also have been in that field, facedown among singed crops, slumped over the body of another boy—only boys, most of them were. She wanted to find out, to turn over every fallen body, check every face until she did or didn't see him, but she couldn't. She willed herself to believe that, somewhere, Askook was alive.

Goodwife Crotchett's glare stole across the circle of onlookers. Before another nightfall, the whole colony would know about the French advance and Ruth's bloody dress, the severed hair lying across Samuel's throat. This time, she would have no one to fend them off but her own iron will.

She inched backward from the flickering embers of her former house. It meant as little to her now as ever it did. The Osbornes' door was opened a crack, and Isabel's embrace welcomed Ruth on the other side. For a moment, everything was quiet. Despair would follow. There would be pain to come beyond the immediate anguish of war. She knew her child, conceived in the budding warmth of an innocent spring, would be born in the harsh cold of winter. Snow would halo the child's head, and Val was right: she would be poisoned, the innocent babe, for all that had come before she'd even taken her first breath. Winter was coming, and with it, the blizzards and famines that ended lives. For now, though, it was quiet.

CHAPTER TWENTY-SEVENTH
Autumn comes; or, the epilogue

At rest, however,
in the middle of everything,
is the sun.

—Nicolaus Copernicus

"What you said about the tides changing with the moon: do you think that's really true or just a coincidence?" Helen asked, as she leaned over her own five-months-pregnant belly and broke some late Hubbard squash from the stalks in the Osborne field. Their gray-blue shells and dry, fine-grained flesh blended into the gray of the land, and if it weren't for their enormity, she'd not have seen them against it.

"If it becomes an occurrence multiple times a day or night at the same hour each time, then it's no longer a coincidence. Rather, it must have some logic behind it. Waves and tides are controlled the same way the stars and wind are," Ruth responded, laboring much harder over her own eight-months-pregnant belly to pull up the late and most stubborn vegetables in the field, mostly cheese squash with its tan-orange skin and coarse pumpkin look. Askutasquash, the Indians had called it— Askook had called it. In her mind, it had morphed to Askooksquash and would forever remain so.

"And you think it is the moon or sun that does this and not God?"

"Aye." Ruth laughed. "I don't think mussel-gathering tide intervals are very high on his list. The sun and moon exist in their place as a center all things draw their lives from. It keeps everything going in turn. Like…a heart, I suppose." Ruth paused. "*The Principia* teaches of lunar gravity. It's gravity what controls the moon, not coincidence. Coincidence controls nothing but fear." She turned back to the squash. "I'd lend you my copy, if I wouldn't get strung up for it."

"Nothing's stringed you up so far," Helen laughed. "I doubt that could do it."

Five long months had passed. Sometimes Ruth felt that if she could explain the sun, the moon, the stars, the tides, the very order of the

universe, she'd figure out how those events and consequences all intertwined to create their own order in turn, and that somehow, there was a
place, a reason, and an explanation for all of it, and in her own understanding of this, she'd find her own order in the universe, an answer to
whys and hows of the past, where they crossed with the hows of the
future. The summer had come and gone, and now the autumn, too, fled
on the ends of the final harvest from the hard soil. She remained at the
Osborne home; her own marshy property had been rescinded under
order of the Mystic magistrate, once it had been deemed she had no
husband to speak for it legally. She kept quiet about the details of that
fateful night of the fire at King's Hall, but it never left her mind. She
saw it in flashes—hair at a throat, a red-velveted rider on a dark horse,
his back to her, taking to a road.

For eight months along, her bearing was small. She sweat harder to
work the chores and required help in more difficult errands; yet, she
refused to leave the hardest tasks undone or to make any excuses for
her condition. Helen never let her friend spend too much time alone.
Melancholy claimed most of Ruth's thoughts. The Stonington Council
made it clear that Ruth's sentence would be carried out, despite Samuel's
death, or perhaps, in honor of it.

She hadn't been blamed for the arson or for Samuel's murder, and
the stolen documents were thought lost to rooms leveled in explosions.
The cropped hair that had lain across his throat had been mysteriously
moved, vanished. She thought of that day often, but despite her efforts
at forgiveness, it was seldom with guilt that she looked back on him
lying there. The time neared when she would depart for the closest
town, disappear in the night, and break the sentence that had been cast
on the child, and this is what replaced thoughts of that day, that fire.
No child of Owen's would serve a master. A promise had been made.
Breaking the chains that bound her would not be an easy task; still, it
would be done.

"You know it is inside of a month now," Helen said, cheerily.

"Both our children will be born in a cold winter," Ruth said. "But
yours will know the warmth of spring."

Helen didn't reply.

"If there are other worlds out there, I wonder if they have spring.
I wonder if somewhere there is an endless winter and somewhere an
endless spring, and how do we cross over? How does one understand
spring when he's known only winter?"

"You mustn't talk of such things." Helen stooped to a broad-bean patch. "Will you never learn?"

"I will never stop learning."

Fairfield came to mind again—what Ruth remembered, shrouded in its gray. And Val, how he'd been there. Would she go there with her newborn child and chance upon him on the way? The past months had been lonely months. Where Askook had once come daily to talk along the stone fence, the forest was now empty. She hadn't seen him since he'd set into the woods with what was left of her heart, but the day after the battle of King's Hall, a red mohawk feather had been nailed to the chopping block by the fence where they'd once nurtured their secret friendship. His flax fields had been sown in the dead of night. And her vanished hair on the battlefield. She took these as a sign that Askook was there somewhere in the woods, distant, unable to reveal himself to her any longer. But alive.

At night, she could sometimes hear the far-off guns of the New English fighting the New French, but none passed through since Captain Lavoisier sent his men charging from King's Hall up toward Canada five months prior. The word along the coast was that the war moved farther north and had abandoned the lower half of the New England Colonies, yet the local folk remained unconvinced. The Viceroyalty of New France was outnumbered and defenseless from the Hudson to Canada. Gossip spread about the Iroquois attack of Lachine, where the cannibalistic warriors tore the unborn babies out of the bellies of pregnant mothers and roasted the children alive over spits, leaving both French and English colonists across the East Coast terrified. Ruth viewed all this with the sort of distance with which one views a stormfront that has moved out over the sea without dropping its rain. It becomes less a frightful thing, but still its darkness bedizens the horizon ominously. She knew the war they were calling King William's War would be bloody and long and one of many that would sprawl and last into the next and the next, then be forgotten as the last and the last, but she wistfully hoped that Lavoisier fired off a few rounds with the English's stolen guns before he was taken down.

Most disappointing of all, Val had not returned. On Sundays between meetings and late in the evenings after chores were done, she rode Arrow out of town to the nooks of The Road to see if she could glimpse a claret jacket atop a familiar mare, but there was no sign. She regretted the night she let him ride off without telling him what his friendship meant to her. He knew, she imagined. But that didn't lessen the ache of regret. Only time could do that now. She looked to the corner of the field where the browning fall leaves of the dwarfish lilac bush lilted, and she breathed out a small prayer for all of them, all of her extinguished lights, that they would glow again somewhere else, if not with her.

"Did you hear that Mercy is getting married?" Helen asked Ruth, startling her.

"Mercy Palmer? To John Breed? That will be good. So many folk are joyous going into winter. It will take the bitter sting out of the cold for everyone." She smiled genuinely.

Helen set her basket down and leaned on the edge of the stone fence next to Ruth. "You don't know it yet, but this child you carry, this boy or girl of your very blood, will take the sting out of it for you, too. You will have unbounded joy beyond any fathom of pain's grasp. You'll never know how you could have lived your whole life without her." Helen took hold of Ruth's hands. "The council wonnot take your child. We wonnot let them. You will have your little girl, and you will watch her grow, and you will teach her of your 'plurality of worlds,' and read to her from your forbade books in languages I cannot imagine, and she will grow into a…strange, knowledgeable…spinster. You will love her, the way she runs toward spring, even more than your memory of him."

Helen laid a hand across Ruth's belly to feel the baby move. Ruth reached a trembling hand to Helen's belly in kind, and the two women laughed.

"See," Helen whispered. "Now would be a good time for you to believe in miracles."

"No." Ruth wagged her finger. "This is not a miracle. It's a view-of-matter. And busy men. You better not teach that child to believe in miracles."

"Perhaps the view-of-matter is the miracle?"

"God's teeth, no. A thing is or is not, and it is simply not."

Thus went their conversation, until Isabel called to the young women to come in for refreshment. Ruth was chilly, and the stiffener couldn't hurt. On her way toward the house, she ruminated. Trinkets from overseas. Real perfume. She missed books and world politics, stories of war and foreign ports. She missed poems in French, the anticipation of something exciting waiting at the harbor. The smell of wet and musty wood and the creaking of docking anchors. Looking forward to something, to someone. There had always stood the promise of arrival; now remained only the promise of departure.

"How many times have I told you to keep yourself hydrated for that baby's sake?" Isabel scolded when Ruth walked through the door, handing off the overstuffed basket of vegetables, heavier than she'd meant for it to be.

"You know I haven't enough toes to count that high." Ruth sat down at the table, resting one hand across her belly and the other on a pewter stein of hard cider. Helen followed, and they made a merry tinking together of their steins, but Ruth's demeanor remained sullen.

"You look worried, my babe," Isabel said when the three women were quiet for too long. "Come, what be the bother?"

Ruth stood from the table and walked into the area where her mattress and trunk were situated. She gathered a few of her belongings, a book: Cotton Mather's *Memorable Providences, Relating to Witchcrafts and Possessions*, an astonishing account of Bostonian Irish washerwoman Goody Glover's episode of witchcraft. Ruth found it amusing, but now where it sat, thrown into the top of her trunk, it only looked unnecessary. The French perfume would go, though. Some leftover lilac seeds. The swatch of dress fabric that still bore Owen's bloody handprint, deeply embedded into the cloth, was stiff and dusty now. She laid it across her abdomen as it had once been, matching her hand to the top of his, pressing it to her. The tiny mirror caught her eye. The metal creature's history sat in its rusting tin edges. She flipped the encasement over to look into the reflection, but where she remembered pinching rosy color into her cheeks, she now looked tired, bleak. She hadn't bothered to stare into its tattling for months. She slid the mirror into the trunk and folded articles of clothing on top.

Isabel looked on. "I knew this day would arrive," she said to Ruth, taking hold of Helen's hand across the table. Comfort where it could be found.

"It grieves me to leave," Ruth said, "but I have no choice. I must go."

A knock at the door interrupted them, disquieting the women.

"God's teeth," Ruth said. "I don't have any more syrup for these addicted women. This is the fourth one in two days."

Isabel opened the door. Hannah Sterry—a young woman of the town whom Ruth knew only from The Road Church and a boisterously celebrated engagement to Mr. William Billings—stood on the doorstep, rigid as a timber. Ruth remembered the guns that had recently gone off in the distance, the intervals between shots getting closer and closer together, and feared the girl was a messenger of war.

"I got word for Mrs. Whitlock," Hannah's mousy voice split the quiet, and Isabel bid her enter.

A shiver ran down Ruth's spine. *That name.* Whitlock. Even in death, her name was attached to him and could not be shaken of it. Hannah and Ruth stood before each other in the kitchen, presently as if preparing to duel.

Hannah said, "I got sended by the council. They request to see you." She reddened as if she did not enjoy her task.

Ruth turned to Isabel. "Oh. Oh, my. You don't suppose that… It couldn't be that they. Well, surely not yet." She paced and scanned between Isabel, Helen, and Hannah. "Oh, Isabel," her voice trailed. "Do you think that it's…"

Isabel nodded curt thanks to Hannah and turned the girl toward the door, shooing her out abruptly. Isabel closed the door with her hands pressed hard against it. She didn't speak. Ruth remained rooted. The floor swelled into uneven mounds on which she had to shift her footing in balance.

Helen rose and walked to her side. "You have to know what they say," she said. "At least find out. Then if you must go," she paused, "*run.*"

Ruth held on to a chair, to Helen, her hands wandering for purchase. "Oh, Isabel. Helen." She shook her head. It was too soon. What if they locked her up, and she couldn't get to another town, to safety?

Isabel opened the door in front of Ruth, ushering as it was necessary.

"Just promise," Helen added softly, with tears already wetting her cheeks, "that you'll think of us once in a moon." The words sounded so final, so sure. She stood on her tiptoes, kissed Ruth on the forehead, then turned the bewildered woman out the door. "Go. Live, you wild heart."

Ruth took a step out the door but stopped. So sudden. Her mind, incredulous, waited for something to break her spell. She couldn't face the council yet. She hadn't intended to face them at all. She'd stayed one day too long. Yet, somehow, a calm came over her when she saw the entryway to the harbor, great sails of great ships off in the distance, all around her aware that the season ended soon, moving as if to a destination. She had to walk past the harbor, but she never walked past it without first walking toward it, and it took her longer to get there than ever before.

She became conscious of how she looked as she always did when she neared the port, where it was already too late to turn back. The dress she wore did not flatter; its tawniness matched her skin, gave her no color. It had been meant for plucking dirty squash heads, and her apron's ashen dullness paralleled in wan ugliness. She untied the apron and tossed it behind her. Let Abigail Billings find it in the path and put it to use. Loam had collected under her fingernails. Stubborn silt permeated her dress collar as if she'd sewn it into the fabric. She couldn't imagine what her face must look like beyond that tiny mirror's telling, the dirt on her cheeks, dust that coated her neckline in thick brown lines that itched. Her hair bounced uncovered, oily and short. Before she could complete her mental list of shortcomings, she was past the harbor, past the long dock, and curving on the swell toward Councilor Burke's. Then she stopped. The air that had been cooled by autumn's coming seemed warmer. Gnats, always swarming into open mouths, parted around her, and she floated through them, untouched. The sun clawed through a passing cloud, and it split the land into fractions of gold and red and gray. Something registered. A flicker at the harbor, and she turned.

There was a man. Her insides leaped and tugged at her and told her to run, but she stayed planted. The figure stood in a sweeping black jacket that stopped at his thighs. Reflective brass buttons adorned the length of the front. She could see the buttons shining from across the dock. His shoulders settled high and, connected by a passant, were graced with gold bullion-fringed epaulets depicting a man of grand rank. He had dark, black hair, but she couldn't make out his eyes beneath the shadow of the beaverskin French cocked-hat he wore. A gold-braided cord hung from it, coupled with a cockade of, at one time, some significance to someone. Beneath the hat, a soapstone pipe hung from the man's lip. She gasped. Beneath his coat, galligaskins—ink-black, full-length fallfronts—covered his legs. They met with knee-high black Spanish leather boots, the right of which was attached with a brace and buckles at the thigh that seemed to be holding the boot up, in place. Ruth regarded the cane in his right hand, his lean into it that rested all his weight against its support. He looked foreboding, to say the least.

Yet, as if on a track, she moved toward him. Cautiously. An apparition on a ghost ship. Afraid a misstep would send her into the water only to find it not water at all, but the dirt floor beside her mattress, jolting her awake. As she neared, he looked up. His blue eyes fulgurated across the dock and onward across the sea in one flicker that electrified everything. She would know those eyes for all time. Yet, the face. Scarred and hardened. But with it a familiar voice cut through the caution, and it was a real voice.

"The council didn't request you, Mrs. Whitlock." He nodded. "I did."

Everything inside her fell to the ground with that voice. Except her fear. Her fear clung to her like a barnacle. Yet, she moved closer, closer.

"I'd scant recognize you without all that hair."

"I watched you die," was all she could think to say.

"Never count a man dead who still has a heartbeat, Ruthie. Your savage friends left me to the care of some French soldiers."

"Captain Lavoisier."

"Of course you're acquainted." He winced at the pain his chuckle brought. "Someone ought to put stones in your stockings."

"I fear it would require anchors." She feared more so that she were delusional as she moved closer still, that any second she would awaken to find him slipping from her sight, her grasp. The way she'd dreamed him night after night, a hundred, a thousand times. Always slipping away. She was close enough now to touch him. She could grasp him, but she purposely stood too far, distrusting, her mind gone. This was the realest dream she'd had; she durst not move an inch to watch it vanish. Over his shoulder, a ship in the harbor was docked too close.

He followed her gaze to the ship's figurehead and the painted words on the side of the prow. "*L'Adultère*," he said proudly. "There she is. As I once promised."

He scratched at a short beard around his mouth and chin that kept the visibility of his marring to a minimum. Gashes at his cheekbones where they'd been split and sewn together had turned to deep impressions. The broken bridge of his nose, not at all smoothly planed as it once was, now bumpy as a rutted wagon trail. A thick scar over his right eye drooped his brow with gentle ptosis. The blue of his right eye was cloudy as it peeked out beneath the squint. Ruth suddenly didn't feel as concerned with her own appearance. He let her look. She'd have to get used to it. She finally put her hand to his marred cheek, rubbed a thumb along the length of a scar, and his flesh was real and sweaty and warm and smelled of salt. He pulled her to him and felt her tears seep through his shirt, and he ran his hand along the curve of her belly and kissed the top of her hair.

"I shudder to tell you the worst of it," he said, "but I haven't a leg below the knee of this boot." He tapped the leather garters holding his right boot in place, braced above the knee and attached to the belt about his waist. "Just a crafted shaft of oak. You'll also find to your fancy that more of my body is scarred than not, and I have the misfortune of deadened nerves that make certain, uh, functions occasionally difficult to perform." He shrugged and scarleted. "My broke nose whistles constantly. My guts give me spastic daily suffering. I've scarce sight in my right eye." He paused, watched her. "I offer all this to you, as Captain Becdelièvre of the barquentine *The Adulterer*."

"Becdelièvre?" she questioned, but then: "Your father."

"My father." He nodded and whispered, "Leave with me now."

Another voice came from the sea behind them. "I'd like to add, to move this process along lest you does watch him die for true this time, that if you refuse him 'cause he be an ugly bastard, I'll throw you over my shoulder like a sack of cornmeal and drag y'aboard the ship kicking and cursing to holy hell. At my captain's command, of course."

Ruth glanced around her captain at the figure stepping from the dinghy beneath the lip of the dock. "Thomas!" she laughed. He'd never appeared in her dreams. This was real.

"First Mate Thomas Hewitt, at your service, m'lady," he said, standing at attention before her, everything else a lifetime in the past. His face was scarred with burns, and he had a limp from a wound that had healed poorly, but he was alive. "*The Adulterer* don't leave without you aboard." He extended his hand to lift her into the rowboat. "We's wide open, so can we—"

"I dare those English to try us," the captain said, as he flipped his cane up into his left hand, and unsheathed a sharp, glistening sword from it. He held the blade outstretched to let it catch the sunlight, and Captain Owen Becdelièvre no longer appeared wounded in the slightest.

⌁

The crew lifted Owen up portside. Ruth took his hand to help him over the rail. He looked at her with indulgent satisfaction, then turned to his crew. "Mettez les voiles pour la France!"

"France?" Ruth echoed, and her ambitions of escaping to a neighboring town blossomed into a picture even grander: ancient cobblestone streets and libraries filled with books and bucolic countrysides of lavender bushes. She imagined Helen going through her trunks months from now, when they'd decided her gone, and reading Newton and Copernicus and French poetry and dabbing herself with perfume, as Ruth pictured the carved Corinthian bookshelf columns and the Cardinal's coat of arms of the Bibliothèque Marzarine. One by one, Owen's crew came up to him, ready for duty, and he issued commands. Ruth was sure she'd never seen him so steady or competent or, strangely enough, handsome.

Thomas said, "Captain, the munitions is secured in the hold, and we be prepared to weigh anchor. I'll take control of the helm and get Guillaume and Laurent underway with navigation, sir."

"You stole Whitlock's guns?" Ruth asked.

"Certainly," Owen said, "and his longbows and kegs of blackpowder and sabers and rum and whatallelse he had, including his lovely widow. I been paid good by your—our—allied friends regarding certain seditious maps from an auburn-hair woman, and a ship to get them out on."

"So she *is* a pirate ship," Ruth said, a little too excitedly.

"*The Adulterer*, like our lands and like her captain, sails under many flags."

"But, the letter," she remembered. A promise had been made to return to Fairfield. She thought of these things now, how hasty this departure had been. "Your poor mother—"

"—is safe in France with the only man she ever loved, Commandant Auguinare Becdelièvre, a recent widower. She inherited his three young girls to raise, so she's as delighted with girls as my legitimate father was to learn he had a son he never knew. As for my brothers, well, see for yourself what a fine crew I've netted, starting with my third mate." He shifted on his cane and pointed across the weatherdeck to Ash Townsend, and Ruth gasped. There stood all five of Owen's brothers manning the deck, right down to Gabriel, alive and fit.

Before she could reply, a crewman came up beside her, extended his arm, and spoke in his best English through his French accent, "Shall I to take Mrs. Becdelièvre below the deck?"

"Non, elle ira où elle voudra," Owen said and waved the crewman off.

Ruth lifted a brow. "Mrs. Becdelièvre?"

"I had to tell my crew something to make them travel across the ocean so late in the year."

"So you told them I am your wife?"

"Yes, kidnapped disastrously by the English!" He grinned as if his plan were the cleverest thing, without a care that his mouth flashed with checkered toothlessness. "For as you see, my dear, *l'Adultère* is French.

My crew is French. And no one here who counts—Thomas doesn't count—knows you are not my wife."

He grinned again, took her hand, lifted his weight off the cane, and rested himself entirely upon her, allowing her support to hold him upright. He kissed her deeply, and her kiss was warm and satisfying, unburdened by haste, and he breathed in the long-anticipated scent of her crushed flowers. This time, she'd wait for it. She'd never rush it again.

"This barquentine is new," he whispered. "She has embarked on but three voyages, and she hasn't yet took a blow. She is fast and sleek. Has perfect planks that still smell of oak and not dry rot. And she is all for you. For our son." Her body released all tension against him as his, in turn, to hers. "Or daughter," he laughed. "God help me."

"You do know this baby's not going to wait until France, aye? I hope you thought to have a skilled midwife aboard."

"Eh." He shrugged. "We've a skilled barber. Now, Mrs. Becdelièvre, to France! There are goods to thieve, people to rob, towns to ransack, empires to desecrate, innocents to spoil…and a few honest crates to exchange in between."

She laughed and swiveled to attention, her eyes bright and her youthful spirit restored. "I shall make it my duty to ransack to my utmost, Captain." She curtsied dramatically. "Who do we pillage and plunder first?"

He cocked an eyebrow and glanced out over the sea's expansive blue, raising an arm and a wicked grin to the eastern sky. "Why, England, of course."

Reference Glossary of Non-English Languages

in order of appearance

ga weg: *go away* [Dutch]

mon petite amour: *my little love* [French]

demoiselle en détresse: *damsel in distress* [Fr.]

hors de question: *out of the question; no way* [Fr.]

grand-maman: *granny; grandmamma* [Fr.]

à ton service: *at your service* [Fr.]

avec plaisir: *with pleasure* [Fr.]

adieu: *goodbye; farewell for a long time* [Fr.]

pour l'amour du ciel: *for heaven's sake; for the love of heaven* (as exclamation) [Fr.]

merde: *shit* [Fr.]

pulsion sexuelle: *sex drive; libido* [Fr.]

c'est fini: *it's finished; it's done* [Fr.]

mäuschen: *little mouse* [German]

tu êtes impossible: *you are impossible* [Fr.]

ça suffit: *that's enough; enough; enough is enough* (as exclamation) [Fr.]

comme tu veux: *whatever you say* [Fr.]

j'en ai marre: *I'm fed up* [Fr.]

un marin français et sa sorcière: *a French sailor and his witch* [Fr.]

égard: *respect* (in a very delicate sense) [Fr.]

j'ai honte d'être ton fils: *I am ashamed to be your son* [Fr.]

je ne me considère pas comme ton fils: *I do not consider myself your son* [Fr.]

cette conversation est terminée: *this conversation is over* [Fr.]

menteuse: *liar* [Fr.]

je te promets: *I promise you* [Fr.]

tu avez ma parole: *you have my word* [Fr.]

alors, pas de français: *then, no French* [Fr.]

à bientôt: *see you soon; goodbye* [Fr.]

parlez-vous français: *do you speak French* [Fr.]

Askook: name, meaning *snake* (**shkook:** *snake*) [Pequot/Eastern Algonquian cognate]

wonnux: *white person* [Peq./E. Alg. c.]

nuk, Ne-wohter: *yes, I know* [Peq./E. Alg. c.]

Waunnuxuk: *Englishmen; English people* [Peq./E. Alg. c.]

kepī'higàn`: *fence* [Peq./E. Alg. c.]

musqáyuw: *red* (Red Forest, proper noun) [Peq./E. Alg. c.]

ohke: *land* [Peq./E. Alg. c.]

bekedum kee [to kee]: *return dirt to dirt* (use land, replenish land, leave it as found) (**bekedum:** *give up; renounce; return*) (**kee:** *dirt*) [Peq./E. Alg. c.]

sunjum: *sachem; tribal leader; chief* [Peq./E. Alg. c.]

Ne-sookedung: *I urinate; I need to urinate* [Peq./E. Alg. c.]

trouvaille: *a lucky find* [Fr.]

debe: *spirit* [Peq./E. Alg. c.]

weektumun: *love someone; someone loved* [Peq./E. Alg. c.]

chauk: *soul* [Peq./E. Alg. c.]

ahupanun: *come here; come; return* [Peq./E. Alg. c.]

cuthannubbog: *seawater; ocean* [Peq./E. Alg. c.]

pechog: *[one's] rib(s)* [Peq./E. Alg. c.]

meyuggus: *[one's] guts/belly* [Peq./E. Alg. c.]

dupkwoh: *night; dark* [Peq./E. Alg. c.]

kunx: *skunk* (**swamp kunx:** *skunk cabbage; swamp cabbage*) [Peq./E. Alg. c.]

inanadig: *maple tree* [Peq./E. Alg. c.]

weeksubahgud: *it is sweet* [Peq./E. Alg. c.]

gersubertoh: *it is hot* [Peq./E. Alg. c.]

woothuppeag: *pail; bucket* [Peq./E. Alg. c.]

nis: *two* [Peq./E. Alg. c.]

nuqut: *one* [Peq./E. Alg. c.]

schwi: *three* [Peq./E. Alg. c.]

wôpáyuw: *white* [Peq./E. Alg. c.]

muttianomoh: *sick* [Peq./E. Alg. c.]

byowhy: *goodbye* [Peq./E. Alg. c.]

Philosophiæ Naturalis Principia Mathematica: De motu corporum: *Mathematical Principles of Natural Philosophy: On the motion of bodies* (book title) [Latin]

Entretiens sur la pluralité des mondes: *Conversations on the Plurality of Worlds* (book title) [Fr.]

oui, monsieur, assez bien: *yes, sir, quite well* [Fr.]

j'en ai fini avec toi: *I'm done with you* [Fr.]

et tu, Brute: *and you, Brutus; and you, too, Brutus* (a line in Shakespeare's
Julius Caesar, 1599) [La.]

oui, Lieutenant-Général, je parle français: *yes, Lieutenant General, I
speak French* [Fr.]

Ne-quonwehige: *it frightens me; it scares me* [Peq./E. Alg. c.]

canakisheun: *where are you going* [Peq./E. Alg. c.]

aque: *hello; greetings* [Peq./E. Alg. c.]

Ne wohter: *I know* [Peq./E. Alg. c.]

Ne sewortum: *I'm sorry* [Peq./E. Alg. c.]

chunche bekedum bunnedwong, nepattuhquonk, do tuggung:
must give up/put down/renounce knives, stakes/poles/pikes, and axes
[Peq./E. Alg. c.]

pakodjiteau: *it is finished* [Peq./E. Alg. c.]

bekedum bunnedwong: *give up/put down/renounce [your] knife*
[Peq./E. Alg. c.]

nuppe: *water* [Peq./E. Alg. c.]

Askuwheteau: *I keep watch; we keep watch* (Name, as addressing himself:
he keeps watch) [Peq./E. Alg. c.]

tahbut ne: *thanks; thank you; thanks for that* [Peq./E. Alg. c.]

savoir-faire: *know-how; knowledge* [Fr.]

Dieu aie pitié: *God have mercy* [Fr.]

c'est ma chance: *this is my chance* [Fr.]

saisis-la: *take it* (as exclamation) [Fr.]

miséricorde: *mercy strike* (a long, narrow knife used since medieval
times to deliver the death strike of mercy) [Fr.]

Je suis le capitaine d'un navire. En français: *I am the captain of a ship.
In French.* [Fr.]

oui, la justice est la vôtre: *yes, justice is yours* [Fr.]

mais pas pour toujours: *but not forever* [Fr.]

Dieu n'a pas de pitié: *God shows no mercy* [Fr.]

Machk: Name, meaning *bear* (**mosq:** *bear*) [Natick/E. Alg. c.]

do kiyo wetun: *and cold wind* [Peq./E. Alg. c.]

wishbium: *get out; avaunt* [Peq./E. Alg. c.]

nuk, sunjum: *yes, sachem; yes, chief* [Peq./E. Alg. c.]

juni shquaaw: *crazy woman* [Peq./E. Alg. c.]

meezum: *gives us; gives that* [Peq./E. Alg. c.]

muneesh: *money* [Peq./E. Alg. c.]

weyout: *fire* (**weyout light sticks:** *candles*) [Peq./E. Alg. c.]

tuggung: *axes* [Peq./E. Alg. c.]

jocqueen: *an Englishman's house or property, as separate from a Native American's* (**ohke of jocqueen:** *the land of an Englishman's house/ property*) [Peq./E. Alg. c.]

keeg: *ground* [Peq./E. Alg. c.]

mudder, nekânis: *no, my brother* [Peq./E. Alg. c.]

nenequdder: *never ever* [Peq./E. Alg. c.]

matwan: *enemy* [Peq./E. Alg. c.]

wōtī'nĕ: *help* [Peq./E. Alg. c.]

chokquog: *a knife-man; an Englishman* (reference to swords of the colonial militiamen) [Peq./E. Alg. c.]

undi, wemooni: *then, it is true* [Peq./E. Alg. c.]

pŭnŭm boshkeag: *lay down your gun* [Peq./E. Alg. c.]

bushkwa: *you shoot* [Peq./E. Alg. c.]

n'shuh: *he kills* [Peq./E. Alg. c.]

ge mŭchŭnŭ: *you perish* [Peq./E. Alg. c.]

ge papoose mŭchŭnŭ: *your baby/ child perishes* [Peq./E. Alg. c.]

towwigoh: *a bastard* [Peq./E. Alg. c.]

Teecommewaas: Name, meaning *striker; he strikes* (**togku:** *he strikes*) [Nat./Narragansett/E. Alg. c.]

Kitchi: Name, meaning *brave* [Peq./E. Alg. c.]

poudre: *gunpowder* [Fr.]

bouilloires: *kettles* [Fr.]

nietsissimoŭ: *tobacco* [Peq./E. Alg. c.]

minshkudawâpû: *whiskey* [Peq./E. Alg. c.]

Matchitehew: Name, meaning *he has an evil heart* [Peq./E. Alg. c.]

Matunaaga: Name, meaning *fights* [Peq./E. Alg. c.]

joyquish: *be quick* [Peq./E. Alg. c.]

wombunseyon, nekânis, kuttabotomish: *if I live in the morning, my brother, I/ I'll thank you* [Peq./E. Alg. c.]

Nuxquatch: *I am cold* [Peq./E. Alg. c.]

mits chauk: *my soul* [Peq./E. Alg. c.]

la liberté sera mienne: *freedom will be mine* [Fr.]

et le tien: *and yours* [Fr.]

son amour pour vous était aussi grand que le monde: *his love for you was as big as the world* [Fr.]

ma chère fille, je te remercie: *my dear daughter, I thank you* [Fr.]

français, oui: *French, yes* [Fr.]

Française ou Anglaise, et où avez-vous trouvé ce cheval: *French or English, and where did you find that horse* [Fr.]

dîtes-moi à quoi vous pensez en français: *tell me what you are thinking in French* [Fr.]

votre plumes rouges sont ridicules: *your red feathers are ridiculous* [Fr.]

pourquoi est-elle ici, Capitaine Lavoisier: *why is she here, Captain Lavoisier* [Fr.]

weshãgunsh: *hair of a beast* (a curse) [Peq./E. Alg. c.]

nous avons un ennemi commun: *we have a common enemy* [Fr.]

l'Adultère: *The Adulterer* (ship name) [Fr.]

mettez les voiles pour la France: *set sail for France* [Fr.]

commandant: *commander* [Fr.]

non, elle ira où elle voudra: *no, she'll go where she wants* [Fr.]

A NOTE ON THE PEQUOT LANGUAGE

It is with sadness as a historian that I say there exists no accurate written form of the Pequot language. As a spoken language, it went extinct when the last native speaker died in 1908, and the language was not a written one. Prior to extinction, it had been a banned language in many parts of New England for over two centuries, and most of it was lost to time or recorded only phonetically by white translators, traders, and early scholars. After the Pequot Wars that wiped out most of the Nation, many remaining tribe members were swallowed into neighboring tribes (generally as enslaved peoples) or later converted to Christianity, thus facilitating the loss of the language.

Pequot is dialectally related to Mohegan (often called Mohegan-Pequot), and has many Eastern Algonquian cognates, including Narragansett, Natick, Lenâpe, Montauk, and Shinnecock. After studying its construction with what little knowledge we have of it, I have reconstructed it to the best of my ability, using mostly early original spellings from translators of the seventeenth and eighteenth centuries, while also putting it into a construct that would both make sense to English-speaking readers and stay true to characters consisting of Pequot Natives and French and English colonists speaking to one another in pidgin contexts.

Early translations include that of: Roger Williams (*A Key into the Language of America*, 1643), Reverend James Noyes (*Pequot Indian Vocabulary*, 1669-79), Experience Mayhew (*The Massachusetts Psalter*, 1709), Ezra Stiles (*A Vocabulary of the Pequot Indians*, 1762; *Wordlist of Mohegan-Pequot*, 1793), and J. Dyneley Prince and Frank G. Speck translating from Mohegan Native Fidelia (Flying Bird) Fielding (*Glossary of the Mohegan-Pequot Language*, 1904). Of additional note are the studies on the Mohegan language by Flying Bird (*A Modern Mohegan Dictionary*, compiled by Stephanie Fielding), *Grammatical Studies in the Narragansett Language* by Frank Waabu O'Brien, *The Dialectology of Southern New England Algonquian* by David J. Costa, and the Yale Indian Papers Project.

There are many ongoing efforts dedicated to reviving and revitalizing the lost language. Each Thanksgiving, please consider helping the Mohegan Language Project or the Mashantucket Pequot Museum and

Research Center. Both are invaluable to this world we all must live in, together—past, present, and future.

A Historical Note

While most of the names in this story, including people, place, and ship names, are taken directly from town records, original maps, journal entries, and old local history books, this story and the characters' depictions are works of fiction. When war in Old World France and England touched the respective French and English colonists in New World North America, it broke the Treaty of Whitehall, an agreement between France and England stating that Old World conflicts would not translate over to New World soil—that North American colonists could remain untangled from the repercussions of the two endlessly squabbling siblings. But war was inevitable; the colonists' lives and livelihoods were still directly tied to their mother countries. The two countries would squabble on American soil, from early colony claims to maritime rights in the War of 1812 to Pacific Northwest border wars, until well into the early twentieth century.

Though most of King William's War took place in the northeastern tip of what is now the United States and the southeastern area of modern-day Canada, skirmishes broke out all along the constantly disputed hazy border between New England and the Viceroyalty of New France, from the Middle Colonies all the way up into Canada and down into the Great Lakes region. The skirmish in my story is based on real events, though very insignificant within the scheme of the full conflict; I've combined real account details from two separate skirmishes into one, however, for plot purposes and have slightly moved the location to suit my characters' needs. The surrounding environs to the rest of the story are otherwise largely untouched.

The main protagonists are fictitious, though everything from their seafaring journeys to their court-appointed punishments to women not being able to own land to the architecture of the houses comes from real people's lives—mined and compiled from the written testimonies and documentation of conglomerated colonists of the time period. I lived for years in New England, married to its history, mired in its myths and legends, falling in love with its ocean and gold-topped buildings and countless miniature cemeteries. This story contains many parts of that history I found and researched there, shining through the veil of others' lives.

The maps and diagrams at the front of the book were hand-drawn and digitized by my own hand, based on public-domain maps and diagrams from the time period, notably those from Thomas Miner's journal. They mix fact and fiction, containing both the properties and landmarks of historical individuals and the properties of those fictitious individuals around whom the story revolves.

Acknowledgments

Special thank you to my partners in crime: Mike Litos, Eric Shonkwiler, Timston Johnston, Taylor Brown, Aline Ohanesian, Scott Phillips, Kevin Catalano, Steph Post, Rilla Askew, Heather O'Neill, Kathleen Rooney, Ethel Rohan, Lori Hettler, Kathleen Grissom, and Ashley Shelby for edits, early reads, and endless inspiration. Thank you to Selma Oeke Algra for accuracy in my Dutch translations and Fanny Dufour Sood for accuracy in my French translations.

I could not have written this book without the inspiration and material of Thomas Miner, Richard Anson Wheeler, the Stonington Historical Society, the Thomas Stanton Society, Laurence Whittemore, Roger Williams, Flying Bird, and James Noyes; read their contributions to history in the form of letters, journals, translations, and firsthand accounts to learn more about Stonington and pre-American Connecticut Colony.

Special thank you to Elizabeth Copps at Copps Literary Services for her boundless enthusiasm and unwavering support. To Ted, for superfandom camaraderie. To C. H. Uties—*mits chauk*. Thanks to all my fam for endlessly believing in me: Mom, Dad, Grandma, Mama Bear Sarah, Mama Karen, Mama Marta, Denny, Ethan, Doug, Nick, Brian, Cammie, Lacy, Melody, all the extended, my German Shepherd Torgo, and my spirit Germy Sheps over the rainbow bridge: Barf, forever my mog, and Napoleon, forever my li'l emperor of everything.

To Jaynie Royal and the team at Regal House, who worked so tirelessly for this book to be born that their efforts were nothing short of a miracle—and I don't even believe in miracles.

To E. G. S.—I wish you could have known what an inspiration you were to this story. I wish I could have told you in person. And to Mrs. Jaworski, who first introduced me to the history of New England through literature but passed before I could ever thank her—thank you. Teachers, never doubt that you make a difference, even when the thanks arrives too late.

To my "patrons" for their endless awesomeness and for helping to make this book happen: Doug Litos, Elaine Angstman, Ted Scheinman, and Sarah Marsh, given in memory of her grandmother, Helen Souders.